THE FOUR MYTHS

Published 2020 by Kettle Books

Cover image © Kettle Books
Cover design © Kettle Books

Kettle Books ®

Inquiries should be addressed to:
Kettle Books
320 Gold Ave SW
STE 620 PMB 1465
Albuquerque NM 87102
VOICE: (678) 348-6320
inquiries@kettle-books.com
WWW.KETTLE-BOOKS.COM

20 21 22 23 24   5 4 3 2 1

Library of Congress Cataloging-in-Publication Data

Names: Reisler, Robert, 1973 – author.
Title: The Four Myths / Robert Reisler.
Description: Roswell, GA : Kettle Books 2020.
Identifiers: Library of Congress Control Number: 2020908688 (print) |
   ISBN 9781734881400 |(paperback) | ISBN 9781734881417 (ebook) |
   ISBN 9781734881431 (hardback) | ISBN 9781734881424 (audiobook) |
   ISBN 9781734881448 (Book I paperback - LIMITED EDITION) |
   ISBN 9781734881462 (Book I paperback) |
   ISBN 9781734881455 (Book I ebook)

LC Record Available at: https://lccn.loc.gov/2020908688

Printed in the United States of America

THE FOUR MYTHS

BY

ROBERT REISLER

MY pen name is Robert Reisler, and I am the author of the book you are about to read. My novel is based on a collection of numbered notebooks I found in the summer of 1999 while on a solitary hike in the mountains. These journals I acquired—written by a man referring to himself as Byron Henning—went on to describe the coming end to this world and were dated from 2007 through 2048 and, therefore, passively claimed they were from the future.

Is the world going to begin to end as this Byron describes? And if so, is there still an opportunity to ward off these events before they come to pass? Are we being handed another chance to reflect on our existence before these coming times?

Regardless of the answers, I felt compelled to produce this book because I have come to believe in the accounts described in Byron's notebooks. I have taken an author's liberty of changing the names and places of several of the notebooks' accounts to protect those persons' privacy, since through my personal research, it does appear they exist and live among us.

And so…on with my work of *fiction?* May it serve whatever purpose it may serve.

—ROBERT REISLER

Book I:

The End of the Beginning

There is a strange normalness to fantasy. There is a normal strangeness to reality. How can so many stories of a fantastical nature, written often by the wildest of men, seem so believable, while countless instances of brutality and heinousness occur in the real world—yet these acts are barely able to be fathomed?

What were you doing when the world ended?

CHAPTER 1

———————◇○⊂⊃○◇———————

"SO, JACK, WHAT'S IN THE BOX?" the security guard asked.

Jack Johanssen worked nights because Jack Johanssen didn't like people. Or rather it was distraction Jack didn't like—and where there were people, there was distraction. The night watchman, Randy Haverstamp, worked nights simply because *that* was his shift. Randy had wielded his nightstick in Jack's building for about a year, and early on in his rental cop employment, Randy had developed a habit of peeking in on Jack's archaeological work, or as Jack saw it, a habit of interrupting Jack's archaeological work. This habit had eventually developed into peering over Jack's shoulder during nearly *every* work break, and Jack had become curious to know whether *any* time of the day was a *good* time to work. Randy's six-foot-five tower-of-a-self didn't help Jack feel any more alone, either. The only saving grace the twenty-six-year-old night watchman had—although Jack would never admit it—was that Randy's excitement toward Jack's work had infected Jack with a small case of the "You-remind-me-of-me-kid-twenty-years-ago-itis." Yet given that Jack was thirty-two, that put the age difference between Jack and Randy at only six years—not really the kind of gap to spawn a comment like "You remind me of me, kid." Randy being only six years younger than Jack made the "kid" reference meaningless, as well, and twenty years ago, Jack would have been about twelve; so this thought was cracking up to be just one more diversion wasting Jack's time in this whole deal.

Randy had returned to college to attain an archaeology degree six months after assuming the role of Jack Johanssen's taller, darker, younger, and "handsomer" shadow. Randy had seen Jack take a lot of things out of a lot of boxes, and his anticipation had only increased with each box, regardless of the contents. The "kid" had explained the work Jack did felt infinitely more interesting than sitting behind a security post for the foreseeable future asking people to see their badges. Randy had reenrolled and had figured if looking at old forgotten crap had inspired him to return to school—forgoing partying this time for studying—then archaeology must be a pursuit worth pursuing.

Jack had been employed by this particular civilian-contracted, US government warehouse for almost five years—his second job since graduating with a master's degree from "somewhere other than Harvard," as his father had often put it before becoming an archaeological relic himself a few years after Jack's graduation. Jack had been valedictorian of his high school, and somehow, this fact alone had solidified in his father's mind the idea that Jack would not stop until he was holding a sheepskin from the greatest university in America. However, Jack hadn't wanted to go to Harvard. Instead, Jack had attended his local state university for both bachelor's and master's degrees, lived at home—quietly—continued a position he'd landed in graduate school in his alma mater's library, where he'd spent about five years researching university collectibles. The warehouse where he currently earned his wages provided him an even more quiet and secluded work environment, at least prior to Randy, and Jack was happy he was not a famous or respected graduate of Harvard asked to teach or speak, or required to do anything of consequence around other people. This wasn't because Jack was a social outcast or was the kind of man who threw up when speaking to women or because he was embarrassed to be in public due to some strange nodule growing out of the middle of his forehead. He was a decent-enough-looking man, standing about five-nine with a good Scandinavian head of sandy blondish-brown hair. And if he'd ever cared to listen, he may have overheard a woman or two mention he looked good in his glasses. They were the dark-rimmed plastic kind; he had picked them because they rested directly on his nose. He hated the oval indentations that glasses with the little rubber pads made in one's nose—not because others might see those indentations, but because if Jack looked in the mirror, they would have reminded him of his father. And the last thing Jack wanted staring back at him under fluorescent lights during every postpiss handwashing was his dead father telling him he should have gone to Harvard because "Harvard graduates, Jack, don't even *need* to piss." No, Jack wasn't the square-jawed, frat-boy, Randy type, but he could have held his own had he wanted to. But he didn't want to, and that's what his father never understood either. Jack loved research archaeology, and in Jack's mind that meant no live people—only books and the long-ago dead…and quiet.

Obscurity had been Jack's major, and he had graduated summa cum laude. After a proving-ground university gig, Jack had walked through the doors of his current employer, reaching the height of his career at the bottom of its warehouse. He was now perfectly content in his underground office, feeling quite accomplished in attaining the goal he'd set out for himself after discovering his field all the way back in middle school while watching a *National Geographic* special on archaeology. Jack would admit the only negative consequence of his choices was his paycheck, which reminded Jack on a bimonthly basis that, regardless of his abilities as an archaeologist, he was not a Harvard graduate.

The warehouse would, however, provide him a lifetime's amount of work cataloging artifacts, collectibles, and other junk Uncle Sam had acquired since he was a baby-sized patriot wearing a baby-sized top hat. These items had been acquired through wars, raids, classified operations, research expeditions, and even donations.

Jack found trouble in only the last means of acquisition. He understood all governments get spoils—but that citizens would, from time to time, bequeath their possessions, even their entire estates, to the grand old US of A? Why on earth anyone who spent a lifetime paying taxes would wish to give even one more penny to the government was the question that lingered with Jack. Jack felt that if he ever drafted a will, he'd bequeath his middle finger, at most. Jack had put off writing a will, for at present it wouldn't amount to any more than a piece of paper whose chicken scratch read, "Please pay off this highly skilled, yet grossly underpaid, archaeologist's debts with any loose change you may find in his sofa. However, since no one knows who I am, and therefore, no one will be around to read this—or determine the location of my sofa—you can all go to hell and kiss my—"

"Jack?" Randy called again. "Hello? The box?" Randy had interrupted Jack's slip into regressive reflection—a defense mechanism designed to hold onto his much-loved silence. Randy had popped in as usual and right on time, corrupting Jack's basement temple of solace…again.

"Did you spend your whole walk down here coming up with that one?" Jack asked, still not bothering to turn his head toward the voice intruding on his solitude. He then answered the kid's inquiry. "I don't know what's in it. I kind of have to open it first, Randall."

"All right, all right. It's just I've got to get back to the security post in ten," Randy replied, "and don't call me Randall." Randy entered the dark office, and after a few steps, he sat on the edge of Jack's desk and crossed his arms. The only light buzzing in the lab was standing on a pole next to Jack's workbench.

"You know, Randy, you always have to get back in ten," Jack said while spinning around on his lab stool staring at Randy over the top of his glasses. "I honestly don't know how you ever talked me into this co-op thing you got going on here with my work."

"Jack, you need me to come in here to remind you you're one of us."

"One of who, Randy?"

"Uh, one of the living," Randy scoffed, "or else after I graduate, my first assignment is going to be scraping your dead ass off that stool and storing *you* on a shelf."

"I think I did just fine for the years before you were hired," Jack answered, turning back toward the container sitting on his workbench, "and the edge of my desk was less worn too."

Randy quickly rose off Jack's desk. A moment later he was rolling his eyes at himself, realizing Jack had won the round. He then plopped his rear back down right where it had been planted before. As Randy returned to his resting spot, he played a sympathy card followed by a brownnoser. "I'm just wanting a little 'hands-on,' Jack. The stuff you pull off these shelves is pretty gnarly sometimes."

"You're still sitting, aren't you?" Jack asked, his back now to Randy, which masked a grin he didn't want the kid to see and was pissed off even existed. It meant he liked Randy and the kid's presence more than he wanted to admit to himself. "Listen, just don't rush me to satisfy your work-shift requirements, okay?"

"All right, all right. *So?* What's in the box?" Randy asked.

Jack sighed. "Randy." He shook his head at himself.

"Yep?" Randy responded cluelessly.

Jack took a moment to peer back over his right shoulder at Randy, wanting the kid to notice his frustration—yet not wanting him to at the same time. Jack tugged at his ear with his left hand, his elbow resting on the lab bench. This habit had started sometime during high school when his left ear began itching at random times and for no apparent reason, somewhere around the same time he'd begun wearing glasses. Figuring Randy deserved another jab for his incessant desk perching, Jack said, "Well, I'm not saying I'm hip, but I think the term 'gnarly' pretty much ran its course about twenty years ago, and why are you so interested in this box?"

"It's a metal one. That means it's one of the older ones, doesn't it?"

It was one of the older storage boxes. The use of metal containers had started in the 1920s. At that time an effort had been made to move items to this type of box from the older cardboard counterparts. Jack's warehouse had begun using plastic containers for newly obtained items starting in the 1980s, but the transplant procedure hadn't been repeated a second time, and he was only to move an article to a new plastic container if he deemed the delicate constitution of the article warranted the effort (and cost). Jack's primary responsibility consisted of recording into a database the contents of the warehouse and drawing conclusions about their nature.

"Well, Randy, you are right about that. The box does appear to be one of the older ones we have here," Jack agreed, looking over the box. "Just give me a sec while I enter it."

Jack turned his focus to his laptop and typed today's date, *January 31, 2007,* and the current time, *23:47,* into his spreadsheet next to the box number, 2347, which he had entered before Randy's arrival. He then entered *M* for metal, into the Box Type column of the document.

Wow. Have I really cataloged that many boxes? Jack thought to himself, looking at the box number, 2347, he had typed.

Randy had already moved around to Jack's side a few moments earlier as Jack had begun to type. He focused on the computer screen while Jack entered the data.

"Ha! Looky there!" Randy exclaimed, throwing his arm in front of Jack's face to point at Jack's laptop screen. "The box number is the same as the time you just typed."

"What, Randy?" Jack said from behind Randy's arm, still surprised by the outburst. He grasped Randy's arm and raised it up and away from his face like a lever. "Really, you're not helping me get my work done."

"Sorry, Jack, but look," Randy continued and pulled his arm from Jack's hand, "*Twenty-three forty-seven*—the time you just typed—and box number twenty-three forty-seven. That crazy, or what? Heh! Things happen like this to me all the time."

Jack succumbed to the directive and glanced again at his laptop entries. The kid was right. The occurrence reminded him of what his mother used to call "kawinky-dinks."

"All the time, *huh*?" he said to Randy, starting to smile but then holding it back, continuing his personal quest to hide any evidence of pleasure derived from the kid's presence as a witness to his work and life. Doing so succeeded in making Jack look and sound less excited—and more constipated.

"Yeah, they do," Randy replied.

"Really," Jack muttered.

The next step was to open the box: the moment Randy was waiting for. For some reason, the conversation had made Jack feel like putting off the moment just to spite Randy. However, Jack had no real reason to keep the boy in suspense, so he lifted the lid. The two men bent over the open box together, seemingly attached to the same invisible hinge, and looked inside.

"Aaaaachhoooo!" Randy sneezed.

"Jesus, Randy!" Jack whisper-yelled, closing the box quickly yet softly, as if he'd been baking a cake in it. "It looked like very old paper! I don't have any interest in you disintegrating it!"

"I'm sorry, Jack," Randy apologized, rubbing his nose violently. "I think some dust got in my nose or something."

"And *you* want to be an archaeologist?" Jack barked. "You know, I may not even take it out right now if it looks too fragile."

Jack's hands returned to the lid again, raising it slowly and steadily. *A guy needs steady, patient hands for this kind of work*, he thought to himself, *and the absence of people—especially night watchmen.* This last thought left Jack feeling a tad guilty. Once the lid was resting in an open position, Jack held up his hand in a Pointer Sisters' *Stop!* toward Randy's face and peered into the box. There lay a scroll.

"*So?* What is it, Jack? *Is* it old?" Randy asked from behind Jack's hand.

"Looks pretty old. But it seems in remarkably good shape considering how *old* it looks."

The scroll, Jack estimated at about twelve inches across, appeared to be made of a parchment-like material. There were wrinkles and creases in what Jack could see of it and, though the edges were worn, he saw no visible tears. Its color was a mixture of cream and maize, dark yellow, and brown. It made him think of what the Declaration of Independence would look like if it were smaller and rolled up. Jack's mind entertained another thought following the Declaration of Independence allusion. The thought was strange, having no real impetus. Nevertheless, Jack thought, *It kind of looks like one of those stereotypical mystical relics possessing magical powers and spells people find in movies.* Of course, his thought wasn't exactly each of those words laid out one after another—it was just the feeling he got. *Magical scroll.* The only other reflection to occur before dismissing the occasion altogether was: *What a weird thought.* Jack moved past this departure from actual work and noticed an information card in the filing slot on the underside of the container's lid. "Well, look at that," he declared, "don't get many of these. Maybe it'll actually tell me what it is."

Jack slid the card out of the slot. Turning it over, he skimmed the card's contents. "Appears to be original—two different handwritings on the card. Must've been transferred from the original box."

"What does it say?" Randy asked hastily.

Jack held the card out in front of him to catch the office light and began to read—well, tried to read—as Randy interrupted him once again.

"No way!" Randy yelped. "Custer's Last Stand!"

"Can I do *anything* here?" Jack retorted. "And it doesn't say that anyway."

"I know, I know, but that's where it's from! Look!" Randy took over the reading of the card Jack never had the chance to begin.

> *Scroll confiscated by Major Reno's troops from dead Injun at Little Big Horn—*
>
> *June 25th, 1876. Attempted Translation—failed. Stored—January 31st, 1877. Transferred to new box: April 7th, 1923. Paul Dunsford, warehouse staff.*

"Now that's gnarly!" Randy concluded.

"Didn't I say that word had run its course?"

"What? *Gnarly?* Never. Gnarly will always reign."

"Okay, Randy."

Randy couldn't contain his excitement. "Can you *imagine?* We're looking at something right here in front of us that witnessed Custer's Last Stand! *Holy shit!* I *knew* I chose the right field!"

"Yeah, I *can* imagine, Randy. It's right here, and I'm looking at it." Jack's sarcasm was lost as Randy gave no acknowledgment to it. Jack gave in, adding, "Yeah, I guess it's pretty neat."

Neat? Did I just use the word "neat"? And after I just got on his case about "gnarly."

Jack continued. "You know we've come a long way in Native American languages. Maybe it deserves another attempt at trans—"

"Hey, Jacky," Randy said.

"Uh, what, Rand-*ee*?" Jack sighed, after once again not being able to finish a thought or task or anything without the kid interrupting it.

Not missing a beat on Jack's patronization, Randy said, "You notice that date? The one when it was moved to this box by Mr. Paul Dunsford?"

"Yeah, what about it?" Jack asked, having no clue *why* he was asking by this point in the conversation. *Why do I keep replying? When am I going to take the "ignore him and he'll go away" approach?* Jack thought, internally admonishing himself.

"Check it out. Write that date in numbers, and you get '4-7-23.' Switch it around to 'year first,' and you get '23-4-7.' That number look *familiar*?" Randy paused, waiting for an answer. He then burst out, "I bet two thousand three hundred and forty-seven's a *prime* number too."

"I don't follow, Randy. What's that about a prime number?"

"Oh nothing, I guess. I'm just saying that besides the box number matching the freaking date, *and* the time you entered it into your spreadsheet there, I just figured twenty-three forty-seven's a prime number too."

Jack lifted his hands in a ready-to-argue stance, thinking to argue if only to accomplish the task of saying *something*. He then let them fall, defeated, his fingers landing on the edge of his lab table. Giving in to whatever this conversation had become, he replied, "Well, Randy, it just so happens it *is*. Twenty-three forty-seven is a prime number. But *why* is that such a big deal?"

"Listen, I've gotta get back to security rounds. But *come on*, Jack. You know all those mystical mysteries always center around some jacked-up thing like a prime number or something. Someone's always saying, 'Ooh, it's a prime number,' or some crap like that." Randy turned and headed for the door. "Anyways, cool one, Jack. Let me know what the scroll says if you figure it out."

Randy stopped on his way out of the lab and turned to look at Jack. A grin surfaced on his face, and a dimple began to form, complementing his well-chiseled smile.

"Now what?" Jack asked.

"Well look at that other date—the date that scroll was first filed away. January thirty-first? Isn't that *today*?"

Randy left, and the door closed behind him with a thud. The gust it produced made its way to Jack's forehead, fluttering his hair and seeming to punctuate Randy's observation and subsequent exit.

A few moments later, the door flew open. Jack turned, startled, and saw Randy had returned. "Yes, Ran—"

Oh geez. One damned sentence to completion, please.

"Huh, Jack. I was just thinking in the hallway and had to come back." Randy chuckled. "Doesn't 2,007 minus 1,876 equal 131, and doesn't 1,923 minus 1,876 equal 47? Gotta run." Then Randy was gone again.

Finally alone, Jack could entertain a complete thought. Of course, he admitted the thought was about Randy. "That kid," Jack said under his breath, letting a smile cross his face, which pissed himself off even in private. "He's sure got energy."

And good intuition, too, Johanssen—don't ya think? Is it "neat" enough for ya?

—◇○◇—

October 3, 2047 CE: Entry 11,725

Things are not going well. I'm probably crazy for even thinking I'll exist long enough to finish writing today's events. The world is ending out there, and the good guys are losing.

All these years, alone in this cabin. There won't be anyone left to even read these notebooks. Why do I keep writing them? Maybe I just hope I'm not crazy, or my visions have a purpose—that they mean there's still hope for a future. Maybe I just hold out hope for Jack and the rest of them. Maybe I do it because I have no other choice, or perhaps I'm too afraid to face an alternative.

Many times, I find myself filling pages like this—convincing myself to keep doing what I've been doing for forty years. I was promised my parents could be saved if I stayed here in this cabin, so that's what I've done. Why do I hold on to that promise? It's been forty years. Probably a lie, anyway. At this point, I just hope I don't die alone on this mountain in a dark and destroyed world. Good night, again.

—Byron Henning

CHAPTER 2

GENERAL CUSTER AND THE SIOUX
JUNE 24, 1876, MONTANA
EVENING

"**I** WAS *BORN* for the cavalry, Reno."

"Yes, George, I *know*," Major Reno answered, "but I think sometimes—what I mean to say is—maybe you forget that you're not immortal. Born, *yes*—but you could die for the cavalry too."

"That's our job, Major," Custer boasted. "We know the risks associated with doing what needs to be done, and we do it. It's just I happen to love what I *do* while I'm doing it."

"What is it again I'm supposed to love?" Reno prodded, simultaneously taking a bite of the meat hanging off the stick on which he was cooking it. While chewing, he followed with, "Is it the riding, the fighting, the clearing out of these Injuns? I forget, George." He swallowed and finished. "It sure can't be the money or the food, and for me, I know it's not the distance from home."

"Reno, my friend, you are home," Custer responded with a smile almost brighter than the fire between them. "Look back over your shoulder. Look past my shoulder."

The colonel was moving his arms like a human signpost, and the major felt compelled to look where they were directing him.

"Look left and right," Custer continued with growing zeal in his voice, "and straight up all the way into the distant end of it all. This land is *ours*. This sky is *ours*. It's all *ours*, and it's going to stay *ours*. God-given. Every step we *take* is another piece of this *home* you're talking about. Home *isn't* where the heart is, my friend. It's where you hang your hat! *Ha!*"

Custer laughed, leaned his head back, and looked into the night's canopy that lay above the two officers.

Custer continued his monologue, unknowingly defining what would one day be codified as Manifest Destiny in American history textbooks. "Shoot, Major, maybe home *is* where the heart is because this whole damned land you see under this big sky of Montana and all the way back to whatever people-infested town you came from *is* my heart."

"Well, Colonel, what can I say?" Reno sighed as he swallowed the next mouthful of whatever animal he was eating (he had stopped caring). "No one ever said you didn't have passion and the ability to convey it. And I understand you, though I don't believe we see everything the same way. Nevertheless, and getting back to your point, especially given the hour and with the big day tomorrow fast approaching—you said you were born for the cavalry. You could have seen this land or conquered it as an infantryman, an explorer, a settler."

"Ah, Major, right as always. But Custer, you must know, was born a *horseman!*"

CHAPTER 3

THE ANCIENT ONE OF THE SIOUX
JUNE 24, 1876, MONTANA
EVENING

decorative divider

AS GENERAL CUSTER and Major Reno were finishing their discussion about heart and hats and land and sky, another conversation was taking place between two longtime friends of a completely different nature in a nearby valley.

"The fire feels good, does it not?" the chief asked The Ancient One.

"Yes, it does. It is a cool night," The Ancient One replied and then stared directly into the chief's eyes. "So ask what you want, my friend. The real reason you requested my company, I assume, was not to describe this fire between us?"

The Great Chief nervously began; he was sure his friend would hear the small shake in his voice. "I have noticed your excessive aging, old friend, and many others—they have noticed it, too."

"Yes. I assumed that to be this meeting's purpose," The Ancient One replied as he looked down into the fire. Raising his right hand to feel his face—a face feeling much different than it had the day before—he continued, "I hope the tribe's spirit is not dampened and it does not worry them too much, especially with this white man Custer bringing his army to attack in the morning."

"You have been with us for generations. The others have come to believe your continued presence has served as a protection for the tribe." The Great Chief lifted his hand, motioning his fingers toward The Ancient One's face. "I can understand upon seeing what has happened to you why they have become concerned." He paused. A few moments later, he decided to ask a question he hoped would have an answer but feared would not. "Do you understand why this is happening?"

The Ancient One hesitated before attempting his reply. "I remember so long ago when I was named only The Scroll Holder. As you know, I became The Ancient One long before you were born, and this fact, Great Chief, must remind you of my age. I am not certain why this change has occurred, but it must be assumed I might soon become 'We Remember Him.' I believe these lines etched on my face, this aging which has come over me in the past day, is a sign. Something is about to happen, and perhaps it also means my time, as well, is…limited."

"Do you *know* this?" The Great Chief asked excitedly and in a manner as

uncommon as his previously wavering speech. His friend, who had always appeared young and had done so for thousands of years before, according to the stories, had transformed into an old man in just a single day. "Did the scroll tell you of such a thing?"

"I have not read the scroll!" The Ancient One rebuked harshly. "You *know* that to be the case!"

The Great Chief quickly apologized. "I'm sorry, I felt perhaps you had—or were *supposed* to do so—now...as things are...different? Forgive me, friend."

"No, forgive me. I did not mean to grow upset." The Ancient One moved his hand to the pouch around his neck and lowered his gaze toward his chest, where the pouch rested. "It has been a heavy burden all these centuries to carry this scroll yet be sworn never to look upon its contents. I do not wish to be tempted now, deluding myself into believing this change in me is cause for breaking my oath."

"No, I suppose not." The chief consoled him. "Forces of an unknown and powerful kind have been at work on you for many of my lifetimes. Many of the great chiefs have sat with you as I do now. I conclude if these forces have decided a different course lay ahead, then who are we to challenge them? We must, therefore, continue on as before; we can only wait and see if another sign brings us understanding concerning this change in you."

"Yes, Great Chief...we must wait. I believe that is best."

CHAPTER 4

MONTANA
JUNE 25, 1876

THE NEXT MORNING HAD ARRIVED. It was the day The Ancient One and The Great Chief had discussed the previous night across a fire. Custer and his soldiers would be approaching soon. The chief was standing in front of his tribe preparing to speak to them, preparing to inspire them, preparing them for their coming victory, and preparing many of them for their deaths.

"Prepare the horses!" The Great Chief began. "The morning has arrived where we will tell the White Man he is no longer welcome near our homes. He has brought many warriors with him, but ours are many more than he believes and many times over what he has brought."

As the chief finished, one of the scouts returned on a horse yelling, "He has split his army into three."

The Great Chief had sent scouts to follow Custer for several weeks after a Sioux spy had warned the tribes of Custer's mission. The tribes had been preparing ever since. The Great Chief was not worried about losing, but he wasn't looking forward to the losses of good young men, and that always went hand in hand with war. Neither was he looking forward to battle, once again being brought to them when they had asked for none.

However, The Great Chief knew of the attack in time to prepare much, and perhaps this would be the decisive blow they needed to keep the White Man from trying again, and then they could, once more, live their lives as they had before.

A concern, however, had nested itself in The Great Chief's mind. The previous day, The Ancient One's appearance had transformed from a young man into an old man. Did this mean the tribe was no longer protected? Did it mean The Ancient One would die? Should the war strategy be altered? Who was this Custer, and what did he have to do with his friend or their destiny as a tribe?

So many questions and answers coming only in the form of guesses and more waiting. *Wait.* The Ancient One and he had agreed to *wait* the night before. But waiting, it seemed, might have only lasted one night, for The Great Chief knew this morning, that the ensuing battle was certain to bring the answers, good or bad, wanted or unwanted, to his questions. Of course, as life had taught the chief, if he lived through the battle and received those answers, they would only be followed by a whole new set of questions.

The scout continued describing what he had seen of the strategy Reno, Benteen, and Custer had embarked upon. "There is a man leading soldiers over the west ridge, and another one leads in the east, but he is further behind. Custer comes down the middle toward the Little Bighorn River."

"We are many, and he is few and divided," The Great Chief announced, responding to the news presented. "We know their position and have the fortune of planning for their arrival. But do not believe we will be victorious too soon. Keep fighting until it is over. We must finish this battle decisively and strongly if we are to send a message to the White Man."

"Great Chief?"

One of the younger members of the tribe was speaking. The chief didn't answer.

"Great Chief?" the brave hollered once again.

After not responding a second time, the chief could see other warriors prompting the initial questioner to ask again. The chief took a breath and answered the question the brave had not yet asked. "You are concerned about The Ancient One's aged appearance?"

The young warrior nodded, and then the others around him began to nod and murmur in agreement. The chief thought how strange it was these braves had the courage to battle against men approaching with guns, but so many had been afraid to address him directly about The Ancient One. Weapons were a powerful force, but it appeared respect instilled fear with an even greater power.

"What does it matter?" the chief asked the tribe. "His appearance is what you see it to be. Do you intend not to fight for our homes and our lives because he has aged? If it is your worry we won't be protected because of his change, how will running from this battle protect us more? And what of the other tribes joining this battle— tribes who have never had a member such as The Ancient One? Put this matter out of your minds, and fight for all Sioux, all the tribes, and fight to protect The Ancient One, as he has fought so many times by your side and your father's fathers' sides to protect *you!*"

That should do it, The Great Chief thought as he turned to leave. And of course, he was correct. *His* army was not populated by a group of paid-for-hire men who smelled badly and behaved worse. *His* army was populated simply by *men*.

—◁◦▷—

Four Winds and Strength From Inside walked courageously and fearfully across the camp toward The Great Chief's quarters. Looks Past the Sky had told them to visit The Great Chief after The Great Chief's words had been spoken to the tribe preparing everyone for Custer and his soldiers.

As they neared, Strength From Inside asked, "What does The Great Chief want with us? We have done nothing which I can remember—this week."

"Not remembering is not proof of having done nothing, Strength," Four Winds replied.

"Are you not a little worried? What if we are not allowed to fight because of some misunderstanding or false accusation?"

"I have more faith in our chief than that." Four peered at Strength. "You must trust your actions as a man will carry you."

"Our actions as men are never in question." Strength From Inside sighed. "Only our actions as Strength From Inside and Four Winds."

Four Winds was twenty-three years old, the son of The Great Chief's lifelong friend, Two Hands Worth Four. He had grown into a strong young man, similar in build to his father. But he was quick. Like lightning, it was said by others, he seemed to be. He appeared and disappeared before an opponent's very eyes when fighting.

Where did he go when he seemed to vanish in a fight? Did he really become invisible? Did he sink into the ground? Did he fly above his enemy? So light he seemed, as he would move, it had been said the winds from each direction were under his very control to lift him into flight. And so he was named Four Winds—a name opposite of what his frame suggested. His large, strong stature confused all the more whomever Four Winds was fighting. That was, if his opponent was conscious long enough to be properly introduced to Four Winds at all.

Four Winds thought for a moment on the fight catalyzing the close friendship between Strength From Inside and himself. It had been the only fight Four Winds had ever lost. And though he didn't lose again, this one loss forged Four Winds's best friendship with Strength From Inside and had earned Strength his name.

Strength From Inside had his child name before this fight. He had been known as Quiet. And quiet he had been, most of the time. Although a year younger, Quiet was similar in stature to Four, and so a challenge between them was deemed a fair one within their training. When Quiet reached the age of sixteen, the challenge was arranged. Quiet believed himself prepared, although he had seen many others suffer quick losses to Four.

When the challenge between the two had begun, Four Winds quickly felt two jabs from Quiet fly by his face. They missed of course; Quiet had tried to catch Four Winds early but had failed to land either attempt. Quiet was amazed by his soon-to-be-friend's speed but was determined to be the first to find victory against this undefeated brave. Quiet's moment came when, just before Four Winds was going to throw his first (and typically last) blow, Four Winds's eyes caught the eyes of Quiet as they were standing face to face. Instead of throwing his blow, Four Winds stood frozen, caught within Quiet's stare. The determination behind Quiet's eyes was so still, so calm, so strong, Four Winds was nearly hypnotized. Quiet's peering felt like a strike to Four Winds's inner core. He felt hollowed out, like a man with no soul riding a buffalo with no heart. The next moment delivered a right hook to the side of Four's head, introducing Four Winds to the ground for the first time in a fight and knocking him out cold.

And Strength From Inside was born from Quiet.

"Do you still remember the time I knocked you out?" Strength chided.

Four Winds replied, "You ask that question so often, it is as if you believe the event has occurred as often as you ask."

"By forcing you to remember, I remind you to prepare for the unknown," Strength From Inside answered. "It's a favor I do you."

"I think it's a favor you do yourself, Strength," Four Winds rebuked.

"Perhaps," Strength agreed, "but to be the only man to have done a particular thing is worth preserving the honor of having done it. And mostly, I remember it in fondness as the day I gained your respect."

"You're fortunate I like you so much, or I would be forced to remind you that it only happened and *will* only happen…once."

"I think you just reminded me." Strength laughed. "But I hope that remains true. You are a great warrior, and I don't mind continuing to be a close second to my hero and my friend."

The two young men arrived at The Great Chief's tipi and asked to enter.

"Here we go." Four Winds sighed. "This better not be your fault, Strength."

Strength looked back at Four Winds with a grin as they began to dip their heads inside the tipi. "I talk much more than I did as a child, so I will have no problem finding the words to ask you, 'Do you still remember the time I knocked you—'"

"Come inside, you two." It was the chief who had stopped their banter.

They entered the tipi. A fire was smoldering in the middle of the circular room, white smoke rising slowly from the charred wood. The Great Chief sat on the right side of the fire, while The Ancient One sat on the left.

Without looking up from the fire, The Great Chief declared, "Four Winds. You are my strongest and finest warrior." He then turned to the other brave. "Strength From Inside. You are my strongest and finest warrior."

Some places in the world may have rendered this set of statements impossible to be true, simultaneously. The Great Chief had made them sound impossible not to be true.

The Great Chief turned from the young men and glanced over at The Ancient One—his mentor, his friend, and the protector of the scroll. He looked down again at the fire. Without looking at the two braves, he stated with unquestioned authority, "You both will fight alongside The Ancient One today. Four Winds on horseback. Strength From Inside on foot. Go and prepare."

"Yes, Great Chief," Strength and Four responded in unison. They stood for a moment waiting to see if more instructions would follow. When nothing came, they turned and left.

They retraced their path back toward the other side of the camp. At the same time, The Great Chief sat quietly in the tipi looking into the fire and holding back the sorrow he felt in knowing he would probably lose a dear friend today and quite possibly the two young men he had just assigned to protect his friend. The Ancient One was aging so quickly, The Great Chief wasn't sure if his friend might die of old age before the battle even began.

Two conversations, unbeknownst to both parties, followed parallel paths.

"It is the greatest honor to be protecting The Ancient One," Strength From Inside told Four Winds as they walked away from the chief's tent, "but I wonder why he is *fighting?*"

"Why are you going to fight?" the chief inquired.

"You know the answer, Strength."

"The answer is the same as it was before, so there is no need to ask again," replied The Ancient One to his friend.

Strength argued, "He has always fought. It would be fine for him to stay back this time. It would not lessen my respect for him."

"I have always fought," The Ancient One continued in his response to the chief's question, "and that will not change today. I am a member of this tribe, and if I am to die, I will die protecting it, as I have lived doing the same."

"You respect him as you do for the very reason he fights today," Four Winds rebutted.

The Great Chief and Strength From Inside both experienced a moment of being renamed Quiet and the issue was closed.

CHAPTER 5

JACK IN THE BOX
THURSDAY, FEBRUARY 1, 2007
LATER THE SAME NIGHT

"Y ou know, Randy, it's going to take me a while just to get the scroll out of the box safely and determine the kind of care I might need to take to unroll it. I can come get you once I get that far."

Randy had appeared back in the lab, seemingly much sooner than his next official break would have allowed. Jack had moved the box into the clean room and had prepared for a more delicate examination, given how old the scroll appeared to be. Jack was making an attempt to keep Randy from standing at his side, bored for the next couple of hours waiting for something to happen. And if Jack was being completely honest with himself, it was more likely an attempt to keep Randy from standing at his side at all. The work he was about to perform was tedious enough without having someone breathing down his neck, making him feel like he had to rush for only the mere fact that they were there.

"The clean room, huh? I haven't seen you use this in a long time," Randy said as he moved aside the plastic of the makeshift room at the back of the office, "but that's fine, Jack. I'll leave you alone for a while. Rounds got boring; I wanted to see it one more time before you started."

"Can't get anything past you, can I? I hope I didn't hurt your feelings. It's just that—"

"No worries, Jack. I understand you. You come off like you only want to be by yourself, but it's not really who you are. You've even fooled *you* into believing it sometimes. The fact is, Jack, you're not a misanthrope. You're an archaeologist. It's a lonely job, requiring a lot of patience, and your dedication to it over the years has tricked you into thinking you don't like people. But really, it's not people you don't like, it's a proper work environment you crave."

"Where'd you get so smart, Randy? Think you got me pegged, huh?" Jack smiled and shook his head. "Don't know, but one thing you said's wrong for sure."

"Yeah?"

"Yeah. I really don't like you."

"Yeah, right." Randy laughed. "You and me would be like Indiana Jones and that guy from *The Mummy* movies if we ever wanted to give up the health insurance and consistent paychecks. We'd be searching for treasures and artifacts that bring the dead back to life and melt the eyes of Nazis, even if we had to go to the North Pole to find them."

"I don't know, Randy. Maybe leave that to someone else. Plus, Indiana Jones didn't wear glasses. I like the comforts of my lab, and to top it off, all the stuff's already been found for me. I just have to go through the boxes."

"Actually, he did, Jack."

"Who did? Did what?"

"Indiana Jones. He did wear glasses."

"Are you sure?"

"Yeah, I definitely remember he had glasses—at least, sometimes."

"Ah, well *there*. I need my glasses all the time." Jack stopped, shook his head at how Randy had pulled him in again. "Why are we even having this conversation?" He turned away from Randy and roll-tapped his fingers on the top of box number 2347 still sitting closed on his workbench. "Just come look at the most excitement you're going to get and get it over with." He opened the box. "There. Take a look, Randy; then, get out. And cover your mouth."

Randy walked over and looked down at the scroll lying at the bottom of the container. "Wow. Just think where this has been. If they got it from Little Bighorn, it was owned by the Sioux. Do you think it's written in their language?"

"Yes, Randy," Jack muttered.

Thanks to Randy, it appears muttering's become my new hobby.

Randy ignored the tone. "I don't know, Jack. I'm just looking at it, and it doesn't really look all that fragile. Take a look."

Jack leaned over, his head next to Randy's, and shined a penlight into the box. "You know, you may be right."

"I think we both just saw 'old scroll' earlier, and so that's all we saw."

"Yeah, I hear ya."

Jack slipped on a latex glove and reached in and gently touched the scroll. It was firm to touch. It didn't crumble, and it wasn't brittle.

Jack sighed loudly. "Huh. I think we can take it out safely and have a look."

"Jack, you're slipping."

"Huh?"

"You just said *we*."

"Yeah, yeah. Now shut up."

Jack curled the fingers of both latex-gloved hands around the scroll and lifted it out. He set it down on a piece of protective parchment. *Amazing,* he thought, *it feels unaged.* It almost made him think the scroll was a fake. Even upon its unrolling, Jack never felt concern he'd do any damage.

After it was unrolled, the two men stood quietly, both staring at it with looks of disbelief on their faces. Randy was no linguistics expert, but he wasn't stupid either. Honestly, one could have been stupid and still have come to the same conclusion that Randy broke the uncomfortable silence with.

"Well, that's definitely not Sioux."

"You got that right, Randy."

"It's Russian, isn't it?" Randy added.

"Yeah. But what the hell would the Sioux Indians be doing with a scroll written in *Russian*? This has got to be cataloged improperly."

"Nope. Remember the index card, Jack?" Randy replied. "It said '*Scroll* confiscated—'"

"Yeah, but it also said 'Attempted Translation—failed,'" Jack retorted. "They definitely could have translated Russian in 1877, so that makes no sense."

"Hey! I'm in a real archaeological debate!" Randy beamed. "College is working, huh? Jack, maybe it came from some lost Siberian tribe that crossed the land bridge and brought it to the Sioux."

"Randy, uh—no."

"I know, but it's got to be something more interesting than some Russian written on some old paper and then misfiled inside the warehouse. That would just plain suck. Can't you translate it, Jack, or some of it? Then we can be sure."

"Well, not just by looking at it," Jack answered. "I'd need to get a couple books from my upstairs office, and my night's almost over. Even if this scroll did come from the hands of the Sioux, they must've taken it from someone else. Settlers or something. That's the only explanation I can think of."

"Ah, go get your books. You can at least start tonight."

"I'll try, Randy. But we'll figure it out one way or the other."

"There you go with the *we* again." Randy winked. "See, Jack, I was right. Indiana Jones and *The Mummy* guy."

"Not one word yet," Jack explained to Randy when the kid returned for the third time since box 2347 had grasped both their curiosities. "I've tried half of the words on this page, and there is not one single Russian word. My Russian is less than good, and I'm tired. It's four a.m. Time to go home. I think I'll have to pick this one up next week. It just seems to be Russian letters, randomly placed on a page."

"Well, Jack, that's weird. Hey, maybe it's code."

"It's gotta be something because it sure ain't Russian," Jack stated, rubbing his eyes. "But I don't think mid-1800s Russian settlers were in the habit of encoding their correspondence." He closed the Russian dictionary and stood up from the stool. He placed the scroll back into the metal container.

Randy watched as Jack closed the lid and latched it. "Well it may not be some ancient magical scroll ready to melt our faces, but at least it's a mystery."

CHAPTER 6

SARAH DUBOIS AND GERARD THE ARCHAEOLOGIST
JUNE 25, 1876, EGYPT

"THERE AREN'T MANY PEOPLE of the millions who have lived, dearie, who can say they've been this close to the Jackal himself."

"O-oh," the girl on Gerard Palton's right arm stuttered as she gazed around the dark and entirely stone-laid corridor down which the two were making their way. The burning torch in Gerard's left hand cast shadowy flickering figures following him and his dearie at the edge of their vision.

"What's the matter, girlie? You getting afraid? No need to worry. Your friend Gerard is here to ward off any evil curses or mummies back from the dead. Ha! Just have another drink, dearie."

"Oh, Gerard," the girl replied. "I didn't think it would be so dark and creepy down here. You said I was going to meet a great king."

"You will, soon. And then we'll dance all around him and show him a little something he hasn't been able to do in a long time. Ha!"

"Oh, Gerard, are you sure you haven't brought anyone else down here like this?"

"Oh dearie, dearie, I swear I've brought no one like *you* down here like this."

"Well, all right. This wine is so good, Gerard. Is it as old as the king we'll be seeing?"

Gerard Palton was an archaeologist, yes, but he was more of a drunk and a philanderer who liked to *say* he was an archaeologist. He did like to dig for things when there was a shovel in front of him and no bottle. Or, as he sometimes thought, he *was* an archaeologist at heart—just one who happened to be better at remembering where he'd left his bottle than where he'd left his shovel. Or maybe it was more that he misplaced his shovel whenever he found his bottle. Or...

Well, regardless, if he had any problems at all in his life, they weren't his fault. They were just the damned circumstances. He sure couldn't help it if he happened to run into a pretty girl every time he was looking for freaking shovels but finding bottles instead.

He was a smooth talker, and that made him well liked. If you made yourself well-

34

liked by the right people and you found some way to keep them happy, you could keep grant money flowing your way for shovel searching and bottle discovering. And every now and then, if you had good instincts—which Gerard had—the workers you hired, who seemed to have a much easier time keeping track of their digging tools, would find something wonderful under the sand.

This was what had happened the previous week. Anubis's tomb. By God, he'd found it. Or by the devil, Gerard suspected. What would God be doing helping a guy like him? But either way, the damned Jackal and his city of Abydos had been found after four thousand years, and it had been on Palton's watch.

The first entryway to be uncovered led straight into the mortuary temple built by Ramses II, the pharaoh whom legend said Moses was responsible for drowning. After a few days of working and freeing the entrance of debris, Palton had discovered the inscriptions that described the temple and its purpose.

The temple had been built by Ramses II in honor of Anubis, the jackal-headed god of the dead. Ramses II had died unexpectedly, though, and his subjects had decided to entomb him there in the hopes that Anubis would heal him and bring him back to rule as the god of the living.

So Gerard had fibbed a bit to his girlie girl. They weren't *actually* going to meet the Jackal, but rather Ramses II. *But you know,* Jackal *sounds so much more exciting.*

The two had made their way to the end of the passageway. Gerard hadn't been in the main chamber yet. He'd sent all the workers home the day before. He might find bottles more enticing than shovels, but a long time ago, there had been a reason he'd gotten into this whole archaeology thing—he loved it. Even after time passed, and he'd come to love other things more—like booze and girls—he hadn't lost his love for archeology. *So whenever I get the chance,* he thought, *why not bring them together for a great time.* Therefore, he'd prepared himself for the big night, found himself a bottle of good wine and a beautiful American girl in nearby Cairo, and headed toward the hole he'd dug for himself.

"It's right through here, Sarah," Gerard said. "Sarah? That's right, isn't it?"

Ah! I hate it when I forget their names.

"Hmmph! Gerard! You haven't forgotten my name *already,* have you?"

"No way, Sarah." He *hoped* it was Sarah; she hadn't exactly answered his question. "I'm just so darned thrilled to be going in here for the first time. My mind is escaping me, darling. Here, have another drink."

"Well, okay. I guess I can understand that. You have a pretty exciting job, although it's a little dark and scary too. Digging up old things is nifty, but the dead people—that's quite *unnerving,* Gerard."

"Well, come here close then, dearie. That's why I'm here—to protect you from all the goblins." And he pulled her close and kissed her before they took their torch and themselves into the chamber.

The inscriptions Gerard had translated contained all the standard warnings about the curses that would befall those who entered the tomb. Ramses II was being resurrected by Anubis, blah, blah, blah, and any who disturbed this important process would invite the fury of both gods down upon their souls, blah, blah, blah. You know, KEEP OUT! NO TRESPASSING! but written in pictures with lots of birds and men walking like Egyptians. Yet, given all the work it must have taken to create these ancient writings, their authors appeared not too bothered with the real truth because there was no mention of what Gerard and Sarah were actually about to stumble across in that dark and forbidding chamber.

—◇○◇—

Gerard had entered the tomb, expecting to see the run-of-the-mill burial chamber: a sarcophagus—mummy placed safely inside; clay jars filled with long-ago-decayed entrails; treasures, statues, and hieroglyphics; and a carving of Anubis, the god of the dead with his jackal head looming over it all, still trying to work his godly magic to bring Ramses II back from his everlasting demise.

Inside, there would be enough gold to dazzle his lady friend into staying and enough "spooky" to keep her clinging. That's not, however, what they saw.

At first the chamber appeared empty, completely void of all the typical artifacts. The inscriptions outside had been completely misleading. As he moved the torch from side to side, Sarah sighed. "This is creepy, Gerard. Nothing's here. Can we go?"

It was very quiet, and he agreed with her—it was creepy. It was a strange feeling, given his career choice and the amount of experience he'd had in these matters, but what was even stranger was whatever it was he heard breathing. Something other than Sarah and him.

"What the…" Gerard let out. He moved closer to Sarah, the opposite action of his scheme; he'd immediately forgotten his original plan had been for *him* to be the brave one.

He swung the torch in the direction of the noise and saw a shape moving toward them with a mummy-like gait. The thing's arms were out, and it was holding something in each hand. He caught a glimpse of its eyes. They were wide and wild. It lurched toward them, groaning.

"Get away! Get away from us!" Sarah yelled and started pulling Gerard backward. "Let's get out of here! Help! Help us!"

Gerard stumbled as Sarah pulled on him, and in his own fright, he dropped the torch and stumbled backward into her, toppling them both like a couple of dominos in the dark. The mummy, or whatever it was, threw itself on top of them. It was still moaning and groaning and breathing hard. Gerard tried to scramble out from under it, but he was sandwiched between the living girl and the not-quite-dead-enough thing atop him.

The thing's eyes rolled back in its head like a shark ready to attack, and the torch made the whites of the thing's eye glow gold. Gerard pushed on the crawling corpse, and it rolled off of him. In some places, its skin felt like slime and in others like sandpaper, and Gerard found himself gagging as he pushed the corpse off himself and then pushed himself off Sarah. He reached down and grabbed the torch he'd dropped during the morbid tackle.

By the time Sarah got to her feet, the thing was up on its knees, breathing heavily on the floor, and Gerard was leaning in to use the torch against it. She screamed, "No, Gerard! Stop!"

"What? It attacked us!" Gerard responded; his eyes were now as wild as the thing's had been.

Sarah came closer and pulled at Gerard, grabbing the torch from his hands. She gasped, "Oh my God! Gerard! It's a man! But look! He's so old! Look, Gerard! He must be a hundred years old. Or more!"

The "man" indeed looked older than any Gerard had ever seen or imagined. So much so, Gerard still felt compelled to think of the man as a "thing" and *not* a man. Out of this man-thing's head grew only a few long strands of white hair. He was so thin, his body seemed to be only a skeleton, painted the color of skin. It was hard to believe he was alive.

Where is there room for any organs? Gerard thought.

Then Gerard noticed the two leather cylinders in the man's hands, and the archaeologist part of him took over. And as he decided to forget about the man's well-being and go after what the man had, it was clear Gerard Palton was not a redeemable archaeologist. He was a selfish, self-indulgent one.

"What are you doing?" asked Sarah as she watched Gerard kneel and start grabbing at one of the old man's hands.

"I'm going to see what he's holding," Gerard said.

"He needs help, Gerard. We should go and get a doctor."

"He'd be dead long before we got back."

"We should take him out of here, then!" she pleaded.

"I just want to see what he's got here in his *hand*!" Gerard was grunting as he touched the man's disgusting skin, but he went ahead anyway with the task of prying the man's fingers from his possession, fingers which seemed to have been so tightly curled around it for so long they had almost become a part of the item.

"Gerard! Stop it!" Sarah bawled. "We should at least try to help him."

"In a minute, in a minute. Really, he'll be dead if we move him. Look at him. I'm surprised he survived the fall."

But Gerard couldn't really care less about the man. He was an archaeologist (and don't forget, a selfish, self-indulgent one). Archaeologists dealt with old and dead things. The items in the man's hands interested Gerard presently. He would be more interested in the man *after* the man stopped breathing.

He couldn't loosen the man's fingers. They were like clamps designed to never release. He pulled at each finger, willing to break them off if doing so would get him what he was after. Gerard's stomach curdled as he felt different parts of the man's hands—decaying sinews alternating with leathery skin. Gerard was picturing freshly dead flesh, beginning to rot, and he tried to shake the image away to complete his objective.

Sarah was standing behind Gerard nearly frozen with fear. She was still trembling from the experience of tumbling to the ground with Gerard and a half-dead man joining them in a dark burial chamber. Struggling with her desire to help the man while Gerard ignored her pleas, she was faced with a choice she didn't like having to make: try and save the man or let Gerard keep going at the poor soul until she became an accomplice to murder. Gerard wasn't listening to her, and he was so intent on getting what the man was holding that he seemed ready to break off the old man's hands to get it. She glanced at her own hands and noticed she was holding something, herself—the torch—and tried to decide what to do to save the man and not get herself killed in the process.

Her panic overtook her, and a moment later she found herself swinging the torch like a bat toward the side of Gerard's head. Within this mayhem, which her evening out had become, Sarah wasn't sure if she'd truly intended what she witnessed next or not; but as the torch hit Gerard's head, she became instantly aware she had lit one man on fire to save the other.

Gerard's hair had been set ablaze along with the linen collar of his suit coat. He was screaming and running through the empty chamber as his face became engulfed in flame. Sarah jumped out of the way as Gerard almost spilled into her in his blazing frenzy. He ran into the wall, rolled against it to face her, and slid down it like a piece of rare meat thrown against glass. Sarah gasped. She recoiled as Gerard's face began to melt exposing bone underneath his cheeks. He was writhing while beating his chest and face with his flaming hands. His screams turned from yelps to gargles and his flesh's color transformed to a mix of blood and black. The fire spread over his convulsing body, lighting his trousers. His fingers on one hand fused into his liquifying face while his shirt material consumed the skin of his other hand. Sarah stood frozen in horror, her arms wanting to reach out to him to do something, anything, if only for the mere fact that Gerard was a human being dying in agony, but she could do nothing. The flames lowered as there became little left to burn of Gerard, or his clothing, and Gerard's convulsions ended. A few small twitches of his legs turned to complete stillness; his charred head slumped to right, and Gerard became the first deceased human relic in his archaeological find.

Sarah couldn't bear to watch as Gerard expired, and she closed her eyes. His screams filled her mind even after there were no more screams, and that was worse than the nearly intolerable smell of his flesh cooking only a few paces from where she stood. She was shaking from the adrenaline coursing through her arteries. She turned and stumbled away, cupping her hands over her ears. She screamed to cover Gerard's howling, or maybe it was only the memory of his howling. She screamed and screamed until she became aware that the tomb was only echoing her own voice. As her yells subsided, they gave way to sobbing. Her chest heaved and she spent several minutes trying to slow her breathing. As she did, she forced herself to turn slowly to view what her action against Gerard had wrought. Gerard's body lay still against the wall on the far side of the room; small embers ate away at whatever remained of fresh meat. The scene was too much for her and Sarah's psyche forced her attention to return to the old man who was kneeling on the ground in the middle of the tomb— *Gerard's Tomb*, she thought, and quickly pushed that from her mind. She moved toward the old man to try and help him up.

The old man's eyes were open and they fixated on Sarah. He seemed disoriented but he didn't appear to Sarah as crazy as he had before. Gerard's finale didn't seem to have had the same unnerving effect on the old man as it had had on her. He seemed unable to rise on his own, or perhaps he saw no need to, and so he stayed on the ground on his knees. Sarah touched his hand and then grasped it, trying to pull him to his feet. The man had little strength, but from his reverse pull, it was clear to her that he did not want to stand. Regardless of Sarah's personal state of panic, she still seemed to be having a calming effect on the man, the way some people could touch an agitated animal, conveying an understanding to the beast that they meant to it no harm. She ignored his resistance and tried again to raise him to his feet. The man needed to get help and she needed to get out of there. Her departure from Gerard's archaeological discovery was way overdue.

"Come on, come on! I can help you to a hospital! Just help me a little." She struggled again. She moved around behind the man and tried to pull him up by grabbing under his arms. She hated the feel of his skin. Spots of milky texture delivered images to her already frazzled mind. She saw her fingers sinking into the man's body on their way to his internal organs, only being stopped from completely disappearing into his torso by rough patches of leathery chain mail substituting for skin. With only a cloth wrapped around his waist, there was little she could do to keep from touching anything but the man's skin.

Still, he wasn't moving. She let go and scuffled around in front of him again, now in near hysterics, and looked at him. "Please!" she pleaded.

His eyes cleared up at her begging, and this time she believed she saw not only calmness but understanding in his stare. The senility seemed to have disappeared for the moment, and the man appeared, impossible as it seemed, almost wise. His look entranced her, compelling her to forget her departure, replacing that goal with a desire to communicate with him. She knelt and watched his thin, limp lips curl into a smile. Instinctually, she smiled back.

The man reached his arms toward her, holding up the two leather cylinders, now forever safe from Gerard Palton due to Sarah's intervention. His fingers uncurled, and as they did so, she heard a most unsettling crackling noise.

If she'd had just a moment more to look into his eyes, Sarah felt she could have read the man's entire life in his gaze. It seemed he could communicate volumes of wisdom with just a look. She understood he wanted her to take what he was holding. She moved, following his silent, almost telepathic instructions, gently taking the objects from his hands.

He closed his eyes, and she watched him fall back into the dark, disintegrating into atoms. It was one more tragic sight in an evening filled with them, and it pushed her toward a mental break she had been keeping at bay for the last several minutes. Her current situation flooded her mind. She was underground, alone in a crypt, two corpses within visual range—or one corpse, rather—Gerard's. The old man had supernaturally metamorphosed into a cloud of dust. The torch was smoldering down to embers—it would be pitch dark inside the chamber soon. One of the dead men here she had killed, and as for the other, she had apparently killed him, too, and now she was holding his possessions.

Sarah knew she had to get out of there before the torch was completely spent. She placed the two leather containers under one arm, picked up the torch, and made her way out of the city of Abydos.

—◇○◇—

The mystery of the burnt-up archaeologist and disappearing scroll holder would never need to be solved. Soon after Sarah's departure, a scaly, clawed, nightmarish creature crawled out of nowhere and ate Gerard's cooked remains, only to disappear again when it was finished. The pile of dust near the center of the chamber where Sarah had received the two scrolls would never be noticed, and thus would never be determined to be of human origin. And none of this would immediately matter, anyway. By the next day, due to a little of the same power which had made a man atomize in front of Sarah Dubois, Gerard Palton—archaeologist, drunk, and womanizer—would mysteriously exist only as a distant and barely tangible memory to anyone who had ever known him, and the dig site Sarah had stumbled out of the night before would be, once again, covered by a sandstorm.

Although Sarah escaped from the Egyptian ruins, her life would soon be in its own state of ruin. She became unable to cope with her failed attempt to save the old man in the tomb, especially considering the effort had only succeeded in killing her date for the night, by setting him on fire. Reemergence of these events as constant nightmares was of no help to her psyche either. And *no one* seemed to remember Gerard Palton. Had she gone *insane?* Had the night even *happened?* It was not long, thereafter, that Sarah Dubois switched from "alcohol for fun" to "alcohol for medication,"—and this was the kind of medication prescribed daily and as often as needed. *Often* intoxicated became *always* so, spiraling Sarah into blackouts and intermittent delirium. During a moment of barely aware self-preservation, she disappeared from the endless streets of Cairo by way of committing herself to an institution for the care of the mentally ill.

CHAPTER 7

JACK AND JON JOHANSSEN
FEBRUARY 1, 2007
9:00 P.M.

"**S**O HOW ARE THINGS going in the city, Jon?"

"Not bad, Jack," his brother replied. "Just pushing the buttons. Reject. Reject. Reject."

"It's that bad, huh?" Jack inquired. "How many books do you read through before you find a good one?"

"Jacky, it's more than you'd care to know. Even when you're sure you've got a hit, you can be surprised," Jon complained.

"Sounds like it's something that just happened by the tone of your voice."

"Oh yeah, definitely," Jon answered. "I'm pretty frustrated right now. I got this great writer kid. We put a book out of his last year. I was expecting another surefire hit. Instead, he gives me this piece of junk I can barely get through."

"We got the same job, different realm, Jon. I have to go through hundreds of meaningless clay pot fragments to find one interesting piece of history."

Jack and Jon Johanssen were brothers—or at least would be brothers for another fifteen hours or so. It was 9:00 p.m. on Thursday, and Jon wouldn't exist anymore by 11:30 a.m. on Friday.

Their relationship wasn't that close. Jon had always been a bit aloof and distant. Jack didn't believe he had received one call from his brother since Jon had moved out of their parent's house and went off to Columbia for his masters five years before Jack had graduated from high school. It wasn't Harvard, but Jack's father hadn't missed following up many of his Harvard jabs toward Jack with "Well, at least your brother went to Columbia." Jack had felt compelled to keep the relationship going over the years, so he forced a call on Jon every so often. He didn't know why. He never got much back. It had always felt like Jon was just going through the motions as part of the family. But Jon was Jack's only sibling, so Jack had kept up the phone calls.

"So, Jon, what's up with this author you say is upsetting you?"

"Ah, it's nothing," Jon replied, "it's just he wrote this amazing FBI mystery—the one I mentioned. We got it published and made a mint last year. Everyone's expecting a follow-up, right? So what arrives yesterday? Derek Dubois, crime fiction writer extraordinaire, sends me his next great *thriller*? Ha! No! Instead it's about his aunt who gets special powers or something derived from some ancient scroll. It's boring. There's no conflict. It's like *Ya-Ya Sisterhood* without the ya-ya or the sisters."

"Doesn't sound much like the first book, that's for sure. What's it about again?"

"I've been over it and I *am* over it; I think I have missed some point, Jacky. But essentially, what I can figure is this lady, Sarah, gets hold of this ancient scroll that somehow gives her the power to stay young. So she decides to travel the world and see some things with her nephew. I haven't got to the end. Probably won't. I really don't see the point. I'm just going to have to tell him to write another book or he's out."

"What a coincidence, Jon."

"What's that?"

"Just last night, one of the boxes I opened contained a scroll. You got me curious now to take a closer look at it. Maybe it can tell me how to catalog this warehouse faster or, at best, keep me young forever, too."

"Well, Jacky, if it gives you the abracadabra to make this guy pump out another thriller, and quick, call me up."

"I always call you."

That slipped out.

"Yeah? Hey, it's nine p.m. Aren't you at work in that basement of yours, usually, by now?"

"Thursdays and Fridays, I'm off," Jack replied.

"That's some schedule. Well, Jacky, gotta go. These books don't read themselves, ya know."

"All right, Jon, but you've known my schedule for—"

Click.

Well, that went like it always does.

Jack and Randy had opened box number 2347 the night before; The scroll from the Battle of Little Bighorn, written in Russian, yet not Russian. However, that had been near the end of the night. After an hour or two of getting nowhere—nowhere slowly—work had ended, and the scroll had left his mind by the time he'd driven home. He was off tonight and tomorrow, and this week he wouldn't be working again until Monday. The warehouse had arranged some huge cleaning crew to scour the place Friday through Sunday this week.

I guess I could go in tonight, just to take a look at it?

He wasn't thinking "fountain of youth," but Jack did like his job for these little curious moments, and if he was being honest, it had been a while since the last one. The call to his brother had made box 2347's contents feel a little more interesting, that was all—an itch that needed scratching, a quote just heard—now needing a movie title attached to it and you just can't quite remember which movie it was…and, of course, there's no rest until you get it, *is there?* And now it appeared to Jack that some non-Russian on some old parchment needed another look before sleep was happening.

CHAPTER 8

JACK BACK IN THE BOX
FEBRUARY 1, 2007
10:00 P.M.

B Y THE TIME JACK pulled into to his parking spot, he'd already heard two different guards at two different checkpoints say, "You in tonight on your day off, Mr. Johanssen?" They made it sound like he'd never done it before, and that made him feel like a government clerk, not an archaeologist. So what if he had never actually done it before? It's not like he had made the decision to never come in on a day off. He'd just not had a reason to yet. Figuring he would hear the same inquiry from Randy, he braced himself for it as he made his way from his car to the building entrance. This rare mood and motivation for his work weren't going to be tainted with any more self-defensiveness.

"Hey, Jack. What—"

"Yeah, yeah, yeah, Randy. I'm here on my day off," he spat and blew past Randy while holding his badge up and heading straight toward the elevator without a glance at Randy.

"That's cool. I'm glad to see ya," Randy replied as Jack flew by, Randy's head moving as he spoke his words like he was conversing and watching the serve of a tennis match at the same time. Randy had to raise his voice with his follow-up because Jack had gotten so far down the corridor. "So why ya here?"

"Sorry, Randy, it's just I heard—ah, never mind," Jack hollered back, still not turning. Jack made it to the industrial-sized metallic doors of the elevator, which carried him to his underground office five days a week and pushed the large black down button. Waiting for the elevator, Jack felt it was so slow, it must have been invented before stairs. He noticed Randy had decided to rise from his stool and make his way down the hallway as well, seemingly not wanting to let go of Jack's surprise arrival.

"I didn't catch you, Jack," Randy said as he neared the archaeologist in waiting. "What'd you hear?"

Feeling an invisible maid scraping egg off his face, Jack decided to give the kid a moment. But he knew the truth would clue Randy into his own pseudoexcitement, and this would ripple into Randy being excited and so forth and so on—Jack knew how the night was going to go before it even got started.

Or so you think, Jack.

Without further trying to explain, Jack admitted, "I thought I might take another look at that scroll you were drooling all over last night. Remember it?"

"Yeah, of course, Jack!" Randy belted. "The one that said, 'Hey, look at me, I bleed prophetic number coincidences and I'm kind of in Russian.'"

"I guess, yeah, that's the one." Jack sighed.

Next, and nearly forgetting he was still a security guard at the facility, Randy followed Jack into the elevator, which had now opened its doors—finally deciding to join the two men after remembering it wasn't stairs. *(And given what the two men were about to be swept up into—not yet realized by either one of them—there's a slight chance the elevator actually did have that thought.)*

"So why are *you* so interested *now?*" Randy asked. "You gave up last night. What happened? Did you start building mountains out of mashed potatoes in your living room?"

"Ha, ha, Randy," Jack laughed. "Uh, no, I wouldn't say that. Aren't you a little young to remember that movie?"

"Reruns, Jack. DVD?"

The elevator carried the men two stories into the ground. Jack hadn't been building vegetable architecture, but this conversation with Randy was bringing back the opening of the box the night before. Combine that with the phone call he'd had with his brother, and Jack started wondering if he ought to consider mashing some potatoes.

Just in case I need them, I mean. That's all.

"I still can't believe you came in on your day off," Randy misfired without knowing it. He was leaning over the workbench where Jack had placed the scroll and several other books. Jack had decided the clean room wasn't necessary anymore.

"Enough already," Jack snapped.

"I think you can't admit you like people, *and* you can't admit you love what we're doing here."

Jack sat up on the stool and raised an eyebrow. "Exactly what *are* we doing here?"

"We're solving an archaeological mystery of an ancient mystical relic!"

"Randy. I hate to burst your bubble, but I think we're just solving the mystery of a misfiling at best."

Randy squinted and looked down at the letters on the scroll. "You know, it doesn't even look Russian. Russian words always seem like they're twice as long as they need to be. These words are shorter, less letters. You know what I mean?"

Jack looked back down at the parchment. "Yeah. I see what you mean. Almost—"

"Almost looks like English, doesn't it?" Randy completed the thought.

"Yeah, or something like it."

"I say we go with English, Jack. First, if the Indians got it from some American settler who was Russian or knew Russian, then the language most probably it would be coded in, if not Russian, would be Eng—"

"—lish." Jack completed Randy's sentence this time.

Jack the misanthrope had just had a moment with Randy the security guard as they answered each other in unison. He smiled at the thought of how excited they both were to be discovering "stuff," and he even forgot to be pissed off at himself for showing Randy his pleasure in the incident. Even if the scroll wasn't magical, it was better than "fragment 12 of broken pot C from dig plot 7 at site 312."

"You know, you're pretty smart, Randy, for a security officer."

"Ha, ha, Jack. You're pretty smart for a government-employed Morlock. But seriously, Jack, let's try English."

"Well, it's easy enough to test your theory out, I think."

"How?"

"Well, let me look at something here." Jack opened back up the Russian dictionary to a page near the beginning showing the alphabet. He started scanning the scroll and looking back and forth at the page he had open.

"Come on, Jack. What are you doing?"

"Just hold on a second."

After a couple of minutes, he looked up at Randy and grinned. "I think you just might be right, Randy."

"Huh?"

"You don't sound so smart now," Jack razzed him. "Listen here. I did a quick check, but I don't think I missed any. The Russian alphabet's got thirty-three letters; English has twenty-six. I didn't find the last seven Russian letters anywhere on the page. It could be a straight sequence code."

"You mean letter for letter? Like first letter of ours to first letter of theirs?" Randy asked.

"Yes, or last to first," Jack replied.

"Well, try it out. Come on!" Randy yelled and slapped Jack on the back.

"You can be as excited as you want, Randy," Jack said after the slap, "but I'm still not buying a whip, and I don't look good in hats."

Jack started working on transcribing the possible code, and after several words, Jack not only could tell he wasn't putting any English down on paper, he was also getting tired of looking at Russian.

"This is hard on the eyes, Randy. Russian has always looked to me like some drunk was trying to tell a story with Roman numerals. I don't think we're getting anywhere."

"Maybe in reverse? Like you said. Our twenty-sixth letter to their first letter and so on?"

"Randy. It was hard enough doing it one way, but I already tried that too. I'm kind of out of ideas." Jack took off his glasses and rubbed his eyes. "I mean, it's definitely a mystery, and that's nice for once, but look at this." He pointed down at his futile attempt at code breaking. "Spinning our wheels and guessing isn't going to get us anywhere. I have taken some cryptography courses, but I've never had to do it for real. I mean what does 'crnf' mean? Or 'hytosqv'?"

And then Jack saw it.

"Wait a second!" Jack's tone had shifted to an emotion more similar to Mr. Eureka's perpetual state.

"Jack?"

"Randy."

"Yes?"

"I can't believe I didn't see this before." Jack sighed.

"What? What didn't you see before?" Randy asked feverishly.

Nah, Jack thought. "Let me see this box." Jack got up off the stool and looked inside the storage container. At the bottom of the box was a piece of parchment the scroll had been resting on.

"There's got to be something more in here than just 'Attempted Translation—failed.'"

He scraped at the parchment, and it came up between his fingers. Underneath it was some paper. The paper looked old—more like Jack would have expected the scroll to have looked.

"What is it, Jack?" Randy was almost panting. "Come on, tell me something."

"I need to get some gloves on." He reached over and grabbed two new latex gloves from the box labeled Disposable Latex Gloves.

"That's not information." Randy pouted.

"Just hold on, Randy. I have a crazy idea, but I don't need to share my possible insanity with you or anyone else unless I'm sure, and then still…" Jack trailed off as he reached in and gently pulled out the couple of pieces of paper lying at the bottom of the box. He laid them out on another piece of parchment next to the one the scroll lay on.

"What are those?" Randy was trying to get a look over Jack's shoulder, but Jack kept leaning in closer, blocking Randy's view. It made Randy feel like a kid being shut out of some parental discussion. He moved around to the other side of the workbench and stretched his neck forward to see the pieces of paper.

"You're going to damage something, leaning over it like that."

"Oh, now you're paying attention to me?" Randy spat. He had a better view now and could see what Jack had pulled out of the box. "Hey, that has Russian writing too."

"Yep. But this was written by someone who tried to translate it in 1877. See the date here at the top? Our Mr. Paul Dunsford didn't seem to care much about listing these additional contents he found in the original box on the index card."

"But what's the big deal?" Randy asked. "So? Someone tried to translate it. We already know that."

"Looks like I'm not the only one to have noticed." Jack laughed. "My God, this is insane."

"What's insane? Jesus, Jack, you're killing me. What does it say?"

"The original translator noticed there was a six-letter word repeated throughout the document more than any other word," Jack answered.

"Why is that important? Maybe the word is like the main subject the scroll is talking about or something."

"That'd be true if it was just any word. These papers prove this scroll is in the right box and indexed properly and that it has been here since the 1870s. But if that's true, Randy"—Jack shook his head in disbelief—"then nothing makes sense all over again."

"What doesn't make sense, Jack?" Randy bawled. "You're not making any sense. That's what's not making any sense!"

Jack pointed to the word in the middle of the paper he had been translating and said, "This word, from when I did the one-to-one reverse sequence letter translation. I have seen this word before."

"But that's not a word, Jack," Randy responded. "What's 'JOTDTF'? Seriously, Jack, what is going on?"

"Randy, that's the word for 'Allied' if it were typed with an Enigma machine, and its settings were all at zero and using no plugboard."

"Huh?"

"Huh is right. In one of my courses on cryptology, the famous German Enigma machine from WWII was discussed. 'Allied Forces' was all over the examples we were given to translate. We studied the machine and its variations, usually setting them at base for simplicity. I recognize that word as 'Allied.'" He pointed once again to JOTDTF.

"Yeah, but it could be a coincidence, right?"

"Could be, but I think a few others look familiar now that I'm looking at it this way. We had to look at examples in German and then the same in English. German, the reason is obvious. English, because it's the other language we all knew. The theory was if you saw it later, you might recognize it. Well, I recognize it."

"Yeah, but who would be using that now?" Randy asked.

"Probably nobody important, but if somebody was thinking they were being creative, we'd still have the ability to say, 'I know what that is.' It's strange, Randy. I never thought I'd actually see it."

"But wait—" Randy stopped, maintaining a questioning look on his face.

"Yes, Randy, I'm thinking what you're thinking. Now you know why I thought it was a crazy idea. How would the Sioux, in 1876, have a document written in Russian, which is really encoded English, which is then encrypted by an early twentieth century cryptograph machine?"

"It's only multiplying the weirdness factor of last night, when we found this thing, by a hundred." Randy was pacing back and forth next to Jack's lab desk. He had replied with a bit of doubt in his voice as if the world where these things didn't happen had been a far safer one and one he'd like to return to. "There's got to be another explanation, right?"

"Obviously. But I guess I should test my theory more fully. But first I've got to get another book from my office: *How to Break the Enigma Code When Native Americans Have Had Too Much Time on Their Hands.*"

"That's funny, Jack. But if this is the real deal, I think we're back to square one when it comes to theories."

"I say we don't go there yet. Definitely a mystery, but let's look a bit further before we start cooking spuds."

"Yeah, agreed. As usual, Jack, I gotta get back to rounds. But when you're done, make sure you get me."

"Will do, Randy."

"See ya," Randy muttered, walking out of the office and looking a bit like he'd lost something.

Like his security blanket.

Jack hadn't let on, but he was already more convinced than the average skeptic that this was, in fact, the *real* deal. He didn't need another book to tell him these Native Americans *had* had too much time on their hands.

Get to work, Jack. This is why you became an archaeologist. He was wondering if he was going to need to buy that whip and hat after all, along with some bags of russets.

And I might need to move the sofa to make room for Potato Mountain.

⎯◇○◇⎯

"Soooo?" Randy asked Jack, poking his head into the lab. He had made his rounds three times just to give Jack some space—but damned if he wasn't going to find out what the hell was up with that scroll.

"Get in here, Randy. It's going faster than I expected. I was fishing through my books in my office when I remembered the damned internet. Being born in the early seventies, I don't always think of Google as my first option when I want to know something. Anyway, I found an online Enigma machine emulator! Incredible. I just chose the type and set the rotors to base position, and *voilà*! Instant translation!"

"*And*, Jack? What the hell does it say?"

"That's what I'm getting to. I don't really know what to make of it. This is either the biggest practical joke there ever was on an archaeologist, or—" Jack paused.

"Or what?" Randy pressed. "Or *what*, Jack?"

"Randy?"

"Yes?"

"I'm a fool. That's got to be it." Jack sighed. "This *is* some sort of practical joke. My birthday's coming up and, ahh! I should've seen it. Damn it! Honestly. How could I ever believe what I've been writing down here could have come from where this box says it came from?"

"Really, Jack? You think this is some kind of a joke on Jack?"

"Maybe even *yours*," Jack accused. "Either way, it's got to be."

"Well it's not me, and really, who would play a joke on you?" Randy asked. "Jack. You work at night—alone. As far as I know, you like it that way and don't ever see anyone else that works here. Do you even have a boss? As far as I know, if anyone gave a rat's ass enough to play a joke on you, it would be *me*, and it's *not* me. Do you think anyone even knows your birthday? When is it?"

"Well, it's not like tomorrow, but it is coming up. It's March second. The big thirty-three…can't believe it…" Jack sighed again. "Randy, it's got to be something like that. It can't be what it appears to be."

Randy didn't answer. He was looking up, toward the ceiling, with his head to one side. He appeared to Jack to be mumbling to himself. A moment later he stopped and stared at Jack.

"What're you doing there, Randy?"

"I don't know. I guess after everything we've been discussing concerning the scroll, my head keeps jumping to look for 'strange' every time I hear a number. I'm thinking you may be right, though—sadly. Even though I still don't know who it would be who would give a shit enough to care about playing a prank on you."

"Thanks. But why do you say I'm right?" Jack felt himself not wanting to believe his own argument, if only because Randy was no longer being the devil's advocate…and there had to be a devil's advocate.

"I'm thinking about your birthday. I did the math. You said you're going to be thirty-three?"

"Yes, that's right."

"So you were born in 1974?"

"Yes."

"So that makes your birthday out to be 3-2-7-4."

"And?" Jack prodded.

"Well—"

Then it hit Jack, and he interrupted Randy. "That's 2-3-4-7 with the digits flipped!"

"Yeah," Randy said. He looked bummed-out. "Our great prime number mystery…gone, huh? Someone probably got your birthday wrong and thought it was February third instead of March second. You know, two-three, three-two?"

Jack paused. "Yeah, and since last night was technically going to be my last night till next Monday, I wouldn't have been here on my 'birthday' they thought was tomorrow. So they did the joke a couple days 'early.'"

"Yeah." Randy sighed again, ironically disappointed as the safety of a *non*mystical world returned.

Randy was right, and Jack couldn't believe he had driven himself in on his night off all excited to be Indiana Jones for this foolishness. He leaned back in his chair, his face stating idioms like "Welp, that sucks," "Guess it was fun while it lasted," and "Move along folks; nothing to see here."

The time had been 23:47 when Jack had cataloged the contents of the box Mr. Dunsford had supposedly transferred on April 7, 1923: 4/7/23. And then Randy had gotten all jazzed about how the fact that 2,347 was probably a prime number. And now Jack's birthday: 3/2/74. Even Jack's current age—thirty-two—*three* and *two* matched the month and day of his birthday. It was all pretty clever. Someone had really gone through a lot of trouble on this one.

Wait a second.

A light returned to Jack's eyes, and Randy noticed it.

"What Jack? You think of who it might be—"

"Randy!" Jack cut him off.

"Yeah?"

"Randy, 23:47 was the *time* that I logged the scroll—last night. Eleven forty-seven last night."

"Uh-huh?" Randy was listening but not following.

"That can't be planned by anyone, Randy. What time I'm gonna do something. And that's what started it—*you* noticing the time matched the box number! If it hadn't been for that, you wouldn't have thought anything about the April 7, 1923, date. You probably wouldn't have even stayed very long. I never would have been all nutty about coming in here tonight on my day off, and there wouldn't have been any hoopty-do about my birthday fitting those numbers in any weird way either." Jack was on a roll now, and Randy was starting to get his point. "And…you can't fake that paper at the bottom of the box, which discussed the attempt at the Russian translation in the 1800s. That sucker's old as shit, and I know it!"

"So you don't think it's a joke?"

"Maybe not."

"Well, what did the scroll say that got you so freaked out about how it couldn't be real, then?"

As Jack's thoughts returned to the translation he had been working on, another thought sideswiped his frontal cortex. "And!"

"Another *and?*" Randy gulped as the mystical world began to return.

"Yes," Jack continued, "and I don't know for sure if this means anything, but—holy shit—I didn't think of this until now. Well, of course I didn't. There can't possibly be a connection."

Jack was rambling, and Randy stopped him. "Jack…what? What connection?"

Snapping out of the conversation with himself, Jack answered, "Randy, the scroll mentions it is one of four others, and it's the fourth one, specifically. And today, I talked to my brother, Jon. He's a book editor, publisher, whatever. Anyway, he said that some author of his just dropped off a book about his aunt having a scroll which kept her from aging and so she went on all these adventures around the world. He said the book was boring and had no point, but I think it might be—"

"Related?! No way, Jack. How could it be? I mean the number thing was cool, but you're taking pretty big leaps here now, *right?*" Randy's voice wavered a bit. He wasn't sure whether he was getting excited or scared. He decided to shelve the debate on which emotion was taking precedent for now. He didn't even know what the scroll said yet. That would clear this up. He'd be able to help Jack bring everything back to reality before their faces started melting or something. This calmness lasted all of about five more seconds.

"Randy?"

"Yes, Jack?" Randy answered. "You know, we're sure asking each other for our mutually undivided attention a lot tonight, huh?" Randy chuckled to lighten the mood. It didn't work.

"This scroll mentions that its keeper will stay young."

"You see? That's nothing, Jack," Randy replied, relieved at first, not having registered what Jack had said. And then, it registered. "It said *what?*"

"Randy, I don't think things are looking much like a joke anymore to me."

"Holy shit, Jack! What else does it say?"

"Well, like I said, it mentions it's one of four, and then it has a title regarding some myth and how bringing them together will affect the world. A person will hold each scroll for thousands of years until it changes hands to another, who will also stay young. Then it gets weird. I haven't finished translating, but so far the rest of it doesn't translate to anything coherent except for one word, which is placed several times within the text."

"What word?" Randy inquired.

"Allied: the word that gave me the clue it was encoded by the Enigma."

"Whoa, whoa, whoa." Randy halted. "Okay, a second ago it was a joke. Then it became like it's not a joke and that's kind of weird, and it might even be mystical or something, but now you're saying it may not only be linked to other scrolls that may actually exist, but their presence is going to change the world. I like the world, Jack.

How's it going to change it? This isn't real, come on. We're sitting here in a dark lab in a government warehouse. We're not on a movie screen. No world changing going on here."

"I mean, I figure you're right, Randy. There's probably *something* to it all, but probably not *exactly* as big as what we're making it out to be. I'll take a few more minutes and finish this up and then we'll take a closer look, okay?"

"Yeah, that sounds like a better idea. I mean, I wanted this whole little thing to be cool and everything, but I'm not ready to become some player in the apocalypse or something. I don't even shoot this gun very well. Let's make this more like a rabbit's foot and less like the lost Ark of the Covenant, *okay?*"

"Yeah, okay," Jack responded blankly, as his attention had returned to the translation.

"I'll make another round and then be back to hear what good luck the scroll brings to those who rub it."

"Yeah, okay," Jack repeated.

"See ya, Jack," Randy said, still trying to stay connected to the archaeologist. He didn't feel much like walking around the warehouse hallways alone as the door closed behind him.

Similarly, Jack didn't feel much like translating the rest of the scroll. Randy would have the privilege of not actually having to read whatever came next alone. Before, when Jack had just been busy translating it, he hadn't been thinking too much, and he hadn't made all the realizations he had just made with Randy. Now he was thinking the Native Americans might *have* had too much time on their hands. And look what had become of *them*. Did *he* now have too much time on *his* hands, and what would become of him?

Is Randy going to return here to see me pulling my heart out of my chest with my bare hands, telling him to drink from it as my eyes roll back into my skull?

All Jack could do was...hope not.

—◇○◇—

"Hey, you're alive!" Randy said, back in the office again like a comfortable saddle.

"Yes, Randy," Jack answered. "What else would I be?"

"I'm not gonna lie," Randy said as he made his way closer to Jack, walking past his perch (Jack's desk corner) without a pause. "I was starting to get mighty creeped out, out there walking around the warehouse alone. I started getting all kinds of ideas in my head."

Jack had swiveled to face Randy, holding his notebook. "Agreed. Felt the same way here. You should hear my thought of how you'd find me when you returned."

"You sound better, Jack. Any more luck with the translation?" Randy was peering down at the notepad in Jack's hands, trying to focus on some words. "Please tell me

54

it said, 'Happy Birthday, Jack: Joke's on You!' or *something* at the end like that, *right?*"

"No dice there, Randy, but there's good news even if there's bad news."

"Uh, Shinola. I never know what to pick," Randy ruminated. "Ah, give me the bad first."

"Okay," Jack said, preparing his answer. "Bad news is this might actually be the real deal. I mean, I'm not sure if it's really going to change the world, but there is definitely something going on here that isn't adding up with math and rulers, if you get my drift?"

"You mean like magic or something? Like real freaky archaeology movie-shit kind of real deal?"

"Yeah, maybe, if you want to put it that way."

"Okay, so that's not too bad of bad news. I mean it makes things weird, but we were kind of hoping it was weird all along, right?" Randy was trying to look on the good side. He'd been having enough of the freak-outs for the last hour or so, and anything to bring back some fun time to all of this, he'd take. "So what's the good news?"

"I'm not sure, but I don't think the scroll is bad or is going to melt our faces off or anything, just because we read it."

"Uh, Jack, I can't believe I'm even having this conversation with you *and* that we are now both actually happy some old document *isn't* going to melt our faces off. I feel even more crazy asking you this, but what makes you think it's not?"

"It said so."

"What was that?"

"I was finally able to translate a few more words. The last sentence here at the bottom says, and I'll read it: 'Jack, I know you and Randy are tripping that this scroll is going to melt your faces off, but it won't, so don't worry.'"

Randy stared at Jack. Jack observed shock on Randy's face, but a moment later, it turned to a face of anger. "Damn it, Jack! It wasn't you! This is all a joke on *me*, right! Shit, I *knew* something had to be up. And *you're* behind it! Okay, everyone can come out now from behind the shelves and shit." Randy had stuck his arms out and was motioning his hands as if to bring an audience of children closer as he looked past Jack to the back of the lab, "This makes a lot more sense. God, why didn't I think of it *before?*"

"It's no joke, Randy," Jack argued. "I wish it were, and I don't know what to make of it at all, but it's no joke. This scroll was taken from the Indians at Little Bighorn in 1876, and it has Russian letters as coded English letters that have been encrypted by a 1900s German cryptograph machine, and it mentions you and me specifically at the bottom. That's all I know. And really, I guess by the time I got finished, that's all I wanted to know anyway—that it wouldn't melt our faces off. And honestly, it seemed to know that that is all I wanted to know *too*. And right now, I'm just fine with that."

"Let me see it. I want to see for *myself*," Randy demanded. Damned if he was going to be the punchline after all of this.

"Here ya go." Jack handed Randy the notebook containing all of his translation work. "Look for yourself."

Randy snatched the pad out of Jack's hand. He scrolled quickly to the bottom of the page the notebook was turned to.

> *Jack, I know you and Randy are tripping that this scroll is going to melt your faces off, but it won't, so don't worry.*

> *sixth*

"You're sure you didn't just write this down to screw with me?"

"Yeah, Randy." Jack laughed. "That's what I'm known for, around here—the clown."

"I don't get it. And what's this last word, 'sixth'?" Randy pointed to the last word Jack had written on the page.

"I don't know." Jack picked up the original scroll and showed it to Randy, pointing toward the bottom. "It's this word here, centered and on a line of its own. As you can see, it ends after that. The sentence to you and me is right above it, then a period, and then this line with the word 'sixth.' Maybe we're missing some of the scroll? The scroll says its four of four at the top, so I don't think it relates to its sequence. We don't have any guarantee that this is everything the Indians had. This is just what was retrieved."

"You mind if I take a minute and look at it?" Randy asked.

"Sure, you can even go sit *at* the desk." Jack flicked his hand toward Randy's typical landing spot.

Randy didn't even blink at the offer Jack had made. He was too lost in reading the translation as he turned and carried the scroll and paperwork over to the desk.

"*And the Fourth being The Horsemen?*" Randy asked, still walking.

"Yeah, I didn't mention it starts out like that," Jack replied. "Hell if I know—and Randy, that's pretty much going to be my answer for everything there, okay?"

"Yeah, yeah. It was rhetorical anyway. Sort of."

"Big word, Randy. Maybe you'll graduate after all."

"Shut up. I'm reading."

"Fine, but if you figure anything out, let me know. My mind hurts."

Jack squinted and rubbed his eyes. He opened them and looked to the left toward his laptop, which was still displaying the online Enigma machine and chuckled to himself.

Bet whoever put that up there on the internet sure didn't think I'd be using it for what I just used it for.

"The myth of the *Hereafter?* What's *that* mean?" Randy was sitting at the desk now.

"Was that rhetorical too?"

"Yeah, yeah. You're right, though. Not much here until the end when it mentions us. It's the fourth of four, the world will change forever, scroll holder will stay young, second holder will too—like you said."

"Yup, then 'Allied,' here and there through the rest until that line at the bottom," Jack followed. "Honestly, Randy, I got nothing," Jack replied. "Seriously, nothing. I'm running on empty anyway, unless I get some food in me. You want to take a walk down to the vending machine?"

"Sure. We'll walk and talk."

"Great. Hope I don't pass out before we get there," Jack scoffed.

"It *is* just like you said, Jack," Randy said, still looking at the pad in his hand as they walked down the corridor.

"I know it is, Randy. You think I'd go through all this trouble to make it up?"

"So where's this second scroll holder that's not supposed to age?"

"Who knows? I didn't pull any mini scroll keeper out of Mr. Dunsford's box," Jack remarked, trying to make light of this all as he fidgeted his quarters into the vending machine.

"Not much of a scroll holder if he's not here. You don't think it's you, do you? And now *you* won't age?"

"Could be, Randy," Jack said as he joyfully bit into his Snickers.

"What? You *do* think it's you?" Randy asked.

"Huh? No." Jack sighed. "Snickers really *does* satisfy."

"Come on, Jack, this is serious."

"Sorry. I just needed a break from all of this." He took another bite, savoring the nougat and nuts and caramel and chocolate. Halfway through Jack's third chew, his expression of eye-closed delight changed to wide-eyed Dr. Eureka again. "Damn! I don't know why I didn't think of it before. Probably information overload—and face-melt fear. I'm going to call my brother, Jon, and find out who that author is. *Another* thing I forgot. *Damn* it. Do I look like I'm getting *old* to you, Randy?"

"Huh?"

"Never mind. It may be a long shot, but what if—" Jack paused at the lunacy of what he was thinking, but then continued anyway. "What if there *is* an actual connection with that author he was telling me about? The one who just finished a book about a scroll his aunt had, which kept her young?"

"I forgot you said that. That's right—no, wait—that's so wrong. Jack, this is too much," Randy said, shaking his head. "Are we actually considering that this thing might be legit?"

"Randy, I'm not considering anything, *and* I'm considering everything. You weren't the one alone in that lab when I translated that last sentence. But I know we won't know anything unless we get more information." Jack turned to return to his office, or to what strangely and quite involuntarily floated across his mind: *My destiny.*

Jack paused in the corridor just outside his lab's door. He looked up at the ceiling and sighed. "Huh. Jon and that author are the whole damned reason I decided to come in tonight and have another look at the thing before next Monday."

—◇◦◇—

What would real people do in situations like this? Perhaps, your gut reaction is "Come on, they aren't actually thinking that scroll is *real*, are they?"

But the answer remains the same, no matter what you think. Real people would do exactly what Jack and Randy did, or what Jack and Randy didn't do, or maybe, real people would do nothing. Real people are unpredictable. Someone else may not have cared enough about the tickle in their mind to give up a night off from work and would have decided to leave it alone. Others might have cataloged the damned thing and moved on to the next box. Others would have laughed about it and gotten a beer. And if any of those reactions *had* happened, many outside observers, such as yourself (if it were possible to have such people to view and comment on all situations) would have chimed in with the opposite gut reaction: "What are you thinking? You can't just walk away and have a beer! All the signs are pointing to the fact that that scroll may be the real thing! An honest-to-God mystical relic with powers! Turn around! Go back and study it more!"

Jack and Randy were real people, and they did what real people do. One of the above. Byron Henning, whom they didn't know, did know what he needed to say to get who he needed to listen…to listen. And, of course, prophecy is still a bitch.

And, just in case the leap hasn't been made yet, yes, Byron wrote the scrolls, or will someday in the distant future—on a little "nontypewriter" he's going to find today, on a desk in a cabin in the woods, about six miles from where Jack and Randy were right now. But currently, as Jack and Randy were reentering the lab after Jack's Snickers run, Byron was just a scared little kid hiding in a camper trailer listening to a disembodied voice.

CHAPTER 9

"**B**YRON?" A mother called out a kitchen window, paused, and waited for a reply. *No answer.*

Again, yelling this time, "Byyyyyyyyyronnnnnn! That boy." She sighed. "I told him not to run off."

"I don't understand," Byron said to nobody. "Why do I have to leave my home? Why do I have to keep walking? I don't want to leave." He started sobbing.

"Stiffen up," the Voice commanded. "Act like a man! You're going to be a hero and save a lot of people."

"Where *are* you? Why can't I see you? I'm only eleven years old. How can I be a hero? I want to go home. This isn't a good idea."

"KEEP WALKING!" was the wind's reply. "Or your parents will die."

"No! Please don't hurt my parents," Byron moaned. "I'll keep going."

"I'm not going to hurt your parents, kid. Your inaction will. Now do what I say."

Prophets. They all have such strange beginnings, don't they? Burning bushes, virgin mothers, appearing and disappearing angels, enlightenment. And nobody ever believes them, do they? They're loony, they're liars, they're power hungry, they're a snot-nosed brat cooking up a story on why he didn't come in for lunch when he was called for by Mom. But in the end, they always change the world. What the rest of us do with how they changed it is up to us, and really, is the whole reason they existed at all.

Later that night, on January 31, 2007, one of this little boy's scrolls would be examined in a government-contracted warehouse. Two others were on the verge of being looked at by a completely freaked-out writer, with his aunt, and a fourth was

59

the only possession a really old—yet young—man had left, as he sat shivering where he was shivering. And a lot of funky stuff had started to happen.

Fairly funky might have been that a whole bunch of numbers seemed supercoincidental regarding a scroll and its movements from storage container to storage container. That little episode had made a security officer by the name of Randy Haverstamp get all hyper about prime numbers and Indiana Jones. Or "funkier" could have happened a couple of days later during a meeting with a publisher, Jon Johanssen, and a writer, Derek Dubois—the day Jack was going to lose his brother. The funkiest, however, was probably the beginning of the whole damned thing. Byron, an eleven-year-old kid playing in the snow and hearing a voice. As he listened to The Voice, he felt compelled to obey it. Whether by fear or by conviction, it didn't matter—he followed it. He was listening one minute, and a few minutes later he was running away from home for good. Byron was off to be a prophet, off to write some scrolls that would somehow arrive in the past only to be looked upon by some people in the present—the present in which he was running away from home, long before the future when he would write them in the first place.

Prophets *do* have strange beginnings.

---—◇○◇—---

"Are you God?" Byron asked while walking quickly down a street, now several blocks from his home.

"Don't ask so many questions. I'm here; you're listening; let's keep it simple." The Voice answered quite unlike what most would expect to hear from The Voice of Prophecy.

"Uh, okay. So where am I going?" Byron asked, his approach to questioning unaltered by the previous advice of The Voice.

"You're going where I tell you. Or—"

"I know, I know, you already told me. Stop saying it."

---—◇○◇—---

How does an eleven-year-old boy wander off in broad daylight, get on a bus with a fake story about needing to get home while not having any change, get ignored by a transit conductor asking for tickets on a train, and then sneak into the back of an unlocked and empty camper trailer at a gas station, all in the course of a typical January afternoon?

Prophecy.

It's the same reason that he's able to stay in that trailer, hidden for two days, eating food from its fridge and using its restroom, only to exit the trailer, unnoticed, and wander off into the woods on the side of a mountain, never to see another human being again. Well, that is, except for the dead one in the cabin he didn't know he was heading to next.

And what a perfect little cabin for some more funkiness to take place this week.

———◇○◇———

"I'm cold. How much longer?"

"You haven't stopped asking questions for two days. Have I given you an answer yet?"

"No, but you always answer."

"Touché."

"What does that mean?"

"Never mind. It's not far now."

"But it's cold, and I'm tired. And scared. Aren't there wild animals? I *am* on a mountain in the middle of nowhere, you know."

Byron had no idea where he was, what state he was in, or where he was going, but he was thankful his mother had made him dress warmly and put his boots on two days earlier when he'd gone out to play. Byron didn't realize that his mother wasn't actually going to make a stink about it that day. It hadn't been that cold, and she knew he would only be out for a few minutes while she was cooking his macaroni and cheese. Regardless of all of that, for some unknown reason, she had suddenly felt compelled to go through the effort of packing him into his snowsuit and scarf and hat and gloves and pushing on his boots.

Can't imagine why.

Three hours walking up a mountain, and a small valley spread out before Byron. The bottom of the valley presented an old cabin—a cabin he would live the rest of his life within.

"Is that it?" Byron asked. "Is that where we're going?"

"Even when we're finally here, you're still badgering me with questions," The Voice replied.

"It is. That *is* the place. Oh, finally." Byron started running as fast as he could down the snowy hill toward the cabin. Still quite a distance away, he tripped, hitting his knee on a rock. He felt glass crumble under his hand as his left palm caught his fall, and his scream hiccupped as he feared his hand had been cut too. Finishing his landing with a roll, up into a seated position, he first held his knee, feeling the tears filling the ledge of his lower eyelids. He was rocking back and forth when he remembered his hand. He pulled it off his knee and, sure enough, saw a little blood. A small cut. He instinctively looked back to where his hand had landed to see what he'd hit. Byron scooted up the hill a few feet to where he thought he might have initially landed. He wiped away the snow with his other hand when he saw the broken glass of a picture frame and a young woman's face peering up at him from a black-

61

and-white picture inside. He picked up the frame and shook it off as he struggled to his feet, not taking his eyes off the woman. His knee hurt, and it caused him to limp the remaining hundred feet or so he needed to go to reach the cabin.

"That'll teach ya."

"Whaddaya mean? It hurts."

"Byron. I've been ignoring your questions, or I've been telling you what to say or where to sit, hide, or walk to for two days. Now it's time to tell you something important."

"Finally," Byron snorted. He was worried. He was completely exhausted. He was completely confused. And yes, he was missing home. But strangely enough, though he had been traveling cross-country with an invisible voice, he'd gotten used enough to The Voice to be rude in return, if The Voice was going to be a jerk.

The Voice continued. "This place is completely secluded. The last person to come across this place was eight years ago. And there isn't going to be a *next* person. Trust me when I tell you that people are going to start becoming a little too busy for recreational hiking."

"And?"

"So what I'm saying is, you'll be alone. You can't be foolish and run around hurting yourself. There isn't going to be anybody around to fix your bones."

"What are you talking about? You mean I'm staying here? When do I get to go back home? How do I save my parents? When do I see them again?" Byron was feeling more fear than he could bear. The Voice was speaking in a very final-sounding manner.

"You don't. You're staying here and you are *not* to leave. Not if you want your parents to live."

The threats again. "What is going to happen to them? Why is this happening? I don't want to stay here alone!"

"GO INSIDE! You knew the deal, or you wouldn't have come this far, so quit your whining!"

The Voice of Prophecy kept *not* sounding like what one would expect a voice of prophecy to sound like. *Where were all the thees and thous?*

"You don't sound much like an angel or God or anything. You sound like a parent," Byron scoffed.

"Maybe that's what you need right now."

—◇○◇—

The cabin was old, but it wasn't dilapidated. Its wood was gray, but its roof looked strong. It had that feel of deserted but not desolate, like someone might be coming back—they'd just been away for quite some time. Shrugging, Byron opened the door to see the inside.

The doorway exposed the entire layout of the one-room abode. Byron found himself standing in the kitchen part upon entering. There was a counter, a sink, and a stove to his left, and a table with one chair farther down ahead of him. Whoever had lived here didn't expect company, it appeared. The thought prodded another question out of Byron. "Does anyone live here?"

"Not anymore."

The rest of the cabin looked like anything he might have seen in a movie regarding old cabins. A few old-school tools and decorations hanging on the walls. An old chair, a couch, a rocking chair. A fireplace, a bed. A hand.

At first glance inside the cabin, Byron hadn't noticed it, but as he focused on the bed, far to the right of where he stood, that is exactly what he saw. A dried, skeletal hand hanging off the edge of the bed from under a sheet. He screamed and turned away as if to grab hold of the owner of the voice. The Voice's corpus was not there to provide a barrier between him and the door he had just entered from—Byron's fight or flight instinct wrestled with whether to shoot out the exit or not. Somehow, the "stay" instinct won. If he hadn't turned away from the hand so quickly, he'd probably have been halfway back up the valley by this point. For if he had scanned his eyes slightly to the right of the dead hand, they would have focused on a head, also. A *dead* head, and not the kind he'd be grooving with. Of course Byron would be dealing with that sight soon enough—even the removal and burying of the whole body. If the voice was The Voice of Prophecy and his boss was the Almighty, then someone was looking out for Byron. For seeing the hand and the head at the same time, in that moment, might have just pushed the boy over some psychological cliff. He was currently under a little more than the average stress an eleven-year-old usually has to adjust to, having just lost his home and his parents due to a voice in his head, which was apparently going to be his only friend in the world as he lived out his life in complete isolation on a mountain, in a cabin, with a dead man to serve as a daily reminder of what his own end would probably be, as well. And this invisible *friend* wasn't too nice, nor was it too forthcoming with information either, and in fact, it had given no guarantees that it was even going to stick around.

"Yes, there's a dead man in that bed," The Voice said as a matter of fact.

Byron was stunned out of his state of panic by how The Voice had explained the situation, as if to say, "Yes, there's some milk in the refrigerator."

"Okay. So why am I here in a cabin with a dead man?" Byron asked in disbelief.

"Because you're going to live here."

"Not with him, I'm not!" Panic started to stake its claim inside Byron's chest again.

"Calm down. Of course not," The Voice answered. "You'll remove him and bury him and then make this place your home. You're going to spend many years here. You'll have to learn how to survive because you're important to the world. So deal with it."

"You said it's for my parents. Now it's the world? What's going on? Why me?"
"Your parents live in the world, right?"
"Yes."
"You figure it out."

—◇○◇—

Byron sucked in some air and turned around to look at his new home again. Calmer, he noticed one peculiar detail about the contents of the cabin that hadn't registered before. There was also a desk, over by the bed. On the desk was a dark object that looked a little like a typewriter. Beside the desk and on the floor was a mountain of notebooks. There might have been a hundred, or two hundred, of them neatly stacked in several piles.

"What are those?" Byron said, pointing at the notebooks as he began to walk toward the desk. The Voice didn't answer. He reached the desk. It wasn't a typewriter. It looked like one but it definitely…wasn't one. He looked at the stacks of notebooks. They looked new, and after picking up and flipping through a few of them, he discovered that's exactly what they were: new. All empty pages. Beside them were several boxes of pens and pencils and several sharpeners. Whoever the man living here had been, Byron thought he must have been planning to do some real writing before…well, *before*. Byron didn't want to think past that. The corpse to the right of him could be thought about later.

Another small, yet older notebook was resting on the middle of the desk in front of the chair and neatly squared with the edge of the desk. It wasn't like the others. This one was leather-bound and looked used. Byron picked it up and opened it. A chill went up his spine as he realized what it was, especially with its deceased owner just a few paces away.

"I think this is a diary."

No answer.

"Hello?"

He turned around, not realizing the futility of the action, and after a few more hellos, Byron found himself ironically missing The Voice's previous nonanswer answers. He now figured they had been a lot better than no-answer answers.

—◇○◇—

Byron stood by the desk for quite some time after realizing he was completely alone. Byron wasn't standing, actually. He was frozen. The mini-thought of missing The Voice's boorishness was replaced quickly with a bona fide, sinking-in reality. A reality placing Byron in a cabin on some unknown mountain, alone, and with a dead body about ten feet to his left.

That pretty much summed up his situation entirely, and frankly, no matter how adventurous one may be (and Byron had never really been all that adventurous), this reality gave Byron the full right to freak out.

While Byron was feeling completely comfortable with his right to be freaked out, his survival instincts planned differently and began their attempt to chip away at his fear.

Arguing with himself, his internal carpenter began chipping. *Chip, chip.* Okay, The Voice brought me here and told me the cabin is mine, and I must stay here so I can save my parents. It's weird, but it's not horrible. *Chip, chip.* Yes, there's a dead body. *Unchip! Unchip!* NO! *Chip, chip.* Yes, there's a dead body, but The Voice said I would remove it and bury it. It's gross, it's creepy, but it is dead. It's not a monster— it's not a ghost or a zombie. It's freaky, and it isn't going to be easy, but The Voice said I would—*what was it that it said?*—oh yeah, remove it, bury it, and make this place your home. Once again, it sucks, but it isn't the end of the world. *Chip, chip.* The cabin's actually nice and clean and comfortable. *Chip, chip.* It's isolated, and in the middle of nowhere—*Unchip! Unchip!*—and I still can't believe everything that has happened—*Unchip! Unchip!*—but *wait.* I haven't been dropped into a cave or a graveyard at night and then been told to live *there. Chip, chip.* This cabin can be a home. *Chip, chip.* Just get rid of the body, *now*—and be done with it. Then, get some sleep. If I need to, I can hike back to the road tomorrow and hope a car comes by. It will then be possible to get home. Yeah, that's a good plan. I might not know where I am, but an adult will, and then I can leave all this behind me.

The fear subsided. Byron started to feel the blood in his arms and legs again, and as he came back to his senses, he realized he was still holding the diary. As he did, it fell out of his hand. He bent over to pick it up and a boom quaked through the cabin, his mind—the whole universe it seemed:

"Do you NOT THINK this is REAL? YOU DECIDE, BYRON, and then think REAL HARD about your PARENTS!"

Byron fell to his knees whimpering and holding his ears as the rebuke came from Mr. Invisible. A moment later, complete silence had returned. It seemed the last part of his plan—the one about leaving and hitching a ride out of there—would need to be abandoned.

—◇○◇—

"I can't believe I just did that!" Byron exclaimed, wide eyed.

It was the first of many moments of accomplishment yet to come, as Byron began learning to live on his own. The macabre nature of this first task made it all the more gratifying.

After The Voice had bellowed its last statement, Byron believed he was stuck where he was, at least for the time being, and if this was the case, then there was one thing that had to be done immediately. He had to get the dead man out of his home. Byron wouldn't eat, sleep, or even pee normally until it was gone. And since he was not a Jedi, he was going to have to touch it.

Pacing the kitchen area, he thought, *How do I get it out of here?*

"It" out of here. That was the key.

The more time Byron spent in the same room as the corpse, the more the body had become an "it" instead of a "him." He stopped pacing and stared at the bed. Plan-making gears cranking behind his eyes, he would work out every step before he started. If he had a plan, then he could tackle the problem. That's what his dad had told him once. *You gotta problem, son? You create a plan, and you tackle it. No plan, no tackle.*

Tackling the dead body and hauling it off in some sort of linebacker move seemed a bit too literal, so Byron kept thinking. *What is my problem? I've got a dead body in the living room!* "Yeah, I know," he asked and answered.

"The real problem is I've got to hold onto it." Byron had begun talking to himself—a behavior that was going to stick around.

"It's too heavy for me to lift. I'm going to have to drag it."

"But if I drag it, I need a path—the shortest path," he answered himself.

The conversation continued.

"I'll have to move the chair by the bed out of the way. That'll make a straight path around the door and to the outside."

"Okay. Step one, make a path."

Byron completed step one. An empty area existed between the bed and the door of the cabin.

"Now what?" Byron asked.

"Umm..." Byron answered. "I grab the hand and pull it onto—"

"Whoa! No freaking way!"

He didn't care much for the argument or the subject matter, but hearing voices was comforting, even if they were his own, given that at present, he was still sharing his space with a beef-jerky human.

"Well, I have to drag it outside."

"Get a towel. You don't really want to touch the hand, do you? That'll make it easier."

"Right. Good. Okay. Step two: find a towel, wrap around hand, pull body onto floor."

"The door!"

"What about it?"

"The door. You need to open the door before you start. That way you don't have to stop once you start—onto the floor, across the room, out the door, away from cabin, and *done.*"

"Right, check. Open door added to step two." Byron nodded his head. "So that's it, right?"

"Ummm. Yeah, I think so."

"Okay, let's do it. The sooner it's gone, the sooner I'll feel better."

"Me *too.*"

Byron laughed. If he'd been older, the last answer to himself might have scared him a bit.

He found a towel in one of the dresser drawers at the far end of the bed—having made an effort not to look at the bed while he had searched. He was happy to see more than the one towel he'd taken because he wasn't sure he'd be able to use that particular towel again.

The moment of truth had come. With step one out of the way and step two started with "Door open and towel in hand," all that remained was "Put towel on hand. Grab it. Pull it. And keep pulling."

He crept slowly toward the head of the bed, arms outstretched in front of him. His face was grimaced, and his head was turned slightly away from the direction he was heading. His eyes were squinting, watching the bed via their peripheral vision. An outside observer might think that Byron was the creepy one. He looked like a zombie going in for the kill of some unsuspecting sleeper. The only issue with that observation was the obvious skeletal hand sticking out from under the covers in front of Byron, which was anything but *alive.* The scene appeared more like *The Living Dead* meets *The Dead Dead.*

Slow steps had only put off the inevitable, and he was finally close enough to be forced into completing step two. Byron bent over slightly, hovered his hands and the towel above the hand, and then he let go of the towel.

Perfect.

The towel had landed, covering the hand completely and hanging over each side.

"Okay, whew! That part's done."

"What are you doing covering up my hand!" the dead man yelled from beneath the sheets. He then sat up with no eyes, his empty sockets looking right at Byron.

"Aaaaaaaaaaaaaaaaaaaaaaaaaaaaah!" Byron screamed and ran out of the cabin. So much for step two.

After about twenty yards out the door, he started talking to himself again instead of screaming at the universe.

"Idiot! That didn't happen!"

"I know, I know. But I had the thought, and that was enough."

"Go back in there and finish the plan!"

———◇o◇———

Right back where he started. It seemed each step in this plan had a rehearsal and a main event.

"I gotta do this. It's getting late—I don't want to be doing this in the dark. I *gotta* do this."

"So do it!" he commanded himself.

"Okay, here goes." He talked himself through it. "I'm reaching for the towel. I am going to close my hands around the towel. I'm closing. I'm closing. I'm grabbing. Oh my God, I'm grabbing. Okay, okay! Now what? Oh yeah, oh yeah. Pull."

He began to pull, but nothing moved. He pulled harder. Nothing. He started throwing his weight into it. Once, twice. Finally something gave.

Yes! He thought. *It's working.* Third time would be the charm. This final pull sent Byron falling backward onto the floor, still holding onto the hand. As he was falling, Byron imagined the body coming too, ready to land on top of him as soon as his butt hit the floor. He immediately let go and scrambled away. Upon standing, still moving away, he tripped backward into the upholstered chair he had earlier pulled further away from the bed to make a path for step two. Now sitting, Byron looked down at the place where the body had landed.

"Oh no." Byron gasped.

"Oh shit." Byron cursed in return.

The body hadn't landed. The body was still tucked away under the sheets, having a nice nap. The body's arm had landed. There are just some things an eleven-year-old shouldn't have to see.

Now step three would need to be reinvented, but only after Byron grew up a little. Staying a child wasn't going to do his psyche any good. Step three eventually sorted itself out to be four essential subparts. The first. Take blanket off body and spread it out onto floor, next to bed. The second. Pick up arm and throw it on blanket. Part two sucked, and so did part three, which was to crawl onto bed with body, getting between body and wall, and push *and push* until body rolled off bed and onto blanket with arm. Part four was obvious. Call sanitarium and ask if he could check himself in. With no phone, he would have to skip subpart four of step three. He would replace this final subpart with "pull body outside by grabbing blanket."

Having somehow made it through subparts one through three, Byron grabbed the edge of the blanket, trying not to look at its passenger, and started yanking. It was hard at first to get the thing moving, but finally it did move, and he was able to keep it going all the way out the door and down the outside step. Byron would never be in school to learn in physics why it's easier to move an object already in motion rather than to start it moving in the first place. But that was okay. He wouldn't need to understand the static and dynamic coefficients of friction for his new career. And given what was coming, nobody else on the planet would really need that information either.

Mentally speaking, the body also became easier to pull. It had become a task—

something to finish. Byron stopped about forty yards away from the cabin. He didn't want to battle a new fear: being too far away from home.

Home...that was funny. He was calling the cabin home.

Something not so funny seemed to have occurred during the drag. It appeared the arm had fallen off the blanket along the journey Byron had just made.

"I'll deal with that later." *Yuck.* "Time to dig."

CHAPTER 10

THE DIARY
SATURDAY, FEBRUARY 3, 2007

A NIGHT HAD PASSED since Byron had filled in the shallow grave of the cabin's previous owner; arm included. He felt braver after his first day's task but not so brave that he would be sleeping on the dead man's bed anytime soon. He'd chosen the couch for now. He had found a huge store of canned food. It wouldn't be enough to feed him forever, but it would be enough to feed him through the rest of the winter and until he learned to hunt—he figured he *would* have to learn how to hunt. How he found the store of food was almost stranger than Day One, requiring dead body removal duty.

The man whose cabin Byron now occupied quickly gained influence over Byron, and not due to some ghostly supernatural power spawned by an insufficient and shallow grave. No. The dead man had left a diary. As if an invisible voice taking Byron to the middle of nowhere and leaving him with a dead body wasn't enough, when the eleven-year-old newly appointed prophet got to reading that diary, he would get a whole new dose of weird.

Byron had woken up late in the morning. He had just sort of passed out the night before as soon as he returned to the cabin after burying the body. So tired, even nightmares couldn't penetrate his subconscious. He'd rummaged the cabinets looking for something to eat and had found some boxes of Little Debbie snack cakes. The Oatmeal Creme Pie. His favorite. It was the first time he'd had a positive thought about the man who had lived there. After eating four of the creme pies, he wandered around the interior of the cabin.

He made a slight second inventory of the place. While doing so, his eyes caught the desk again and the diary upon it. Byron took it and started reading, and he didn't stop. This diary was to be his Saturday. This diary was to be a tad more interesting than "interesting."

The man had been a German who had moved here after World War II. He had been part of something called the "SS," but he had hated it. Not being proud of this, he had punished himself with a life of solitude on this mountain. He had written his diary in English as a protest to his time served in the German elite. The man had been married, but she had died during the war, and page after page was devoted to his love

70

for her. As the diary entries continued, they spoke less of his daily doings and regrets in life and concentrated more on his love for his deceased wife. Gaps for months would occur; then there were days of pages, one after another, about her. The man recalled every moment he could remember and would curse himself when he couldn't remember more. He would repeat her name, Lucina, writing only her name for pages like a lovesick teenager. He would end these stints of writing with the torture he felt from remembering her and how sorry he was for her death—she had died in a car accident while coming to visit him while he was on leave. A declaration of his intention to stop writing about her due to the emotional pain it was causing him would be followed by pages of apologizing for ever wanting to stop. Another gap in time and then more lovesick drivel.

The final entries, written in 1998, spoke of an event that rattled Byron more than the story of this man's life had.

> *Oh my God, Lucina. I am dreadfully sorry! I don't know what to do. I have gotten too old. I can't do anything right. I've searched and searched, and I can't find it anywhere. What will I do? I just wanted you with me. I've always carried your picture with me when I went for firewood or food. You're all I've got left in the world, if there is a world left. Oh Lucina! I dropped it! I lost it! I lost your picture!*

"What?" Byron called out. The event he had just read had hit too close to home.

Byron looked up onto the desk across from where he had seated himself on his couch/bed. There he had placed the broken picture frame he'd cut his hand on the day before. He had set it down on the desk to pick up the diary right before the invisible Voice of Prophecy had disappeared.

I found Lucina's picture, Byron thought.

He read on. But page after page of anguish for not being able to see her anymore became too much to read. Byron wished to God he could put this poor soul out of his misery and give the man the picture he'd found when arriving at the man's cabin.

"I swear if there was a way I could give it to you, I *would*," Byron yelled at the diary. This man had lived nearly seventy years alone as self-inflicted imprisonment with only his dead wife as company. It was real. Byron had never read anything so real, and its diversion from the types of books he had read from the school library was not a welcome surprise. He didn't fully understand the themes of deep guilt and atonement and regret or why someone would punish himself. As for loss, however, Byron felt the loss of his own family, making this man's loss something to which he *could* relate. He decided to turn another page, only to find that what had rattled him before was nothing compared to what came next in the journal. The entry was dated a few weeks after the loss of the picture.

> *Lucina, dearest Lucina, I got you back! It's a miracle! I can't describe it. I don't know why I deserve it. But I got you back! It's the most amazing thing, and I don't know how to believe it, but I must. There's no other explanation. He knew! He knew about this diary. He had your picture! He knew my whole life inside and out. He knew everything! I have so much to do. I'm old now, Lucina; I don't know if I can leave the woods. I don't know if I can make it back. Oh, how will I? But I promised him. I promised him I would. I have to. He brought me you! You would have liked him. He was a good man. He seemed to really care. And understand. He understood my loneliness, my loss. He walked in and out of my life from nowhere. He was magical. But he said he couldn't help me further; he couldn't undo my life or bring you back to me. But he brought me your picture! And that's all I really wanted. That's all I really deserve, if that! But I have it now. And I will help this Byron. I will try my best and do what he told me to do. You got my word, my boy. You brought me my Lucina.*

No matter how much one tries to explain Einstein's Theory of Relativity to most high school or college students, rarely anyone gets their head completely around it. But compared to what Byron had just read, grasping Einstein would be cake. Byron's eleven-year-old mind could have easily slipped away, never to return, upon reading this last passage. Luckily, it didn't. Luckily, kids his age—in this age—are a little more prepared for weird. Movies and video games can help a lot if your kid is going to be a prophet.

Might keep that in mind.

"Whoa!" Byron said and dropped the diary. "What is going on?" This was Byron's reaction, for better or worse, instead of comatose-ness.

He rose from the couch and started pacing the room like he had done the day before, looking back at the book on the floor and then pacing some more, sometimes with a questioning look, sometimes with an astonished look that even had the beginnings of a smile. As he made about his twentieth pass across the inside of the cabin, something familiar caught his eye on the shelf next to the fireplace mantel. He couldn't believe he hadn't noticed it before. He stopped dead in his tracks and just stared.

This time for sure I'm going down. I'll be someone's loony uncle who never talks, soon enough.

Upon the shelf, leaning back on its stand, and having been placed at a slight angle to the run of the wall was the exact same broken picture frame with Lucina's picture inside, which Byron knew was lying on the desk behind him. Byron didn't go into a coma, though, as one might expect. Instead, he turned around to make sure what he knew *was* what he knew. He was right. He picked up the picture on the shelf and ran it over to the one on the desk.

Same frame, same picture, same cracks.

"Holy shit," Byron croaked. A lot of *holy shit* moments would happen around February 3, 2007.

In three days, Byron's life had become weird. That was simply it: weird—the new definition of his life. Invisible voices appearing and disappearing, him becoming a mountain man and burying dead bodies, picture frame paradoxes. His mind had survived it all with no risk of catatonic slippage in sight. Therefore, he did the only thing that seemed logical: he sat down and continued his reading of the dead man's diary.

There wasn't much left. What was left was very beneficial to Byron, but, yes, still weird. The man believed himself to have been visited by Byron, or someone who said he was Byron, and this visitor had told the man to get his home a tad more prepared for a posthumous visitation.

This Byron had requested that the man venture out of the woods and into the closest town to collect various items. The subsequent sojourn had resulted in many of the items Byron now possessed. Byron learned of a massive canned food store in a crawlspace around the back side of the cabin. A cabinet in the kitchen was stocked with lots of medicines, bandages, and other first-aid paraphernalia. The stacks of pencils, pens, sharpeners, and empty notebooks by the desk had also been placed in the cabin because of this visitation. Lastly, the diary contained a detailed description of how to use the typewriter-looking thing to encode messages. At present, Byron had no idea why he would need such a device or all the stationery, but he was thankful for the food and the three spare can openers that had been placed in a drawer for him to find.

The journey itself had damned near killed the man. His diary spoke of having to walk for miles before being picked up by a trucker. He'd had to go to a bank to exchange his sixty-year-old American currency. He'd used everything he had to buy the items and hire a taxi to drive him and the items to a place close enough he could carry the boxes of items back to the cabin, making several trips, but far enough away so the cab driver would not have the slightest idea of where to look for the old man's home, just in case he was that curious a cat.

Byron couldn't believe what he had read. Was it possible? *No, it couldn't be.* Some other Byron had convinced this man to practically walk himself into his own grave and only for having been given back a picture of his wife. *But wait—what about the two pictures? Was* that Byron, him? Were these things he would do—or *had* done? Eleven-year-old Byron wished the Voice was back for just a couple more questions.

CHAPTER 11

Derek Dubois and Jon Johanssen
Friday, February 2, 2007
11:00 A.M.

Derek Dubois cautiously sat down in one of the two paisley upholstered chairs facing the huge oak desk of his editor, Jon Johanssen. It was their first face-to-face meeting in almost a year, and nothing much had changed, including his nerves. The meeting's professional purpose was to gather Mr. Johanssen's thoughts on Derek's recently completed second novel. Derek's personal purpose was to fulfill his desire not to be viewed as a one-hit wonder of an author, making this encounter more nerve racking than the first meeting. In that meeting, Derek had arrived already knowing he was being published. That meeting had made Derek feel as if he were in a dream, waiting to be pinched. This meeting had Derek feeling awake and waiting to be knocked out cold by Jon Johanssen's possibly negative opinion.

"It's good to see you, Jon," Derek stated casually, following his words with a forced smile. "I guess I'm ready to hear what you have to say about the second book. Don't make it hurt too much."

Jon Johanssen was a large man. He had the kind of size one might expect a man in his position of power to have—the kind of size for which large oak desks were most likely invented. Natural intimidation had opened doors for Jon that remained closed for others with a similar education. Size matters. Always has, always will. However, regardless of this maxim, Derek was only moments away from discovering size mattered not, at least for today.

"Derek, I don't know what to say," Jon Johanssen stated without expression. "This one's just not going to cut it. It's not like your last book. That's what I was expecting. I'm sorry, Derek, but we can't get this one published. Frankly, I wouldn't even know how they'd market it. You just can't go from bestselling crime drama to a mystical fountain of youth scrolls, and I'm not even sure if that's *even* what this is about. I mean I *read* it, but I just don't get it."

"All right, all right, Jon," Derek said defensively. "Ouch—you talk like a publisher!"

"Derek," Jon responded dryly, "to the author, the editor *is* the publisher. Without my buy-in, no publisher will know it exists."

Derek had been nervous, but he'd become defensive almost immediately upon hearing Jon's opinion. The emotional investment and the effort it had taken to complete the book, regardless of opinion, had created a sense of needing to be recognized for the work alone before being critiqued.

"Well, I made you enough money off my first book—you could take it a little easy on me. You're not the one who just spent the last year of his life putting that book you're holding to paper."

"Derek, it's my job. I only speak what the people out there would say," Jon said, pointing his finger out the floor-to-ceiling windows to his right, which were masquerading as a wall. Johanssen's size and gesture created such presence, it swayed Derek to turn and look, expecting to see all crime-drama readers levitating outside of the high-rise building, nodding their heads in agreement with Johanssen. Shaking his finger at the floating readers, Jon continued, "*They* want another FBI thriller. Do you want me saying that in *here*, or three million saying it out *there*?"

"Well, if they all say it now, they'll break your window," Derek replied, not believing he'd said the thought in his mind out loud.

"What was that?" Johanssen fired back.

"Nothing," Derek said, letting it go.

"Derek, you just can't follow up your last novel with this. It's missing something anyway."

Derek snapped again. "Like what?"

"I don't know—a point, maybe?" his editor retorted coldly.

"Thanks a lot."

"Derek, they're going to read two pages and be like, 'What's the hell is this?' You need to cater to your audience when you're a new author. The people who picked up your first book—they did so because they were already interested in the genre, and the marketing persuaded them that last little bit to give you a try. Besides them, nobody knows who you are yet. So you need that audience base, and, frankly, so do we. The publisher can't fill all the Borders and Barnes & Nobles with prints of your book only to have them go from hot in week one, returned in week two, and thrown at the discount stack, week three."

Derek turned to look out the window. He saw the skyline of New York City—this time, minus the floating readers. Defeated, he asked the window *(not Jon, because the city was less intimidating)*, "So what do you expect me to do?"

"Well, Derek, if it wasn't for the success of the last one, I'd be wondering whether to keep you signed because this just isn't good writing. If it were, I might tell you to try submitting it to one of the several fantasy publishers. But I can't even recommend *that*. I really don't think their readers are going to care about your main character. She doesn't really *do* anything. Where's the conflict?" Jon picked the manuscript up off his desk and waved it at Derek. "I think you need to shelve this one for the time being. Perhaps you can pick it back up in a few years, and maybe then you'll see what I'm talking about. As for right now, you're going to start over and produce a book along the same line as your first. I'm sorry if that wasn't clear between us, but if you want to have another book published, that's what you are going to have to do."

"I guess I don't have much of a choice," Derek submitted. "Do you mind if I take that with me?" He stood up and reached for the manuscript Jon was holding.

"What?" Jon asked. "Oh, th—"

Poof.

Jon Johanssen would have finished saying "Oh, this?" if he hadn't turned into a plume of dust.

Nope. Size didn't matter—told you so. Not today.

"Whoa! Whoooooooaaaaaa! Holy—"

Derek Dubois would have finished saying "Holy shit!" if he hadn't fallen backward over the chair he had just been sitting in. The paisley chair toppled over, and a moment later Derek found himself on the floor, feet sticking up in the air. He had returned to his previous seated position, only rotated ninety degrees backward.

What the hell just happened? Derek thought.

He scrambled out of the chair and onto his elbows and knees, still behind the chair. His chest pounded like a bass drummer had rented it as practice space. He quickly looked over at the office door to see if anyone was around. No one. He turned back toward Jon's desk and slowly rose his head above the inverted seat of the chair. As Derek's eyes crested the edge, he hoped his sight would prove nothing had occurred other than him making a fool of himself. This, however, was not to be the case.

His editor wasn't there. The manuscript lay in the middle of the large oak desk. A few of the top pages had blown out of place from what was otherwise a neat stack, as a result of the slight impact the book had made when it landed on the desk. Landing on the desk because the manuscript's holder had broken apart into a gazillion particles before Derek's eyes a few moments earlier.

Oh my God, it really happened.

There was no editor, and Derek could see a gray residue on the desk. He turned his head again toward the door, expecting to be jumped by twenty police officers, all hollering at him to "freeze and move away from the dust cloud, buddy— slowly…slowly." No cops, though. Instead, only silence.

I have to get out of here, he thought. *I'll figure this out on my own. I'm not relying on some police officer to believe I had nothing to do with it.*

If Derek hadn't been a participant in this freakish event, he may have realized a pretty good premise for his next novel had just materialized. Or dematerialized, that is.

Derek stood up and grabbed the book off the desk, arranging the pages as he did so. He shook the manuscript off over the desk, fighting back the urge to vomit as the dust, which had been some part of his editor's hand, or arm, or maybe even head, floated down to the desktop. He turned and headed toward the door. As Derek opened the door, he sighed with relief at seeing a lobby as empty as the office he wished to exit. An apparent early exodus for Friday lunch was his ticket out of there. Making his way to the elevator, Derek ignored a fleeting thought that perhaps fleeing the scene might be the wrong decision. Panic isn't called panic for no reason.

He proceeded to the elevator and pushed the down button between the two golden ornately decorated elevator doors. Waiting for an elevator—long enough on normal days—had Derek feeling as if he were waiting for Otis himself to invent the damned thing.

The left elevator finally chimed and opened. An older man in a suit and a child, possibly his granddaughter, looked at Derek from inside the doors. Poe apparently had sublet his chest from the drummer, and Derek attempted to will away the word "guilty" most certainly stamped across his forehead.

"Hi," he muttered and then lowered his head and assumed the second of two possible elevator stances. The first stance is to focus on the numbers above your head, counting to the floor you're headed to. The second stance is to look down at the buttons, studying the cryptic open-door and close-door symbols as if you're seeing them for the first time and are intent on deciphering them. The fact is most people choosing the second elevator stance actually take the time to redecipher those two symbols, finding a small satisfaction in discovering, once again, which button would hold the doors open and which one would close them. Derek's concentration on the buttons and their meanings, even in his current state, proved this act to be a modern human instinct, for it seemed Derek couldn't keep from deciphering the two symbols, even when running from the scene of a crime, or disappearance, or disintegration, or whatever it had been.

The elevator quickly closed the gap between floor numbers thirty-one and one, but Derek still felt it was taking too long. The old man and his small companion evolved into telepaths, probed his mind, and completely understood what was going on with their fellow passenger. The doors opened, and Derek stepped out, heading directly for the revolving exit door, all the while expecting Grandpa and little Jenny to begin screaming "Stop that man! We *know* what he did!"

Outside. He was there. He'd made it. And with no attempted citizen's arrest like he had expected from Deputy The Little One. Derek turned left down Fifth Avenue, making his way to the subway, where a few more terrors awaited him.

Emerging from the subway off Canal Street, Derek Dubois had confirmed Jon Johanssen's death *had* been the result of a crime—*Derek's* crime. Two more people had gone up in smoke in the tunnels. Derek realized his hands moving toward people was the cause of the involuntary manslaughter he was guilty of—now, times three.

The subway cars had been sparsely populated, or the first death might have caused a stampede inside the train. Derek had reached for the pole, and the woman seated nearby had simply and silently disappeared, her ashes softly settling onto her seat. Derek turned around quickly, instinctively pretending nothing had happened, but the event had gone unnoticed, and the maneuver had not been needed. Person number two disappeared as Derek reached for the stair railing leading up to Canal Street, causing the man on the stairs in front of him to go *pop* or *poof* or whatever. The stairs were empty; thus victim number three went missing—*forever*—with no witnesses, as well. Although Derek felt anything *but* lucky, he guessed in some strange way, lucky is what he was.

With his manuscript now pushed down into the back of his pants and his hands shoved deep into his pockets, he reiterated his only goal in life: get home.

I've got to get home! And without killing anyone else.

CHAPTER 12

JESSICA FINDS SARAH DUBOIS
APRIL 7, 1923, CAIRO

———————⊸o⊂⊃o⊶———————

ON THE SAME DAY warehouse worker Paul Dunsford was removing a scroll from a cardboard box and placing it into a metal one, Jessica Resden was going to be removing her long-lost sister from an institution in dusty Cairo and taking her back home to New York City—well, taking her sister and a couple of scrolls her sister happened to have back home.

"It's her. Oh, Howard, it's really her! I *found* her! I found her!" Jessica Resden sobbed as she looked at her older sister seated across the cafeteria from where she and her husband, Howard, were standing.

"How can that be, Jess? There's no way that can be her," Howard Resden argued.

"It is *her*. I'd know my sister anywhere."

"That woman is not a day over thirty, Jesse. Your sister was three years *older* than you." Howard didn't enjoy dashing Jesse's hopes, but there was no way possible the woman eating at the table across the dining room from them was Jessica's seventy-some-year-old sister, Sarah Dubois.

Except for the fact that there was a way. He just didn't know it.

"It's her, and I'm *going* to go talk to her," Jessica demanded and took off toward the lady they had spotted.

"Jesse, I know you want it to be her. I know you do. But it's impossible. [*No, it isn't, Howard's mind replied to himself, acting out his wife with annoying accuracy.*] Don't go upsetting that woman. [*I won't.*] Jessica! Let's ask someone first. [*Hmm? Did you say something, Howie?*] Maybe they pointed out the wrong patient."

No they didn't, "Howie". Oh boy. No they didn't.

Howard walked back toward the door they had entered to confirm the information they had been given. He glanced back at Jessica and he wasn't surprised to see her continuing her walk of defiance to his pleas to wait a moment.

"Oh, Jessica, you never listen. Just hold a moment, will you?"

Well, that fell on deaf ears, he thought to himself when his wife's movements refused to display the slightest pause in reaction to his voice.

"Well, at least talk to the lady *gently*," Howard half whispered across the distance Jessica's conviction had already created between them. "I'm sure she doesn't know you. You don't want to set her off or anything. Good grief. I'm just checking with the nurse so we can find the patient we *are* looking for."

I'm talking to myself again, aren't I? he thought.

Jessica was hearing her husband. She always heard him. She loved him. She loved him because he let her be her and not because he forced her to follow his instructions. And although he would never admit it, he loved her because of why she loved him. And in the end, that's the only way real love works. They had been going at it like this for thirty-nine years. Her spunk and his support fueled their relationship. Howard would tell her no, she would say yes, he would say okay, and then she'd do it like she was going to anyway, proved by times like this, where he wouldn't say okay and there she was—off doing it. And there were times he would say do it, and she would say she didn't want to do it anymore just to get that cute little "Good grief" out of him…and then…she'd do it.

What was "it"? That's a simple enough question to answer. The "it" was something Jessica Resden had set her mind to do, culminating in Howard Resden being dragged along for the ride as an accomplice—or at the very least, a guilty bystander.

They had been together on a lot of missions finding adventure and life in the world, but one mission superseded all others. When a clue arose as to where Jessica's sister might have gone, all other plans were put on hold. She had been missing for forty-seven years, and Jessica had never given up hope. Howard had given up long ago, but he had never let Jessica in on his secret. He didn't need hope to be happy, but he did need Jessica's hopeful heart to be happy. And every adventure and every wild goose chased had forged their bond a little more.

Still halted in the middle of his journey to the nurse's desk, Howard spoke again to Jessica. "You want me to come with you? I don't really feel all that comfortable about you going and talking to a stranger in a mental institution, you know?" Howard waited for an answer he knew wouldn't come. "Oh, good grief. Hold up there; I'm coming." He didn't see it, but the corner of Jessica's mouth curled up in her trademark grin.

They approached the round table where the young woman sat eating her dinner. Lifting a carrot on a fork to her mouth, the woman caught Jessica's eye and looked up at Jessica. As soon as it happened, the woman lowered her gaze again back toward her plate, and Jessica proceeded to sit down across from the woman she knew was her sister. Howard followed, as usual.

"Now slowly, Jess."

"Are you my sister, Sarah Dubois?"

"Well, Jessica. That was slow." Howard scoffed.

"Shush."

Howard rolled his eyes and shook his head. "Good grief."

Jessica spoke again to the woman. "It's me. I'm Jessica, your sister." The woman didn't look up. "Sarah? Talk to me, please? I've been looking for you for forty-seven years. *Please* tell me it's you."

Howard leaned over and whispered, "Jessica, Sarah would be seventy-four years old now. Leave this poor girl alone."

"You know, she looks just like her." Jessica opened her purse and fumbled through it. She quickly produced a picture and handed it to him. "Tell me you don't believe it's her."

Howard took the old photograph he'd seen a thousand times and held it up, comparing the live and still versions of whom Jessica was wanting to be one and the same. He had to admit the eeriness of the similitude. If the lady eating her carrots before them had been laughing or smiling or even talking, there might have been some room to doubt. But the lady had no expression on her face. The picture matched perfectly. The two sisters in the picture had taken the shot a long time ago when standing still was required during lengthy film exposure. People rarely smiled due to the difficulty of holding one for more than a moment.

It was impossible, of course, that this was Jessica's sister, but if Sarah Dubois had an identical twin born two decades later, this was her.

"See, Howard. I know you see what I see."

"Yes, Jesse, I do, but *still*. Her *age*, dear?"

"Sarah?" Jessica continued, prodding the girl. "Please say something. Tell me who you are. I know you're not Sarah Palton like the register said. You're Sarah Dubois, and you're my sister, and I'm taking you home."

Howard's jaw dropped open as he heard "Jessica?" escape the woman's lips.

"Yes, Sarah, it is me. Oh dear God, is this where you've been all these years? What happened to you?"

Sarah didn't say much after that, and this provided Jessica with few long-awaited answers. There had been enough recognition between the two sisters that Jessica and Howard were able to help Sarah gather her personal artifacts and have her check herself out with them. How she had ended up in a mental institution in Cairo, Egypt, Jessica didn't have the first clue. The last time they had seen each other had been in Paris around 1875. Now it was April 7, 1923. For now, how Sarah got there ceased to matter. Jessica would be returning to their childhood home in New York City, this time *with* Sarah after more than five decades, and that was enough for Jessica Resden. Of course, a certain lonely government warehouse worker, Paul Dunsford, would be going home in a few hours also, after another long day of transferring the contents of cardboard boxes to metal boxes.

—◇○◇—

The ship taking Jessica, Howard, and Sarah home plowed through the Atlantic near the same course on which the *Titanic* had unfortunately met its doom eleven years to the month earlier.

"Frigid water, Jessica. It must have been a horrible night when she sunk."

"Oh Howard, will you ever stop mentioning the *Titanic*? Every time we get on a boat for the last ten years, it's the same thing. You know, you'd say it if we were in a rowboat and fishing in a river."

"I can't help it. We were supposed to take that ship home. Ride the largest ship ever built by mankind. The ship that God couldn't sink! And if we *had*?" He paused for a moment. "That would have been our last adventure."

"And you always say that, too, and then *I* always say to forget about it. We got that lead on Sarah, and we sold our tickets, and that's that."

"But it's different this time."

"What is different, Howard?"

"Well, this time, we *found* Sarah, and she hasn't aged a bit since that picture taken in Paris you've been carrying around all these years. I don't call that normal. I'd call that strange, or a miracle or something. And when you combine finding her in this strange state with the fact that exploring that lead relating to her kept us off that doomed ship, it's enough to make it stick around in my mind—tossing and festering it. I keep telling myself, '*Howard*, go over it again. Try to find some meaning.'" He paused, waiting for some sort of recognition that he was making a good point. None came, as usual. He knew he loved his wife because if he didn't, he knew he'd push her right over the railing of the ship for not saying he had a point. He knew she knew, but it wasn't her style to be so obvious. Her style was not to let on that she knew, so that he could love her all the more for knowing she knew that he knew she wasn't letting on.

"Well, Howard, I'm just glad to have my sister back. You can go on dreaming about your miracles. It's miracle enough I found Sarah to satisfy me."

"Don't you even wonder? Why she's the way she is? And she hasn't said anything but your name. Look at her over there on the chair." He pointed at the umbrella-covered table where they had just eaten lunch on the deck of the cruise liner. "She just sits there, holding onto her bag. What happened to her? What's she been through? How did she end up in that institution? She checked *herself* in there, Jesse. Why does she still look like she's in her twenties? Don't you want to *know*?"

"Well I'm not going to know any of those things unless she tells me, so I'm not going to worry about it right now."

"I think she saved us from sinking to the bottom of the ocean," Howard replied. "That's what I think."

There. He had said it even if it didn't make any difference—or sense, for that matter.

"Howard, you and your imagination. You make life so interesting when you're busy trying to get me to listen to you." Jessica smiled and took his hand in hers and rested both hands back on the railing of the ship. "We've gone a lot of places in our lives, and you've always been there for me, and I love you for that. I hope you're okay with ending that life. I need to take care of my sister now. You know that, don't you?"

"Yes. I know, Jesse," Howard answered his wife while looking out over the ocean as the wind fluttered his gray, yet full, head of hair. "It was never the places we went. It was who I went to those places with. It was your soul and your heart and your drive. If you'd ever done laundry, I'd have enjoyed watching that too. And honestly, Jesse, I'm sure you'll still find ways to ignore my good advice and cause trouble in New York."

"You know, my sister was a lot like me back then. I don't know where she went after we met our father in Paris, but the fact that she ended up in Egypt without us knowing about it doesn't surprise me in the least. But she was, umm—more of a free spirit than me. I set out to *do* things. She just drifted with the wind and currents. Wherever they took her, that's where she went. You would have liked her less, I think. If I drive you crazy, she would have put *you* in that place we found her." Jessica chuckled at her own thought and then noticed her sister again, sitting at the table under the umbrella.

"Oh, Sarah," Jessica said, "where did you go? I hope I get you back. I do hope to get her back, Howard. I really do, and I don't care if I ever understand anything else. I just want her back. But I'm still so very happy to see her again."

"I know you are." He paused and lifted his arm to place it around her shoulders. Pulling her close and kissing the top of her head, he reassured her, "Never had a mission we didn't accomplish, huh?"

"No. Not now. Not anymore, Howie."

CHAPTER 13

SARAH AND DEREK DUBOIS
FEBRUARY 2, 2007
12:30 P.M.

—◇○◖◗○◇—

"THINGS ARE *NOT* GOING WELL, Aunt Sarah!"

"What's wrong, Derek?" Sarah had to fight hard to get the words to come out.

"I don't know. I *think* I killed three people today. I don't know how; I mean I didn't *do* anything. I was moving my hand toward—"

Stop! Derek internally yelled at himself.

Derek had started to take his hand out of his pocket in order to mimic the gesture he was describing and stopped himself cold, shoving his hand back, down deep. "I know it sounds crazy, but I really think I—I think I killed them just by moving my hand out toward them."

"Wh-what happened? Tell me," Sarah Dubois asked, still struggling to speak.

Derek was pacing the room. The house he had grown up in had always felt like a haven: safe, peaceful. However, after today he felt there would never be any safe haven for him again. To be faced with having actually killed someone was such a dramatic shock to the senses, he barely believed it was really happening. Derek kept trying to open his already-open eyes, praying that somehow, he was reaching the end of a nightmare.

If I just shake it off and try to stretch my lids open just a little harder, I'll wake up.

But instead, only pacing in front of his aunt, he continued, panic increasing on his face with each step he took.

"I don't know what happened," Derek began to explain, "I was talking to my editor. I was hearing him rip apart the book I wrote for you. You know, the one where I take you on all the adventures you wished you could have gone on with this power of unending youth you seem to have. Anyways, Jon was telling me how he couldn't publish it. 'I can't publish this, Derek. It's got no point! Give me an FBI thriller.' The next thing I know, I'm asking for the manuscript back. I reach for it and he—oh my God, Aunt Sarah! He just turned into a cloud of dust right in front of me! I swear it. He just disappeared! I didn't mean to. I was mad, yes, but all I wanted was the book back."

85

Immediately, Sarah looked horror-struck. One hundred and thirty-one years of mental stress times fifty seemed to enter her eyes, making her, for a moment, not look twenty-seven any longer, but one hundred and twenty-seven. She thought hard, trying to remember so long ago. *Had it really happened?* It must have. She had spent most of her life locked up and afraid of herself because she had done something—something bad. The memories flooded in, images she hadn't thought of in several lifetimes. She quickly squeezed her eyes shut, trying to shut off the faucet of recall.

—◇○◇—

Some people are built for killing. Some live to kill. A few of us experience the act of killing in self-defense. If any of the latter group were asked, they would usually explain that killing—even in self-defense—is not easy to live with afterward. A remaining group, those who kill by accident, tend to live with a grief akin to dying themselves, living an unending cycle of their mind perpetuating the idea that just around the bend is the ability to do something different, something that will reverse *everything. If I just think it through one more time.* Most of us, fortunately, never partake in the ending of a fellow human being's life, and although modern people see death and murder on TV all the time, actually killing someone is a whole different genre of drama. Desensitization to *Watership Down*–style violence and a lot of rabbit sex is one thing. Actually entering the rabbit hole is quite another.

Derek was coming close to entering that tunnel, and Sarah could see his eyes scanning for the entrance. She didn't need any visitors in here. There was barely enough room for her to crawl through the ever-encroaching walls built of grief, self-hate, and disbelief.

Sometimes a chance arrives at the doorstep. Sometimes a person feels they have done something very bad—something they could never make up for—yet they get a chance. Not a chance to rectify what they have done, but rather a chance that allows them to know their life was not lived completely in vain. These chances are rare, and when they come, they don't come easy; and furthermore, they can be very easily missed. Some people notice these chances but don't believe they are worthy enough to take them. Others take them on the belief that for a moment they may be of use to someone. And if they truly love someone else more than they hate themselves, they may just succeed.

Sarah loved Derek. He was her great-great nephew, and he had always been there with her in her house his whole life. He had grown up around her and had never made her feel like she was some dark and crazy family secret. And now he needed her. As she watched him pacing back and forth, her eyes followed him, growing older with every trace they made of his movements. A look of wisdom came over her face like one that had formed on a very old man she had once seen in a tomb. *I remember him. He was happy with me, not fearful. He gave them to me; I didn't take them. He was ready to go; I didn't kill him. And Gerard was bad—I gave that old man a moment of peace before he died, not terror.*

"Oh God, Aunt Sarah!" Derek was still continuing his rant. "And then on the subway, and then on the stairs! I'm so sorry. How did I do this *thing?*"

She let out a scream, and it stopped Derek's pacing like a heart attack. One thought surfaced in Sarah Dubois's mind, and although she had spent over a hundred years locking up her mind, this one thought seeping through the keyhole seemed more important than all the thoughts she'd spent decades repressing.

Oh, please don't let my life become his.

"*Derek! Stop!*" Sarah yelled and stood up from her chair as if gravity had reversed itself temporarily.

Aunt Sarah, as an authority. This was something new. The thirty-five-year-old Derek froze in front of his twenty-five-year-old-looking aunt, lips slammed shut, eyes turned to Sarah and waiting to hear any other command she may have. He didn't have time to marvel at the sight he was witnessing before she began to speak.

"Derek. I can't tell you for sure what is going on. But I can tell you that you are not crazy, and you are not bad, and you are not the only one in this family this has happened to. I need to tell you something. Something I myself am just now remembering." Sarah continued, "Derek, it happened to *me*. I have seen a man turn to dust. And my hands were reached out toward him."

"What?" Derek gasped. "How can this be? I'm trying to convince myself I didn't see it, and now you're telling me not only did I see it, but *you* have seen it? My aunt— the one who doesn't age and never speaks *now* tells *me*, 'Derek, don't worry, you're normal because you're just like me!'"

"Get hold of yourself, Derek!" she shouted.

"How can I? They're dead, Aunt Sarah." He sobbed and fell to his knees with his head in his hands. "I can't get the image out of my head." He sobbed. "I'm reaching out to them and they disintegrate. I keep wanting to reach out and save them, and then that idea petrifies me because of the gesture."

"I know," Sarah said and touched the top of his head. "You can't take it back. I know the feeling, believe me, Derek, I know."

He continued to cry. "I just want to grab them and put them back together. I'm so sorry, I'm soooo sorry!"

"I don't know the *why* behind anything, Derek, but I will tell you my story if you'll let me. Maybe together we can figure out a way for both of us to stop punishing ourselves."

Derek composed himself slightly upon hearing the hope in her voice. Also settling in was that his Aunt Sarah was speaking normally for the first time in his life, and maybe he shouldn't miss it, just in case it went away again like in that movie *Awakenings* he had watched with her—made her watch with him—several years before. He got up off the floor and moved to the couch next to Sarah's chair, trying to erase the day's images from his mind long enough to concentrate on his aunt. He sat looking up at Sarah, who was still standing. His jaw dropped as he thought, *I know she has never aged, but she really looks like she's in her twenties now. She's younger than me!*

Sarah began to tell the events of her life. She explained how in 1876, at the age of twenty-seven, she had fallen in with an Englishman who had invited her to come to Egypt soon after she had met up with her sister and father in Paris. She had run off with him, not telling anyone. Soon after arriving in Cairo, she had taken off on her own as she normally did, leaving the Englishman to wonder why he had bothered. She then explained how one night, soon after, she had met an archaeologist (who was really more of a drunk). She had been drinking, and he had convinced her to go down into a tomb he had recently discovered and be the first two humans to set foot in the place. He hadn't really interested her so much, but the event did, even though the farther they went into the tomb, the more uneasy she had begun to feel about the whole idea.

She then explained to Derek the events occurring in the darkness, which had changed her life forever.

"Oh my God. Aunt Sarah? That is where you got those two scrolls?"

"Yes," she replied.

"So this Palton guy? Is he one of those guys we read about falling 'victim' to a curse for opening an Egyptian tomb?"

"That is just one of the many mysteries that happen to surround that part of my life," she answered. "I made it out of that tomb just as the torch was losing its glow. Somehow, I made it back to my hotel. The emotions—oh, Derek, fear, remorse, confusion, and more fear—they consumed me, and I collapsed for a couple days in my bed. When I awoke, I didn't remember where I was at first. When it came back to me—I can't believe all of this is coming back to me; I had forgotten all of it, it seems, until just now—anyway, when I got my bearings, I half expected the Cairo authorities to show up any minute asking me about Mr. Palton. Nobody ever did. When I finally ventured out of the hotel a few days later, it appeared that no one even knew of him or his dig site. I waited a long time before returning to the tomb dig. But when I got there it was gone. The sand was completely smooth, and it didn't look like anyone had ever dug there."

"Nobody even looked for him? Didn't he have financiers?"

"I never dug that deep into it for obvious reasons, Derek. And by the time I even found the nerve to go near the site, I was already heavily drinking, drowning the consuming guilt I had from killing Gerard and the old man. I couldn't get Gerard's screams out of my mind or the smell of his burning body. I don't know how long it was until I checked myself into that mental hospital my sister eventually found me in.

Maybe Jessica obtained the records, and they are still around somewhere to tell me how long I was there."

"January 31, 1877, Aunt Sarah." Derek added, "I've seen the records."

"Oh? Seven months I wandered? Goodness. I think I experienced long periods of lost time. I just remember there was one day I woke up in an alley somewhere in Cairo. My mind cleared a little that day, and although I wasn't myself, I felt some responsibility to not end up dead. I don't think I thought past that, but now I feel like I knew my family deserved better than to just find me dead on the streets or never at all."

She walked over to her dresser and opened a drawer. Sarah turned around holding up a canister in each hand. If there were anyone alive on earth who had been alive in 1876, when she had last held them like that, they wouldn't have been able to tell the difference between 1876 Sarah Dubois and 2007 Sarah Dubois. She was the spitting image of her young, beautiful self who had taken those two articles from an old man who had fallen away from her, turning to dust, 131 years earlier.

Sarah ended her story. "And I think I owed something to that old man who gave me these."

"The one who turned to dust?" Derek asked.

"Yes. I don't remember it happening the moment my hands reached out toward him, but as soon as I had the scrolls, he smiled and fell back into atoms."

"You've never let me see them. What's written on them?" Derek asked, continuing with more questions. "Did anyone else in the family ever look at them? I know I've asked all these questions before, but you've never been the answering type, Aunt Sarah."

"Derek, I so wanted to talk to you, to tell you more. I know I had those emotions. I felt warmth somewhere down inside when you would tell me about the beautiful places you were writing me off to in your book. I just couldn't find my way out, to link those emotions with coherent thought. The answer to your question is no. No one, including myself, has ever looked at them. Early on, I felt too guilty about the whole affair to ever look at them. Yet I couldn't throw them out. And I guess over the years, everyone in the family was so concerned about my emotional state that whenever I would show agitation about anyone going through my personal possessions, I think they just left them alone."

"Aren't you curious, now?" Derek said softly. "I mean, especially after today's events?"

"Somehow I do believe the time is finally here."

—◇o◇—

Sarah and Derek sat side by side on the couch. The couch, like everything else upstairs, was antique. The upstairs apartment had been created for Sarah by her sister,

Jessica, after she and Howard had brought Sarah back from Cairo over eighty years earlier. Jessica had died from an infection only three years after returning with her sister. After that, Howard didn't last much longer without his Jesse. Before Howard died, he contacted Sarah and Jessica's younger half brother, James. James was only about thirty at the time, the product of a marriage late in Sarah and Jessica's father's life.

James Dubois had been recently married. It was 1927, a couple of years before the Crash. Being given a house by a half sister's dying husband he'd barely met was something he couldn't pass up with his new bride, Sophia, a French girl he had met at the University of Paris a few years earlier. Howard had explained to James that although the Dubois home was fully his, taking it would require the caretaking of his older half sister, Sarah, whom he had never met. James took the offer and moved himself and his new bride from France and made a life in New York City. Having no interest in the American stock market and owning a home with no debt, they survived the Depression better than most. Howard died soon after James and Sophia had moved in, almost a year to the day of his Jesse's passing.

Sarah lived in the upstairs apartment. Sophia loved taking care of her. Sarah wasn't an invalid. Even though she moved slow and not often, she would help sometimes with the cooking of meals and the cleaning. When she was standing, she would do all right, although she remained quiet. And if there wasn't a specific thing for her to be doing with Sophia, then she would sit in her chair by the window upstairs in her room. Sarah didn't change with the times, nor did she react well to anyone changing her room, her clothes, or really anything regarding her quiet existence in the Dubois brownstone.

That life had continued in pretty much the same way until Derek's father, Richard, was born. Sarah would sometimes hold Richard as a child. Richard grew up with the secret of his *unaging* aunt as well. He met his wife while studying at New York University. Richard Dubois and Derek's mother-to-be, Sandra, carried on with the family responsibility. Derek was born in the early 1970s and grew up around Sarah, just as his father had.

Perhaps it was the being in on a secret, or Sarah's unchanging beauty, or perhaps both, that intrigued everyone privy to the situation and drew them to her, but nevertheless, someone had always been there to look after and protect Sarah Dubois. Derek had played around Sarah all the time growing up and had considered her his best playmate. He would read books to her in her lap after he had learned to read, and as he grew, he would tell her the events of his day most nights before going to sleep. When Derek decided to write his first book, he found the most creative environment was right there in his aunt's upstairs room. He would talk to her about the story and bounce ideas off her and then pretend she was answering. He would read the story to her as he wrote it.

After his first book's amazing success, Derek had been able to quit his much-hated job and devote his full time to writing.

Derek could remember upsetting his aunt only once in his entire life. One day he was looking for some paper to jot some ideas on, and he came across the two scroll containers in one of his aunt's drawers. He had just opened the cap of one of them when she came out of the bathroom and saw him in the act. She had let out a yell and hurried quickly to him, pulling the containers from his hands.

Derek's creative juices started flowing after seeing the rolled-up scroll inside the canister. He combined Sarah's reaction with the articles, and the idea spawned for his second book—the one Jon Johanssen would later hate. Even more so than the first one had, this second book had brought his voiceless aunt and him even closer together and probably was responsible for her recovery today—and his salvation.

And now, he was seated next to her, taking the scrolls out of their containers. But this time, he had Sarah's permission.

"Don't you think any of the family ever had curiosity get the best of them? At night while you were asleep or while you were taking a bath or something?"

"I think your father was the only one who ever noticed them, and he respected my privacy. He was a good man, Richard. And you are the same way. Did you ever take them out just to get a look even after you decided to write a book based on them?"

"I sure wanted to, Aunt Sarah. The more I wrote about them having a power to keep you young, the more I started to believe it myself. But I loved you so much. I didn't want to ever risk seeing you upset again like that day I opened the canister. The look in your eyes—I didn't like it."

"*See?* You didn't, and they didn't."

"Yes, I see," Derek replied as he started to unroll the first scroll. "I can't believe we're doing this together." After unrolling it, he paused for a moment before speaking. He had expected hieroglyphics or something akin to them.

"Russian?" Derek called out the unexpected, and yet the obvious. "Aunt Sarah, this is Russian."

This occurred about thirty-one hours after two men in the basement of a civilian-contracted government warehouse made the same observation on a similar document.

CHAPTER 14

JACK AND RANDY MEET SARAH AND DEREK
SATURDAY, FEBRUARY 3, 2007

"WHAT WAS *THAT*?" Sarah Dubois asked. It was the next morning, and Derek and Sarah were seated, having breakfast—a routine ritual only changed on this day by the fact that Sarah Dubois had been speaking throughout the meal.

"I think someone's knocking on the door," Derek responded.

"*Well*? Don't you think you should answer it, Derek?"

"Yeah, I was about to, but now I'm wondering," Derek sighed. "No one ever knocks on our door. I'm remembering yesterday now. What if it's the police? What if they're looking for my editor? *I* was the last one to see him alive!"

"Derek, you did nothing wrong, and there isn't anything that can remotely connect you to it, not even a body. Collect yourself and answer the door, or you may *give* them reason to suspect something."

"Yeah, you're right. He just disintegrated. I can't believe I'm *saying* that. But I didn't touch him. There's nothing to tell."

"Then go!" She directed him to the door with a pointed finger.

A few moments later, he was at the front door of their three-story brownstone. He looked through the peephole and saw two men in plainclothes.

Detectives. Damn! Derek thought.

Cautiously, he unlocked and opened the door, trying to grind a smile into his face to replace the look of fear he knew was plastered across it.

"Hi, gentlemen. What can I do for you?"

The two men looked at Derek and then at each other. The one in front, closest to Derek was shorter, about five-nine, around the same age as himself, Derek felt. The one standing behind this man had a boyish face but appeared to be in his late twenties, regardless. He was as tall as Derek but had a bigger build.

The shorter one spoke. "Are you…" The man paused. "Are you Derek Dubois, the author?"

"Uh, yes. That's me."

Great, it is the police, Derek thought. *Don't look guilty!*

Derek spoke again, trying not to look guilty, knowing he was failing miserably.

"The one and only! You're not a crazy dangerous fan or anything, right? 'Cause then I'd really need to be going!"

"No. We're not crazy fans. My name's Jack Johanssen, and this is my friend Randy."

Johanssen? Derek thought. *That's my editor's last name. I don't think these are cops. And he said 'friend,' not 'partner.'*

"Well, that's good. I don't need my thumbs sawed off or my legs hobbled just yet. How…how can I help you?"

Shit! Is it bad that I'm not showing recognition at the name Johanssen? Guilt, valid or not, sucked the same.

"Ha!" The shorter one let out a slightly nervous laugh, "Well, the thing is. I'm a scientist—well, actually—I'm an archaeologist, and—"

"He's your editor's brother, Mr. Dubois," the taller one interrupted. "We just wanted to talk to you a bit because he—your editor and *his* brother—is missing."

"Really? Uh…that's…I just saw him the other day. Yesterday, in fact."

Jack chimed in quickly. "Listen, pardon my friend here before you slam the door in our faces and think you need a lawyer. I just want to talk to you for a couple minutes or so. We're not accusing you of anything—just trying to retrace Jon's steps."

"Okay, I guess. Sure." Derek offered them the opening to the brownstone. "Come inside and sit down. I'll try to help with what I can."

They walked into the foyer, and Derek led them to the sitting room and motioned for them to take a seat anywhere. "Are you sure he's missing? Like I said, I just saw him. I had a meeting with him at his office."

God, I hope I'm not stuttering.

Derek continued. "Ha! He was actually ripping my book apart. Told me I had to write another one. Seems funnier now than it did then. Well, I mean not funny, I mean, if he's missing. I'm just say—"

"That's all right. Don't worry," Jack said, stopping Derek's attempt at normal conversation. "Mr. Dubois, I don't have a clue where my brother is. His secretary told me last night she hadn't seen him since his meeting with you before lunch. I was able to get your address from his files. I hope you don't mind."

"No, of course not. Just don't sell it on eBay!" Derek let out another nervous laugh. Every laugh felt tellingly nervous.

Jack continued, "And honestly, for all I know he just decided to take a vacation and not tell anyone. He wasn't exactly the best people person in the world."

Randy snorted.

Derek attempted his next lie.

"Maybe he really hated my book that much and quit being an editor."

Jack paused at Derek's joke, and Randy saved the day again. "Mr. Dubois?"

"Yes? Uh…Randy, was it?"

"Yes. That's me. I'm Randy, and this is Jack. You're Derek. I gotta know if what Jack told me is true."

"True? What is true?" Derek responded beyond puzzled.

"Would anyone like some tea?"

"Aunt Sarah?"

Well, maybe Sarah saved the day.

Sarah entered the sitting room with a tray of tea. She was obviously younger than Derek. The way she carried herself, the way she'd done her hair, *and the clothes she was wearing*…she looked like she had just stepped out of a photograph from a hundred years ago, or more.

Randy appeared to gulp as if he'd just swallowed his own tongue—if anyone had been watching.

And someone was watching. Byron was watching. Every event in this book was watched, or this book wouldn't exist. But you'll learn about that later.

With all the men in the room hiding behind some mask, Sarah, with her demeanor and dress, appeared more a Beacon of Truth than a Presenter of Tea.

Jack had partly deciphered a scroll stating that its holder stays young. Jon had told Jack that Derek had written a book about a "Fountain of Scrolls aunt." Jack and Randy looked at Sarah as if she were a ghost. Maybe it wouldn't be the scroll that would melt their faces…maybe it would be her. If she had offered them mashed potatoes instead of tea, her words might have produced a full Medusa effect, instead of only their stone-cold stares.

Holy shit, this thing might be for real, rippled through both their minds. *Probably,* their minds added. Their minds needed to make room for "probably," just to stay sane.

Derek was looking at the two men, trying to comprehend the source of their shock, when Jack started to speak. "Mr. Dubois, you're going to think I'm crazy, and if what I have to say is complete nonsense to you, then throw me and my friend out the door. But I've got to say it. I have just spent three nights dwelling on this thing, and now that I see your aunt, I just need to say it—say it and get it over with."

Randy started to stop Jack but then stopped stopping him.

"Okay. So what do you want to say?" Derek asked blindly—more blindly than he even realized, given what was coming.

Jack opened the left side of his jacket with his left hand to reveal the inside of the jacket to the group, making sure they saw there was no weapon he'd be reaching for. He still came off like he might be revealing a bomb and timer, wires and all.

Instead of a detonator, Derek noticed a small cylindrical canister sticking out of the inside of Jack's inner pocket. He watched Jack pull it out. Sarah and tea had become completely ignored for the moment. Sarah set the tea down on a table, doing her own ignoring, and came in closer to see what these two visitors were doing.

"What's that?" Derek asked one moment too late. By the time he finished asking, a scroll had slid out into the shorter man's right hand.

Sarah gasped then covered her mouth, attempting to reverse the sound she'd made.

"Uh-huh," Randy affirmed her shock. "There's no escaping this now. We're all in this."

"What do you mean? All in this? In *what?*" Derek asked honestly. Honesty felt much better, and he thanked the universe for the opportunity to give some.

Jack began. "This scroll, I believe, might look *familiar* to you? I believe you might have one also. Really old, possibly in Russian that doesn't quite look like Russian? If I'm correct, you also have no idea what it says but have a pretty good idea it's keeping your aunt there stuck in the 1870s. Well, I've translated this one, and if you would be kind enough to tell me the truth, maybe we can *all* get some answers, and I might actually sleep again."

Derek looked over at his aunt, who had moved to sit next to the men on the couch.

As if that didn't give anything away.

She gave a look to Derek, a pleading look, and nodded. The men hadn't noticed. They were staring at him, waiting for an answer.

Derek sat for a moment in silence. He spoke, taking Sarah's nod as permission. "We do."

"Do what? Mr. Dubois?" Jack prodded.

"We have a scroll. We have two, in fact. And…you're right. We don't have any idea what they say. But how did you know?"

"Two?" Jack said, almost gulping. "Randy, that's three out of four right there."

"Uh, yeah." Randy didn't know how to do this conversation anymore.

Jack continued. "I'm sure if you put a little thought to it, you can probably fill in most of the pieces on how we led ourselves to you. That is, if I help a bit."

"Okay, then help," Derek begged.

"Besides the fact that our scroll says it's number four of four and that the scroll's keeper will remain young, my brother happened to—"

"Your brother told you about my *book!*" Derek yelled.

"Now you're getting it. I put two and two together and took a leap."

"But what made you think there was anything valid to the relic? Do you have a relative that doesn't age *too?*"

"No, I don't. Neither of us. I'm an archaeologist, like I started to say before. I research items collected over the years by the government. I came across this scroll on Wednesday night. It was collected during a survey of the aftermath of the massacre at Little Bighorn in 1876.''

"Eighteen seventy-six!" Sarah burst out of her silence.

Randy and Jack jumped at her exclamation. The shifting of their weight on the cushions made her end rise, and she bounced with them.

"Your aunt sure knows how to interject. Geez," Randy said, embarrassed. He looked at her as she balanced herself from the aftershock of the two men's surprise, and this time he didn't stop looking. Sarah looked back.

"Okay," Jack said, breaking the moment. "So it seems 1876 has meaning beyond Custer and my scroll? I want to hear more in a second. Shoot, I'd like to see your scrolls in a second. But you asked what made me pay a tad more attention to all these details?"

"Yes, I did," Derek answered, wanting more.

"The scroll is at least one hundred and thirty-one years old, and it mentions Randy and me by name."

"What?" Sarah and Derek said together—and once again, Randy and Jack jumped together.

It was Saturday afternoon, 1:31 p.m., February 3, 2007, when Sarah and Derek and Byron had a "What?" moment together. Byron had just read about a certain dead man's loss of a picture in a diary.

———◇○◇———

"It had your *names*? Holy shit!" Derek burst out, completely mystified. "Oh, I'm sorry, Aunt Sarah." Derek apologized for the language. Far away, Byron was only a few moments away from saying the same exclamation once he noticed there were two identical broken picture frames in the cabin.

"Yes, and it was written very 'conversationally,' if that's a word?" Randy chimed in. "I mean, here we are looking at this relic that appears to have powers or be, uh, I don't know what, mystical or something, and yet it's written like how I'd talk to you. It's weird."

"He's right," Jack said. "I don't understand what is going on, either, but we're here, and you seem to know what we're talking about. Do you think we could see the other two scrolls?"

Derek looked again at Sarah. Sarah was looking at Jack. Jack was looking at Derek but then switched his focus to Sarah, noticing she was looking at him. Randy had been talking a moment earlier by moving his eyes back and forth between Derek and Sarah, but now they were resting on Sarah, and he hadn't moved them since Jack had started talking.

Breaking the three men's stares at her, Sarah spoke. "Do you think you can translate mine?"

"Yeah. I think so," Jack answered. "Are the letters Russian?"

"Yes," she replied.

"Well, then, there's a pretty good chance they came from the same source and are hopefully encoded the same way."

"Where was it you said you worked again?" Derek asked.

"I work for a government warehouse," Jack answered. "Why?"

"It's just my aunt has been cooped up in this house for nearly eighty years and has only recently become aware of the world again. I just would like it very much if the government was not so much interested in this that she becomes imprisoned somewhere like an animal to be studied."

"No, ma'am," Randy broke in, answering to Sarah as if she had made the comment. "No one is going to take you anywhere. Jack works for the government, yes, but he's doing this research on his own time." Randy turned to Jack. "That's right, Jack? Isn't it?"

Randy's statement made Jack realize he hadn't much considered the state of his "officialness" on this research trip.

He *was* employed by the US government. His job was to catalog and research the relics within the boxes in the warehouse. Now that he thought about it, Jack assumed the government likely felt most of the items would hold little or no interest to anyone outside a circle of PhDs in history. He most certainly believed if any of his supervisors or their supervisors believed there might actually be something truly powerful, like the Lost Ark of the Covenant from the first Indiana Jones movie, they would probably be down in Jack's lab looking for it themselves. Jack supposed if he was to find anything of that sort that they, of course, would want to know about it. However, Jack also thought the reason he had never contemplated a situation like this was because nobody really believed in this sort of thing, and if nobody believed in it, then there probably wasn't any precedent on what to do if it happened.

If what happens? Jack thought.

Well you know, if some archaeological find is discovered to have special powers or something.

Oh, yeah. And so each of these items, on this long list of special powers yet to be discovered, all roughly do the same thing, say the same thing, and affect the world in the same way, right?

Well, no, but—

And so, all these millions of relics lying around with "mysticalness" stamped all over them have a standard set of government-approved procedures to always follow, when one is found? Perhaps something like: "If said archaeologist comes upon a relic that has secret mystical powers, please call supervisor at once because a supervisor will always know better than aforementioned archaeologist. Especially, if the supersecret relic has something specifically referencing you. Your supervisor has his set of procedures to deal with just that sort of thing. It is important you adhere to these procedures so you don't go misinterpreting the meaning of said relic and start feeling you're important to the damned thing and end up getting too big for your britches.

You know, that kind of general procedure.

Yeah, Jack pretty much figured he was on his own here—definitely in the realm of "Figure this thing out for yourself." This wasn't work-related anymore.

"Randy's right. Don't really think this is anyone's business but ours, right now. And by that, I mean, given the nature of these things and what we know so far, we should only proceed together if we are in agreement."

"Then it's agreed. I'll go and get them," Sarah replied and stood up from the couch. She walked away from the men with a natural grace and beauty, and Randy's jaw hung a bit as she left the room. Jack didn't notice Randy's jaw because he was experiencing a tad of the same mandibular joint condition.

"Your aunt's quite the special woman," Jack said to Derek. He then noticed Randy still frozen in his state of awe. "Randy, you look like a hypnotized puppy dog."

Randy snapped out of his gawk, and Derek spoke up. "So, uh, you guys want some of this tea?"

"Sure," Randy replied, "Sarah prepared it, right?"

"Do you even remember the scrolls and the lost ark and—" Jack rolled his eyes.

"All right, then." Derek got up and poured glasses of tea from the table Sarah had left the tea sitting on.

"I'll have one too, I guess," Jack conceded. "It'd probably do me some good. Calming effect or whatever."

Derek finished pouring a second cup. The room had become silent except for the cascade of liquid flowing out of the teapot and into the cups and that sound had all captivated the three men's attention as they were caught in thought and surrealness. If the scene had been being filmed for a movie, a director would have just ordered his Russian cinematographer to stay on the pouring teapot, having commanded, *"Stay there, Aleksi! Right there! Right now, it's all about the teapot. The damned teapot's the only thing in the universe. You got it? Aleksi? Don't you lose it! Hold. Hold. That's it. Cut!"*

Derek carried the cups over to the couch where the two visitors were still seated.

("Stay on the tray, now, Aleksi! Close in on that tray.")

"I'll bring over the sugar and let you handle that part," Derek said, breaking the contemplative silence. He handed the first cup to Randy, stretching his arm out toward "Jack's friend," for that's all Derek really knew about Randy at this point. Randy was reaching for the cup when suddenly he witnessed a look of horror on Derek's face. Then Randy felt the heat hit his stomach.

"Ahhh!" Randy let out a primal yell, jumping up from the couch shaking the hot tea off his torso.

Derek's hand had frozen as he had moved the cup toward Randy. The halt in motion had caused tea to leap from the cup onto Randy's midsection by way of its own inertia.

"What the hell happened to you, man?" Randy was holding his shirt away from his stomach.

Derek's eyes flickered, and his state of silent panic became verbal. "Oh! Thank God!" he gasped.

"Thank God?" Randy yelled back, "Thank God for *what*? I'm lucky that didn't go into my face! Where the hell'd you go?"

"I…I'm sorry. Are you hurt? I didn't do anything to you, did I?"

"What?" Randy asked again. "Yeah, you did something—the tea's what you did." Calming down, Randy concluded, "It's okay now, though. Don't worry about it."

Derek seemed to relax a bit.

"Wait a minute. You really *did* zone out, didn't you? Are you all right?" Randy asked.

"I'm really sorry. Yeah, I guess I did. You're not burnt, are you? I've been a little on edge the last few days concerning Aunt Sarah and those scrolls. I think I'm actually glad you guys showed up, now that I think about it."

"It appears so, that you've been on *edge*," Randy confirmed. "I've never seen dread like that on a guy's face—ever—and all you were doing was handing me some tea."

Derek responded with silence, only to be broken by the reentry of Sarah with her scroll cases, one in each hand.

—◇○◇—

"Well, here they are, gentlemen."

"Oh, Aunt Sarah," Derek immediately turned to his aunt and said, "You missed a bit of excitement. I accidentally spilled tea all over—uh, Randy, correct?"

"Yes, Mr. Dubois, the name is Randy. It's no big deal, though," Randy replied, looking at Sarah the whole time. "As I said, don't worry about it."

"Actually, why don't you call me Derek? I think there's a rule that once a man's spilled a beer on you, you get to call him by his first name. Tea's close enough."

Randy laughed back. "All right, *Derek*. Maybe tea is close enough."

Walking up to Randy, Sarah asked, "Are you okay? You're not burned or anything are you?" She was lightly tugging at the wet part of his shirt.

If anyone had been watching Derek, they would have seen him freeze again. He was looking at his aunt, yet not seeing his aunt. She was acting differently, and for the first time, he truly didn't see her as older than him, as his 150-something great-great aunt. Instead, he saw a young, attractive girl. And he felt guilty attributing those qualities to her.

Sarah was feeling what her nephew was seeing. But there was a new feeling too. In her first youth (*is that what you'd call it?*), she had been about the game, the play, the enjoyment of it all. She wasn't looking for anything but the world to open itself to her eyes. The idea of love, or anything like it, wasn't a journey for which she would be buying a ticket. However, now, it appeared, falling in love might suddenly be feeling natural, normal, and worth exploring.

"No, I'm fine, really. It was a little hot but no burns," Randy replied.

"Don't make so light of it, Randy," Jack muttered, not being able to help himself.

"Well, maybe Derek has a shirt you can borrow?" Sarah said, not hearing Jack.

"I'm fine. I think it's going to dry all right here soon enough. If we all go out or something, maybe I'll look into it."

"Where we going, Randy?" Jack couldn't resist asking. "Out, was it?"

"Huh, Jack?"

Jack stood up, standing like a chaperone at a middle school dance next to Sarah and Randy. "Does anyone in this room remember anything about those two articles Miss Dubois is holding? If you don't mind, Miss Dubois, and Randy, if you are sure you're fine and don't need a burn unit called, I'd love to take a look at the two relics the lady has tucked up under her arm that's been keeping her young for over a hundred years."

"Oh. Oh, no," Sarah said, "Here you are. Anything you can do or find out would be great." Sarah's focus had shifted back to her possessions. "As you can imagine, I have many questions as well."

Sarah eagerly pushed the canisters into Jack Johanssen's hands. *Now the keeper of three mystical scrolls,* he thought to himself, not knowing whether to chuckle or run crazy into the street, never to be heard from again.

"Well, Randy, look at this. Three of the four right here in my hands, three days after we found ours. A scroll a day, they say."

Sarah raised her soft eyes up toward Jack as he made this observation and asked the obvious. "So where's the fourth?"

BOOK II:

DAVIS AND HACKER THE TRACKER AT THE TOP OF THE WORLD

CHAPTER 15

AND THEN THERE WERE TWO
JUNE 25, 1876

THE ICE STRETCHED FOR MILES in every direction. Hacker began to wonder if he remembered any other colors besides snow white, sky blue, and the brown earth tones of his clothes and the sleds. The sky was overcast today, leaving only two of those colors in this long-overstayed reality. He couldn't imagine how heaven was going to be so great if it only offered the hellish hue surrounding him on all sides. He hadn't attempted a trip this deep into the Arctic before, and he wondered if he'd made his first real mistake. To ignore this notion, he pushed another thought into his mind.

If you finish this trip, the payoff will make it your last.

This attempt at mind trickery didn't change the fact that *he* knew the *crew* knew he was lost. They hadn't said anything yet, but he was sure they were thinking it, and he figured they'd be saying so soon enough. The dogs didn't look too good, either, and that wasn't helping his situation.

He'd been lost for at least two days. The damned compass had stopped working, and the stars were of no use if it was going to be cloudy every night. They didn't travel but in the day, anyhow, and the sun, when it *was* visible, didn't do much for him at such a high latitude. Regardless of all of that, for some reason, Hacker felt nothing was *supposed* to be useful. This gut feeling gnawed at him like frostbite and even scared him a little. *I don't get lost—or scared, for that matter,* he thought to himself, *so what the hell's going on?* It felt like something was at work to make him lost, and if that were true, it didn't give him much hope of finding a solution to their predicament or his treasure.

"Mr. Hacker, sir?"

"Yes, Davis, what is it?"

"May we go for a walk?"

Hacker understood what Davis meant by "walk." Knowing the conversation needed to happen, he didn't badger Davis for bothering him. Hacker stood up on his sore legs and followed Davis away from the sleds.

"I know what this is about, Davis."

"Yes, I suppose you do. The others have begun to notice—"

"You don't have to tell me, Davis. They're all shakin' in their snowshoes that I might be lost, *right?*"

"Well—"

"Listen, Davis, I don't get lost. Hacker the Tracker's my name," Hacker interrupted boastfully and dishonestly. He knew right away he didn't buy his own con any more than Davis, as displayed by the unimpressed look upon his first mate's tired, windblown face.

Hacker figured he'd better bite the bullet and nip this in the bud right now before it degenerated into a mutiny, getting them all killed out here in the middle of nowhere.

"All right, Davis, I guess the time has come to have a talk with the crew."

"Davis here says you dumbasses think I'm lost! Is that true?"

Only silence was returned by those he was addressing followed by a few glances back and forth at one another.

"Well? Is that it? Speak up, boys! This is your only chance. You bring it up later, and I'll shoot you for treason!"

Hacker's crew stood there wide eyed, not sure what to think. Collectively, they wondered if Hacker had really meant "treason." Was that really the correct term? Mutiny, yes. But *treason?* None of them remembered viewing Hacker as the leader of some tiny traveling country.

Hacker, on the other hand, was laughing as he interpreted their stares to mean each was thinking, *So is he still gonna shoot me if I say something now—it just won't be for treason?*

Ah, what it must feel like to be in their position…poor boys.

Hacker thought it was pretty amusing to watch them all squirm. If he was going to come clean and admit something that had never happened to him in thirty freaking years, then the least he could do was get a good laugh out of the deal.

"Ah, haaaaa! Shoot! Now that's priceless!" he spewed. "You all know I'm lost. You all know we're gonna die up here if we don't figure out where we are. You all know that your very lives depend on this conversation right here and now. And none of ya's got the guts to say something to me about it."

He waited a moment. Still not hearing a peep out of them, Hacker boasted, "I know I'm a hard ass, and you're probably all figuring you'd rather live a couple more days in this snow than have me shoot you now, but in my book, that just makes you a bunch of pus—"

Craaaaaackkkkkk!

"What was that?" Davis shouted. "Did you hear that?"

The others agreed when the sound came again, this time louder and longer.

Craaaaaackkkkkk! Craaack!

"Ah damn! It's the ice!" yelled Hoppins.

Hacker stepped in. "Everybody, effin' quiet, and hold still. Which direction did it come from, Davis? And don't be wrong."

Davis thought for a moment, and then he raised his left arm and pointed. "That way, yes, that way."

Another cracking noise erupted. It was closer, and everyone realized Davis had pointed in the correct direction.

"Gear up. Quick! We head that way!" Hacker commanded, waving his arm in the opposite direction of Davis's verdict.

"Mush! Mush! Come on, you dogs!" Hacker shouted over the almost-deafening continual cracking of ice. It seemed to come from all directions now, drowning out all memory of any other sounds heard before. If Hacker had had much time to think, he might have contemplated the futility of yelling at the dogs. Even with their more attuned ears, it was most probably the whip that was influencing them to mush and not the sound waves of his voice traversing their auditory canals.

Hacker looked back to see the other sleds. The other four were still there. He had half figured he would see everyone behind him quickly being swallowed up by the ocean, given the sounds he was hearing. Where was it coming from? Before, it had been behind them. But now it was so loud, he assumed he'd be driving his sled down into an unseen crevice just ahead of him at any moment. There was no longer a way to know which way was the right way to go. They were five brown specks in a sea of white, above and below, due to the overcast skies, and an erupting thunder filled his entire reality. He just hoped—regardless of how loud and epicenter-less the cracking was—that there had been a sound reason why they'd left in the direction they had. And of course, that "loudness" didn't necessarily have anything to do with the speed of fissure travel.

"Come on boys! Keep up!" He waved his arm back at the team and pulled it forward as if he were grabbing an invisible rope that had lassoed all the other sleds and he was bringing them along for the ride.

Davis wasn't so concerned with his "president's" leadership, his motivational arm motions, or his cries of support, if there were any—it's not like he would be able to hear them anyway. Davis wasn't too concerned anymore about whether a mutiny was going to happen. Or which side he would have chosen: stand as second in command with his captain and die honorably, or become captain and live with a reputation he would never have dreamed of acquiring: mutineer. Davis wasn't worried about the other sleds, or the team, or anything else, really. Well, there was that one thing, wasn't there? Davis was pulling up the rear of the team, and someone had decided to join him. His name was Impending Doom, and he was swimming.

———◇○◁———

Impending Doom didn't mind the cold water of the Arctic Ocean. And walking took way too long when you were trying to reach a poor soul out past-timing on a dogsled. And when you had such a quickly traveling crack in the ice sheet plowing forward effortlessly opening the water for you, there was no better choice of travel.

Impending Doom was not Death. Death was some distant cousin he'd never met on his mother's side. I. D. didn't go looking for a "next name on a list"—how boring that would be. I. D. liked spontaneity. He'd show up out of the blue when things were going just horribly wrong for some chap.

This crack was moving up one of these chap's backsides, and I. D. was just riding the waves and waiting to hear that phrase he'd heard so many times before in so many different tongues but rarely got to hear completed. He usually just heard "Oh shi—" and then there just wasn't any time to waste. Impending Doom had to assume his alter ego: grow up, get to work, get busy and do his job—however you wanted to put it—and become just plain old Doom.

———◇○◁———

Davis was mushing and looking back over his shoulder about a hundred times a minute. The fissure was chasing him feverishly, and no one else could even tell. He would be gone, and the rest of the team would notice sometime later that "oh...Davis is gone."

The sleds were spread out with at least thirty feet in between each, alternating left and right sides of an invisible line between Davis's sled in the rear and Hacker's at the lead. The ocean was opening behind Davis, and it was so loud he thought his ears would start bleeding and his brain would explode well before he died a wet frozen death.

Did he really have enough time at this moment to think of his family? To ask questions like "Why did I choose this as a livelihood? Why did I stick with a captain like Hacker? What fool's errand was this, and am I really going to die alone at the rear end of a dogsled team at the top of the world?" It seems he did have enough time to think these things. And several more things, as well. "Did I ever tell my mother I was sorry for breaking her vase? What did I eat for dinner last night? Shoot, I really can't remember." It appeared to Davis that no matter how fast impending doom could move, a mind could move faster.

Ahead and then back, he continued to look, swiveling his head. As the opening gulf gaining on him reached below him, between his legs, he felt a compulsion to say two words he never would have wished to be his last on earth.

"Oh shi—"

Impending Doom was as nondiscriminatory as he was spontaneous. He was literally riding a wave at present, but that's typically what he did anyway. Went with the flow, that is. Whatever the circumstances befalling some poor soul, he would just drop in and do what needed to be done when the time was right. But he never knew when that time was right until he knew. He'd just know, ya know? And that's why he loved his job.

I. D. was just about to reach up between the two sled runners and yank that sucker, Davis, down into the depths. He thought he'd gotten a clue it was "that time" when Davis looked down at him and said, "Oh shi—"

"—iiiiiiiiit!" Davis finished yelling down at Impending Doom as the crack in the ice took a sharp right, out and away from under Davis's sled, leaving him safe for the moment.

"What?" Impending Doom thought for a moment. But then shook that off quickly and said, "Hell yeah! That's what I love about this job! Now that hasn't happened in a long time!" It appeared Davis's fate wasn't in the books yet.

Davis made a dead stop once he saw where the crack in the ice was headed. As he stood there, thankful to be alive, he couldn't begin to understand what he felt about what he saw next.

The opening in the shelf had veered forward again and then cut left. It seemed to be gaining speed and purpose, if that was possible. It jumped forward and swallowed sled four in an instant. Andrews was gone. It then swung right, yet still forward, directly toward the next sled in line. Cutter's sled disappeared swifter than Andrews's, as if practice had helped make perfect. Five had become three, and Davis was about to close his eyes in horror and sorrow when a ledge of ice sprung out of the shelf further ahead like an ejected tectonic plate during an earthquake and slammed into the side of Hoppins's body, knocking him off his sled and up into the air. Before he hit the ground, the ocean had opened below him, welcoming him for a dive. Davis could have sworn this third occurrence *(murder?)* looked like the ice was just having fun now, and he would have been willing to swear he'd seen a hazy hand reach up from the ocean, catch Hoppins midair, and pull him straight down into the Arctic. But of course, he couldn't admit to himself he'd seen that, could he?

Davis could hear again. The utter stillness of the ice shelf had returned. It appeared the fissure had completely halted, having taken two sleds, Hoppins, Cutter, and Andrews as booty. Up in the distance, about three hundred feet ahead, Hacker had stopped as well and was looking back at Davis with his hand resting on the top of his head in a posture of survey and disbelief. Davis looked back at Hacker in bewilderment, with a little relief arising from not being left completely alone. Next, Davis's mind entertained a strange thought he would never fully understand: "I've met Impending Doom. I know the feeling he gives, and I'll take his cousin Death anytime."

—◇○◇—

Sure as hell you will, thought Impending Doom about Davis's thought. *You seemed like a wimp to me anyways. Choose some style if you got to die, man. But if you want the old drab and dreary "I have come for you. It is your time," then fine— look up my distant relative when you get old. Ha!*
Then I. D. had some poor souls to attend to who were about to be in dire straits elsewhere, and he was gone.

—◇○◇—

Hacker turned his head to see what was going on behind him. Hacker didn't see Andrews's sled. He looked harder, squinting, trying to maintain his balance as his sled continued to move at a rapid pace in the opposite direction of his current line of sight.
Oh my God! Hacker's mind gasped, not having the time to form the words on his lips as Cutter disappeared into the ice. But when a block of ice jutted up at an angle and shot Hoppins into the air like a cannonball, Hacker had turned around and yelled, "MUSH!" louder than he had ever yelled anything…ever. He missed someone playing catch with Hoppins's body a second later. And it's a shame, too, because he was so much closer to Hoppins than Davis, and front row seats are hard to come by when you're a working man. A man like Hacker probably deserved to be haunted by that sight more than Davis, anyway. At least Davis had been farther away, allowing him to later retain the luxury of second-guessing himself. Life isn't fair, but mercy sometimes makes up for the disparity.
"Mush! Dammit! Mush! You effin' dogs, mush!" The ice had quit moving halfway through Hacker's command. Hacker felt somewhat ridiculous hearing himself screaming, "You effin' dogs, mush!" as stillness returned around him.
"Whoa!" He pulled on the reins, slowing and then stopping the dogs. They were panting rapidly, glad to get a rest from his whip. Their ears were even more relieved to get a rest from Impending Doom's Wild Ride Extravaganza.
After coming to a stop, Hacker turned back again. He pulled the hat off his head, wiped his face, put his hand on his head, and scratched his scalp through his sweaty

hair, looking perplexingly back at Davis's sled.
Thank God, I'm not alone.

CHAPTER 16

ALWAYS HERE AND THE INUIT
JUNE 25, 1876

———◇○◯◯○◇———

"HURRY, FATHER, come quick!"

"Yes, as you wish, My Sweet Mother. And where is it that we are going?"

"Oh, Father, it's terrible. It's terrible, you'll see. He's over there"—she pointed—"behind Cold One's camp."

Father quickly followed his daughter to the other side of Home Now to see what had her so troubled, and he was feeling quite worried by the time they arrived at their destination a couple of minutes later. My Sweet Mother had been speaking in a panic during the whole trespass. Statements such as "Not him!" and "Oh, Father, his arm, and his hair!" and "What could this mean?" had helped to further his worry.

As they cleared the back side of Cold One's camp, Father beheld a most wretched sight. Always Here was on the ground on his back. Most of his hair had fallen from his scalp, and it littered the pure snow around his head. Worst of all, it seemed he had broken his upper arm, bad enough so that a large piece of bone had ripped through the skin. Blood oozed from the wound, and Always Here lay unconscious.

I hope he's only unconscious, Father thought.

"Is he alive?" Father asked in the calmest voice he could muster.

"Yes, Father, I believe so. I felt him for chest motion before I ran to you, and he was alive then. But Father? Father, what does this mean? Always Here can't *be* hurt. So how is it that he *is* hurt, Father?"

"I don't know. We'll have to answer that later. Right now we must tend to him so we don't lose him. Go tell Strong Arms and your brother to come quickly and to bring blankets. We must move him inside and keep him warm. And we need to fix his arm."

"Yes, Father. I'll be back with them."

Father looked down at his old friend who, until this moment, had always looked as young as his seventeen-year-old daughter who had just run off. They had been friends since Father had been a little one, back when his name had been The Son. Then, Always Here had been his mentor. Later, Always Here had become his peer once The Son had become Father and leader of the tribe. "Oh, my dear old friend," Father uttered slowly with his wise, authoritative voice, "what has *happened* to you?

How is this even *possible?*"

He felt his own forehead and wiped the same hand over Always Here's scalp, which was mostly bare now. His head felt warm, considering its lack of protection, and that worried Father more. A fever had come.

"Here they are. Here they are, Father. I brought them." My Sweet Mother had returned. Strong Arms and The Son stood with wide-eyed stares of disbelief at the sight of Always Here lying on the snow.

"Father, what is this?" Strong Arms asked shakily.

"Yes, what is happening, Father. Do you know?" his son asked in succession.

"No, I do not know. That will have to be solved but not now." Needing to snap these two young men out of their shock, he took charge, as his role in the tribe demanded. Regardless of how he shared what they were feeling, Always Here needed help, and he aimed to provide what he could to his friend. "Hand me the blankets My Sweet Mother—quickly. And Strong Arms, take one of them and lay it flat, here, next to Always Here. The Son, take the other end and help Strong Arms."

They did as they were told. Father wrapped two of the blankets around Always Here. He then instructed the two boys to help him carefully lift their friend onto the last blanket so they could all carry Always Here with it.

"All right. Everyone take a corner. We'll move him to his home."

—◇○◇—

"Always Here…Always Here. Are you all right?"

Always Here could swear he was hearing the voice of a mystical seal riding a brilliant ribbon of dancing sky shines. He was trying to open his eyes, and as he did, the blurriness cleared. He saw My Sweet Mother, who might someday be Mother Leader, peering over him.

"Oh, Always Here! You're awake. I must go get Father. But you stay here…and stay awake…I'm going. Maybe I shouldn't leave you? Oh, what do I—"

"Go, My Sweet Mother. It's all right." Always Here loved her concern—such a young, innocent soul. One of the brightest he had known since a time almost too long ago to remember he thought. How long had it been…four, five thousand circles of the sun?

"Oh, okay, all right. I'll be right back. I'll be right back, Always Here." She ran out of the hut.

"Father, Father!" My Sweet Mother called out as she ran up to her father. "He's awake, he's awake, Father! Hurry, I didn't want to leave him."

Father had been discussing the recent strange events with Strong Arms and Questions Father. He turned toward his daughter's voice. "Ah, good, come, let us go to him. Perhaps he'll have the answers we are searching for."

Strong Arms held the canvas open for Father and Questions Father and entered

Always Here's home behind them. Strong Arms felt quite honored to be asked to join this meeting of such obvious importance. He took a seat off to the right side of everyone, not quite fitting in his spot because of his massive size. He was trying not to appear as the most noticeable person in the room, as he usually was. His father had been Strong Arms before him. His father never mentioned having ever sat in such a council. Battle planning, hunting considerations, yes, but a matter of tribe history or a Father's decision? He didn't think so.

The Circle's meetings were always and had always been populated only by Always Here, Father, Questions Father, Mother, The Son—if Father had a male child—The Other, and My Sweet Daughter—if Father had a female child—once she was old enough to be referred to as My Sweet Mother and later, Mother Leader, if she had a child.

Presently, Father and Questions Father had not chosen one of the tribe's sons to be The Other. My Sweet Mother had gone to find Mother, and The Son had been sent on an unknown mission. Strong Arms, therefore, sat with the three remaining men with titles for such a meeting. *Was this significant?* he wondered.

"Strong Arms, come close and join The Circle." Father motioned his hand for Strong Arms to join them. "We may not have much time, and you should be a full part of this council."

"Yes, Father, but I do not see why—" Strong Arms stopped himself, realizing it was not appropriate to be prolonging this portion of the conversation, given that time may be a precious commodity.

"We will talk more later, Strong Arms, but for now join The Circle and be attentive," Father responded and then turned to Always Here.

"Do you know what is happening, my dear friend?"

"I do not. The arm is set well. I thank you, though I can barely remember what it is like to have a wound."

"Is there any reason you can think of? How did your injuries happen? When did you take on such age? The sounds in the distance—did they play any part in this?" Father was hastily asking questions, and the fear in his voice was apparent. Always Here looked older than any man he'd ever seen.

"I know very little of my purpose outside what you know. Protect the scroll and stay with the tribe." Always Here coughed and grabbed his arm in pain as his body jerked. "Too many circles to count have I resided among your people. I can only scarcely recall the short life I lived before arriving with you. I only have the scroll to prove, even to myself, that I came from somewhere else."

"And the sounds, the great thunders off to the west? We were just discussing them. I sent The Son and White Bear to see what they could find."

"I was observing the sky and its odd whiteness behind Cold One's camp, where you found me. I felt a strange feeling, one of tiredness, weakness, come over me. I looked at my hands, and they were as you see them now. Aged. I touched my face and my head, and my hair slid out into my hands. I became disoriented, and that's when the thunder came. It appears you heard it as well. I stepped backward in surprise and stumbled in my newfound elderliness. My arm must have become damaged in the fall. That is all I can tell you."

"We do not want to lose you!" Questions Father exclaimed. "We must do something, Father. There must be something. Are you sure we are not to read the scroll, even now, Always Here?"

"No! That is one thing we *cannot* do!" Always Here demanded, and then he cringed in pain. "Oh, the arm hurts. I apologize, Questions Father—and always true to your role." Always Here managed a smile.

Always Here continued. "I know only one rule, and after so long, I believe I have guessed at a second. First, the scroll must not be read, by me or anyone of the tribe. Your safety and your fate depend on it. Second, I have come to believe that it cannot be my purpose only to hold onto a document forever that is never to be read by me or any of the people I serve. What meaning could there be in this? It is my belief, no matter how long it has been and how constant our existence in this state has become, it must come to an end eventually. If the scroll is not to be read by us, yet we are to protect it, then reason tells us it must be meant for someone else. And given my present appearance and injury, the weather, and the unknown sounds over the horizon, I believe there is a good chance The Son and White Bear may return with more than information."

"You believe that the one the scroll was written for is out there, right now?" Strong Arms blurted out in concern for The Son and White Bear.

"Yes…I do," Always Here answered calmly.

"So we wait," Father concluded similarly to what a Sioux chief and *his* newly aging friend had done the night before, thousands of miles away.

CHAPTER 17

DAVIS AND HACKER AND THE INUIT
LATER, JUNE 25, 1876

"GET DOWN, THE SON! You have a lot to learn about not being seen."

"Okay, White Bear. That's why Father approves of you as my friend, I'm sure, The Son had replied as he ducked down behind the ice.

The two youths were looking across the white plain at two other men struggling to control three teams of dogs. The men looked tired and defeated. It seemed that unfortunate events had also happened to these men.

"They have lost a man in their group, The Son. They won't make it if we don't help them. There is nothing in the direction they are going. They seem to be committed to maintaining their third team of dogs, and that is slowing them down even more so."

"We don't know these men, White Bear, and I believe it may be no accident that they appear just as Always Here has had such misfortune."

"What should we do?" White Bear asked. "If we go back to get permission to bring them with us, we may lose them by the time we get back, or worse, they could die. Father and Questions Father want answers. These men may have those answers. I believe they will not hurt us given their situation, and we can more than handle any ill will they may have once we get them back to Home Now."

"I don't like these men, White Bear. They are strange, and the larger one is not a good man, I am sure."

"How do you know?"

"His dogs wince at the sound of his voice. They are used to being beaten by him." The Son turned to White Bear. "We take them back. But we keep careful, all right?"

"Agreed," White Bear said.

"Once we expose ourselves, I am in charge, as that is my expertise. Do not raise your spear unless you see me do it first—no matter what. Understand?"

White Bear agreed again.

The two boys circled around in front of Davis and Hacker undetected, under White Bear's instructions to stay low and upwind of the dogs. They had dressed in white fur, given the nature of the mission.

114

"Davis! Pull out your gun!"

"Why?"

"There's someone up ahead! Quick!"

"How do you know they're hostile?"

"I'm not waiting till you're dead to find out."

"Wait. I see them now. I think you should lower your gun."

"Why?"

"They have their hands up. I think they are trying to appear friendly."

"*Appear*'s the word, Davis. I won't be surprised again today." Hacker struggled to pull out his gun with his cold hands. They were cramped in a gripping position from holding on to the sleds for so long.

"Sir, I am sorry to argue with your authority, but considering there is no one left of our team to hear me do so, I feel it won't hurt your authority too much. We are barely moving, we're lost, we're shaken. We don't have enough food to get back to our base, even if we knew where that was. This great treasure you believe is up here is not presenting itself. So if there is a good chance we're going to die anyway, or better, a chance we can get the hell out of here alive, I'm willing to take the risk of accepting their help if they have any to offer!" Davis stopped, surprised by his own words escaping his lips.

"Davis, you've shown some spine twice today, my boy. Maybe there's a captain in you yet. Not while I'm alive, mind you, so don't go runnin' off, or I'll shoot you. I need your instincts too much. Hell, look at that! You've even got me admitting I need you. What a day, Davis; what a day. Ha! I guess if I bring you along for your instincts, I'll follow 'em, despite your insubordinate tone." Hacker put his gun away.

Not your day, Hacker. Who's leading who here? he thought.

The two men stopped the dogs, stepped off the sleds, and raised their hands in the same manner as the boys coming toward them; they began closing the gap between.

Hacker hadn't put two and two together just yet, but his treasure was presenting itself—the only way a small treasure in a vast sea of nothing could. With a loud thunderous announcement, a disaster, messengers appearing out of nowhere at a time when you had little hope left, and of course, the telltale of all...when you least expected it.

—◇○◇—

"Where do you think we're headed sir?" Davis inquired.

"Where the hell do ya think?" Hacker boasted.

Great. Hacker was back. "Yes, sir, Hacker sir," Davis replied sarcastically. He was not amused. Hacker's arrogance was about as useful here, given their situation, as thin ice.

Hacker didn't much care for Davis's tone, but he knew Davis was his closest thing to a friend, teammate, fellow soldier—however he wanted to look at it—that he had out here. It was probably better not to push him too hard by getting on his case about an insubordinate tone of voice. He had handled the men smartly before. Of course his "handling" had been interrupted by a big hole in the ice that inadvertently killed all the other men. But all in all, he had believed it was going well and would have continued to go well and in his favor. He hadn't remained captain all these years because he didn't know what he was doing.

"Davis, these two Eskimos are not to be trusted. We'll follow them because we have no other choice. But you and I need to stick together if we're going to get out of this alive. We have no idea what these people want with us."

A little bit of the "you and me" and a little bit of the "fear the unknown" made for a healthy "us against them" soup.

"We shouldn't automatically assume they're hostile," Davis retorted. "Perhaps we will read the wrong intention and get ourselves killed."

What kind of pepper was his first mate adding to this broth? "Ah, yes, Davis, but we don't want to be caught unaware because we get too comfortable." Fight pepper with a little salt.

"I think they look friendly enough and are willing to help. If we play our cards right and are friendly in return, maybe they'll show us the way out of this block of frozen hell."

Come on, Davis, you're ruining my brew here. Better turn up the fire, but not too hot. "You're an ignorant, naive man, but I like you anyway, Davis. You just remember who's in charge here if you really do care about staying alive."

Why am I here with this man? Davis thought to himself. *Have I needed work this bad, for this long? And why am I hungry for soup?*

Davis and Hacker continued on with the two young ice dwellers. Davis continued to contemplate the day's events. It was a wonder in this desolate place they could come over some mound of snow and ice and see any signs of civilized life. However, these boys had come from somewhere. How the hell did they show up when and where they did?

The dogs ran back and forth around the men, feeling stronger, despite their mutual exhaustion, after having been unstrapped from the sleds and allowed to run free— especially free from Hacker's whip. Deep in their dog psyches, they yearned to never see a dogsled again.

—◇○◇—

"The dogs are happy. Do you see, White Bear?"

"Yes, I believe they will stay with us, regardless of these men's fate." White Bear paused for a moment. "The Son? What do you think they are talking about back there?"

"The bigger one is telling the smaller one he's in charge."

"How do you know?"

"How do you know how to hide in the snow?"

"I don't know. I just have always been good at it."

"I am good at understanding others, White Bear. Men like him always try to maintain their authority. Also, imagine you were in their situation. He is making sure he stays in control because he doesn't want the smaller one getting him killed."

"Killed? How?"

"By us."

"We're not going to kill them," White Bear stated with some doubt, now that this was a topic of conversation, "*are* we?"

"Of course not. But they don't know that. They only know they are lost and alone, that we are leading them somewhere they don't know, and to meet people they've never met, and for reasons unknown. He knows he is at a disadvantage if we have less-than-noble intentions."

"If that is what he is thinking, we should be careful not to give him the wrong impression."

"I would agree with you, White Bear, but I also believe events may be beyond our control. It is strange these two appear just as Always Here is experiencing such a change."

"Are you worried we will lose Always Here?" White Bear asked.

"I don't think we should talk any more about him. He should not be the topic of speculative conversation."

"Forgive me, The Son," White Bear said, embarrassed, "I see Home Now."

"Let's prepare our new friends."

The Son turned back toward Hacker and Davis. He motioned with his hand for them to come nearer. He thought showing them Home Now would comfort them and possibly put them in good spirits. He was still worried about the larger one and how he might react, given his fears.

Davis and Hacker walked a little faster up to the two boys. As they got closer, they could see a camp off in the distance. Both thought of warmth and food, regardless of whatever other emotions had been debated.

The Son pointed at Davis and Hacker and then at himself and White Bear and made a motion meant to convey they all would be going to the camp.

Hacker nodded in understanding and looked at Davis. "I guess we know where in the hell we're going now."

"But not where in the hell we *are*, right?"

"Right," Hacker mumbled.

They approached the camp. Scattered tribe members stopped and looked at the four entering Home Now.

"Stop staring!" The Son shouted. "Look welcoming to the strangers."

Hacker put his hand down on his gun at the shout. "Davis," he whispered, "be prepared...for anything."

The men and women changed their expressions into forced smiles, which made them appear even less genuine to Hacker.

"I don't like this, sir," Davis said back.

"I know what you mean."

"I don't think you do, sir."

"Well, then, what *do* you mean?"

"I mean, I don't like your suspicious mentality right now. I think it's going to get us into trouble. I think they are trying to be nice. They are probably as afraid of us as we are of them. Yet these two have still apparently offered to help us."

Hacker just couldn't figure out what had gotten into Davis. When had Davis flipped the tables on him and become in charge? Davis had always been useful as appointed advisor but times seemed to be a-changin'. What to do, what to do? Give him an inch he's gonna take a mile. Get into an argument with Davis right now, and they're going to make a lot of Eskimos very nervous.

"Davis, you and I are going to have a little chat later about chain of command. However, for now, advice noted." Hacker took his hand off his gun, and the forced smiles seemed to become a little less fake.

"Go tell Father we have arrived with two men who are very different from us. Find out what we should do with them."

White Bear heard the order and followed it. He didn't get halfway there before Father was already on his way. The news of their arrival had traveled fast. Father had been watching Always Here go in and out of consciousness, getting more aged every moment. The fact that The Son and White Bear were returning with strangers seemed to be no coincidence. Perhaps they were here to help the situation. Or perhaps they were the cause of it. Either way, he needed to find out.

"That's got to be their chief, Davis," Hacker said as Father came around the back of one of the canvassed homes with White Bear. The two were walking calmly, and Hacker felt awe and threat from the aura of strength and wisdom emanating from the man approaching Davis and him.

Father approached Hacker and then stopped, facing him a few feet away, and smiled. Hacker peered into Father's eyes, trying to read him and gather his intentions. He wasn't going to be intimidated. Well, he wasn't going to *show* he was intimidated.

"White Bear tells me you have lost some of your men and are in need of help. Possibly you are lost?"

Hacker watched this chief—if that was, in fact, who he was—as he spoke these words. The chief first motioned toward the young one who had run off to fetch him. Then he had pointed at Davis and him and then looked off in the distance, presumably discussing where they had been found.

"Listen, I don't understand what you're saying, Chief, but we don't want any trouble." Hacker then pointed at White Bear and The Son. "We came with these two because we are hungry, and we don't know where we are." Hacker turned and patted a hard pat on Davis's stomach and then pretended to feed something to his own mouth. He then pointed back toward where they had come from and made a wide motion, trying to describe the vastness of the area. He didn't have the first idea how he was going to get directions from these people that would be effective enough to get them home.

Father didn't understand Hacker, either, but he picked up on the hungry part. He pantomimed to Hacker he could get them food to eat, and Hacker responded with a nod.

"We're going to get some food, Davis. You better start finding a way to communicate with these Eskimos. I've got enough things to handle. I don't need to spend all my time here playing charades."

Father turned toward his son. "The Son, you bring them to my camp. Tell your mother to bring them something to eat and drink."

He turned to Hacker and Davis. "You will go with The Son and White Bear." Father moved his arms in a way to show them to follow the two boys. He then turned and left.

The authority this man had Hacker envied. It was magnificent to witness. The command felt in his presence radiated from him like a second sun—a much-needed second sun, given their environment. In this leader's presence, it took every bit and strength of will Hacker had to not feel lowered to the station of the two boys whom he was now following again. It made him angry to feel so weakened, especially given every other mishap he'd been through recently.

The Son wasn't going to question his father in front of anyone, but he was conflicted by the decision to bring these strange men into the presence of Always Here. He didn't trust the bigger one, and Always Here had not been in good shape when he had left Home Now to investigate the loud sounds that had been heard by the tribe. He would bring the men but would attempt saying something to his father alone before taking them inside. He motioned for Hacker and Davis to follow White Bear while he went and informed his mother that she would need to bring food for the men.

Hacker, Davis, and White Bear began walking away from The Son, who had disappeared into some makeshift-looking canvas abode. Hacker observed the small cooking fires and children and mothers dressed in fur as they passed along their trek to wherever it was they were being led. He couldn't believe these people lived here all of the time. They had adapted amazingly well, but as for him, he was up here to get something, and when he got it, he was heading right back down to New York, where at least summer existed part of the year.

And then he knew. Perhaps because food was on its way or because he wasn't so completely concentrated on trying to figure out where on God's white earth he was or maybe because Davis had finally decided to shut his trap for a few minutes, allowing him to think, but Hacker finally drew a conclusion worthy of his experience and a similar conclusion, in nature, to what this tribe's leaders had drawn in regard to Davis and him.

The treasure's here. Dammit, how could I be so blind? This can't all be coincidence, he thought. The compass stops working; then he has a feeling he was supposed to be lost. There's a lightning bolt of a crack in the ice, which apparently had his team on its hit list, and then out of nowhere, these people show up and bring them home for dinner. Well, hopefully not *for* dinner.

And not to mention he was supposed to be the guy who could find the things that can't be found, and this was the hunt meant to prove it.

There isn't anything that can't be found more than a thing that finds you first.
About time, Hacker; about time.

CHAPTER 18

HACKER AND MR. SIME
EARLIER THAT YEAR OF 1876

"I BROUGHT YOU HERE to see me because I hear you're a treasure seeker. What kind of treasures you go after, Mr. Hacker?"

A man dressed in a suit that was way too clean for the establishment in which he was sitting sat across from Hacker and was leading the tracker into a conversation. He didn't truly need his questions answered.

"About any kind," Hacker responded. "They all got value, or they wouldn't be called a treasure, now would they?"

"Who do you think you are, Hacker? I'm about to give information leading you to your 'next find' in what I assume is a long list of failures by the look of you, and you want to be a smart-ass! Jacky, get rid of this bum!"

"Hold up a minute. You can shove me off like I'm some jackass if you like, but you obviously have a reason you were willing to give me what you brought me up here to give me. I think you know enough not to judge me by the look of me, and you know I got something you—or the people that work for you—don't got. So you don't want to cough it up, that's fine; I'll walk out of here right now. No need for Jacky there to lift his little finger. So I'll be going now unless you want to allow both of our personalities to sit here at this table and get me what I want and get you what you want *done!*"

Hacker stood up from the rectangular wooden table. Hacker's height towered over the seated party, and he knew even Jacky was thinking if he didn't have his gun, he didn't have much ability to do anything to Hacker that Hacker wasn't going to allow him to do. Hacker's breadth dwarfed everyone in the bar, and this had always worked well for him in commanding authority in a group, whether he had earned the right to or not.

"Davis!" Hacker called to his second, who was standing across the pub waiting for the little meeting to end. "Let's go!"

"Yes, sir, boss!" Davis hollered and started to pick up the pack he had brought in containing items you don't leave with the horses: mainly money, papers, weapons, pictures, maps, socks, booze, and of course, good luck charms if you had any. Most did.

121

"All right, Hacker, no need for dramatics. Sit down. I understand both of us got to be in charge. That's why we're in charge."

Hacker sat down, feeling like someone had pushed him down by the head. He didn't like the feeling, but its blow was lessened by the next line he heard.

"You're right—I *do* need you."

"Damn right you need me, or you wouldn't have me here talking to you."

"Right, right. But the nice thing about power? Usually you can set things up so if you *do* need something, the other fella needs something from you too. And you do, Hacker. You need my intel. So now that we've both held up our testicles and dangled 'em, let's get down to business."

The man continued. "You've got instincts, and you're the best tracker around from what I hear. People say you find things that others don't find, so I'm calling you in to find a thing that ain't been found. You got a buyer already. You just got to go hunting, and your payment awaits. Ten thousand and supplies for the retrieval, and you can negotiate up to fifty thousand or forty percent of the find's intrinsic value, the lower of the two, once I know what it actually is."

"You're telling me you don't even know what I'm searching for? What the hell kind of treasure's that? How will I know when I find it?"

"That's what I'm getting to."

Meet Mr. Sime. He runs the show in Maine. It's 1876 and he's the big shot. Worked his way up. His family had once been big shots here, ran a shipping company. But that had been some ways back. He'd had to bring the family name back to glory again. He'd started out a tracker like Hacker. He'd tracked for fur; he'd guided settlers; he'd given good advice on how to make it in the Northeast to newcomers and immigrants. Soon he found the legwork could be done by others, and that's when his advice had become a little more expensive to newcomers. One could get good advice on how to live up here, how to farm, how to keep the Indians happy, and most of all, how to keep Mr. Sime "protecting" your interests if one just paid a little extra tax to Sime's annual budgetary needs. It was good business. He treated the people well—as long as they paid him. And he never took so much that they hated him, but everyone was aware of what would happen if they decided only the government deserved taxes. You'd be leaving Maine a little stiffer and a little deader than you had come in. But shoot, he had only had to do that a couple of times to get the message across. Mr. Sime considered himself a businessman who was doing a benevolent service to the people. He found and provided the commodities and protection that a community needed to survive and progress in an "up close and personal" way the governing politic could never match.

All in all, Mr. Sime was, in some twisted way, not so bad, given the period and dangers still existing in less populated areas of the wilderness. Not so bad as power-hungry, self-deluded underground leaders go, that is. He had only killed two settlers, their dogs, their animals—well, and their families too. Okay, Mr. Sime knew as far as the Ten Commandments went, he was probably a bit in the red, but all in all, when compared to others of his type, he wasn't too bad. He did care about his people and tried his best to do right by all who did right by him. And he kept his word, and people respected him for that, even if they feared him as well.

"Mr. Sime, let's get to it, then. Your James over there found me and drug me up here to your lovely state of Maine saying you've got a job for me." Hacker was shoving his thumb back over his shoulder, referring to one of Mr. Sime's henchmen. "You know what I do; you've heard of me; you bring me here. I'm listening. I've checked you out, and from what I hear, you're a man of your word. So let's get to it. What do you want me to get, and where is it?"

Hacker was losing his patience. Conversing in a back-and-forth manner with another alpha male when both needed the other and hated admitting it was like walking in quicksand. You could see your destination and you were hell bent on getting to it, but the harder you went toward it, the further out of reach it became. Somebody needed to lay down flat fast and let the other walk over him, or no one would be getting to where they needed to go.

Simeon, or Mr. Sime to everyone else but his dead mother, knew how to play this back-scratching game because *that* was pretty much his job. Give the other an inch, and yeah, he may take a yard, but you may gain two.

"Hacker, I like you already. You're tough. You know who you are and what you do best. I'm not patronizing you either. You're Hacker the Tracker, they say, and even though I was a tracker myself, nobody's calling me Mr. Sime the Tracker. I want your instincts and your well-oiled machine of a team on my payroll, at least for this one job. But after I feed you what I know, you're the boss of the mission. All you need to think of me as is a paycheck of ten to fifty thousand dollars waiting for you when you return."

"Jacky?" Mr. Sime looked up at his bodyguard. "You can go stand over there with James. I've got some real business to do here with Hacker."

"Jacky" nodded and walked over to the bar near James and Davis. Mr. Sime leaned in across the beer-stained table toward Hacker and, with an almost-boyish grin, said, "How long can you stay alive on the ice?"

—◇○◇—

"You don't have to answer that, Hacker. It's rhetorical. I gotta story to tell, and every story needs a—shall we say—a bait 'em and hook 'em."

Hacker was about to punch this fool in the face, but it seemed that he was finally getting around to telling him something worthwhile, so Hacker gritted his teeth, clenched his fists under the table, and forced out, "So you got me, Mr. Sime. Tell me your tale."

"All right, I will," Sime pontificated. "There's been a chain in my family for five generations. My father's father's father was too young to understand any context to my great-great-great-grandfather's dying words, but this is what he said. He told my great-great-great-grandfather when he was just twelve years old, the following: 'You find the dirt up north, where there's only ice, and you'll find——'"

"Yeah? I hear ya. Keep it coming, Mr. Sime. Find what?"

"That's it, Hacker. That's all he said. You find the dirt up north where there's only ice."

"Yeah?" Hacker nodded. "And you'll find...what, Sime? You'll find what?"

"That's it. I told you already. Nothing more."

"That's it?" Hacker asked more for effect than anything, half hoping to make this fool reconsider his story so this trip to Maine didn't turn out to be a complete waste of Hacker's time.

"So I ask, can you do that Hacker?" Sime continued. "Each one of my grandfathers and my father went searching for it or sent someone searching for it. Nobody returned. I figured it's too cold, and there's not enough to go on; most likely they all must have succumbed to the elements."

Hacker, now furious, balked. "You're telling me you want me to go find some dirt at the top of the world because your grandpappy told you to do it? And to top it off, every single one of your crazy relatives that went off gallivantin' around in the snow died doin' it? Why the hell would I want to go find some dirt and risk *my* life doing it *too*?"

"Because of this." Mr. Sime reached through the neck of his shirt and pulled out a chain. Hanging from the chain was what looked like an animal made of gold. Sime pulled at the chain; it came off his neck, and he held it out to Hacker. Hacker reached for it and picked up the golden figurine with his thumb and forefinger. It just about covered half of Mr. Sime's hand.

As Hacker brought it closer, he could see the gold was fashioned in the shape of a dog. It was a crude similitude, but a dog nonetheless.

"Heavy. Feels solid. So what's this all about?" Hacker asked with a little more curiosity given the new variable, besides *dirt*, just added to this little venture down memory lane of this bozo's family tree.

"It is solid. It's pure gold, and that is what my great-great-grandfather had pushed into his hand as my great-great-great-grandfather was spilling out his final words." Mr. Sime paused, looking to see if Hacker seemed interested enough for him to continue.

"Uh-huh?" Hacker didn't know where this Mr. Sime was going, but he'd come this far. Might as well let this Mad Hatter finish.

"The way my father and his father and so forth figured it was, as you may have guessed, you find the dirt where there's only ice, and you find the gold that made that dog."

"Oh, Sime. I've heard of wild goose chases but, shoot, none like this! I mean you might as well hand a goose to Davis over there and tell him to push some golden eggs out of it! You got anything else classifyin' in the 'worth hearing' category—or is this bullshit it?" Hacker couldn't believe he'd just climbed three states to hear this garbage. "I mean if your long-lost granddad found this dirt in the ice and got this little piece of bow wow"—Hacker dangled the doggy in the air—"why didn't he bring back the rest of the gold carved into a big pile of dog shit?"

"We've asked that same question," Sime interrupted.

"I hope *exactly* the same question," Hacker barked. "How 'bout all you father-and-son Simes come up with *this* idea, while you're doin' your askin': Old Grandpops was a loon dying from the crazy age. Seems the obvious choice to me! Ha!"

Ignoring Hacker, Sime continued. "We figure he was never actually there, but that he came by this information somehow and decided to pass it on before he died at the unexpectedly *young* age of thirty-two."

"Oh, that's great. So I'm going to take my team into the middle of nowhere searching for something that doesn't even make any sense on fifth-generation hearsay. Come on, Sime, you must've known I wasn't this crazy. Why'd you waste my time bringing me up here? I don't even like lobster."

Hacker had dropped the "Mister" from this idiot's name a couple of comments back and didn't figure he'd be restoring it anytime soon. He tossed the chain and pup onto the table and started to get up again, deciding to make sure he used his size to make his departure as humiliating as he could for this nutcase.

Mr. Sime runs the show in Maine. Hacker's in Maine. So Mr. Sime runs Hacker. That's the rules. It was time to gain that second yard.

"Guess what I heard was *wrong*."

"What's that?" Hacker asked midway to a full rise from the table, unable to complete his bold exit.

"I heard you were the man who could find things that can't be found. Now if there ever was a hunt for something that can't be found but I know is there—I know it—it's the dirt on that ice that's got that gold! You're the man, Hacker. Find what can't be found. Prove it. Prove it to yourself, prove it to me, to your crew, to your mommy, I don't care who. You know somewhere in that tracker heart of yours my story's got some merit. Somehow it means more than a kook's ramblings, and you want to find it as much as me."

And now why not gain a third yard. Or a mile.

Sime continued, "And tell you what. I'll give you thirty thousand dollars, even if you come back with nothing!"

So much for his grand departure. Hacker sat back down for a second time, unable, it seemed, to get out of this conversation in a manner of his choosing. This guy was starting to feel like the boss between the two of them, and that didn't sit well with Hacker's subconscious. He felt forced to continue onward with this ridiculous proposition.

"Why on earth would you do that? I could just go sledding around with Santa Claus for a few weeks, come back down with nothing, and collect my thirty grand?"

"You're not a man that would do that Hacker. You and I both know it."

"You may think you know me, but money can change a man, and that's a lot of money. It could do an awful lot of changin'."

"You can't exchange a man's first love with his second," Sime said. "We both want one thing more than money."

"What's that?"

"We both want to find that dirt!"

Give an inch, take the whole damned circumference of the earth.

Sime was right, Hacker conceded. If Hacker had been asked at that moment why he had agreed to the mission presented him, he wouldn't have been able to determine if it had been because Sime had gotten the best of his ego or if he really needed something like this "dirt" to track. Maybe a little of both. Maybe he needed to prove to this man that his name meant something, and he needed to find for himself if his profession was more a gift than it was a nicely honed skill.

"Davis! Come on!" Hacker bellowed this as he stood up again from the table, this time reaching a full powerful rise, half authoritative, half tantrum. He reached the door of the pub with Davis close behind, stopped, and turned back to look upon the dank saloon. Many a man there looked as if they were drinking themselves out of any challenges in life, deciding to feel good about it, and then dribbling to one another over and over about the one amazing thing they'd done at seventeen, each listener wondering if he was hearing a new story, his own story, or a dream he'd had the night before. One thing was for sure—to Hacker, at least. *I'm not them*, he thought. At this, Hacker yelled his answer to Sime's proposal across the dark room. "I'll be in touch about the supplies I'll need!"

"You'll hear from me too."

"Not if you hear from me first. Ha!"

"Don't worry, Hacker. I'll send someone by to collect your list."

"I'll get that list to you. No need to bother Jamesy or Jacky there."

"All right, so you'll be hearing from me," they both yelled in unison.

Each lion had his roar.

—<o>—

The ground was firmer here at this Eskimo camp, and it was easier to walk than it had been out on the drifts. When a man could plant his feet on firm ground, he felt more like a man, and Hacker was feeling more like a man. Food was on its way. He wasn't lost anymore. It might still be correct to say he didn't know where he was, but you didn't feel lost when you were no longer wandering aimlessly. Most importantly, he had figured he was close to his prize. Davis was still acting too big for his britches, but Davis could be handled. Hacker was a leader being taken to a leader. There was no army guard here, but their procession across the camp felt important. Silence existed here like it had out on the ice shelf, although their march was surrounded by others who were half going about their daily business and half peering at the party of three heading toward the chief's home.

Feeling more like a man felt good, but feeling more like a man hadn't provided Hacker with any precognitive ability—he didn't realize every solid crunch of his boots on that firm earth was bringing him another step closer to his death. Two other men elsewhere on planet earth were feeling very manly and were also to be dying that day. Why not him too? But Hacker knew nothing of a battle at Little Bighorn nor of the city of Abydos, and he never would. So his man pride parade continued. He kept his eyes sharp, almost forgetting the one clue he had, although at this point he didn't think it mattered. His treasure was out to find him, not the other way around. Nevertheless, Hacker thought he should probably keep his eyes peeled for some dirt, given he had the other half of Sime's clue covered. "Where there is only ice" had been part of Hacker's life for quite a while now. That part? Definitely covered.

They neared what was likely the chief's tent. Extra animal furs decorated the entrance and what appeared to be a guard stood outside. The boy Hacker and Davis were following had been joined again by the one who had split from their group earlier. The one just arriving made a friendly motion for Hacker and Davis to wait, and then the boy disappeared inside.

The Son entered his father's home, where he had still lived only the year before. He was hoping to ask his father to reconsider letting these two men near Always Here, who had since been carried to his father's home. Upon entering he saw Always Here along with Strong Arms and Questions Father. It was interesting to see Strong Arms at The Circle. Had he been chosen as The Other? Regardless, if he was to have any chance of saying anything of his opinion, he'd better do it quickly. Questioning his father in front of the tribe was not allowed, but at The Circle, anyone with a concern could voice it. Questions Father typically was the only one who did this, or at least was usually the one to instigate such conversations. After that, others at The Circle may take the opportunity to then add their opinions. Being the youngest, The Son had never begun a discussion like this, but he had hoped, given the extremely strange circumstances, he may be safe from too much humiliation.

He approached The Circle and sat down. Father immediately spoke. "The Son? Where are our visitors?"

"They're outside with White Bear."

"Bring them in. We are waiting, and they are waiting. Is your mother informed?"

"Yes, I am." The Son's mother was entering the tent, her arms holding two baskets, presumably with food inside. As the smell from the baskets reached The Circle, the presumption of food was replaced by certainty. "Why are those men standing outside in the cold? Bring them inside. If they are hungry, we should get them eating. Food is good for relations, not cold air."

"I was just asking our son to bring them in." Father answered his wife and then turned toward his son and said, "Go get them."

"But, Father—"

"Get the men, son. No more delay."

And that was that. The Son had tried to stop something not meant to be stopped. Valiant effort, kid…really. However, the events of June 25, 1876, by the Gregorian Calendar's count, were going to proceed with the same momentum and certainty as the earth spinning on its axis or the moon moving through its phases. "But, Father" being spoken was the furthest anyone anywhere got that day to halting prophecy. And prophecy, when it is real, falls under the same category as any universal law Newton, Einstein, or Kepler might have discovered. As unchangeable as the mass of elements or the speed of light, prophecy, if put to the scientific method, would be as real as mathematical fractals. The nature of prophecies, however, makes them a little difficult to study, as such.

If truly categorized, prophecy would fall somewhere within a general interpretation of Heisenberg's uncertainty principle, which states that you can never know the speed and position, simultaneously, of an electron because the instruments used to measure one measurement force you to forfeit the measuring of the other. We know the electron exists and has a speed and position because both can be measured, but both values can never be known at the same time, so in a way, the electron will always elude us. And so, too, prophecy provides us with the same conundrum. To see prophecy occur, one needs a very broad view. In human experience, this usually comes in the form of hindsight and historical study. However, by this time, the events have already transpired and therefore cannot be "measured" directly. Those involved in—and going through—the events constituting a particular fated "happening" are present and available to study the prophecy firsthand, but they never see the bigger history they are helping to unfold, and therefore, all the great data and observations are lost to unawareness.

The third group, if present at all, are just as unfortunate at providing anything concrete toward describing prophecy as a mathematical equation. This group constitutes those who believe in a prophecy and see the events unfolding before their eyes that lead to said prophecy's prophetic occurrences. Sadly, these people are rarely believed by others and typically never get to be involved in the actual events of the prophecy. Regarding this endeavor to study the numerics behind prophecies, this group is never populated by anyone who has the slightest desire to get out a ruler, microscope, calculator, or prophecy-o-meter so as to gather anything remotely needed for applying the scientific method.

The Son, being part of the second group, had too narrow a view of the history of the universe to see how big a part he was playing within it. He was feeling only failure as he got up from The Circle to go fetch the two men he had left outside. However, *we* have the benefit of knowing he should have been proud. *We* know that out of everyone on earth, he was the only one, anywhere, who attempted to change any of this day's events.

Nevertheless, on this day...

Three not-so-good men were going to be killed while they tried to get some scrolls. Four very old Scroll Holders *were* going to vanish into dust as they lost possession of their scrolls. Four ancient scrolls were going to change hands. Three other decent people were going to walk away with some scrolls who *were not* expecting to do so when they had woken up that morning. And no one and no thing was going to stop any of it.

That's why they call it prophecy.

CHAPTER 19

AND THEN THERE ~~WERE TWO~~ WAS ONE
LATER, JUNE 25, 1876

"HE'S MOTIONING FOR US TO GO IN," whispered Davis to Hacker.

"Actually, he's telling his friend to bring us in," Hacker whispered back, speaking just to be *more* right.

"Right." Davis rolled his eyes. He was losing patience with Hacker. "Either way, we're going in. And that woman who just went in's got food. I can smell it."

You get your food, Davis; I'm getting my treasure, Hacker thought to himself, his mind now far from feeding his belly.

The boy who had remained outside with them held back the canvas, presenting the entrance to tangible warmth. Hacker and Davis took the cue and ducked inside. The older woman who was carrying food had done the same a minute before. Both men received a chill down their spine produced by the change in temperature they experienced as they entered. Hacker tried to hide the effects of the shiver and managed only to make himself appear paralyzed.

A fire crackled in the center. Hacker saw the man he believed to be the chief along with the other boy, two men, and one really old fellow who appeared to be injured. The woman was off to the side taking food out of her baskets. Hacker secretly began to care a bit about eating when he saw it.

As Hacker's stomach began to growl, he caught sight of something, barely able to believe his eyes. *Mr. Sime, if you could see this.* It had been one thing to hear such a crazy story from the man who had sent him to this area of the world whose only export was frostbite. And given the tale, he was still amazed he had come. If his men had known the details, there would have been mutiny long before he had become lost. He imagined the scene. *Come on men, we're looking for dirt. I know it's up here somewhere! Keep your eyes peeled. You see anything brown and it didn't come from a polar bear's ass, you best point it out in a hurry! That's our treasure!*

And then he'd have been shot.

The thing about the discovery he'd made at the far end of the hut was that it couldn't be misinterpreted. He didn't have to ask himself a question like, *Is this the dirt Sime's talking about?* The only way this could *not* be the dirt Sime had been talking about was if Sime hadn't mentioned dirt at all.

Behind the fire sat the chief, and behind the chief sat a plant. Plants don't typically grow in ice, and this plant held true to that principle. This plant was growing in some dirt. Now, if it had just been any plant in any dirt, perhaps Hacker would have needed to investigate a little further. However, there was a third caveat to the situation at hand. There was the plant. There was the dirt. It couldn't be the same plant that had made it to these people with the dirt. Most probably it was that plant's great-great-great-grandchild. And then, of course, as just mentioned, there was the dirt. Nothing special there. Lastly, there was the pot. Except the pot wasn't a pot at all. It was a crate. And this crate had a signature. It had writing stamped on the side: Crafting Fish Company. Crafting—that was Mr. Sime's last name. Simeon Crafting.

Am I really seeing what I am seeing? Sime, you crazy storyteller. Well, all I can say now is there damned well better be gold buried in that crate.

But then again, Hacker thought, it didn't matter. He was promised thirty thousand anyway. On the other hand, he figured Sime might be less apt to pay out, regardless of his word, if Hacker only brought back a plant in a box.

He had had no idea what he was going to find if he ever found it, and this sure wasn't what Hacker had expected. The crate was a two-foot cube, and it was obviously important enough to be kept by the chief. It would hold a lot of gold, even if some of the volume was dedicated to holding dirt for the plant.

There was going to be no way he would be allowed to examine the contents of that crate. Additionally, there was no way he was finding his way home without the help of these people. He would have to think this through.

Better eat first. Maybe an idea will come.

Davis and Hacker were instructed to sit at The Circle. They were given dried meat that had been warmed and water to drink. Nothing was said to them while they ate. The others ate, too, probably in an effort to make Davis and him feel comfortable. They were a patient people, Hacker thought. Given that two strangers had just arrived at their home out of nowhere, they held back from conversation for a good twenty minutes while everyone finished their food. Hacker tried to keep his eyes off the crate. Once, he found himself staring at it, and he felt the old one recognize where his gaze had focused. He looked away, as if he had just been glancing around at the surroundings. He didn't figure it was any big deal, considering that the crate had English written on it, and it only made sense that someone like Davis or him might notice that.

What Hacker didn't notice in the old man's eyes was true understanding. The old man, to Hacker and Always Here, to his people, knew his time had come and that these men had brought his end with them.

"Always Here," Strong Arms said when the last of the food had been eaten, "can you advise on how we may learn something from these men, given our languages are different?"

"Strong Arms asks a good question, but I feel everything will present itself soon, and answers will come."

Strong Arms had been told earlier in the day that he had, in fact, been chosen as The Other. The Other was a tribe member whom the rest of The Circle picked from the tribe. Always Here picked who would be "Questions Father," the impartial and wise advisor to the leader. Then there was the family of the chief—Father, Mother, The Son, and Mother Leader (or My Sweet Mother if she was still childless). The Other was the one member who had free rein to say anything and at any time, because he was the representative of the tribe. The tribe had always been taught that The Other would never need to fear retribution for acting on his role.

Strong Arms had been somewhat intimidated by the other members of The Circle prior to being picked as The Other, but he didn't hesitate for a moment to prove to himself and the rest of the tribe that what they had been taught to believe about The Circle was true. Therefore, he decided to be the first one to start speaking concerning the new arrivals. He wouldn't continue to be so bold just for the sake of being so, but he had to know if what he had been taught was true.

"You believe if we just sit here and wait, something will happen?" Strong Arms responded.

"Yes, that is what I believe."

During this exchange, Hacker had become frustrated. They were talking among themselves about Davis and him. At best, this banter would produce these natives agreeing to be guides for Davis and him to return home. It's not like they were going to offer tribe membership or cough up their most beautiful daughters for marriage. The way Hacker figured it, all possible endings did not include him leaving with that crate.

Then, his plan came to him. It wasn't the greatest plan, but it was the only plan, as he saw it. And it wouldn't work if Davis didn't back him. Given their current relationship, he wasn't sure if that would happen, but he hoped the surprise of it would put Davis into automatic first-mate mode.

He was wrong. Oh well. At least Hacker had found the thing that can't be found and had died knowing it.

Hacker's size and gun, masquerading as authority for the last time, lasted about two minutes before he realized his end was near. He'd stood up, pulled out his pistol, and grabbed the old man with the broken arm and yelled, "Davis! Get over here! We're leaving with the gold in that crate!"

"What? What are you talking about? What the hell are you doing? You're going to get us killed!" Davis had said and stayed seated.

By this time, Strong Arms had stood and grabbed his spear and was aiming it at Hacker. The guard from outside rushed in when he heard raised voices. Seeing Strong Arms focused on the big one, he raised his weapon on the seated one.

At this, Davis instinctively pulled out his gun and pointed it at the quickest aim, given his position: the chief.

"You going to get on my team now, Davis? This crate here's what we came looking for. We take it and this old bastard and get ourselves led out of this frozen hell. Grab one side of it, now!"

Davis struggled with what to do next. There had been no time to think about the situation Hacker had created. The Eskimo with a spear raised at Hacker was yelling something at the one who had come from outside. The old one was clutching something around his neck and looking right at Davis. The chief was looking at the woman, and the woman was crying for everyone to calm down, most probably upon seeing the coming death of her husband via Davis's weapon. Two others rushed in from outside, and their glances showed internal debate while they assessed the situation and decided whom to direct their weapons toward.

Davis rose. He had little choice but to attempt to escape Hacker's stupidly manifested plan. Just then, the one sitting to the side of the chief spoke to the one aiming at Davis. He navigated the strong one's spear from Davis's direction and directed it toward Hacker. Then the old one, with eyes focused on Davis, reached calmly toward Davis's gun. He placed his hand gently on the gun and pushed it down. Davis allowed this and realized he had ceased being a target.

Hacker started yelling at Davis and was pressing his gun into the temple of the old, injured Eskimo.

"What the hell are you doing, Davis?"

"I'm sorry, sir, but you're being a fool. I suggest you lower your weapon before you get yourself killed."

Hacker didn't see a way out, and Davis was looking for a way out. Hacker needed help carrying the crate if he was going to escape with his hostage. Davis needed to do something to further distance himself from his maniacal captain if these people were ever going to trust him after this was all over—whatever *this* was. Hacker was looking at the four poised to strike against him, and Davis saw an opportunity to change careers by raising his gun and firing it at his boss.

"Ha!" Hacker's voice had belted a last laugh as Davis's bullet entered his skull. As fast as lightning, one thought raced through Hacker's dying mind. *The ten little Indians song doesn't end this way!* Hacker's disbelieving stare at Davis never left his face as the hole in his forehead started to bleed. His gun-yielding hand dropped to his side, and his powerful form fell to its knees. A moment later Hacker was facedown on the ground. Hacker didn't feel his head hit the firmly packed snow—the snow that had recently been the cause of propping his ego up again—but he wouldn't have felt much like a man anymore, anyway, if he had.

Davis had spent a lot of years with his (now former) employer, never thinking it would have ended like this. It's funny how things work out. For some reason,

Hacker's banter and posturing and leadership style had really started to rub Davis wrong the last few days. Not enough to kill him, but obviously not enough to keep from killing him either.

"Goodbye, Hacker," Davis said under his breath. Davis wasn't sad, but the relationship had lasted long enough to deserve a closing statement.

All weapons were lowered, and as the adrenaline subsided, everyone began smiling in the release of stress. Davis dropped his gun to the ground between his feet. Strong Arms sat back down at The Circle. White Bear had been one of the three standing near the entrance. The Son told him and the others to remove Hacker's body, and they proceeded to do so in a manner that made removing dead people from the chief's tent appear commonplace. Of course it wasn't, but the event hadn't really hit anyone's psyche yet, so everyone went through the motions of giving and following orders.

Questions Father told Davis, "Thank you," even though he wasn't understood. The chief reiterated this to Davis, and because of the repeated word and tone, Davis figured he knew what they were saying—especially when the woman proceeded to say the same thing.

Davis didn't know how he felt about being thanked by strangers for killing someone he had known for such a long time. It was like saving a child by shooting your rabid dog. It felt good and bad and right and wrong, all at the same time. One good thing, though. These strangers were a lot more likable at first meeting than Hacker had ever been in fifteen years.

The only one present who didn't resume his original place was Always Here. He remained standing where Hacker had been holding him next to the crate. He didn't have the strength to stand on his own, but he was standing nonetheless. He didn't have the strength to dig his one good hand into the dirt and pull out a canvas sack like the one around his neck, either, but he did that too. He placed it under his bad arm, and everyone but the chief looked surprised as he took the one hanging from his chest and flung it into the fire—with strength he also did not possess.

And Always Here didn't have the strength to walk around the fire to hand Davis the sack he had pulled from Mr. Sime's treasured soil—but he did it anyway. Since he was far into the negative concerning his own personal power, given all these impossible tasks he was completing, Always Here felt fortunate he didn't have to find the strength to turn into dust as Davis took the sack from his hand.

Then everyone except Davis had to find the strength to fight back tears.

"Oh my God," Davis muttered, "I'm so sorry." He didn't know if he was responsible or not, but he felt responsible, and the gloom entering the air after the old man's disappearance affected Davis to the point he felt himself fighting tears with the rest of them.

Not a word was spoken for several minutes. The members of The Circle all had the same thought cross their mind: *What did Always Here's name mean now that he was gone?* Always Here had made them feel like their people would always be here. Was this the beginning of their end too? Father broke the silence by saying, "Someone should find our new Scroll Holder a place to sleep."

Strong Arms, as tribe representative, stood up and told Davis to follow him. And strangely, Davis understood him, not just in inference, but he understood the language. Davis didn't flinch at this event. "Strange" didn't much affect him anymore.

CHAPTER 20

APRIL 7, 1923
FORTY-SEVEN YEARS LATER

⊲◦⊂⟋⟍⊃◦⊳

"WHERE IS OUR FUTURE, MOTHER? I can't find him anywhere." The Son had a look of impatience on his face only found in younger members of the tribe. He wanted his favorite playmate and was not happy to find him missing.

"You ask that question often, and it always makes me smile," Mother Leader responded.

"Why is that, Mother? It doesn't make me smile. To me, it only means I can't find my friend."

"When you speak these words, you have one meaning in your mind, but I have two."

"Mother? I don't understand. Please tell me where Our Future is," The Son replied, only making the tribe's matriarch smile again and let out a small laugh. "Why are you laughing at me?"

"My dear, I'm not. I promise you. However, you did it again. Oh, the youth are so delightful. And so similar in meaning to your question."

"Please explain to me what you are saying." The Son looked at his mother with inquisitive yet impatient eyes. "I want to be as wise as you and Father are."

"Don't worry, Son. You will be and when your trials come, you will learn who you may become."

"I want to be Questions Father!" The Son interrupted.

"Well," she replied, "If you are to become Questions Father, I know you will have no problem speaking your mind.

It had been many generations since The Son had desired not to be Father upon reaching The Age. After Father had died, Mother Leader's brother had died before taking a wife, leaving The Circle with no Father and no The Son. After Mother had died, My Sweet Mother had become Mother Leader, assuming the roles of Father, Mother, and Mother Leader, and had become leader of the tribe. Questions Father now advised her. Now her son could be the next Father. If he became Questions Father and she had no more sons, the role of Father may leave the family. To become Questions Father required giving up the birthright The Son had to be Father. Very few ever had the desire or courage to do this at the young age The Decision was required. To choose to follow the path of Questions Father contained within it three caveats viewed by some as unattractive. First, one may have to wait much longer to be a member of The Circle. Second, he would be giving up his future son's right to be Father. And third, one was accepting the fact he may not be chosen by The Circle for the role of Questions Father at all.

Mother Leader continued. "As for your question, as long as you continue to ask me where our future is, it means we do not yet know it—and that, in turn, means there is still hope we have one at all."

The Son sat for a rare quiet moment, trying to understand his mother's words. Then, he spoke. "I see the two meanings in my words. I do, Mother! But we will always have a future, correct?"

"That is to be seen. All people wish this to be true. Our people believed we would always have a future as long as Always Here was with us. But when Our Future came to be with us, Always Here had to leave us, and we became less certain."

"The stories of Always Here you have told me make me smile. Why was the tribe not angry with Our Future, since it was his coming which made Always Here be: no more?"

"Because we are a fair people. It was not Our Future's intention that Always Here leave us. As you know, it was Our Future who tried to save Always Here. We do not understand everything, but we do believe it was time for Always Here to leave us, and it was time for Our Future to join us."

"Our Future does not look like us."

"That is because he did not come from our people."

"Then why is he named *Our* Future?"

"He did not always have this name, just as Always Here did not always have his name either. I did not always have my name, and you will not always be The Son."

"Yes, but why is he *Our Future*?"

"Because once Always Here left us, taking with him one belief about our tribe, we took on another belief."

"And what is that belief, Mother?" The Son asked.

Mother Leader closed her eyes, remembering her own young days when all these events took place when she herself had a different name—when she had been My Sweet Mother and had gone running to find her father after finding Always Here on the ice with a broken arm. "The tribe believes our existence has been tied to the scroll ever since Always Here arrived with it many thousands of circles of the sun ago. We believe the passing of the scroll from Always Here to Our Future is also important to our existence. We believe, for whatever reason, this transfer that happened is inextricably linked to what is to become of us. And so, your friend is…our future."

The Son reflected on his mother's statement, foregoing his typical impatience, and thus showing signs he may have what it would take to be Questions Father one day. However, after this reflection and the subsequent filing of her words' meaning in his mind for use in some distant time, he looked back up at her and asked a question that only showed the innocent curiosity of his youth once again.

"What was Our Future called before?"

And again, she smiled, for his question once again had two meanings, and once again, one meaning was unknown to him.

"You're smiling. Did I do it *again*?" The Son asked with a sigh. He was frustrated with his lack of ability to understand the subtext contained within his own dialogue.

"*Yes*, you did, but don't be upset. I will answer them both. The answer to the question you don't know you are asking is—our future was Always Here. But the answer to the question you are asking—"

"Yes?" The Son immediately prodded, this time with a response manifesting true impatience, completely unaware of yet another double meaning in the very answer his mother had just provided.

Mother Leader grinned again, taking a moment to reflect on the rareness of conversations such as these. Taking her son's hands lightly in hers, she calmly replied.

"His name was Davis."

—◇○◁—

Craaaaaackkkkkk!

Our Future was taking his daily walk. Each day over the last week, his walk had taken him further from Home Now, and the distance he had reached today could almost be called the start of a journey. A familiar and destructive sound had just occurred over the horizon, pushing chills through his body not spawned from the cold. A distant memory had instigated that shudder, and he thought through the recall it produced: *I really am quite distant from where I started.*

"In more ways than one." Our Future swore he heard the statement float through the wind.

"Aaaaaaahhhhhhhh! Hellllllppp!"

Are those screams? Did I just hear someone? It was probably the wind again, Our Future thought. *Did I just hear English?*

Again, the ice erupted with a loud cracking sound, but this time the ground quaked violently beneath him. He lost his balance and let out a similar scream to the one he thought he had heard a moment before. As Our Future lay on his back looking up at the blue sky and feeling the ground continue to rumble beneath him, he had a feeling of foolishness rush over him. *For over forty years, I have felt like because of this scroll, I am somehow important, and yet look at me now.* On his back on the ice, he did not quite feel like the future of anything, except perhaps the future definition of iniquity. *Maybe I am just "Davis."*

The ground stopped moving, and complete silence fell over the ice plain.

The tribe had named Davis "Our Future" many years ago, but he had always felt to be more the Idol of the Present among the curious youth. He had never had any answers for them when they would ask him and then ask him again, "What is our *future*, Our Future?" No matter how many times his response was absent, they stayed enamored by his story. He figured they were more intrigued by how different he looked than anything. He brought with him no answers about what lay ahead, but he did bring proof of an unknown world outside of the reality they knew. No one had ever ventured outside of Home Now and chosen not to return.

Today, Davis was more clueless than he was used to. More so than all the times he'd been bereft of answers for his young tribesmen. Davis didn't know he was about to kill two birds with the proverbial stone as he pulled himself up to his feet, lost in thought, deciding to head home. Davis didn't realize that the sound that had landed him on his back was bringing with him something resembling an answer to the children's unending inquiry about their future, and simultaneously, would clue them into a fallacy they had regarding their past.

Surely The Son would be looking for him by this time, so he got moving. Davis was completely unaware the future of the tribe was following him, proving Davis's forty-six-year-old namesake with every step. For when Our Future began to walk, so did the unnoticed man behind him. And that man would be bringing Home Now a new friend. Well, maybe not a friend, and maybe not a new one, at that.

Impending Doom wasn't showing up just yet. He had been a little busy wiping out his second group of dog mushers in less than fifty years just out of Davis's visual range. Then he was off to London to prove how fast some schmuck's life could flash before his eyes when his horse got spooked by lightning. Next, he had to pay a visit to a poor slob who'd just noticed his child's tricycle had tripped him, bringing the corner of a concrete stair closer—very quickly—to his face. If that wasn't impending doom, what was?

Impending Doom had several similar stops to make before he was to venture to Home Now. He never knew what lay ahead. He would come and go so quickly; sometimes, he barely remembered where he'd just been.

And honestly, I. D. didn't care. His job was like his name. He was all about the now, the immediate—the *impending*. His job was the complete opposite of caring. Fear of death...fear of death followed by actual death...change of fate...it was all the same to him. He didn't care where he went. Even failing to correctly guess who was checking out and who wasn't didn't faze him. This was a good thing, because that "saved-at-the-last-minute shit" was always happening. He was only *Impending* Doom, which of course, did not necessarily necessitate actual Doom.

He thought to himself, *Thank goodness I get to see the actual Doomed ones through to the end. Because if that half-wit, Boreville, twice-removed cousin of mine, Death, got to come along and clean up what I got started...that, I might actually care about.*

CHAPTER 21

JUNIOR ARRIVES
APRIL 7, 1923

---◇○◠◝◞○◇---

"IS THAT MR. HACKER?" The Son whispered to his mother.

"*Shhhhhhhhhhh!* Don't speak!" Mother Leader shushed back.

"He has a gun just like the pictures Our Future has drawn. I saw it."

"Please, The Son. You must be quiet." Mother Leader pulled her son close to her breast, hoping to calm him and praying it would have that effect. "That is not Mr. Hacker, but he is very dangerous. We must be quiet, or he will hurt us."

"What about the others?"

"Please. No more questions right now. Your mother is in danger." It pained her deeply to create the dread she witnessed in his eyes upon her making this comment, but it seemed the only approach available to halt his inquisitive nature—a nature that at all other times had been a sign of his potential, not one of his imminent doom.

---◇○◇---

Did someone just think the word imminent? Well, that was close enough to "impending" to make a certain *monster* feel quite comfortable he was at the right spot at the wrong time—well, the *right time,* if one were looking from his perspective.

He'd been in this quaint, transient village above the tundra called Home Now for quite a while. Not all visits had a swoop in, swoop out nature. In certain circumstances, Impending Doom could linger somewhere for hours, or even more. Though rare—and a much slower process—these times had the potential to be a whole hell of a lot more fun for I. D. So damned much terror and unending, all-encompassing fear. *So much!*

Watching how fear of the inevitable, when it looms, can eat away at a person's being was like watching cancer on fast-forward. First, the shock phase. Second, the negotiating phase, followed, finally, by the fear phase. These, always followed by the shaking, begging, pleading, and crying phases, in various order, on repeatable loops, or all at the same time. When there was time allowed for the screaming phase to show up, I. D. found it the most fun to watch.

Yes, there were those few maggots out there who got stronger the more impending doom you threw at them. And sometimes that strength gave them hope, and a doorway would open for them, cueing the exit of I. D. But sometimes it wouldn't, and at the last minute, they would see their doom coming, succumbing to it with a yell or a whimper, depending on how real that apparent strength truly was. When this happened, I. D. didn't mind the maggots so much. *It's sort of fun to watch those tough types still get what's shown up at their doorstep, no matter how much they strutted.*

This stop, in particular, had—so far—been a pleasurable mix filled with all types of responses, situations, and subjects. It appeared the men of this tribe were proportionately full of maggots, and the women seemed to have maggot blood, too, but the women were having some trouble—trouble controlling the fear they felt for their children. Aside from these individuals, it appeared to I. D. that he was here to shower a whole lot of impending doom on a village, a tribe, a way of life…gosh…on a whole slew of things.

And in what form had all this impending doom come to Home Now?

It had shown up in a man who had followed Our Future back from his daily walk. It had shown up in a man who had just walked away from his own freak-show sled accident an hour before—an accident that had sucked into the Arctic Ocean every sled on his team along with every mate with whom he'd traveled to this forsaken place. I. D. didn't mind this tough guy, though a maggot he was. This man was an exception.

Yes, this man may have been all badass, as his entourage had wailed and moaned as they were suctioned into their chilled, wet graves, and he may have even opened that door of hope previously described, walking away from the disaster. However, because this maggot had lived, I. D. was getting a second showdown, and it appeared as if it would doom everything in sight. An O. K. Corral of the North had come to Home Now.

Meet the maggot. His name was Junior. Now, how in the world could some half-frozen man named Junior be responsible for lassoing our old acquaintance, I. D., against a whole tribe of people? And even more importantly, why was Junior at Home Now in the first place?

It's all in a name, right? "Junior" was only what this man was *called*, but it wasn't his proper name. Nah. This man's father had possessed a bit too much ego to have a son with a name like Junior. Nevertheless, his father hadn't been able to resist naming his kid after himself, thus requiring "Jr." being stuck to the end of the kid's name. And, subsequently, Junior's dad couldn't resist calling him "Junior" afterward, pandering to the ego that created this whole mess in the first place.

Junior maggot's given name was Simeon Crafting Jr., and he had heard a little story from Papa Sime. Dirt, ice, gold, a great-great-great-grandpa, blah, blah, blah, yes…but he had also heard about one too many men coming up here to find it and never being heard from again. And by one too many, I mean one particular Hacker too many.

Junior had heard that several descendants of gold-gasping Grandpa had searched for the family treasure and never returned, but it was Hacker's story that had intrigued him and prepared him. His father had told him of a man fifty years earlier who had been sent on the errand of finding Great-Great-Great-Grandpa's gold. This man was known to be able to find things no matter how difficult, but more importantly, this man had been offered thirty-thousand dollars even if he had come back with nothing. Yet neither Hacker nor his crew had ever returned.

This bothered Junior. Even a man who needed to prove he's "the man who finds things that can't be found"—would he really let himself die trying on what was probably a fool's errand, anyhow, when $30,000 lay waiting for him back in Maine? But Hacker hadn't returned. So Junior assumed this treasure was still there, waiting to be found. But something had compelled this Hacker fellow to keep going, keep pushing, keep from returning to collect. Had he found a clue and decided to keep going, maybe took too much risk for the thrill of accomplishment?

Maybe it hadn't been the ice and cold that had taken Hacker out. Maybe this treasure existed, and someone was protecting it. Maybe Hacker the Tracker hadn't come back for his $30,000 because he hadn't been allowed to do so. Someone up there on the ice had decided a different fate for him.

The answer as to how this half-frozen, lone man named Junior was about to hold so much power over the people of Home Now is—drumroll, please—there just happened to be a lot of advancement in personal firearms since the 1870s. It was 1923 now, and Junior had come equipped.

Hacker had been one man with a pistol and a colleague wavering in loyalty. Junior Maggot had a machine gun and a few personal explosive devices called hand grenades. Well, more than a few…and more than one machine gun. His motto was Be Prepared, like the damned Boy Scouts—even if you're going to do a whole lot of killing of a whole lot of people, unlike a Boy Scout.

A few minutes before Junior had arrived with his inherited ego, The Son had been at the edge of Home Now watching, waiting for Our Future to return. He had seen Our Future appear, but Our Future hadn't been alone. Another man dressed in strange clothes was following Our Future. He had something large in his hands and was pointing it at Our Future. Another one of the same was hanging off his body. It looked like a weapon. The man also had two *guns?* Strapped to his chest. The Son thought *guns* because he had seen pictures drawn by Our Future about the day Our Future had come to Home Now. This scene on the ice didn't look good, and The Son had run back to his mother to tell her.

When Mother Leader heard the news, she had poked her head out to look. She had to duck back in quickly because Our Future and the visitor now appeared to be a lot closer than what The Son's description had portrayed. That's when the yelling started.

"All right! All right! Everyone better come out here now if you care about this guy. He sure don't look like no Eskimo I ever saw, but he's dressed like one, so ya better get out here!" yelled the man behind Our Future. Mother Leader heard this but did not understand it. She then began her effort to quiet her son's questions, which began a second later.

——◇○◇——

"I don't know how the hell it could possibly be you, Davis, but I'll be damned if it isn't. I did my research on you and Hacker and the little escapade my father sent you on. I've seen pictures of you both. If you want anyone to be left alive in this little home you've made for yourself, then you'd better get everyone out here. *Now!*"

Our Future hadn't been called Davis or spoken English for so long that he couldn't be sure this event was happening. He thought maybe it was a dream. *Maybe I hit my head when I fell on the ice, and I'm still out there floating in oblivion.* But like a pinch that doesn't wake you up out of a dream because you're not dreaming, the gun jabbed in his back hard enough to make him fall to the ground again didn't wake him up, either, because Davis wasn't sleeping. As he struggled to stand up again, clawing at a new pain in his right kidney, Davis dually toiled with understanding the English just spoken and the decision on whether to follow its instructions once its meaning registered. Ironically *(or suitably?)* it seemed to Davis (a.k.a. Our Future) that he was, at this moment, holding the actual future of Home Now in his hands.

Perhaps, I should have said no to the name...

"You don't look any older than you did in pictures from fifty years ago, Davis!" the man screamed. "What the hell they got up here? And where's Hacker? Or do I now know why he didn't come back with my father's gold?"

"What do you want me to do? Answer your questions or call the people out?" Davis pushed the words out slowly as if he were shoving a heavy English dictionary from the back of his brain to its front. He realized this guy didn't know Hacker was dead. That might be helpful, so "Buy time and think" was the strategy at hand.

"What are you, Davis, a smart-ass?" the man barked from behind. "I couldn't tell that from the picture. Ha!"

"No," Davis answered, "I just want t-to do whatever it is you want me to do." Davis stuttered intentionally in a submissive tone of voice, though this wasn't hard to fake since his English was still making a comeback.

"Well, what I want you to *do* is get everyone out here and get 'em lined up! And if that son of a bitch Hacker's here, he better come out unarmed, or I'll start shooting the children first. This here's a Thompson machine gun, Davis. You ain't seen one of

144

these. Twenty rounds the first second I pull the trigger and every second after that till you're huntin' polar bears by yourself!"

Davis didn't know anything about handheld guns like that, but he decided to believe the man. Maybe coming clean with this man would help. He was, obviously, here for something. Maybe if he got it, he would leave. Then a thought hit Davis.

Wait a second! He said his "father". This is Mr. Sime's son!

CHAPTER 22

THE STORY OF THE CRATE
JANUARY 31, 1877

H ACKER HAD NEVER TOLD his men what it was he was searching for after they'd agreed to exchange horses for dogsleds. He had offered them a payout from the guaranteed thirty thousand upon return. They didn't know the exact figure Sime had given Hacker, but Hacker had always paid what he said, so for the portion Hacker had offered his crew, they had taken him at his word. Davis hadn't learned the object of Hacker's quest until soon after Hacker's demise. Knowing the truth of what had become of this fantasy treasure and knowing the amount of gold would not impress this armed man, Davis's heart sank. If this maniacal progeny of Sime was here for it…things weren't going to end well.

Very quickly after Hacker's death, Davis had fallen easily in love with the people of Home Now. They were pleasant and calm, especially when compared with his recently deceased employer. He couldn't imagine venturing back to America, alone in the Arctic, or being responsible for making one or more of the tribe accompany him as a guide. Regardless, there wasn't much of anything to return to anyway. The tribe had offered him a place in their family, and he had taken it. Given the hard life he'd lived till then, Davis couldn't fathom a better life anywhere else. He'd saved them from Hacker and, at the same time, had apparently become the new bearer of some relic they held dear. This transfer of the relic had instilled great trust in him from the tribe. The trust could be seen in their eyes, and soon he had become part of their inner circle.

Time and events moved slowly in Home Now. *Soon after Hacker's demise* was, in reality, several months later. On a day like any other had been since arriving at Home Now in June 1876, Davis was requested to join The Circle, and this is when he first learned about the gold. They had not only waited for him to learn their language (the understanding of it he'd gained right after Hacker was killed had faded after a few days as magically as it had come to him in the first place), but also, after hearing the story, Davis became aware they spoke rarely about the subject.

The day Davis had been given the name Our Future by Father was the same day he'd learned about a great many things.

As Sarah Dubois was checking herself into a sanitarium in Cairo, Egypt, Father, of Home Now—the Far North, was motioning to Davis to sit down at a fire. As he did so, he told Davis, "You are Our Future."

Davis was taken aback. "What do you mean? I am only a man. I can't be that important."

"You misunderstand me." Father looked steadily into Davis's eyes and stated very clearly in their tongue, "That is your name now. You are no longer Davis. You are *Our Future.*"

"But why?"

"For a great many reasons," Father replied, "but mostly because we believe what is to become of us is directly linked to your arrival at Home Now."

"I wish I understood," Davis said humbly. "What gives you this idea?" Davis had not forgotten about the strange end of Always Here, but as the months had progressed, it had become easier to rationalize the day's events as, if anything, less mysterious, less significant.

The scroll Davis had taken possession of, although obviously special to the tribe, didn't seem to have any real value. Davis had looked at it many times. It was some document written in Russian. How they had gotten hold of it, God only knew, but it wasn't insane to think that at one time or another a Russian might have made it to the Arctic.

"Is it because of this?" Davis held up the canvas containing the scroll hanging around his neck. "I know it has some special significance to Home Now, but honestly, it is just a document written in a language of another people who look like me. How did you come by it?"

"It's true. You don't understand many things." Father smiled, for without a mirror, Davis hadn't noticed a few other things, as well. Father continued, "Always Here—"

"Yes." Davis interrupted. "Exactly what happened to him that day? Please tell me I'm remembering something that didn't really occur."

"Always Here had his name for a reason, just as you do now," Father answered. "He was named as such because he had been with our people for thousands of circles of the sun. And he had looked young like you, up until the morning you and Hacker came to Home Now. It may have been some time since you have seen your face, but although it has only been a few months, you look younger and healthier than you did when you arrived here the day Always Here left us. I believe being the new protector of our scroll has affected you more than you realize."

"What—"

"Yes, Our Future. You are now called this because as long as Always Here was with us, he stayed young and our tribe was protected. However, since he is no longer with us, we don't know what lies ahead. We believe your arrival was the reason Always Here aged and disappeared from our lives that day, and that the key to our destiny is within you."

"That scroll is not thousands of years old, Father. Like I said, it's written in a modern language...called Russian."

"Always Here was forbidden to look at the scroll, and what you say may be partly true, but you will also see over time that what I say is *also* true."

"Father?" Davis asked.

Father seemed to be in a forthcoming mood today, so Davis was taking the opportunity to get a few more answers of a concrete nature.

"Do you know what Hacker was searching for up here, and do you know what he thought he had found in that crate? He couldn't have been looking for this scroll, correct? I mean if what you say is true, it does seem to have power—a possible fountain of youth, even—but I don't believe there is any record or legend at all concerning your people's tribes and any supernatural powers. I also don't think anyone at Home Now knew the scroll around Always Here's neck was a decoy, except for perhaps you, let alone Hacker. So why was Hacker so interested in that crate?" Davis motioned to the crate, which still sat in the room near where the members of The Circle were now having this conversation. "And by the way, how did you come across being in possession of a Crafting Fishing crate from the 1700s?"

"Lots of questions about our past coming from Our Future." Father was grinning at his own play on words. Father was one of the few at The Circle with a sense of humor. "I will tell you."

—◇○◇—

"As you call them, back in your 1700s, we were much the same tribe we are today. However, except for Always Here, none of us alive now were alive then, of course. At that time, a young member of the tribe took it upon himself to leave Home Now. When The Age comes, our youth are sent to survive in solitude for a time. Before this youth I speak of, none had ever decided not to come back. Most of Home Now believed the boy had succumbed to the elements, but Always Here believed he had left to find his own way, perhaps as a challenge to himself.

"We did not see the youth again for nearly two cycles of the sun. That's when we all learned of the story I am about to tell you.

"The boy's name was Far Look. He always had a look in his eyes as if he was looking right through you and on to the distant horizon. Was it only the shade and shape of his eyes creating this illusion? If it was, then perhaps the giving of his name predisposed him to look beyond the horizon for his own future, and this eventually led to his prolonged disappearance.

"Far Look told us a great many things, as well, upon his return to Home Now, of

148

which we were previously unaware."

CHAPTER 23

FAR LOOK'S JOURNEY
AUGUST 3, 1752

"FATHER," Far Look said to the father of the tribe. "I have returned!" Far Look was ducking his head inside Father's home during a meeting of The Circle.

"Yes, Far Look, we know...for...you have returned," Always Here answered, lightly mocking Far Look's youthful exuberance which, apparently, had not left the boy despite his journey.

"Yes, I have, and I bring with me a gift for Home Now." Far Look's head then disappeared outside from where it had just come. He returned shortly with two guards carrying the Crafting crate, which appeared quite heavy. They brought it to the center of The Circle next to the fire, and the two departed.

"What is it, Far Look?" Father asked quickly. He was not sure whether he was impatient with anticipation for the boy's story, the unknown gift, or a lingering annoyance with the entire situation. Far Look had left Home Now without informing anyone, only to return and behave as if he had never left. His demeanor showed no sign of awareness that his leaving had, perhaps, had an effect on his people.

"Yes, Father," Far Look said and then paused, as if to create a moment of anticipation. "It is—"

"Where have you been, Far Look?" Father could take no more and cut the boy off, ironically keeping the knowledge of what was in the crate hidden from The Circle and himself for a while longer.

"I have been where other people, not like us, live. I almost died getting there, but there is a world of people you would not believe. As long as I can recall, I had wondered if the whole world was white, covered with ice and snow and water, and I needed to see for myself. I took my supplies and dogs when I left for The Rites, and I never looked back. I just kept going in between the rise and fall of the sun. It wasn't easy, but I used the skills taught to me by the elders, and I survived. Until I came to a different land. The ground turned hard and brown, still cold, but I saw a plain before me like no other I had seen. One day, when I felt I could go no more, I met my first pink man. He was a guide of some sort. His name was Pickland. He gave me food I had never tasted before and offered to take me to *his* kind of people's Home Now. It was a place called Maine."

Far Look described the structures, the clothing, the inventions, and the ships. It made little or no sense to anyone in The Circle except for Always Here. Always Here did not understand the details of the things of which Far Look spoke of, but at a time long ago, he had seen strange things as well. A pink man had appeared out of nowhere and given him a scroll and told him to go to the people of Home Now.

"I had to earn a device called money to get the food and shelter I needed. It is a concept hard to explain. But in that place, if you do work, then you are given a thing called money. This money you then give to others so they will give you what you need. It is difficult to understand the need for it, but the process seems to work for the pink people. I worked loading ships. They are large sleds—some as big as three Home Nows—which float on the water taking people and their belongings to distant places on the other side of the water!"

"If it is so great, then why return to us?" Father said in light disgust. He was interested to hear of these things, but he feared it might plant the seeds of leaving into the minds of other youth wishing to see this world Far Look spoke of, and that could destroy the tribe. Father contemplated adopting a policy of not naming children names connotating distant places and journeys, from here on out.

"Because, Father, it was exciting, but it was not Home Now. I knew I had accomplished what I set out to do, and that was enough. I needed to return to my people."

"We are happy you have returned, Far Look. Why did you not tell us you were leaving?"

"Father, I ask that The Circle forgive me, but I believed if I had said so, you would have stopped me. Was I incorrect?"

Father attempted a response. Wisdom and fairness were not always easily combined.

"Far Look. You may be right in that we may have said no. At first, that is. However, part of having trust in The Circle comes from trusting it to make the best decisions for the tribe and for it to listen to the tribe when making those decisions. Everyone in the tribe must trust The Circle to do this and do it well, because without that, the tribe has no wisdom and no protection. You should have come to us with your concerns. Your decision to leave may have been postponed, and perhaps someone would have accompanied you of more maturity. Your family may not have been so distraught either. By leaving without warning, you put your people at risk. We searched for you. We waited to move Home Now longer than usual, waiting for you. We also don't know if you have attracted attention to Home Now by your interaction with these other people you describe. I do not know if we are the only people who have a member like Always Here, but I do believe he is here because we are special. Does this make sense to you?"

It was a good answer for being spoken without preparation. Far Look only combatted it with one sentence.

"Always Here is here for a reason which does not involve us staying separated from the world forever."

The rest of The Circle paused, as if they all took the same breath at once. Far Look's statement somehow rang true in each of their hearts like a subconscious telepathic truth none of them were aware of, or had spoken of until now, but they all knew it nevertheless. Perhaps Far Look was correct. His journey may have been stopped by The Circle, in an effort to protect the tribe, but perhaps it was Far Look's unscheduled departure that was needed to bring about the destiny of the tribe. This supposition was truer than any of them suspected.

"The Gift," Father said, breaking the uncomfortable silence and returning the conversation to the object Far Look had placed before them. "We can talk more later concerning your deductions about Home Now and Always Here. What is this gift you have brought the tribe?"

Far Look rose and moved humbly toward the crate. He opened it, pushed his hands into a mound of dirt, and pulled out two large rocks almost the same color as the sun.

"Gold," Far Look announced. "They call it gold, and the pink men believe it to be very valuable. I met a man who played a game called poker. He owned the ships I worked on. We became very good friends, and he taught me to play this game as well. Although he would always play with large amounts of money, he never let me lose too much. I believe he liked the risk. He seemed like a very comfortable man who wanted to be doing something else with his life but was not able to do so because of his situation. Perhaps that is also why he liked me. He felt my story mirrored his own emotions."

The Circle listened intently.

"Mr. Crafting almost always won. Once or twice I won quickly before he had bet too much. It was still enough to feed me for weeks. Those were good wins. But near the time I was feeling the call to return to Home Now, I played a game with him that went like no other had before it.

―◇○◁―

"Well, Far Look? Are ya' playin' or are ya' foldin'?"

"Playing, Mr. Crafting, playing."

"Well, ya' bett'r know what yer doin', or ya' may be workin' them ships longer than ya' want and miss yer opportunity this season to return to this Home Now ya' keep talkin' about returnin' to."

"Yes, sir, Mr. Crafting. I don't want to lose too much; that is true. But I am playing."

Mr. Crafting had taught Far Look poker. Mr. Crafting liked risk in poker because he didn't get much risk anywhere else. Mr. Crafting didn't believe Far Look had a better hand, but he wanted to humor the boy because the boy seemed to have a good hand that he wanted to play. Mr. Crafting didn't believe the boy had learned the art of bluffing, and Mr. Crafting was correct in his assumption. Mr. Crafting would let the boy risk his leaving Maine this season because that made the game worth it and didn't hurt the boy too badly. And why not? Mr. Crafting had a pretty good hand.

The boy did not fold. The raises went back and forth, and the boy was in for months of work where only his bare necessities would be paid for. He would miss the opportunity to leave this year, and if he wanted to return home with anything more than what he had arrived with, he may have to stay an additional season. Mr. Crafting played cards with the boy because he was different, because he liked him, because he reminded him of himself, and because the kid liked him back and wasn't afraid of him or his authority. But Mr. Crafting also played cards because he liked playing cards. No one had money like him, and he couldn't place the kind of bets he did with Far Look with any of the other ship hands he had. It just didn't seem appropriate.

The love of risk, waiting for the sure hand, and the excitement of the game culminated with Far Look staring across a table covered with raises. Far Look's savings, notes mentioning extra weeks of work, Mr. Crafting's coins and office belongings, and one piece of paper in particular, which mentioned the contents of a safe under Mr. Crafting's desk. The kid probably had a four of a kind—a completely respectable hand—and the boy deserved to be able to play and risk his money and time with a hand like that. The unknown, the pace of the raising, and the thrill of the play had taken hold of Mr. Crafting to the point where the gold in his safe was worth the risk to see how this game played out.

With a jack high, straight flush, what difference did it make? Mr. Crafting thought as he showed his hand.

Then the boy spoke.

"Isn't the royal flush the best hand you can get, Mr. Crafting? That's what I have, right?" And Far Look showed his cards.

"Ha!" burst out of Mr. Crafting's mouth, making such a noise that Far Look could have called it a yelp, a burp, or a laugh, and he'd have been correct. Mr. Crafting shook his head as he looked down at Far Look's cards, as if to shake his eyes back from blindness. "Uh. Yeah, kid…it is, and you *do*," Crafting replied with a gaze in his eyes akin to the kind of look that had gotten Far Look his name in the first place.

Far Look broke the silence filling the room and said, "What'd I win? What's in your safe, Mr. Crafting?"

Mr. Crafting probably wouldn't be too proud of Junior Crafting waving the machine gun wildly at Far Look's descendants a couple of hundred years later because the long-since-passed Mr. Crafting had been a fair man. He showed Far Look the chunks of raw gold in the safe and said they would be held for him until he was ready to leave. Mr. Crafting was a little relieved he didn't keep *all* of his gold in that safe, as he was not sure he would have bet any differently if he had.

Far Look knew about gold and the value these people attributed to it. He would have no way of using all its value to buy goods and then transport them all to Home Now by himself. Therefore, Far Look decided to take the gold itself back as a present instead. He hadn't lost his savings, so he used that to buy his return supplies. Before Far Look left with an inconspicuous Crafting Fish Company crate filled with dirt and Mr. Crafting's gold, he also carved a small golden dog as a parting gift for Mr. Crafting for his kindness and honesty.

Mr. Crafting was completely fine with this exchange throughout the rest of his life. However, unbeknownst to Far Look or Mr. Crafting, the rest of Crafting's life was to be only another few months. He would soon after contract a mysterious illness. On his deathbed in a fever dementia, grasping the golden dog and gasping to his young son, he would push the dog in his son's hand and follow this action up by saying, "You find the dirt up north, where there's only ice, and you'll find—" But as we know, he never got it all out.

CHAPTER 24

THE FUTURE OF HOME NOW ARRIVES
APRIL 7, 1923, CONTINUED

———◇○◯◯○◇———

NO. THINGS WERE NOT going to end well.

That's what Davis was thinking as it registered to him that it was Sime's son who was here to claim his family's heirloom gold. Things were not going to end well because even if the people of Home Now wanted to give it back, which they surely would in order to make this gun-waving lunatic happy, there was almost no gold left to return.

After Far Look returned with his gift, The Circle discussed for some time what they would do with the yellow stones. There had never been any gold in Home Now, nor any other precious metal for that matter. Eventually, it was decided that since somewhere there were people who believed gold to be valuable, then it should be left as an offering after a fruitful hunt. The earth gives to them; they would give back to the earth a beautiful piece of itself.

Hunters began wearing leather necklaces with chips of Sime's lost gold. When a prey was slaughtered, the hunter would leave behind the gold they were wearing. After two hundred years of following this tradition, there was only a small fragment of gold left in the crate besides what was currently being worn by the tribe's hunters. Unless Sime's son had a hankering to go on an Easter egg hunt for little fragments of gold located under snow and ice over several hundred square miles of the Arctic...things were not going to end well.

"I said, *get* these people out here, *now!* And Hacker, too, unarmed!" Sime's son repeated quite earnestly, his volume raised high, scaring the tribe even more.

"Okay, okay," Davis muttered. The English still felt odd as it escaped his lips. "But I think there may be a problem."

"And what's that, Davis?"

"Hacker isn't here right now. I don't know when he'll be back, but if you don't want to be startled, you better be somewhat on the lookout. He is armed."

Davis was grasping at straws. Anything to stall and keep this guy's mind occupied. He could not let the craziness he observed in Sime Jr.'s eyes manifest itself as a mass murder.

Junior wasn't happy about what Davis said. He wasn't *really* happy about anything right now. He wasn't happy about losing his crew. He wasn't happy he'd seen something *doing* the losing of his crew. He wasn't happy that Davis didn't look a day older than a fifty-year-old picture had pegged him. He just wasn't happy. Junior didn't like it. Didn't like anything. But he was here; *he* had made it. So Junior figured he'd get what he came for and get the hell back home.

"The gold, dammit! Get them out here and tell them to bring the gold now! I don't got time to bullsh—"

"Okay, okay!" Davis repeated. Davis was afraid Our Future was about to make a big mistake for the tribe's future, but Junior was starting to look trigger happy, so Davis knew he had to do something. He started calling the tribe to come out and stand in a group. He called for two of the men to tell The Circle to come and bring the Crafting crate with them.

"That's better," Junior called. "Now which way do you think that bastard Hacker's going to be coming from? And don't lie! I'm sure I can pull this trigger long enough to shoot several of those children and their mothers before I fall from a surprise shot from your boss."

Adding more to the story he was winging, Davis said, "Well, given the sun and the time of day. Uh, he's on a hunt with a couple trackers. They probably won't be back till late, so they'll want to follow the path—" Davis was now making fingering motions as if to solve some math problem floating in the air before him. Davis pointed randomly to the left and concluded fictitiously, "Umm. I think from that side of camp."

"All right. I see the crate over there with my family's name on it. Tell them to bring it over to me."

The Circle had arrived with the crate. Junior hadn't seemed to realize the implication of only one person carrying the crate who didn't appear too fatigued by doing so. Davis motioned for the young man to bring it over.

"All right! Finally, something. After all this damned way!" Junior knelt on the snow, machine gun still pointed keenly at the tribe. "Davis, you go stand over there with the rest of them. You're making me nervous. You don't want me nervous."

Our Future was getting scared. There wasn't a Hacker coming to save them.

And even if Hacker was coming, he'd shoot Junior and then shoot some of the tribe, anyway, just for not telling him about the gold. Then he'd leave with the crate, regardless of the fact that there was barely any gold contained within.

Davis thought it funny his mind could have such a strange thought at a time like this. Davis also seriously doubted "save them" was anywhere close to the right words to use, even in regard to dead fake Hacker. No, this wasn't going to end well. No Hacker the hero, no Always Here with magical powers of protection, no arsenal of hidden weapons, no gold, no hope. Our Future was about to watch the tribe and himself become No Future. No Future at all.

156

"Well, goddamn! The legend's goddamn right. Here's some dirt, and goddamn, there ain't nothing but goddamned snow anywhere else around." Junior started moving his hand through the dirt. "Davis, you're a goddamned idiot. Why would you and Hacker stay up here when there's all this goddamned—"

It appeared that Junior liked to take his Lord's name in vain pretty much as he pleased. There didn't seem to be any pattern or order in which certain things needed to be damned by his Creator and others didn't. Then the clincher making this day pretty well damned by Junior's God occurred when Junior pulled his hand out of the dirt with the small remaining nugget of yellow stuff that had brought him all the way to Home Now all the way from Maine.

"Goddamn! Where's the goddamned gold?"

This was the moment Davis hadn't been waiting for.

"There's only this one goddamned little rock!"

Davis stood speechless. Silence drifted through the setting. Even Junior had shut up for a minute as he figured what to do next. A gust of wind swept loose snow through the gap between Junior and Davis and the tribe. A creature anticipating every single one of their moments had been the real cause of that gust. An illusion of slow motion was created in this single moment of silence, but it wasn't peace and tranquility being born. A human game of dominos was all that awaited them, Davis feared. Regardless of his stall tactics, nothing had been reversed. Davis looked at the tribe members and could tell they were all depending on him. He was Their Future. He would have the answers.

Davis had no answers, as he had so often told the children.

Davis pushed through the fear to say something. "Yes, uh…see, not all the gold is there." Davis's mind gears were cranking hard. Then Davis caught Daring Rush's eyes. Daring Rush hadn't made a kill at the last hunt. He had come back very distraught over the matter, and Davis remembered him talking at great lengths of the attempts he'd made, only to fail at bringing the tribe food.

Daring Rush has a necklace, Davis remembered.

"The tribe wears the gold also." *Yeah, this was good.* "The men wear necklaces for good luck while hunting. I can have each of them bring you their necklace." *This was going to buy him more time.* Junior wouldn't want to get too close to the crowd, so Davis could send the men with gold pendants over one at a time. Maybe even send some of the men back to their homes to "look" for theirs.

"All right, Davis, now we're talkin'!" Junior snorted. "Send 'em over here. Slowly!"

Davis spoke in the tribe's tongue and told the men wearing gold around their necks to go to Junior and give him the necklace. There hadn't been a way to say "in a line" or "one at a time," so the men began to push through the women and children all at once. Junior got one look at this and raised his gun at the tribe, showing more aim and determination.

"Hey, hey, hey! Wait a damned minute! You send them over here one at a time, Davis! Hands out, holding the gold and droppin' it in the crate. Got it?"

Davis quickly stopped the men and got out in front of them. He took Learning Heart by the shoulders and guided him toward Davis, explaining what to do with the necklace. Learning Heart walked slowly toward Junior, taking off the necklace and holding it in his hand with arms outstretched. Davis then took Rigid Back and explained to him to wait until Learning Heart had returned from Junior. He made further pantomimes to show the other hunters to continue this pattern.

Junior held steady aim on the hunter coming closer. Both men's eyes were locked as if each held a gun. However, Learning Heart didn't have a gun. He only held the light for Junior's fuse.

"What the goddamn is that?" Junior yelled out as Learning Heart opened his hand to show the necklace before dropping it into the crate as he had been instructed to do by Our Future.

"Davis? I'm talking to you, Davis, goddammit!" Junior's words were pure fury.

"Yes?" Davis called, trying to hide the fear in his voice.

"Davis. Is this the whole tribe? There can't be more than forty men standing there, and only about half of 'em moved when you told 'em to get their butts over here!"

"Uh, yes, this is everyone, I swear," Davis answered. He didn't know these were the words Our Future was meant to utter to truly be true to his name.

"Well then, you'd better start praying! Because that necklace your friend here dropped in the box ain't got much gold bigger than a goddamned fleck!" Junior was looking fiercer than ever. "You better tell me there's more gold somewhere in this camp! More than twenty more of these goddamned *flecks*!"

—◇○◇—

Well, when things aren't going to end well…well, let's be honest…nobody says that phrase when they are dying from old age, calmly and with acceptance, comfortable on their deathbed, surrounded by loved ones. People say that phrase when things just have that look. You know. The look like everything's about to hit the fan. And when that "everything" goes to the extreme, an old friend gets called.

What a scene! Impending Doom thought as he swooped down from nowhere (*everywhere*) to this arctic wasteland. He'd been watching and waiting for that signal transforming so much "impending doom" into "time to party."

How time moved for I. D. wasn't exactly the same as earth time. He was in his own moment but out of the moment. Able to observe as if time was stretching out slowly before him, and he was strolling down the line taking inventory of each word, action, scream. It wasn't precognition. He was just as surprised at events as they unfolded as anyone.

This Junior guy's really pissed! I think he's going to shoot that boy. Oh well, looky.

158

He did. There. The bullet is leaving the gun. Time to go to work!

—◇○◇—

"Wait!" Davis screamed. But it was too late. The bullet shot Learning Heart right through the back. His chest exploded as Davis looked on in horror, and then Learning Heart fell to the ground. A slight breeze seemed to come out of nowhere, and Davis could have sworn he saw something black move between Junior and himself.

That's one shoved facedown into the snow! Ha! Who the hell said this wasn't going to end well?

"Better tell me there's gold somewhere, Davis! Tell me now where it is! It's goddamned hard to pull this trigger with a soft finger!" Junior was losing control from the journey, the day's events, the stress that Hacker might return and get the best of him, and the seemingly small bit of gold he was going to walk away with, for all his trouble. *And how the goddamned am I going to walk away, anyway?* He had no gear, no help, no food.

"The gold—" Davis's voice stuttered, and Junior fired another shot, this time randomly into the crowd gathered behind Davis.

"No!" Davis yelped. "The gold is—" But honestly, Davis was so panicked, he didn't know what to say. The tribe was screaming and starting to turn and run.

Junior let several rounds go. The bullets were flying past Davis. Impending Doom was having a field day. Junior was losing it.

"Not good enough, Davis! I'm shooting till you tell me I'm leaving with more than fairy dust and pebbles!"

"It's—" Davis started another lie.

"Not good enough!" Junior held down the trigger. Davis turned and saw so many of his friends dropping to the ground. Some had been close and had stood still in a frozen panic. Others fell as they ran, now to be frozen forever on the icy ground. Before the grenades started landing behind Davis—yes, Junior had started throwing grenades, as if to say, "I brought 'em; I'm gonna goddamned use 'em"—Davis swore he kept seeing a shadow in the air, causing his friends to go down. Step one, bullets. Step two, a shove.

To make the point!

Do I hear laughing? Is someone enjoying this? Davis shuddered on the inside.

Some of the tribe had gotten out of firing and grenade range (*Really? Had this fool really used grenades?* Davis thought), but many more lay dead, or in pieces, or severely wounded behind Our Future, who felt more like Our Destruction at present.

"There *ain't* no more gold, is there, Dav—" Junior stopped midsentence. His head made an unnatural jerk. The Thompson fell from his hands, making no noise as it landed on the snow. The returned silence had demonstrated this. Davis didn't know what was going on; he didn't wait to find out. He rushed at Junior, leaping over the crate, and took the madman to the ground. Davis was glad to find out he only was taking what *used* to be a madman to the ground. For Junior was as dead as a dead man could be when he's dead.

—◇∘◇—

Whoa! Looks like the ball's changing hands! I. D. realized as he knocked the life out of one more falling Inuit hit by Junior's rampage of bullets.

Impending Doom's stretched-out, wide-lens view of events had given him ample opportunity to see a lot of impending—*yet oh-so-unsuspecting*—doom sneaking up behind Junior. But he was Impending Doom...so of course he would see this.

Awwwww. Poor guy don't know what's coming, I. D. thought. *I am! I'm coming!*

—◇∘◇—

The Son wasn't going to have much of a tribe left, let alone grow up to be Questions Father. Half of the current Circle would be dead by the end of the day, but the young boy's heroism could have made him Father, Questions Father, The Guard, or some new post related to greatness and bravery the tribe hadn't invented yet. Against his mother's wishes, The Son had taken his father's spear and crawled out of the back of their home underneath the canvas. Mother Leader had known to stay and not go when Davis made the call for everyone to come out. She and her son had seen the danger coming, as opposed to everyone else. Mother Leader had tried to keep her son quiet—make him stay—but he threatened to scream if she didn't let him go. It had been an empty threat, but it had worked.

She had let him go.

And go he did. The Son crawled out of his home and began to crawl on his stomach in a wide, imagined circle to Junior. He crawled and crawled quickly, but always just out of visual range of the epicenter of trouble. He crawled out of the camp, far to the right, and came far around to the back of the camp, finally coming straight up a line to the rear of where Junior stood. Creeping closer to Junior, The Son had arrived close enough behind Junior to be seen if the wild man were to turn around. When the first shot went off and he saw Learning Heart fall, The Son froze. He had never seen anything like that, and he had become paralyzed with fear. He thought he was next. He knew he would be seen. The man would turn around and do the same to him. He was afraid to turn around and crawl back out of sight. That, for sure, could also attract the man's attention. The Son buried his face in the cold ground.

Then the next shots were fired. His head popped up, and he saw more of the tribe fall. There was yelling, and then the gun started killing everyone in sight. The man didn't seem to have any desire to turn around. He seemed only to have the desire to destroy everyone. The Son still couldn't move. The sounds were so loud. The grotesque sights foreshadowed what could happen to him. Then the explosions began. Too many people were dying, screaming. Finally, The Son's instincts to save his family took over, like they would for Davis a few moments later. The Son sprang up from the snow. He was roughly twenty feet behind Junior. He ran silently and raised the ivory spear and plunged it into the soft lower part of Junior's back.

———◇○◇———

Look at that kid run! I like him! I like him a lot! Bring on that doom, kid! Impending Doom was full of glee seeing The Son running at Junior. *Guess you're going down next, Maggot Jr.!* and he flew in to help Davis knock this last Crafting descendant to the ground.

———◇○◇———

Junior's insides lit on fire. He froze in pain, and his gun fell from his hands. He wanted to turn in reaction to the blow, to see what or who had caused the agony he was now experiencing. He could only freeze, hoping, praying to his god of damned things that the pain would end. As the fall to his knees commenced, Hacker's airborne cohort, Davis, collided with his chest. Junior fell backward, and the spear currently shoved into his right kidney, liver, and right lung dug in even deeper. It twisted, grabbing and swirling some intestine like a fork in spaghetti. No type of screaming would have sufficed to convey Junior's pain, so more fittingly, he produced no sound at all. The back end of the spear hit the ground as well, sliding out sideways away from Junior's body. Junior's insides were being pushed angularly as the tip of the blade pierced the inside front of his rib cage, burrowing its way out of Junior's body on the opposite side it had entered, and bringing "blood and guts," as they say, along with it.

Even Impending Doom didn't have to do much on this one. It seemed he was held back for most of the process, only to watch with glee as Junior experienced internal poisoning, shock, and death. Then I. D. did "the tap," and Junior was over.

———◇○◇———

Who was gloating?
Davis tried to shake this strange thought as he lay upon the corpse of what he hoped would be the last of the Crafting Clan he'd ever encounter. He looked up. He had the strangest feeling someone *or something* was above him patting himself *or itself* on the back for a job well done or for enjoying a *party.* As Davis turned, he caught a glimpse of a black figure in the air. Then it was gone. Davis felt a chill, knowing he had seen what he had seen, and he had seen it during Junior's killing spree too. He closed his eyes to shake it away and remembered he had felt that presence

one other time, hadn't he? A long time ago, during the dogsledding tragedy that had landed him at Home Now.

When Davis finished his disbelief and opened his eyes again, he saw The Son standing there looking down at him.

"I did it! I stopped him!" The Son cried.

Davis now understood what had happened. He was getting to his knees and he saw the spear jutting out of Junior's left ribs, displaying a chunk of Junior's liver, apparently, as a trophy for its efforts. Davis realized he had been lucky the spear had exited where it did. A few inches to his left, and the spear could have "trophyized" a bit of Davis as well. It was over, and that was all that really mattered now. The Son was just ten years old, but whoever was left of Home Now owed their lives to him.

"Yes, you did. Now help me up so we can go help the others."

CHAPTER 25

THE END OF OUR FUTURE
A WEEK AFTER THE KILLING OF JUNIOR SIME

———⋄∘⟨⟩∘⋄———

"**E**XPLAIN TO US why you say you should leave, Our Future?" Mother Leader asked. She was one of four members left in The Circle. There was her, her husband, The Other, and her son. The Other was new as of today because the previous tribe representative had been killed the week before by the man who had taken so many of the tribe with his weapons. Questions Father had also been killed. The Son had been inducted after the massacre. Never had anyone so young joined The Circle.

"Mother Leader, I don't want to leave either, but it is something I know I should do." Our Future, who was feeling a lot more like Davis lately, tried to explain his reasoning. "The recent events have shown I do not bring with me the same protection Always Here brought to Home Now. I have also been thinking a lot about what your father told me Far Look had said. It doesn't make sense for Always Here to have brought you this scroll, protected your tribe for thousands of circles of the sun, to have never read it, and then to die, only to give it to me so I could then offer no protection whatsoever to Home Now. I think this scroll has a purpose, and I feel it is important I search out what that purpose is."

"Far Look's actions brought that man here. If he hadn't left, You and Hacker wouldn't have come either," Mother Leader said, postulating that the tribe would have been protected indefinitely had Far Look not gone off on his own.

"Yes, Mother Leader," The Son interjected, using her title for The Circle, the way he guessed he was supposed to, "but didn't Always Here start to age when Our Future was close to Home Now? If he was meant to protect the tribe forever, then why did he die and give the scroll to Our Future?"

The Son seemed to have the kind of head on his shoulders he was going to need to become Questions Father, after all. Everyone looked at the boy, almost in the same way a Circle, long ago, had looked at Far Look.

"The Son is right," Davis declared. "I think these events were meant to happen. I think your tribe was meant to protect the scroll until it could—" Davis had no words. What was the scroll for? What did it say? How did it keep its holder young? What did it have to do with him? Why the hell was it in Russian? What was it all about? Then

163

again, that's exactly why he needed to leave—to try to find these answers. "—could be, uh, *used*. For *whatever* it's going to be used for."

Mother Leader looked down. She was thinking. She was agreeing with Our Future for more than one reason. Nothing really made sense about the scroll, but what Far Look had said and The Son and Our Future were saying made the most sense of anything.

"Our Future. I believe you were named correctly. A future is a future, as good or bad and as short or long as it may be. I believe in what you say. You must leave and find out its purpose. Home Now is very reduced in numbers, and I am not sure we can survive. It may be time that we leave also. Start a new life among the pink people, such as yourself. I believe your coming brought this future to us. And I believe the scroll and its purpose will be the lasting part of our future."

"Do you really believe there are not enough of you to survive?" Davis knew it was true, but it helped to argue the point, if only for hope's sake.

"Yes. And so we will leave with you," Mother Leader said unexpectedly and decidedly, "and when we reach that new home, we will say goodbye to you there, and you can take our future with the scroll and do what you think is best."

Mother Leader had decided on a plan, but a week before on April 7, 1923, too many cooks had been in the kitchen; too many children's hands had been in the cookie jar. Too many people had touched some scrolls, made some decisions about scrolls, or changed the directions of people's lives associated with those scrolls, and that had tipped the teapot just a little too much.

The last mystical tea to pour out as that teapot fell over was another gift from Davis's oft-returning and unrequested acquaintance, Impending Doom. He'd be sending just one last ice catastrophe Davis's way for old times sake, so to speak, and it would swallow everyone from Home Now into a icy and watery grave only a few days after embarking toward their new existence.

Well, it'd swallow everyone, that is, except for Our Future.

And we all know there's got to be a double meaning in that...

BOOK III:

THE FOUR MYTHS

CHAPTER 26

AND DAVIS MAKES FIVE
FEBRUARY 3, 2007, CONTINUED

EVERYONE SAT DOWN, keeping their eyes on Jack, hoping he would provide an immediate answer. Sarah had everyone thinking about Scroll Number Four. Given the strange circumstances that had brought the group together, each was wondering if there would soon be another knock on the door. Sarah and Randy sat to the right of Jack on the couch. Derek had returned himself to the chair across from them, having pulled it away from the wall and closer to the coffee table in front of the couch. Jack opened the first canister of Sarah's and pulled out its scroll. It looked to be of the same makeup as the first one, and as he unrolled it and surveyed it, the assumption was validated. Completely the same, except in content. All in Russian that didn't look like Russian. The same organization of lines at the top, which looked like titles, and headers, and—

"Huh?" Jack muttered to himself.

"What is it?" The three others piggybacked his muttering.

"Nothing really, or who the hell knows, maybe something, really. But, regardless, here at the bottom," Jack said, as he pointed to where he was looking near the bottom of the parchment, "yours has a single centered word by itself also. Like ours."

"Hey, I noticed that before, too," Derek burst in. "I couldn't read them, obviously, so all I could do was focus on the look of them. I saw them for the first time yesterday."

"You just saw them for the first time this week?" Jack asked, puzzled. "I thought you wrote a book about them?"

"Well, I had stumbled across them a while back, but Sarah caught me opening a canister, so, honestly, I only saw the rolled-up version. That's where the idea of the book came from. I never actually got to see them until yesterday. So, yeah, yesterday."

"Oh," Jack replied as a thought entered his head, "On the second?" *Two scrolls found on the second* rumbled through his mind like a bulldozer being driven by Randy's disembodied voice proclaiming, "Prime numbers, Jack! Prime numbers!"

"The second?"

"Second of February," Jack replied.

"Is that significant?" Derek asked.

"It's just interesting," Jack said.

"The other one's got the same layout too," Derek added with a waver in his voice precipitated by the confusion he felt from Jack's responses.

"Good. Consistency will help solve the mystery," Jack replied, deciding to take a look at canister number two's contents.

After unrolling the second scroll, Jack could see Derek had been speaking the truth. *Possibly the truth from on high at this point*, he thought. Jack didn't know what was going on or if he should really be going all Pentecostal in his mind, but too much was adding up here, and if you see a math book in the kitchen, that's what you have to call it, no matter how much you may have wanted to find your mother's recipe for her comforting apple pie. And so, on went the sermon in Jack's mind. *Speaking the Truth! And Praise—*

"You've got internet, right?" Jack asked Derek, breaking his own silly thoughts while pulling his laptop out of his bag.

"Yes, wireless. The password is Sarah1923 with a capital *S*."

"Hahahahahahahahaha!" Randy burst out laughing in a slightly maniacal, slightly fake manner—only fake in sound, that was. "*Nineteen twenty-three?*"

"What's the laugh for?" Derek responded.

"Yes, Randy, why are you laughing?" Sarah followed.

"Because I don't care anymore!" Randy exclaimed and laughed more. "I really don't." Randy had been having his own silly thoughts about the whole experience, and hearing the year "1923" had put him over the edge. He calmed himself a little, realizing he was probably scaring his hosts, and he repeated, "I'm sorry, but really, seriously, why 1923?" Randy thought he might be losing it, or at the very least, he just didn't know *what* to think anymore. *Is this really happening?*

"Well, if you're asking, you must have a reason, and I'd like to hear it," Derek started. "But if you want to know, that's the year my other great-aunt, Sarah's sister, Jessica, found Aunt Sarah and brought her home. April 7, 1923, to be specific. She had been missing about forty-seven years."

"Hahahahahaha! Jack? You hear *that?*" Randy was shaking his head. "Derek and you both found these scrolls *this* week, and looks like Old Mr. Dunsford and Great-Aunt Jesse were lovebirds too!"

Jack had been starting his laptop furiously and listening to this craziness all at the same time. It was all beginning to be a bit too much to process at once. He was going to need to diagram it out soon if facts like this kept rolling in.

"Yes, I hear Randy," Jack said, "and I don't really know what to say. My brain is starting to hurt."

And my heart is starting to race.

"Who's Mr. Dunsford, Randy?" Sarah asked while looking right into Randy's eyes, which seemed to calm him down a little.

"Sarah, there's a lot to tell you, and it appears you have a story, too, but Mr. Dunsford is our 2-3-4-7 man. He was just another warehouse worker like Jack here. Except he wasn't as smart as Jack it seems, because he didn't figure all of this out. But anyway—"

"Well, remember, Randy," Jack cut in modestly. "Mr. Dunsford can't necessarily be blamed. The Enigma machine wasn't exactly on his radar in 1923."

"Enigma *machine*?" Derek asked. "And what was that you said, Randy? Your 2-3-4-7 man?"

"See? There's just too much going on here," Randy croaked.

"It would seem so," Sarah replied to Randy. She then looked at Derek. "What's an Enigma machine, Derek?"

"Umm…well…"

Randy saw Derek struggling and decided to help. The poor guy didn't know where to start, let alone know why the topic was even relevant or why he had decided to land himself in the position of explainer.

"Sarah, I promise you Jack's going to explain everything, in order, in a sec," Randy said. "Right, Jack?"

"Yes, Randy, I will," Jack answered as the online Enigma machine loaded in his browser.

"But back to your original question, Sarah," Randy continued. "Mr. Dunsford happened to refile the scroll Jack and me found in the warehouse on the very day your sister located you: April 7, 1923."

"Mr. Johanssen?" Sarah said, breaking her eyes from Randy momentarily.

"Yes, dear?" Jack replied, stopping for a moment from having already begun transcribing the Russian letters located at the bottom of each of Sarah's scrolls into English.

"Eighteen seventy-six was when I found the scrolls in Egypt. It's also the year I went missing, at least to my family. I think it was June. Several months later I checked myself into a mental hospital in Cairo. That's where my sister eventually found me."

Jack looked up this time and asked cautiously, "Since we're on dates, anyhow, you wouldn't happen to mind telling us when exactly you put yourself away, so to speak, would you?"

"Don't say it was January 31, 1877, Sarah." Randy said, his elbows resting on his knees and eyes focused on the floor between his thighs and shaking his head. "Oh, hell, say it. What difference does it make now? I already believe I'm King Tut, probably reincarnated to see the invention of fusion power." Randy just kept shaking his head while staring at the floor. He had one more comment to speak, to her, to anyone, to the floor, even. It didn't matter. So, he said it to Jack. "And Jack, you heard her say June 1876, right? I sure hope there's not another Last Stand in all of this, and you're Custer. Or worse, me."

Me too, thought Jack, not wanting to verbalize his answer, just in case acknowledging Randy made his supposition more possible. "Thanks, sort of."

"How did you know?" Derek asked, stunned by everything he was hearing. But this especially. For these two visitors to relate to a random date like that...well, it was a bit too queer. "I'd think you guys were screwing with us if I hadn't already seen the power of these things in Aunt Sarah's longevity."

"So, that *is* the date, Miss Dubois?" Jack asked.

"According to papers Derek found, yes," Sarah answered.

"Everybody's finding a lot of papers," Jack said.

When Sarah spoke, a combination of intelligence and grace flowed from her, making anyone listening not know whether to hang on her every word for the pure sake of knowledge and insight or to cave in and just get to falling in love with her already. Fortunately, for Jack and Randy's friendship's sake, Jack wasn't really interested in love at the moment. Randy, however, was losing his concentration on all matters at hand every time she uttered a word.

"Well, it just happens to be the date our scroll..." Jack paused for a moment and lightly chewed on the inside of his bottom lip. This break created a new world order; everyone previously hanging on Sarah's every syllable now switched their focus. The age of Jack the Oracle had arrived, and it was time to pay attention. The Oracle spoke. "Okay, I'm not really thinking anymore about things in a 'just happens to be' sort of way." *(Yes, Oracle speak to us. What is it you have to say?)* "The date you filed yourself away in a mental hospital seems to be the same date our scroll was filed away in the warehouse for the first time after being found at Little Bighorn. And, yes, if either of you happen to remember, that battle took place in *June*—June of 1876." *(We see. Feed us more. Make us whole.)* "Looks like all three scrolls were checked in for safekeeping at the same time, and then got a little safer again about forty-seven years later. Yours, in this house—mine, in a metal box." *(We understand. But we want to know more. We have questions...)*

"What's the meaning of all this?" Sarah begged. "What the purpose? Why me? Why you?"

"Hell if *we* know, Miss Dubois," Jack responded, trying his best not to laugh like Randy had done earlier, fearful he may not stop. He couldn't get prime number math out of his head. Jack's "hell-decorated" ignorance had broken the spell he had placed on his comrades a moment before. He was only Jack again, a guy as confused as they were. "I sure hope we can find out. I'm going to translate these words at the bottom of yours first. They're a bit intriguing—the way they are laid out, the fact I was able to translate them compared to the rest of the words. It's got to mean something. A clue. Something. Ours said 'sixth.'"

Everyone remained quiet after Jack's last statement. The Oracle was born again in the group's subconscious. The mention of a specific clue, a direction to take…perhaps they may be only a step away from an answer—at least, one of the answers, and one answer was far more than any of them had ever had before. They watched Jack type on his computer. They looked back and forth between it and the two scrolls he had laid out on the coffee table. He had used various articles from the table to hold down the corners of the scrolls to keep them from rolling up themselves. A couple of marble coasters, a *New Yorker*. These were the types of tools a modern Oracle used, it seemed. They didn't know Jack felt like no Oracle—only a man wishing he could unload some of the weight on his mind and use that too.

It didn't take him long to translate the two words on the two scrolls. He had noticed before that one of the scroll's "bottom clue word" had been hyphenated. Jack had never imagined that an ancient mystical scroll would contain something like a hyphen. A normal person would most certainly use this hyphen discovery to convince themselves the scrolls weren't ancient and weren't mystical.

Well, cross "normal" off my list of redeeming qualities, Jack thought.

He studied his translation of these simple words where they sat, separated by a few spaces each, in the Notepad file into which they had been typed. A quick study, and he didn't think he needed to translate the top of the scrolls to figure out the sequence of Sarah's scrolls. Jack leaned over and sat his laptop on the floor beside his left leg. He took a moment to rearrange the three scrolls on the table, in the order he felt appropriate. The others watched in wonderment, each deducing Jack's reasons for doing what he was doing. Witnessing action with apparent coherent thought behind it, in relation to the scrolls, was mesmerizing.

"Jack?" Randy could hold his curiosity no longer. "What are you doing? I feel like our entire lives hang in the balance of the next words you say."

Jack ignored Randy, focusing on his task. He had realized the scroll on the right, with the hyphenated Russian "word" was most probably the first or second scroll, and the one on the left was the second or third of the four. *Mine is the fourth— of course, of course.* Rearranged now, Sarah's two scrolls were swapped and lay to Jack's left, his and Randy's to his right.

He glanced down at the laptop screen by his feet and back at the scrolls. A small grin tickled the right side of his mouth.

"Come on! Dammit, Jack, what do you see?" Gasket blown, Randy was now in need of a mind mechanic.

Jack turned his head to look over to Randy sitting to his right. Jack's elbows were resting on his knees like Randy's had before, but instead of looking down, his hands were hanging, fingertips slowly tapping each other. His smile widened.

"Randy," Jack began, "I'm not sure if we're missing the first or the third scroll, but I think I might know where it is."

"Really?" Derek jumped. "*Already?*"

Derek's surprise was echoed, almost immediately, by Randy's and Sarah's own versions of his exclamations.

"Really?" Sarah and Randy asked.

Had Sarah just grabbed Randy's hand? Jack's subconscious noticed.

Somewhere deep in Jack's mind, one of his brain cells asked this question, given that Jack's peripheral vision had caught the act. The question went unnoticed by all his other brain cells, however, because they were too busy firing back and forth to one another, all jazzed by what Jack felt he had surmised concerning the missing scroll. Those cells began an explanation. "Well, so far, the scrolls' language hasn't been very cryptic—once you get them translated, that is. Ours even sounds like it could have been written by Randy here. I mean the line that speaks about Randy and me even uses the term 'tripping,' as in 'You're tripping, man.'"

"So? What do you see?" Derek asked, not sure why he was excited about finding a fourth scroll when he didn't even know what scrolls one through three were for. "Does it say where the fourth one is?"

"Yes, Mr. Johanssen," Sarah chimed in, now more curious than ever, though she didn't quite understand what "tripping" meant and why it was such an important word.

"Yes, ma'am. And, really, call me Jack."

"Only if you'll call me Sarah. I may be old, but I'm not old."

Should I be scared I know what that means? Jack figured it was the only time anyone had said anything like that and meant it...literally.

"Okay, Sarah." Jack obliged with the use of her first name. He lifted his right hand, and, pointing in succession to the three words, one on each of the scrolls, he said: "Twenty-first...Street...Sixth."

"That is what those words say?" Derek asked, somewhat rhetorically, getting it, not getting it, believing him, not believing him, slowly decaying into insanity, holding it together via survival instinct.

"It sounds like an address," Randy announced—a bona fide Dr. Watson in training. Clarifying his statement he added, "Or rather, an intersection."

"Or rather an intersection." Jack jinxed Randy as he spoke the same words. If this group of theirs was being brought together for a reason, and all were meant to come to an understanding together for a reason, it was working. *We ain't fakin'...whole lotta echoin' goin' on.*

"Yeah," Derek said, still following this strange conversation—wanting to, not wanting to. "But it's missing the 'and,' you know, like Twenty-First Street *and* Sixth?" Derek stopped. "Wait. That's just a few blocks from here."

"I know. If it's a New York address, that is. And at this point, why would it not be, given everything so far?" Jack continued, "Here's my thought, take it or leave it. I think you're right, Derek. And if we're missing the 'and,' then that would make Miss Dubois's—sorry, *Sarah's*—scrolls, number one and number two, and ours, four, and the missing one, *three*. I think number three's at that intersection, and given how the line I had translated in our scroll reads as if it was speaking to Randy and me, right at that moment, then I say we all go now and look for it."

"You mean *before* we translate the rest?" Sarah asked. She wanted to know everything they said. They had taken her life. They had given her life. She didn't know how she felt about them, but she wanted to understand them and know what they said, know if they said anything about her...gave some meaning to all she'd been through. And the thought of going outside scared the life out of her. She hadn't left the house since arriving there in 1923. She didn't know it, but she was squeezing Randy's hand tighter. However, Randy knew it.

"Miss Dub—uh...Sarah," Jack said, "I can't say I understand these things. But I think we need all four to understand them completely. I didn't need anything but a couple sentences on ours and a string of coincidences to find you and Derek and these other two scrolls of yours. I think, as crazy as all this still feels, these things are telling us to go now and find number four."

"Which is actually number *three*, right, Jack?"

"Yes, Randy, most probably," Jack affirmed.

"I don't think this is the outing I need to change shirts for." Randy grabbed at his tea stains and turned toward Sarah. "Let's go and see. Okay?"

As she looked back at him, Randy thought how strange it was to suddenly realize he was falling in love in the midst of all the craziness confronting him. But he was. And since she was still holding his hand, he felt she might just be too.

"Oh my dear goodness. Do you see that?" Sarah gasped on the streets of New York.

This was the second time Sarah Dubois had repeated this statement in the past twenty minutes. The first as they had reached Seventh Avenue. Looking down the "Av," as they had come around the corner from their street, the scene of what New York City had become since she had arrived there in the 1920s opened before her. Number one "oh my dear goodness," check. Number two came as she caught the sight of a man sitting on the sidewalk on the other side of Twenty-First Street.

Currently, the group was huddled together at the southeast corner of Twenty-First and Sixth and looking across Twenty-First Street at the busyness on the other side.

"Yes, I see," Jack responded.

Randy gasped as well, finally focused on what Sarah had drawn their attention to. "Do you really think there could possibly be, a *scroll* in *that*? I can't believe it. I can't believe we just came out here, and it's that freaking obvious!"

"I know, Randy. But only to us. No one else seems to care at all—mystically and literally."

Jack was referring to the complete lack of compassion or awareness of a dirty homeless man with a long beard seated against the wall across the street from them. Across his chest, tied with a rope at each end was a satchel of some sort, which looked like something you might buy in a Native American curio shop, yet more genuine and more aged. The bag was longer than it was wide. It looked as if it'd be perfect for holding a rolled-up document on which were transcribed the secrets of humanity.

"Hey, look closer," Derek spoke up, "past the filth and the beard. He doesn't look that old, does he?"

Randy's eyesight was better than Jack's, and as they both focused in on the man, Randy agreed with Derek. "You're right, he looks like he could be *thirty years old* under all of that."

"Not in his eyes," Sarah added. Her eyesight appeared to be the best in the group attending this party going on at the Sixth Avenue Club. She knew the look on the man's face all too well. She'd seen it in her own mirror. "He's seen too much for thirty."

"Well, if our guess is right, he's probably seen too much for *one hundred* and thirty," Jack said. The tone of the conversation now becoming eerie.

"One hundred and thirty-one, Jack," Randy had to add, as Mr. Prime Number Math Coincidence Man Avenger.

"Right," Jack acquiesced followed by a chuckle amounting only to a quick holding of the breath and then a quick expulsion from the nose, creating a sound that tended to up the eerie factor by ten in situations such as these.

Needing to step out from under the Umbrella of Eerie, Derek asked, "*So?* What do we do? We can't just bum-rush the guy. If he's not who or what we're looking for, we'll scare him to death, and if he *is* who we're looking for, then he might be like Aunt Sarah was and—"

"—we'll scare him to death," Jack finished. "I know."

The four of them stood there on the corner, all trying not to stare and looking all the more like they were staring. The New Yorkers passing by their huddle didn't notice them except for an annoyed few needing to change gears and circumvent their group as they desperately tried to follow White Walker's command as he conducted humanity from the traffic pole's Walk/Don't Walk sign. Regardless of the attention they were giving the man in question, he had remained oblivious to their presence and, apparently, the presence of everything around him.

"Well, it doesn't look like he's going anywhere soon. I think we have a couple of minutes to think about this," Jack proposed. "But, Derek, keep an eye on him anyway. With all this traffic going by, I don't want him to sneak away."

"I got him in my sights," Derek said.

Randy raised an idea. "Jack, wait a minute. These three scrolls we've got look the same, right?"

"Yes?" Jack replied. Suddenly, he thought he knew where Randy might be headed with his question. "Right, Randy. So we go over there and take ours out. We start looking at them right in front of him, and if he's our man, he'll recognize them."

"And we'll see him recognizing them."

"Yes, and maybe, he'll snap out of it like Aunt Sarah did." Derek had jumped in, liking the idea.

"Perhaps," Jack replied. "Sarah, there's a good chance that something similar to what happened to you happened to him, but he never had the idea to check himself into an institution."

"Oh my God," Sarah responded in horror. "To think, I could have ended up like that for a hundred years in Egypt. Oh, the poor man."

"You didn't, Sarah. Thank God." Randy tried to comfort her.

"All right, let's do this thing. The light's changing. We should go." Jack stepped into the street, motioning for them to follow White Walker as well, as the idol beckoned them to the other side of Twenty-First Street. Jack was now on a mission to get this thing solved.

Or a mission from God.

The Blues Brothers, Jack? Really?

Well, it is New York.

The Blues Brothers were in Chicago, Jack.

Oh, yeah, right. So, whew! It isn't a mission from God.

As he stepped onto Twenty-First Street, Jack thought that sometimes his reflections didn't merit acknowledgment, and so he kept these little conversations to himself.

Problem was, the next thought *did.*

But it is. Isn't it? Chicagoans and New Yorkers may hold their respective cities to be dear, distinct, and noninterchangeable. However, regarding important world-changing prophetic missions blended with Jack Johanssen's personal reflections, it appeared their feelings mattered—not so much.

The four crossed the street and veered slightly right to head themselves a little deeper into Twenty-First Street. They stopped in front of, and a few feet away from their man in question. The man had his back against the wall, completing the caricature every New Yorker would deem "just another building and just another bum"—every New Yorker, that was, except for the ones currently blocking the sidewalk in front of the seated man. They believed he might hold the very mysteries of heaven and earth in the small satchel hanging around his neck. Jack lowered himself to a crouch, acting as if he was trying to get at something from his bag. Opening the canister would be in direct line of sight of the man, who still appeared to be oblivious to their presence.

Jack pulled the top off the white cylindrical container he had retrieved from his bag, reached inside, and pulled out one of Sarah's scrolls. The other three watched the bum's eyes intently. They wouldn't be earning any Oscars for Best Actor in an Inconspicuous Part today. Jack unrolled the scroll and faced it slightly toward the direction of the man as he pretended to look it over.

—◇○◇—

Coming out from a tunnel or waking from an intense dream or turning on a light switch you've been searching for in the dark all feel about the same as awakening from a seventy-year, semicomatose state. Or so most people say. Essentially, part of you is still in the dark—the dream, the tunnel—and part of you is not. For a split second, you're in neither light nor dark, and then you're no longer where you were, but you're not quite sure where you are. And then…you know…*ya know?* And most of the time…for at least a moment, you remember, also, where you came from, what it was like before. As was the case for Our Future, a.k.a. Davis, a.k.a. homeless bum. He was all three of these people, but just a moment before, he had been none of them. Or was it some of them? He wasn't sure. And why did he leave the tunnel? Did he want to? Hadn't he been comfortable there? Isn't that why his mind had walked into that dream, that dark room, in the first place?

The answer was simple. Sarah and Davis both cared about someone or some people more than themselves. Sarah had waited decades for her nephew to be born and grow up, had grown to love him through his love for her, and then she had to watch him nearly lose himself in the same fear she had succumbed to, in order to find her way out of the darkness.

Davis's hope in finding a purpose to his life as keeper of Home Now's scroll had all but disappeared as he had watched an ice crevice swallow his people and feed them to the deep waters of the Arctic Ocean. He had been wrong to come up with the idea of leaving the tribe to find answers. This action had spawned their decision to leave with him. Perhaps if he had stayed, a way for them to rebuild and grow their numbers again would have materialized. Our Future had destroyed Home Now and its people. There was no answer. There was no reason. There was no mission. There was only sadness, loss, guilt, and emptiness. How many times had he wanted to throw away the scroll in the hopes that he would begin to age again and be able to accept the same fate as his people? But he hadn't been able to do it. He enjoyed convincing himself his inability to discard the article stemmed from his own fear, his own inadequacy to be able to do the right thing and just let himself die for the mistake he'd made. But deep down inside, he knew this wasn't the reason for his inaction. This scroll had protected them for thousands of years, and it was all that was left of them. For whatever reason it existed, Davis had misunderstood it and destroyed the tribe with his ignorance. But before he had entered their lives, the scroll had protected them, so he knew he needed to protect it. And perhaps, that was a more fitting punishment. To wander the earth, unable to die, punishing himself for his ineptitude. But the scroll had some kind of message on it too. Maybe, one day, the scroll could be interpreted or understood by someone, and Home Now's story could be told so they wouldn't disappear from the annals of humanity before they ever had a chance to be a part of it in the first place. That someone appeared to be kneeling in front of Davis right now, and that someone was holding a light switch that, oddly, looked like a scroll.

—◇○◇—

It could not be missed by any of the four of them. The man's eyes had lit up like a flashlight had been turned on from inside his skull and it was running on Energizer batteries. But not the normal batteries sold in stores; these were from a certain bunny's personal stash.

"Oh my God!" Randy burst out. "It worked!"

"He's coming around, you see?" Derek observed.

"He's done come around already, Derek," Randy cried.

The man started to smile as he looked at the scroll Jack was holding. The man lifted his right hand from where it had been resting on the sidewalk and slid it up the side of his hip, over his abdomen, and rested it on the bag draped across his chest.

"It's in there! He's got it. This is incredible." Derek couldn't believe what he was seeing.

"Let's help him up," Randy said to Derek, and he started to walk toward the newest member of their club.

Randy got to one side of the man and lightly took his arm. The man appeared to be grateful and gave it freely. Randy looked up at Derek and noticed that Derek hadn't moved.

"Come on, man. Get your hands out of your pockets and help me."

Derek looked back, shaking his head. He had the same scared look in his face Randy had seen earlier when Derek had delivered a cup of tea to Randy's lap.

"What's the problem, Derek? You seein' ghosts?"

Sarah saved the day again. "Randy, he can't. I'll explain later when we get back. Jack? Could you help Randy?"

"Sure." Jack put the scroll away and threw his bag over his shoulder. He was interested now, more than ever, to know what was going on with Derek. After Sarah spoke, Jack had noticed her hands were in her coat pockets too.

Jack went around the other side of the man and took the arm opposite Randy. They pulled together, and the man slid up the wall to a standing position. The man was dirty, and he didn't smell good either. If it had been a hot day in June instead of a crisp day in February, the smell may have been too much—enough to make the group give up their new lives as Raiders of the Lost Scrolls and leave their latest

177

cohort on the sidewalk where they'd found him. Jack thought for a moment how ironic it was that this man could be the most important archaeological find ever, and everyone around them had about as much awareness of this fact as they had about what was going on in Pago Pago.

Prophets don't descend from the skies, Jack. They rise from among us.

Yeah, I guess they do, if you believe in that sort of stuff.

But you do, Jack. You do.

While New York wasn't noticing Davis awakening from his coma of depression, *the group* didn't notice something as well. As Davis's "head light" turned on, all four of his soon-to-be new best friends heard—for a moment—a child yelling out in pain. However, not realizing the profundity of the event or that they were the only ones in New York to hear it, none of the group mentioned it, as it barely registered in their conscious thought. It was New York City and the middle of a Saturday afternoon. There were a lot of noises, and this one sounded distant. Perhaps this one had come from around the corner or from the window of an office above them. All five in the group were simultaneously aware of many sounds from second to second. They were, of course, in the same place at the same time, and, of course, this would be the case. And they were doing something important—they couldn't possibly be expected to pay attention to every little thing, especially a noise they barely knew they had heard in the first place.

Of course, the only difference with this noise was that it wasn't coming from around the corner or from a window, or even far away—sort of. Because no matter how distant it "sounded" it was actually coming from right in front of them. It was coming from the man they were helping to his feet.

—◇○◇—

"Aaaaaaaaaaaaaah! Owww!" Byron grabbed his head and then covered his eyes. The pain that hit his head as he finished reading the diary had come out of nowhere, and it felt like a headache, an earache, and a blinding light in his eyes, all at once. This is what happens when telepathy/prophet-hood-ness, or whatever, gets turned on in one's brain.

This is how the visions started. The sounds were overwhelming. Byron's quiet cabin had suddenly become taxicabs, a subway, the center of a city, only amplified by about twenty. The bright light of day hit his eyes, and he couldn't make out anything but moving blurs of grayish blue in the blinding whiteness. He rolled off the couch and onto the floor, still clutching his face, begging with what was left of his conscious mind for whatever was happening to end.

After a few moments of intense pain, he felt someone grab his arm. A moment later, his other arm was taken. He felt himself being pulled up and off the floor. The initial shock and pain began to subside as he found himself seated on the couch once

178

again.

He fell back against the couch, and his eyes rolled to the back of his head. His eyelids closed. The whiteness faded, and the blurs took shape. The sound lessened, too, and his mind returned to him. Instead of seeing the inside of his cabin on Mount Wherever, he was seeing an intersection in a big city. He saw four adults—three men and a woman—and they were helping him cross the street.

Who are these people? Where am I? Am I here? What are they doing to me?

The next moment, they weren't helping him any longer. He was seeing these people from a different angle now. It appeared they were still helping *somebody*—and, in the same way they had been helping him. A man who looked homeless was being walked down the street, each of his arms draped over the shoulders of two of the men in this group. Byron felt like he was walking next to them and then like he was watching a movie of them. He tried to look down to see his hands, but he couldn't see them. He was there, but he wasn't there. He was experiencing their environment, yet only watching it at the same time. He tried to speak to them, but they couldn't hear. And when he tried to speak, it felt unnatural, like walking across your living room but upside down and on a thread. It was unsettling, and it made him want to watch and listen rather than comment and interact.

—◇○◇—

"Hey, he's walking with us, Jack!"

"Yes, Randy, I know."

"Hey, man, we're not here to hurt you or anything," Randy told the man as they traveled back toward the Dubois home. The man's arms were draped around Jack's and Randy's shoulders. Sarah and Derek followed behind. "We're just taking you back to these folks' home where we can all get to know each other better concerning these documents. The lady behind us, we think you have a lot in common with, so don't worry, okay?"

"All right," said the man.

"Holy Shinola! Jack! You hear that? He answered me!"

"Yes, Randy, I heard."

It seemed old times were here again.

"It's not far now. Just up here." Randy nodded his head toward the building up ahead surrounded by other brownstones just like it. "You gotta name, buddy? I'm Randy, as you probably heard. Randy Haverstamp."

After a moment, still shuffling between Jack and Randy, the man turned his head to answer Randy, stagnant breath armed and loaded, and calmly uttered, "Davis. I'm Quincy Davis."

"Well, nice to meet ya there, Davis, Quincy Davis," Randy answered back, "nice to meet ya. Holy moly."

Listening, Jack had to admit again that he liked the kid—no doubt about it, he liked him. But, of course, the admission was only to himself, and…he still hated that he did.

A few minutes later, they were assembled back inside the Dubois family home. Davis had been sat down in a chair to the side of the sitting room's couch. Everyone looked back and forth at one another. The Sitting Room Sequel didn't appear to have changed much in plot. Everyone knew what they had gathered for, and everyone wanted to get to it, but no one appeared to want to be the first to bring it up, or more likely, no one knew how to bring it up. After a while, Sarah spoke first. For being as quiet as she had been for as long as she had been, she was making quite a name for herself in the talking department of their organization.

"Mr. Davis, now that we are all together and safe in my home, I think we have enough time to discover all we wish to discover from each other. I think, then, that you have plenty of time to take a nice bath and get yourself feeling a little better. I can make you some soup, and my nephew, Derek, will get you a fresh set of clothes. You all look about the same size. Then we can discuss."

Her statement about size was partly true. Jack was shorter by at least five inches compared to the other three men, and, of course, the silent, invisible eleven-year-old observer in the room was much shorter than Jack.

Davis had been coming around more and more as the brisk walk to these people's home had progressed, and although he still felt like he was waking from a really long dream, he was feeling more like himself again. More like himself—meaning, that is, the man he had been over eighty years ago—but still himself, just the same.

He hadn't talked in so very long. Rising from the chair to accept the lady's offer seemed a much easier task than speaking. As he opened his mouth to answer Sarah with "Yes, ma'am, that sounds nice," his mouth felt like it was full of yarn, and his mind was having trouble figuring out which words to put first. Eventually, and after a bit of stuttering, he got it out almost perfectly. Things were brightening up for Davis. He could feel it. And they could see it.

"Well, then, Mr. Quincy, sir, let Derek and me show you to the washroom. Derek?" Sarah turned toward the rear entrance to the sitting room with an authority General MacArthur would have followed.

Again, Davis replied as he began to move, "Yes, ma'am. Thank you, ma'am." Davis hadn't been called Quincy since the last time he'd seen his mother, in 1868. He had no idea how he felt about it.

Davis followed Derek and Sarah out of the room. Jack and Randy watched as the others left them alone. Jack spoke. "Well, I think he might be our man, Randy."

"Yeah?" Randy inquired.

"Well, he's sure got 1800s manners," Jack replied.

"Yes, sir, he does." Randy chuckled and rolled his eyes at his own joke and the absurdity of everything.

—◇○◇—

Byron sat erect on the couch, his eyes wide open, jaw hanging. He shook his head as he became aware of his cabin surroundings again. "Whoa!" he said out loud and to no one.

Any prophet will tell you that the first out-of-body experience is the worst. And for the most part, they're telling the truth. What they mean is, getting your head wrapped around the experience, going through it with no previous frame of reference, and then trying to figure out what to do with it and understand it—that's the unsettling part. Asking yourself if it really happened, if you're crazy, if it was just a dream, did you eat some bad spinach...grappling with your own sanity...these are all very difficult things. What they don't mean by "the first one is always the worst" is that later experiences are somehow, better, *easier.* No, the experience just becomes familiar. One can get used to getting on a horse, but if the horse keeps bucking you off, you don't start to enjoy it. Byron had a lot of places left to go with eyes rolled up in the back of his head, his butt sitting on the couch—and those places were going to be a lot more harrowing than some nice lady's living room or the streets of New York. Lucky for him, he didn't know this yet. One kind of needs to get used to riding, even start to like it a bit before being thrown onto a bronco. And whoever was doing this to Byron knew that too.

Standing up from the couch, he started pacing the cabin, a new pastime of his. He asked questions to himself and received silence in answer. In the days and months ahead, these questions would continue to pass by without being answered, and then new questions would replace older ones. He wouldn't have a lot of time to think up answers, anyway, as his life was about to become very limited in the realm of variety. There would be sleeping, and there would be viewing. "Viewing" is the name he would eventually give the experience he had just had. Of course, there would be eating, firewood gathering, and hunting as the canned food ran out and the winters came and went. And there would be a lot of writing. Any questions or concerns left haunting him after these activities would surface only as doodles, side margin scribbles, and footnotes in a stack of notebooks he would slowly start filling. Currently, they were sitting on the floor beside the desk in his cabin, and they contained nothing at all.

—◇○◇—

Chicken. Egg. Who knows, right? *Age-old question.*

After a week or so of these *viewings,* Byron had decided to start writing the experiences down. Did he do this because he felt obligated to capture the lives of the people he was witnessing, especially as things got progressively stranger and out of hand for all of them? Or had he been influenced by the stack of empty notebooks, along with their accompanying boxes of pens and pencils, which had all been staring him down since first he had arrived at the cabin? This stationery, of course, was only there because Byron, as an older man, had apparently appeared and told the dead man buried outside his cabin, the man who had already been dead when Byron arrived at the cabin, to buy the stationery for him when he visited the old man in the past, which...*ha!*...Byron would apparently be able to do sometime in the future?

Who knows? Who cares? Right? Shoot...would Byron have thought to bring back the picture he had found outside the cabin to the old man if he hadn't read that it had been so darn important to the man in his diary that Byron had brought it back? *Who knows? Who cares?* It happened. Deal with it.

For whatever reason or motivation, Byron did start writing his *viewings* down. He tried to be as detailed as possible, but as he aged and matured through natural processes and living vicariously through so many lives, his writing and attention to detail improved even more. As time went on and the *viewings* increased, he found he was not seeing everything in the order in which the events happened. Writing helped him keep it straight in his mind. He was jumping into different lives, different continents, even different eras. As he returned to the same places repeatedly, apparently to gain information from different perspectives, the bigger picture started to unfold to him.

Byron began taking time to diagram his notebooks, correlating them to each other with a number system he developed. Actually, he didn't completely develop it on his own. He had a little help from himself. Soon after he began documenting his *viewings*, Byron even experienced viewings of *himself*—in his cabin in the future. He learned to hunt, diagram his notebooks, and even how to shave, all from future Byron. As the years went on, shaving became the least useful skill he learned. Chicken. Egg. Chicken. *Age-old question.*

And just another question without an answer.

Jack and Randy were sitting quietly in the sitting room after Derek and Sarah had left with the newly found Scroll Holder. Jack was beginning to lay out their scrolls and set up his translation office on the coffee table again when Randy stood up and raised his hands to the sky.

"Who the hell wrote these things, Jack? I mean, is this really happening?" He was speaking to Jack but really wanting the answers to come from God or the universe, or something benevolent.

"I don't know, Randy. Pinch me or something and see."

Randy leaned over the table and reached out his fingers toward Jack's arm. Jack looked at what Randy was doing and slapped his hand away.

"Ouch, Jack. That hurt!"

"What the hell are you doing, Randy?"

"I was going to *pinch* you! You told me to, and I sure as shit wanted to test it out."

"Randy, we're not sleeping. I think I wish we were, but we're not." Jack shook his head and began to rub his eyes. "I really didn't think you puking out the Prime Number Spreadsheet Manifesto on Wednesday night was going to land us where we are right now."

"Well, me neither. Should've kept my mouth shut. Do you realize we just found some ancient document with our names in it? And then it led us straight to some bum in the middle of New York City who had a scroll just like it? Huh? Jack? Do you *realize that?*"

"Of course I do, Randy. It happened to me too." Jack sighed. Jack's next thought wandered to whether or not he should speak of their hosts while they were out of the room. He decided to risk it. "Randy? You notice anything...I don't know...funny about Derek and Sarah? I mean, nothing bad—I see you've kind of got the eye for Sarah, and she's a pretty thing, don't get me wrong—but I'm just curious. You notice anything, anything at all?"

Randy developed a concerned look on his face, his eyes zeroing in on Jack's. Jack wasn't sure if Randy was about to get upset in an attempt to defend Sarah's honor, or if he was just thinking about the question. Randy broke his stare and looked back toward the exit through which the other three had just left.

Randy whispered, "You mean about how all of a sudden they won't take their hands out of their pockets?"

"Yeah, exactly. I'm glad I'm not the only one who noticed it," Jack replied quietly.

"What do *you* think's going on?"

"I don't know. They weren't doing it when we met them. When did it start? Do you remember?"

"Not sure, Jack." Randy thought for a moment, rewinding the last hour or two in his mind. He began talking, mostly to himself. "Well, I definitely noticed when he wouldn't help you with that Davis guy."

"Yeah, I know," Jack answered, "but there's something else. I can't put my finger on it."

"Wait!" Randy whispered excitedly. "The only other strange thing that's happened today, well besides every frickin' damned thing that's happened today, was that look on Derek's face when he spilled the tea on me. I don't think I've seen him move his arms since then."

"You're right. I saw that, but then Sarah came in the room with the scrolls, and things got normal again," Jack agreed. "But that look wasn't fear that he was burning you, it was coming from somewhere entirely diff—"

Sarah and Derek entered the sitting room again. Sarah didn't have her hands in her pockets anymore, but Derek unmistakably did.

"So, gentlemen, what were you talking about?" Sarah asked. "It sounded pretty serious. Is it something about the scrolls, or perhaps our friend upstairs?" It took one look into her eyes to know she had noticed Jack's and Randy's hushed tones. Her eyes would have made Randy confess to murdering his own parents if he'd done so.

"I'm sorry, Sarah. This is just a pretty crazy day. I think we are all a little on edge about what this is all about. Jack and I, well, we—"

"Miss Sarah, what Randy is trying to get out is this. I think whatever we have all discovered here is possibly really big. Really *real.* I believe we are all good people here. Even that character upstairs seems like a decent enough man. I think if we are going to proceed together, then we need to trust one another. And be honest with each other. Don't you agree?"

Sarah and Derek stared at Jack. Derek looked at Sarah. The look of "Yes, we've got something to say" on Sarah's face was unmistakable to Jack and Randy. It was Derek, however, who spoke.

"I did it," Derek said, almost sounding panicked. "I'm so sorry."

"What, Derek? What'd you do?" Jack asked back.

"You want to know why I've got my hands in my pockets, right?"

"Well, yes, that's sort of what we were getting at," Jack said, amazed his inquiry had produced such quick results.

Randy followed up with, "Yeah, that's it, your hands. And yours, too, Sarah…sorry." This quick apology appended to Randy's accusation came freshly squeezed right out of his heart and proved that although Randy might not know the definition of the word "meek," he could darn well embody it.

"No, that's okay, Randy." Sarah was consoling. "I agree with Jack. I think we do need to be able to trust one another if we are going to finish translating those scrolls together."

Derek was still noticeably upset. He was sweating and had a look of regret, even the look of what was appearing to Jack and Randy as guilt forming on his face. "Your brother, Jack. I don't really know what happened. I was reaching for my manuscript after he told me he didn't like it, and I don't know. As I put my hand toward him, he just…oh God, he just…" Derek broke down.

"Just what, Derek?" Jack led, trying to get Derek to finish.

Derek was sobbing by this point. Any other person in his situation might have had his hands up to his face, crying into them, but Derek's were still firmly planted in his pockets, which made the scene look even odder than it felt. What Derek said next ran up the odd meter more. "He just…turned to dust. A pile of dust! I didn't know what to do. I just grabbed my book and ran out of there. And I know it was me,

184

because it happened again when I was on the subway and again coming out of the subway. Two more people just disintegrated in front of me when I put my hand toward them."

"Oh my God!" Jack fell back on the couch. "Jon's dead!"

"Yes. I'm so sorry," Derek responded, still standing and still weeping.

Jack didn't know what to feel. It was a shock, to say the least. He didn't know what he was expecting Sarah and Derek to come clean about, but he hadn't remotely considered it would have anything to do with announcing his brother was dead and that one of them was responsible for it. Jon and he hadn't been super close, mainly because Jon was a pretty distant type of fellow who didn't put a lot of effort into familial relationships, but he was still Jack's brother.

Jack stayed silent for another minute, and his reflections were broken when Derek couldn't take the silence anymore and spoke again. "I'm really sorry, Mr. Johanssen," Derek pleaded. "Really."

"No, no, Derek, that's okay." Jack couldn't believe he was consoling Derek. "I mean, obviously you didn't mean to do it."

"No, of course not!"

"I know, I know," Jack repeated, "but it's still hard news to hear. I thought you were going to tell us you were both lepers or something. Not that Jon's dead. God."

Randy broke in to try and give Jack another minute. "So that's why you spilled the tea on me, right?"

"Yes, Randy," Sarah answered, trying to give Derek a minute also. "He told me about it. Both of us had forgotten about this"—she paused—"this power...or whatever it is...when you arrived out of the blue today. That was the first time he was putting his hand out toward either one of you, and then he remembered. That's why he jerked."

"But, Sarah, you don't have your hands stuffed in your pockets, so what do you mean by 'both of us'?" Randy asked.

"I'm not sure, really. Maybe I should. But I think it doesn't happen to everybody. When I came into the room, my hands were all over your shirt and out toward Jack sitting next to you. I didn't even think about it until later. But both of you are still here, so I figure you're both safe around me. I guess Derek doesn't want to take the risk that you're also safe around him."

"Well, thank you, Derek." Randy gulped. "I think I'd rather not be dust today, or a guinea pig."

"So you're not upset with me, Jack?" Derek asked wearily.

"No, Derek, I'm not. It's hard. Jon and I weren't like super brothers, but he was my brother, you know. It's not easy news. But what I am worried about is what exactly is going on here. Up to now, as far as Randy and I knew, if there was any funny business with these scrolls that reached outside of what is the 'normal and explainable,' it hadn't taken the shape of danger yet. In fact, one of the few lines I translated that made any sense was the statement to Randy and I that we didn't need to worry. I don't know. What you're both telling me now is that maybe we didn't have to worry about our faces melting off, but there still may be cause for *some* worry, after all."

"Oh, I hope not," Sarah replied. "I think we've all been through so much already. Perhaps we should just put them away and forget all about them."

Jack thought about her idea. It seemed attractive. But was it feasible? Was it even *possible?* He wasn't much into fate and destiny, but he had a strange feeling they might have already passed some point of no return concerning fate and destiny.

"Miss Sarah, that sounds great," Jack said, "But I think you know it's not possible. This isn't just about curiosity. I don't think we're just a bunch of cats sitting around, waiting to be killed. You've got a nephew there that looks damned scared at what's happening to him. So scared, I wonder if he'll ever want to be near strangers again without his hands in hiding. I think he deserves to try and understand what the hell all this is about. And then there's the man upstairs. You saw his face when he saw our scroll. It was like seeing—physically—the very definition of hope. I don't know what he's been through, but I think a man just came back from the Phantom Zone and only because he wants to know what the purpose of these things are. Shoot, my brother's dead. I guess I'd like to know why myself. And you, Sarah, I don't think you care so little about why you've outlived everyone you ever loved sitting alone in a mental institution in Egypt for fifty years. I think too much has happened to all of us here to even consider what you're proposing. I don't mean to sound derogatory. I think your idea is coming from the heart and a desire to put this all behind you and go on and try and find some normalness in your lives again. I just don't think it's necessarily going to be possible to care that little, at least until we know what's written in these scrolls. Do *you?*"

Sure talking a lot for a misanthropic recluse, Jack. What's up? Did you take a "No really, I'm a leader" pill, this morning?

Listening to this, Sarah realized hiding from what was locked inside the coded messages of the scrolls was not going to make anything better in their lives. She had taken the biggest risk of her life to save Derek the day before, and now it was time to take another one.

"No, you're right, Mr. Johanssen—I mean, Jack. I do not care so little."

⎯◇○◇⎯

"I thank you much for the clothes, ma'am. They fit perfectly."

Quincy Davis/Our Future had entered the room showered, shaved, and smelling of Old Spice. He was wearing brown slacks and a white collared shirt. With the brown shoes and dark-blue tie finishing the touches on his reformation, no one outside of the little sitting room would have been able to tell he had been a bum on the streets of New York City not an hour before. And he had come to the room prepared, remembering to bring the one mandatory relic required of guests at this particular gathering.

"I think you folks will be wanting this, correct?" And Davis held out his party favor.

⎯⬦○⬦⎯

"Mr. Davis! Oh, you look so nice," Sarah said, turning to greet him and simultaneously pushing her hands into her dress pockets. Davis didn't notice her hands disappearing or the tinge of jealousy that flickered across Randy's face after she spoke.

Davis was an attractive man, slender and over six feet tall. His hair was long from his time on the streets, but he had combed it back, and it was still partially wet, so it didn't look as long as it was. He had a nice smile, and although sadness still hummed deep in his eyes, he appeared to be about the brightest soul in the room at the moment. A gleam shone in the forefront of his eyes, and it was one of hope, like Jack had mentioned. Perhaps Davis was the hope they all needed for a better future.

Davis was still awkwardly holding out his scroll, and Randy knew quite well Sarah and Derek weren't going to take it from him, so he stood up and crossed over to Davis.

"Thank you. Quincy, was it?" Randy asked as he took the man's offering.

Davis thought for a moment at the question. *An old name, yes, but it felt new, and this was a new start…a fresh start. With new friends.* A new name for a new start. "Yes, Quincy! At your service. And you are Randy, correct?"

"Yes, and Jack there is on the couch. And you know Sarah and Derek Dubois."

"Yes," Davis agreed and redirected the conversation back to the scroll. "So, it's in Russian. I showed it to a Russian. He said it was gibberish. Not one Russian word."

"Yes, Quincy," Jack responded from the couch, "we know. It's a bit more complicated than that. I'll explain later, but I have managed to understand how to translate it."

"Unbelievable." Davis stood, bewildered to hear the statement he'd given up long ago at ever hearing. "Well, there's mine too." He nodded at Randy. "Please, do your magic."

Jack received the scroll from Randy. Jack unrolled it and placed it on the table in front of him in the space he had made for it between the other scrolls. Space number three. Jack noticed right away there was something different about Quincy's scroll. At the bottom, there appeared to be two lines, centered and separate, from the passage above, unlike the single line on the other three. Right away, he could tell that the first line, which consisted of a three-letter word, was the word "and," as he had

187

previously assumed it would be, thus completing the location they had found Quincy at. *Twenty-First Street and Sixth.* But the second line was longer and looked like a sentence, except for the last three letters, which were spaced out and single. Jack guessed at what those might be and hoped his guess was right.

It was.

Getting to his task, he translated the line with the help of his computer. Jack read the translation out loud, *"Jack, I know you need the initial setting for a three-rotor Enigma to complete the bulk of the translation. It's J O N."*

"Holy," Jack said moving his head back and forth slowly like it was running on a pendulum gear assembly. "Randy. This is it. It's the real deal, and it's what we needed." Jack sounded like he'd been hit by a train and lived.

"What do you mean?" Sarah asked.

"Well, we weren't entirely forthcoming with information either. To be honest, I was never able to translate the entire middle section of our scroll. However, the part that I did translate led us to you, who I believed had a scroll like ours. I didn't expect two, but regardless, I had a hunch that locating another may help in further translation. My hunch has paid off."

"You mean you might have gone through all of this and we might not have known anything more?" Sarah asked. "That was a pretty big gamble you took with our emotions, Mr. Johanssen." It seemed for the moment that shock had removed the first-name basis between her and the translator.

"I know, and I'm sorry. And I'm not throwing stones, but it appears you both may have taken a little risk with our bodies? So let's call it even? Quincy's scroll gave me the code I need to translate everything. I say let's get on with it."

Jack was looking up at Sarah and Derek waiting for some sort of approval, acceptance, forgiveness—whatever it took to make them all one big happy family again. He figured they'd be spending a lot of time together after today.

You're on a roll, Jack. On being right, that is.

—◇○◇—

Jack worked for the better part of the evening transcribing all the Russian letters to English ones, so they could next be decoded on the Enigma with the setting J O N. Excited and dedicated as he was, he eventually gave way to sleep, on the couch, head back. The others had done the same, one by one drifting off as Jack worked. They all had equal desire to know the outcome of Jack's efforts, but the day's events had taken their toll replacing zeal with *z*'s.

The next morning, the group easily forgave Jack via mutual guilt for having not completed his task the night before. Sarah cooked a nice breakfast. Waking up in the morning together and eating breakfast made them feel like a family, and they acted like one. The five of them laughed and joked about experiences from the day before and almost seemed to be able to ignore the strange and negative circumstances that had brought them together in the first place. A break from the strange was what everyone needed, and Sarah's breakfast had seemed to do the trick.

Derek sat directly across from his aunt, careful not to put his hands in the direction of anyone else at the table. Sarah was equally cautious in regard to Quincy, since she considered herself lucky she hadn't killed Randy or Jack. She began to think…of any others in her family during her long time inside the Dubois family home, or anyone in the institution in Cairo, or anyone that she could remember for the months she wandered Cairo after her night in the tomb with Gerard. Sarah's mind drifted further away from the breakfast as she once again considered a thought she'd had a few days earlier.

He was happy with me, not fearful. He gave them to me; I didn't take them. He was ready to go. I didn't kill him. Gerard was bad—I gave that old man a moment of peace before he died, not terror.

She thought harder about the moment, trying not to wince at the memory while she sat at the table with the others.

I was on my knees, and he held them out for me, and then I reached and took them. Then what happened? He smiled. Right. And then what? He fell backward. And then? Wait, he fell backward and then turned to dust! Is there more?

Her mind was tugging at her memory. Had she been confused by the years and the horror and the guilt and even by Derek's experience?

Wait. I touched him. I tried to help him up. I held his hands! He didn't die or disintegrate or anything because of me!

"Oh my," Sarah gasped.

Derek responded, followed by Randy. "What is it?" They both asked, a moment out of step with each other.

"Derek, I don't think I'm like you. Or did what you did, or can do it. The man in the tomb. I remember. I'm not responsible for him turning to dust. I know that now."

"What man in the tomb, ma'am?" the newly named Quincy inquired—*Name number three, scroll number three. Why not?*—and put a bite of some *really* good eggs into his mouth.

"I was in a tomb, in 1876, in the Sacred City of Abydos, when I acquired my scrolls. They were given to me by a very old man. After I took them, he died. But not just a normal death. He fell back…into nothing. Or became nothing, rather. Only dust."

"Ashes to ashes," Quincy replied.

"Yes," Sarah answered.

Still chewing and placing new bites of these fine eggs in his mouth, Quincy continued, "Eighteen seventy-six, you say?"

"Yes."

"Interesting," Quincy said, with yet another bite. He was careful to raise his hand in front of his mouth as he spoke. He wanted to follow good manners in the lady's presence, but he couldn't remember the last time he'd tasted a meal so much like the home he'd grown up in. "That's the year I got my scroll, and the same thing happened to me. Always Here was his name. He had been with this tribe of Eskimos for centuries. When I arrived, he looked like the oldest man in history. He handed me his scroll and disintegrated into dust, just like you described. It was the strangest thing I ever saw. I guess I started to think of it as, not so abnormal, after several years went by and it was clear I wasn't aging in just the same way the tribe had described the life of Always Here. I sometimes wondered if that'd be my end, too, one day."

"This is too crazy. Jack?" Randy blurted out. If Sarah was going to fall for Randy, it wouldn't be for his cool-cat charisma; it would be for his boyish charm. "You gotta finish your task in there." Randy pointed to the sitting room. "These two have lived like completely parallel lives! Why are we different? Why does *she* have *two* scrolls? You think the answers are in there, Jack?" He pointed and pointed again in the direction of the scary acquired relics.

"I don't know, Randy," Jack responded. "I guess they'll tell us everything, or they'll tell us what's important, or they'll tell us nothing at all. I'm banking on the middle one, though. I assume if your questions are important to our purpose in all of this, then they'll probably be answered. Let's finish Miss Sarah's nice breakfast, and I'll get back to work with a full stomach and a clear head."

Jack had none of the answers yet seemed to articulate the answers needed when required. Jack's answer had allowed them all to continue eating and talking trivialities, feeling as normal as they could for a while, each doing their best to ignore the red herring of their common experience. Derek had a few thoughts of worry creep into his mind concerning this power of his, which he seemed to be the only one possessing. He was selfishly hoping, most of all, the scrolls would have some answers for him.

"You're all not going to like this one bit. I don't like it one bit either."

"What aren't we going to like, Jack?" Sarah asked this as she entered the room where Jack had been seated for the better part of the morning and early afternoon.

Randy had been sleeping in the chair across from Jack, passed out from the early rise, Sarah's food, and the uneventfulness of Jack's silent efforts at his computer. Derek had paced awhile in the sitting room after breakfast and then left Jack alone to go take a nap as well. Davis, now called Quincy, had been sitting in the kitchen talking with Sarah, each of them explaining their lives and stories to each other. He had offered to help her clean up the breakfast dishes and to cook the late lunch she was preparing, but she wouldn't have it. "Just sit down and go on with your story, Quincy.

It's fascinating; keep going" she would urge when he'd try to be helpful, causing him to break from his tale of Hacker and Home Now.

"Randy, wake up." Sarah nudged Randy's shoulder, and he jolted.

"What? Huh?"

"Randy, go upstairs and get Derek. Jack's done, it appears."

Davis had followed her out of the kitchen and was leaning against the back wall.

"You finished the translation, sir?" Quincy asked Jack.

"Quincy. Call me Jack, please. I don't think I've ever been called sir, and I don't think I'll start now. And if these things are telling the truth, I don't think I want to be a *sir.*"

"I'm sorry. Old habit, it seems," Quincy replied. "Even though I spoke another language to the people on the ice for fifty years, I guess the tree grows how the twig's bent?"

"Yes, it probably does, Quincy. I'm sorry, too, for jumping on you. I just think we ought to all be friends and keep it on a first-name basis starting right now."

By this time, the footsteps of Randy and Derek could be heard racing down the stairs. Everyone in the sitting room waited for them to enter. They entered as if the hallway had given birth to twins, with one final hell of a push.

"Well?" Derek asked quickly, and sitting down, looking very childlike with his hands still shoved in their places—place one and place two.

"Well, first of all, the only good news I've got is for Derek," Jack announced to the room. His gaze settled on Derek, and he continued. "I think you can take your hands out of your pockets."

"Because?" Derek inquired further.

"Because Simon says," Jack said. "Because these things told me you could, and I wouldn't risk myself turning to dust if I didn't believe them."

"What about me, Jack?" Randy burst in.

"You don't have your hands in your pockets, Randy."

"No, Jack, I mean what about the risking," Randy scoffed.

"You're fine, too, Randy. I wouldn't risk you either, *usually.*" Jack turned to Quincy. "You, too. We'll all be okay."

"Before I do anything, what does it say first?" Derek begged.

"Yes, Jack, read it first," Randy agreed. "And did you mean you only have *bad* news for the rest of us?"

"All right, both of you," Jack answered. "I can see there's no good way to begin, so I think I should just start at the beginning. But for you to get some relief, Derek, let me start with you, now that I think about it. I don't know; my head's spinning. And all of yours are going to be soon. Not sure if that makes me feel better or not."

"Thanks," Derek replied, having heard nothing after Jack said he'd tell him more.

Jack began. "It appears there's a little bit more to this world than we thought.

And"—Jack paused and looked out the window facing the street, creating suspense in the moment although he hadn't intended to do so—"a little less."

"What do you mean?" Randy asked.

"It appears that not everyone is really a person."

"What does *that* mean?" Derek prodded for more.

"Well, take my brother, Jon, for instance. It's hard to admit, but considering what you were able to do to him, he was just filler."

"Filler?" everyone else asked.

"Yeah, according to these documents, there are people such as Derek here who will gain the ability to discern between complete human beings with souls and the rest of the walking bodies, which just fill up space and make the world what it is. Full of people, operating, and crowded."

"That's absurd!" Sarah responded.

"Perhaps. But no more absurd than your nephew can turn others to dust just by pointing at them, or that you and Quincy are over a hundred and fifty years old."

Silence filled the room. If Jack had ever been a stage actor, he would have been experienced with the power to push an entire audience's emotions one way or the other with each line delivered, and how remarkably similar that felt to his current experience in the sitting room of the Dubois home.

He continued his monologue. "The scrolls also say that everyone in this room are real people, which makes sense to me since we all seem to be connected to their discovery. So, like I said, Derek…"

"Okay, okay," Derek answered. "If you really think it's all right."

Derek took a moment to breathe in deep. He closed his eyes and slowly pulled his hands out of his pockets. Opening his eyes, Derek looked around the room. The worry on his face was not fading.

"Point them at me." Jack requested. "Somebody's got to give you some peace."

Derek hesitated another moment and then slowly raised his hands in the direction of Jack. Nothing happened.

"I trust Jack," Randy followed. "Point 'em over this way."

Derek took Randy's instructions and proved a second time either Jack was correct, or Derek had lost whatever gift or curse he'd acquired.

"I guess that makes me number three," Quincy said from the kitchen chair he'd carried in and placed at the far end of the coffee table. "Do it. Zap me."

"Ha, ha. Funny," Derek replied, his heart still racing from the two previous trials. "I still feel like I'm playing Russian roulette with friends and the phaser's set to vaporize."

As he raised his arms toward Quincy, Randy yelled, "Noooooo!" and Derek almost fell backward as he recoiled his arms. "Sorry," Randy said, "couldn't resist."

Derek steadied himself; with it being clear that Quincy was going to remain among those who are solid, everyone in the room started laughing. Randy's practical joke was breakfast part two and a second gift to the group to feel normal again. As they were laughing, Derek was letting some pressure out of the barrel, himself, by throwing his hands at each of them like a magician and saying "Pow! Bam!" and producing more laughs as the recipients of his gestures pretended to poof themselves into oblivion to assist Derek in his stress flush. Even Jack had forgotten, for the moment, about his brother in his happiness for Derek's revelation.

"I don't know how I feel about knowing about this 'filler' idea, but I'm happy you're all safe around me, and that I guess I haven't really killed anyone of real human makeup. Did I just say that?"

"I'm with you, Derek, and sadly that is about the best news any of us are getting today, I think," Jack prompted.

"I'm still sorry about Jon," Derek said.

"Thanks, but a lot makes sense, now, somehow, concerning Jon and me. I don't know if a normal reaction is to feel better or worse, but I do feel better."

"What is coming next?" Randy intruded. "What do those things *say?*"

Jack eyeballed Randy. "Oh, I don't know, Randy, your typical ancient scroll banter, end of the world, Armageddon, apocalypse, Stay Puft Marshmallow Men, and 'welcome to the first day of the rest of your life'—what's left of it, that is."

"Oh great!" Randy balked. "I thought it was going to be something remotely interesting. Now you're saying it's just your run-of-the-mill prophecy of the end of time. That's all it says?"

"Well, I'd agree with you, Randy, except for one point you seem to be overlooking."

"Yeah, what's that?"

"Well, two points," Jack said, correcting himself. "The first, you can't help but overlook, because I haven't said everything that's in the scroll. But the second should be a little obvious to you."

"Well, it isn't, Jack, so fill me in before I just grab your computer and start reading myself."

"Randy," Jack said, "just two days ago you said you didn't want them to say anything about any apocalypse. Now, you're like, 'That's all it says?'"

"Well, Jack," Randy replied, "I guess now that you're saying that's what they say, it just feels less real—more made up."

As the sentence escaped Randy's lips, Quincy and Sarah turned their heads in unison to face Randy. Sarah was seated on Randy's right, and Quincy was on his left, and Randy didn't feel the heat of their bidirectional stares at first. Eventually, he noticed Sarah's and then turned to find Quincy looking at him from the other side.

A shudder ran up his spine.

"But it is real, isn't it?" Randy gulped, and his eyes returned to Jack again seated behind his laptop and across the coffee table. "These two prove it." He waved his thumb back and forth to Sarah and Quincy.

"The end of the world," Jack reported, "is a punchline. It's the end of a joke or the plot of every blockbuster due out next summer in theaters. Or there's always some new group declaring it's just around the corner—a corner that turns out to be more of a roundabout going nowhere or a path to mass suicide—anything but the actual end of the world."

Jack stopped speaking, sounding in his inflection like he would say more, but he didn't. As the group waited, something opposite in nature to his odd comments began to resonate inside of them in a place no one ever likes to go. The place in your mind that creeps up on you sometimes, saying, *There's more to this than you think* or *Damn, don't you find life's a little too coincidental?* or *Remember, there are no atheists in foxholes.* This group didn't have the luxury of responding the way most do to these kinds of thoughts—that is, with, *Honey, can you pass me the remote?* or *Yeah, I'd like the number seven super-sized, please* and then going about the rest of their day.

The feeling they were feeling was elongated, stretched out, enveloping, and this made them *really* experience what they were feeling. It would have been the perfect time for Jesus to appear before them walking on water and explaining how they had just won some fabulous door prizes for realizing the world is more than it seems— and at this point, they would have believed what they were seeing had that happened.

Jack continued. "I joked, Randy, when I answered you about their contents because it very well may be the last joke we ever get to make concerning the subject. I don't think any of us have given any real thought to what the scrolls might *say* because we were all too busy waiting to see what they said."

Sarah looked up with her sweet eyes and calmly broke the rising fear eating away at everyone's sanity. "Jack, dear? What *do* they say? All of it, please? It's time."

"All right, Sarah." Jack took a deep breath and held it for a moment, letting it out by slowly pursing his lips together as he did. He chuckled to himself slightly. "Heh…here goes."

CHAPTER 27

THE FOUR SCROLLS
FEBRUARY 4, 2007, LATER

"**O**KAY, as you know, there's four of them. My original guess of the order was correct. Randy and I discovered the fourth. Sarah, you had the first and second, and Quincy, yours *is* number three.

"I had been able to translate a few lines at the top and bottom of ours, and would have been able to do the same on yours, Sarah, except for I jumped to the bottom quickly, as you know, which then led us on our leap of faith to find Quincy there."

"Thanks again, Jack," Quincy interrupted.

"You're welcome, *sir.*" Jack fired this Davis's way in his never-ending partially conscious endeavor to keep things light. "All right, anyways. Quincy's had what I needed. There were a couple sentences at the bottom, which gave me a key setting for the Enigma, allowing me to decode the remaining bulk of the scrolls. It mentioned my name and told me the codebreaker was my brother's name. J-O-N, Jon."

"Unbelievable," Derek muttered under his breath.

"Yeah, it would have been, except for Randy and I had already experienced our personalized message three days ago. I guess I was a little more prepared after that. It's still crazy to me, however, to think that *this* one," Jack pointed down to Davis's scroll unrolled on the table, "was in *his* possession"—and he motioned his hand toward Davis—"for over a hundred years, some of that in the Arctic, and ours was filed at my work for the same amount of time, and all that while they had my name written on them. It'll take a while for this to sink in. I'm still getting over everything else that's sinking in."

"Continue," Randy pushed.

Come on, Jack. Jack was feeling the push from everyone.

"Okay, so I used the code, and it worked. Of course it did, or we'd still be at square one. Anyway, each scroll has a header or a title of some sort. Each one relates to a particular idea, or what the scrolls call 'myths' that humanity will be faced with. Going in order here, we've got the Myth of Man, the Myth of Monsters, the Myth of the Here, and the Myth of the—"

"Hereafter!" Randy exploded, performing a nice one-eighty from *Armageddon's* frightened Buscemi to *Bring It On's* entire cheerleader squad. "I remember reading that, Jack! I asked you what it meant, *remember?*"

Jack looked at Randy, giving him the "Can I continue, please?" look.

"Sorry, Jack, keep going," Randy muttered, silenced by Jack's look. Sarah smiled at Randy. Randy smiled at Sarah. Their mutual attention quickly returned to Jack, however, when Jack started speaking again.

"Yes, that's right, Randy. You did see that. I had translated that part. Also, if you remember, at the very top there was a small phrase. It reads, '*And the Fourth being The Horsemen.*' Well, the other three say, '*The tribe of Caleb,*' '*The Kingdom of Anubis,*' and '*The people of the Malamute.*'"

"Wait a second," Derek said.

"Looks like you picked up on it, huh?" Jack responded, looking above his glasses.

"Picked up on what?" Randy asked.

"Come on, Randy, you figured out the whole numbers thing the first night. *Think* about it?" Jack prodded.

"I don't know," Randy whined.

Derek made his attempt. "It sounds to me, Jack, like its talking about three dogs and a horseman. If that's not referring to the end of time, then I don't know what does."

"Right," Jack said. "But if you recall, that's not exactly the sign from Revelation, which I think you're pulling from. Yes, there's the *three-headed* dog, Cerberus, that guards the gates of hell, but that's actually Greek legend—not biblical, *but* it is the Four Horsemen of the Apocalypse that are a symbol of the end of days in the Bible."

Derek nodded, agreeing with Jack. "Right, you're right."

Randy was still hung up on the subject. "Where do you get the three-headed dog from?" Randy inquired.

Jack ignored him for the moment and continued with Derek. "It's actually ironic that you picked up on it the way you did, by mixing and matching the traditions. It appears that's exactly what these scrolls are all about—human myths and how they will play a part in our own destruction."

Sarah gasped. "It says we will be destroyed? All of us?"

"Not exactly, but as Sam Cooke said, 'It's been a long time coming, but *a change is gonna come.*'"

"It's been too hard living, but I'm afraid to die," Derek added. "I think I relate. So Jack, you really think this is all for *real?*"

"I *think* you know that even better than me, Derek, though I appreciate the effort to disbelieve. That's me about every two minutes," Jack replied. This statement forced Derek to lower his eyes to the ground and shake his head in disbelief. He then began nodding in acceptance, a posture becoming quite common to their little group.

"Who's Sam Cooke?" Quincy asked.

"Where are the three dogs?" Randy asked.

"What else does it say, Jack? *Please,*" Sarah asked.

"Quincy, you first. Sam Cooke is a twentieth-century African American singer. He sang a song, among many, called 'A Change Is Gonna Come.' It was a song related to the struggle for civil rights for black people in this country that was still continuing well into the 1960s, which is when he sang that song." Jack then looked at Randy. "Randy, *Caleb* comes from the word *kelb,* which means *dog* in Hebrew. Anubis was the Egyptian God with the head of a jackal, and a malamute is an arctic dog breed possibly used by the Inuit people who live above the Arctic Circle—people like the ones Quincy was with when he got their scroll. We used to call them Eskimos."

"Now to Sarah's question, which was 'What else do they say?' I believe I can safely say, hers is the question we all care most about. Am I correct?"

"Yes…" Randy trailed off, not sure if he had just been informed or scolded.

"Uh, Jack?" It was Quincy stopping the progress this time. "I don't know if this means anything, but Hacker and me were using malamutes on our trip up north. Upon arriving at Home Now with the three remaining sled dogs, the people of Home Now took them in. I remember our dogs were distinctly different from theirs. That means their scroll saying they were 'the people of the Malamute' was with them a long time before they got any malamutes."

"Well I guess that would be proof number forty-two in this thing," Jack retorted. "I think I'm just going to start reading, if that's okay with everybody?"

Everyone nodded in unison, and Jack began to read.

"Scroll number one. This is yours, Sarah, or one of them."

The Tribe of Caleb,

The Myth of Man

This is the first of four scrolls. If you are reading this, Jack, it is because you have found all four. I knew you would, but good job anyhow. Humanity is on the brink of a new chapter in its existence, and this scroll will help explain what you are all about to witness. Throughout the Eons, beliefs have been created, plagiarized, misused, and distorted. Sometimes they have been used for good, many times for bad. Beliefs are what lie within the spiritual side of the human being, but just because the human being has a spiritual side does not mean their spirit is good. It may be full of light, like your new friend Sarah, sitting there, or it may be black and cold. Many people suffer from the worst kind of belief, the myth that they are better than others. Whether it be their bloodline, their race, the shade of their skin, or the knowledge they possess, they look down on those who are not of their kind or as gifted as they are. Of course, every human being has moments of this kind of foolishness, but some are consumed by it. Some do more than feel this pride from time to time due to human imperfection, and, instead, they act upon it, hurting others, or conspiring to hurt others. These are the worst kind of people. The myth that one kind of man is better than another kind of man or that vanity has any place being in a human will soon take shape in a very real way on this earth. Those who are plagued with these misguided beliefs will slowly decay into various degrees of hideousness. They will be ashamed of themselves. They will be shunned by most, and they will feel the torment and shame they have inflicted on others. Perhaps they will learn, but most will probably not.

Twenty-First

"*Okay?*" Randy asked. "So, what's that supposed to mean? I thought everything was explained. Whoever wrote it seems to like you, though, Sarah."

"Randy, your jealousy will have to wait," Jack responded. "We still have three more to go. And I think they'll help."

"Okay, then. Go on, go on."

"I think I will," Jack answered.

"Number two of Sarah's."

The Kingdom of Anubis,

The Myth of Monsters

This is the second of four scrolls. Since you're reading them, in order, to Derek, Sarah, Randy, and Quincy, I'll just get on with it. I'm sure they're anxious. This one's simple, Jack. Humanity's full of its monster stories. Full of its beliefs about demons and the hell on earth they'll bring at the end of time. The Antichrist is some random family's little boy on a tricycle, the dead rising, the ghost of their dead mother just wanting to cook one last pancake in her kitchen. There's just no end to it. And the longer human beings exist, the more complex and detailed, and scary, the damned things become. It's like they want it to be real. Okay. If people are really waiting for the end to come and all this hell to be unleashed, and they seem to be, because they all have their sextets out measuring the angle of the sun, waiting for the signs, so they'll be really prepared. All they need to do is study the books, and pictures, and ancient cryptograms. Maybe Dan Brown can even write them a book that explains it all, so they'll even know what special ancient knife they better have on hand in order to be the last man standing, alone, on a dead earth, with no monsters, and no people, but...at least they made it. They knew what to expect, and they were prepared. So prepare.

Street

"Now what's that supposed to mean, Jack?" This time it was Quincy. "Listen, I'm in no mood for any demons from hell to be showing up at the door. I just lived quite a long time in my own personal hell, and I'm not too keen on living through another."

"I hear you, Quincy," Jack replied, "and I don't really know what to say. These documents are at least one hundred and fifty years old and seem to be thousands of years old if the stories behind them are correct. Yet I just translated them with a device that wasn't invented till about ninety years ago, and they've got our names in them. Whether I like it or not, I'm starting to lean toward the 'We may not like it, but it's happening anyways' side of the aisle."

"Damn it, Jack," Randy said. "The damn thing told us not to worry, that our faces weren't going to melt off. That sounded good, even comforting. Now, you're saying Freddy Krueger's coming to town."

"I don't like this any more than you, Randy. But I think if ours had told us the whole truth, we might not have come looking for the other three. I guess I'm glad I know, rather than not know...I think. Let's move on."

CHAPTER 28

THE BATTLE OF LITTLE BIGHORN, REVISITED
JUNE 25, 1876

WHY DID CUSTER LOSE the Battle of Little Bighorn? Historians can gather facts, surmising what they may from sparse accounts reported by those who witnessed the aftermath of the dismal failure, but no one can know for sure. No one alive today can be in that moment in history. Well, that is, except for one man, a man named Byron, to whom we owe the knowledge of this entire event.

Byron's visions allowed him to write the battle's accounts in his journals. The day was a pivotal time in history. An ancient holder of a scroll was about to expire, and this would unleash, for a few moments, a power contained within that scroll. Jack's group was about to learn all about the contents of scroll number four and how it was going to play with humanity's beliefs, making everyone automatically aware of every false belief they believed, and how untrue they actually were. This scroll power unleashing would occur in two other places on earth this day as well, and Byron would, eventually, view those occurrences too.

In this vision of Custer's Last Stand, Byron learned there are two types of men: Secure and insecure.

If nothing of the supernatural had occurred, and if better planning and higher commitment to the mission by all commanders had been displayed on the side of the US Army, the fight might have gone considerably better for the White Man, even if, in the end, they still were doomed to lose.

The Battle of Little Bighorn was destined to be a numbers game, though no one has ever been correct about the nature of those numbers.

The side with more soldiers was victorious. The Native Americans did possess the overwhelming numbers and, thus, were…victorious. Aware of Colonel Custer's plans, they had prepared to meet him with an insurmountable force, impossible to defeat. So there is nothing more to understand, correct?

Major Reno was not necessarily convinced Custer's plan was well conceived, and perhaps this caused him to lag the morning of June 25 a little more than he should have. Perhaps Reno directed his troops the long way around the West Ridge. And what of Major Benteen? Well, though a devotee of Custer, Benteen just wasn't that good at navigating Montana, and it took him a little longer to arrive—a little too long.

Thus, Custer and his men, being the first on the scene, where the Sioux were waiting for them, were wiped out relatively quickly by an overwhelmingly unfair ratio of Indians to White Man.

Case closed, *right?*

Wrong.

What's not understood is there actually *was* a chance for Custer to be victorious— even without the absentee officers and their respective troops, and even with being so completely outnumbered, American Indian to American soldier.

Strange things were at work that day. The fourth of four scrolls was about to change hands for the first time in five thousand years. And, for a moment, just a little bit of the information contained within those scrolls became a part of reality.

The groups of men, Indians and soldiers, fighting on the battlefield near the Little Bighorn River on June 25, 1876, were suddenly aware of how dead wrong any of their untrue beliefs were. The amount of disorientation, despair, and fear that consumed each man in the following moments was directly proportional to the amount of sincerity, security, and humility each possessed. Essentially, the stronger the character of the man, the lesser the effect of the event.

A man has beliefs he holds dear; they define him—beliefs that help guide or rule his decisions. Some men hold these beliefs out of sincerity, others out of arrogance, and some out of ignorance. A man gains security from his beliefs, even if it is a false sense of security. They help to give him his sense of place in the world and serve to guide his understanding of it. All that happens around him will be filtered through his beliefs. Beliefs don't necessarily have to be about God or a Supreme Being; they can be part of any category. However, for an idea to *be* a belief, there needs to be some emotional attachment to it. A belief isn't just a piece of information a man is indifferent to yet holds to be true. A belief is not just an acceptance of a fact. A belief is something that *matters.*

If Custer and his soldiers had only had a proportionately greater number of *secure* men than the Sioux, then the outcome may have been different for them. Of course, the law of probabilities was still against Custer, given that his men were heavily outnumbered, but no one said it was *probable* for him to have been the victor, only that it was more *possible* than one might have thought, given what *really* happened.

Were the Sioux a special race? Were they somehow born with more integrity than the White Men coming to fight them? The answer is no; they were as human as anyone else. But sometimes the values one culture or group teaches and holds dear might promote more character than another. It's not a given that nineteenth-century American culture was teaching less positive values than that of the Sioux. Maybe it was, maybe it wasn't. However, *if* America was, its effort was not represented by the majority of Custer's Seventh Cavalry.

—◇○◇—

"Oh my God! Oh God! Nooooooooooooo!" screamed a soldier in horror as he realized there was nothing special about being white.

"Mommy!" screamed another private who was confronted with knowing he was not the son, between himself and his brother, whom Father loved best.

A somewhat sociopathic recruit turned his weapon on a few of his fellow countrymen before an arrow buried itself in his skull, ending his rampage. The belief his mother loved him and didn't fear him had been nullified by the scroll's power.

"Oh dear." A sergeant who believed his wife to be completely loyal said this to himself right before he put a bullet through his own head, having realized his belief was the exact opposite of the truth.

Silence came from many who just passed out on the spot because they were incapable of handling the fact that nothing they believed was actually true.

When George Armstrong Custer realized his middle name had no destined significance to his accomplishments in life, that his great country of America had no more business treating the Indians the way it had than it had the Africans, that his belief that all this land was somehow his birthright was wrong, and that his first dog, Latsy, never really liked him, the colonel stopped in his tracks. Most probably, this last disintegration of falsehood is what beat the strength out of the man.

⋖>○⋗

Up to the moment of supernatural clarity produced by the article in the possession of The Ancient One, Custer had been fighting quite bravely and successfully, though he was feeling outnumbered and had been wondering where his reinforcements were. If he'd had much of a chance to think, he would have realized the fruitlessness of his situation. However, he was focused on each moment as it happened, which required his utmost attention if he was going to stay alive as long as he could.

During the fight, his eye was caught by an Indian up the hill from where he was fighting who seemed to be nearly a hundred years old; nevertheless, he was trying to fight alongside his tribe. Custer intended to fight his way to that Indian and kill him. Custer figured the man to be some elder of significance and decided that killing the old Injun might gain his army some ground by disorienting or disorganizing the Sioux.

Through some quite impressive battling, Custer had made it to the Indian. It appeared two braves, one on a horse and one on foot, were guarding this man. They fought valiantly and impressively against Custer. Eventually, the colonel had been forced to finish them with his pistol instead of the more entertaining process (by way of the sword).

As Custer stood face to face with the elder, the hellish battle continued around them like a tornado devouring men's bodies and souls with each rotation. Now that he was closer to the man, Custer was taken aback by how old the Indian looked now.

This new perspective had Custer feeling the Indian might die of old age at any moment, saving Custer the trouble of killing him. The Indian dropped his tomahawk and began tightly grasping a pouch tied around his neck. It looked significant to Custer—perhaps like a flag. Killing this Indian and capturing this article may produce the effect the colonel was hoping for.

Custer reached his arm out and grabbed at the pouch. It didn't take much to get it away from the old man, regardless of the strange realizations starting to pour into his head the moment he held it in his hand. After seizing the pouch, he might have noticed the old Indian disintegrate into dust before him, if he hadn't been so concerned with his childhood dog's indifference to him.

The rest of the battlefield grew completely silent and still for a few moments after Custer attained possession of the pouch. It is unfortunate this particular event was not seen by any living witnesses, for it would have produced many exciting debates among future historians.

Although all the Sioux who were fighting realized instantly many of their spiritual beliefs simply weren't true, most of them were able to accept they had been wrong and pick up the battle where they had left off. It seemed that courage, honor, integrity, loyalty, and protecting their homes and families were all still valiant beliefs that *were* true.

Four arrows ripped through Custer's body while he was struggling to get over his boyhood dog's lack of interest in him. Before he hit the ground, the Sioux warrior on a horse who had been protecting the old Indian, and whom Custer had thought he'd shot and killed, rode by and secured the pouch from Custer's hand.

The brave, known as Four Winds, had been able to grab the pouch, though a bullet from a Seventh Cavalryman had buried itself in his brain a second prior. He didn't get two more gallops before falling off backward from his horse, the pouch still clutched in his hand—a pouch later to be picked up by Major Reno, surveying the decimation that had become of Custer and his men.

The battle was over soon after General George fell. The men who had started this day by battling Indians were now mostly battling their own personal demons—and were doing so without a leader. They never reorganized into an army. Most died without even remembering what they were fighting for or whom they were fighting.

CHAPTER 29

FOUR WINDS ARRIVES
FEBRUARY 4, 2007...STILL.
(FOUR SCROLLS, FOUR MYTHS, FOUR WINDS,
FEBRUARY 4TH...WHY NOT?)

"OKAY JACK, GO AHEAD. Keep reading. What's next?" Randy prodded.
"Next is Number Three." And Jack continued his reading.

> *The people of the Malamute,*
>
> *The Myth of the Here*
>
> *This is the third of four scrolls.*

"This is yours, Quincy. Jack looked up and nodded his head at Davis. "Forgot to mention that."

"Thanks, Jack."

"Ah, come to think of it," Jack continued, "guess you understood that, given the title. All right, anywho…"

Anywho? Jack thought to himself. *Did my grandmother just pop out of my mouth? I hope that is a not a sign that means something.*

He began.

> *There were four Scroll Holders chosen to protect four peoples. Caleb, Shusaab, Always Here, and The Ancient One were their names. They should be honored, for they gave up much so that people could have their Armageddon. Caleb and Shusaab suffered the most, and only their personal insanity relieved their suffering after being entombed for all time in the dark, silent crypts of Abydos. All four completed their tasks on a day when they began to age uncontrollably, and on a day when three others, separately, would arrive at each Scroll Holder's location and try and take their scroll. There was the stranger who would die*

trying to take a scroll, and additionally, there was a stranger who would be given the scroll and live on afterward. Hacker and Gerard are gone. Sarah and Quincy live to sit with you, Randy and Derek, as the new Scroll Holders. A third stranger, Custer, is gone as well, but Four Winds got your scroll, Jack. He did not live, like Sarah and Quincy. He was killed by one of Custer's men's bullets. Myths aren't always consistent, you know, but then again, maybe, somehow, it does make sense. I'm sure someone will make total sense out of this by looking at it from this angle or that angle. Strange why so many people have such a strong desire to believe in things that make so little sense or spend so much time on ridiculous prophecy deciphering. Why not believe in things that do make sense, like loving each other, helping each other, taking care of people who can't take care of themselves. Sorry, I get distracted. So, no, Four Winds didn't live like Quincy and Sarah. But he's here now—so maybe this one does make sense after all.

"Huh?" Randy asked, only to be cut off by a knock at the door.

Knock. Knock.

"I was wondering if that was going to happen," Jack said to himself and shook his head, letting out an airy under-the-breath laugh. He even entertained a slight roll of the eyes as he contemplated how right he'd been in his guess. *A genius, worthy of Harvard,* he thought. *Dad, you'd be so proud…unless you were filler…geez.* Jack pushed away the eerie thought and said, "Derek, you might want to get that."

Derek stood up. "You don't think?"

"Actually, I do think. And I also think you might want to open the door. The guy's probably a little scared," Jack responded. "Oh, and you don't need to worry about your hands with him either."

Derek stared at Jack, too puzzled to argue, knowing he'd only lose the argument if he tried. And the argument would really be with himself and not Jack anyway. It was like being inside a paradox of a paradox. He turned and left the sitting room to answer the door without saying a word, feeling like he was a robot servant or on autopilot.

When Derek got to the door and opened it, he wasn't exactly sure of what he'd expected to see. And by the looks of the young man standing on the other side of the doorjamb, it seemed the feeling was mutual.

It was a Native American, taller than Derek's six feet something, with an extremely muscular body, even more apparent from the fact the man was wearing next to nothing. He was covered in warrior paint, complemented by an extremely authentic-looking outfit consisting of a headdress and long leather loincloth. He looked like he'd just stepped out of a history book and into twenty-first-century New York City. John Dunbar may have been fictional, but his words describing the magnificence of the Sioux were now unmistakable fact—if Derek was, in fact, truly seeing what he thought he was seeing.

"Come in?" Derek struggled to say it at all, let alone calmly, to the brave. He made the universal motion for *"Enter"*—or at least what he dreamed up in the moment to be the universal motion for entering. Derek had assumed the man would not be able to understand him, but he was wrong. This became apparent when the man answered.

"Thank you," he said, and he entered the brownstone. He walked past Derek, and Derek found himself following his new guest into the sitting room, where he was to make an announcement.

"I am Four Winds. I am here now. Byron said you would be here and that you are friends."

"Byron?" Jack asked.

"Byron wrote the scrolls," Four Winds answered.

"Well, that's good to know," Jack replied. "And here I thought I was sitting with all the information. Please, Four Winds, come in. Quincy, can you bring in another chair?"

"There is no need." Four Winds held up his hand to stop Davis. "I will sit on the ground." And he sat on the floor.

"We were just reading the scrolls for the first time out loud," Jack explained.

"I know. Byron said you would be when I arrived. Continue with your task."

"Okay," Jack replied, thinking one long *Ummmm*, just because it seemed appropriate to pause, reflect, and momentarily go bonkers. Then Jack continued. "But would it be all right if I ask you a question?"

"You have just asked a question. But you may ask another."

Jack laughed at the young man's good humor, considering, well, considering everything...

"We just learned you were actually killed. Was that incorrect or—"

"No, it is correct. I was visited by Byron the morning before a great battle we were to have with people of your kind. With soldiers. He looked like you, but he did not act like those men. He said the white soldiers' leader would take something from our eldest. He told me, no matter what, I was to gain possession of it when that happened. He said I would live longer than I could imagine if I did so."

"You *believed* this Byron?" Jack asked.

"He had magic. He appeared and disappeared in the air. My name is similar in meaning, but I do not do what this man could do."

"So? Was it the truth or a lie? Did you die, or did you live?" Randy entered the conversation with the new arrival.

"Both, it would seem," Four Winds answered. "This Byron said after I take the item from the soldier leader, there would be a door, and I should hit it and enter it when it opens. They will be reading papers he had written, and they will be expecting you. They will be your friends. Byron did not tell me I would be shot in the head by one of the soldier guns before I arrived at your door. I am glad for this omission. It would have made the task he demanded of me more difficult."

"Unbelievable," Randy responded. "All of this is very, very, very—"

"Unbelievable, Randy?" Sarah interrupted with a smile.

"Yes. It is," Randy replied back with a smile, his angst diffused once again by her very reemergence into the dialogue.

"It's nice to have you here, Four Winds." Jack picked back up his laptop, which he had set aside when Four Winds had knocked at the door. "I am sure there is much we can tell each other. But it appears the right thing to do now is to proceed with my reading, so I'll continue." And he read.

> *You have now met Four Winds. And all three of them are together at last.*

Jack looked up and glanced around the room. The scroll was obviously referring to Four Winds, Sarah, and Quincy. He thought to himself, *The lives these people have led.* And he laughed inside, as the word "unbelievable" floated across his mind too. A crooked smile landed on his mouth as his attention returned to his laptop.

> *It is not that beliefs and legends are inherently bad. Humanity will not be destroyed because it had its superstitions, its hodgepodge mix-and-match belief systems, its complex array of hypocrisies. Humanity is human. It is what it is. And the universe is what it is. And God, I assume, is who He is. Humanity has its eras, and this is the next one, and it appears, perhaps, to be the final one, and humanity's myths will play a role. I do not know why. The good of the world cannot be blamed for the bad, and they are forced to deal with the bad every day of their lives. They are given the tools of perseverance, patience, love, forgiveness, and what my mom called a stiff upper lip in order to handle what the bad brings their way. Soon, they will be given new tools. Some will gain control over the earth, wind, water, and fire.*

and

Jack, I know you need the initial setting for a three-rotor Enigma to complete the bulk of the translation. It's J O N.

"The four elements," Derek said to no one, "the Myth of the Here. Ingenious. Terrifying. Only the good get that, right? That's what it said? I hope they *stay* good. Power corrupts. Haven't you seen *Spider-Man? Smallville?*"

"Number four, Jack," Quincy urged. "If we're all going to be fighting for our lives tomorrow, I want to get this over with and get another one of Miss Sarah's meals into me."

"Oh, Quincy." Sarah laughed.

Randy, obviously panged by jealousy again at having missed an opportunity to compliment Sarah, awkwardly threw in, "Yeah, me too."

"Oh, Randy, stop it," Sarah replied, shaking her head and giving him a wink.

Jack looked back at his laptop.

And the fourth being the horsemen.

The Myth of the Hereafter

This is the fourth of four scrolls, which, when finally brought together, will change the world forever. The scrolls had the power to keep their bearers young for thousands of years, and also the second bearer, but no longer does that hold true.

Jack stopped reading and interjected, "That's all I had been able to translate of ours until today, except for of course the couple lines at the bottom about my face not melting off."

"Our faces, Jack." Randy interjected.

"Yes, Randy. Our faces not melting off."

The others gave a nod of acknowledgment *(what else could one do in a conversation like this?),* and Jack went on with the discovery.

They will not help you live forever. Use them for their intended purpose. They are for your information and in line with all that has brought them into being. They are the symbol for all of humanity's beliefs, right and wrong, its superstitions, ridiculous and credible, and its need for signs and proof, though little does the human race ever care, even when presented with signs. These scrolls will largely go unknown by most—as if they would have helped if seen by all. The sea of people is divided into three groups. There are those who choose good over evil, and there are those who choose evil over good. There are those who help make the world go around. These people just fill up space. To anyone, they are human, but to the universe, they are dust. Your brother, Jon, was one of them. And Derek need not worry, because none of your group make up any of this third section of the population. Derek is a Discerner, and there will be others like him who will have the same power to tell who in a crowd is real and who is not real with just a wave of their hand. It would be best not to use this gift recklessly.

People believe so much in a life beyond this one, or they don't. And some waver in the middle. But whoever we are, we usually believe something strongly about something. Sometimes we're right, and sometimes we're wrong. We claim we want to know truth, the real reality. Do we ever wonder what would happen if we were actually given that information? Knowing the truth would come with the opposite, too, correct? Could we deal with finding out what the lie was? What if we were just presented with the truth of that which we were completely wrong about? I guess you'll see.

Jack, I know you and Randy are tripping that this scroll is going to melt your faces off, but it won't, so don't worry.

Sixth

"I skipped over the word 'Allied,'" Jack finished, "which is littered throughout our scroll and was my first clue on how to decipher them in the first place."

Silence had returned to the sitting room, making the name of the room all the more fitting. Each mind in the room was thinking their own personalized thoughts related to the life they had led up to this point. Sarah had been listening, but ever since she had learned of who that man had been in the tomb—and it now appeared there had been two of them trapped there—she hadn't been able to escape imagining the dread of their ordeal. *How horrible,* she thought, *to be in that place, in the dark, for so long.* For the first time, she actually felt good for having arrived there with Gerard and having done what she had done. It was a relief like almost no other she had ever experienced.

———◇○◇———

Quincy Davis had a lot of things on his mind as well. Jack mentioning Always Here made him think of the people of Home Now, and that brought sadness, but then hearing the scrolls' contents finally brought some meaning to their existence and the answers he had been longing for all this time. The people of Home Now had been destroyed, but perhaps they had remained in existence much longer than they ever would have and long enough for their people's story and lives to be known and loved by others—even if they were only the others sitting in this room. It also appeared that somebody named Byron, who was privy to a lot more information than they were, believed the people of Home Now to be important. Another thought drifted across his mind, and he found himself voicing it.

"I think I've seen one of those monster things, or heard it, or felt it or something."

"Really, Quincy?" Jack said surprised. "Here? Already?"

"No. A long time ago. I lived through three horrible experiences of human destruction. Once before arriving at Home Now with my employer, a man named Hacker. Another when the people of Home Now were almost completely wiped out by an act of human carnage. And again when leaving Home Now with the remaining members of the tribe when I lost them to an icequake. Each time, I would have sworn there was something there with me. I saw or felt *something* during moments throughout all three of these experiences of death."

"Like what?" Randy asked.

"I can't say for sure. It's been so long since I thought about it, and I really didn't give it much thought then. There wasn't anything to think about past a lingering feeling." Quincy tried to remember the day with Hacker and the crew out on the ice, and then the image of Hoppin's death arrived on point. "When the ice was breaking up around us and we were trying to outrun it on the sleds, there was a moment when it seemed to me the ice was alive."

"Alive?" Randy begged.

"Yes, like it was *trying* to kill," Quincy continued. "Hoppins, one of our men, flew up in the air as he was knocked from his sled, and he didn't seem to continue to fly in the direction he was heading either. It was like he was caught, and then pulled straight down into the ocean. I swore to myself I didn't see what I saw, but there's more. It wasn't just *like* he was caught. I know I saw a hand."

"A hand?" Randy was beginning to sound like a backup singer to the story.

"Yeah, and when it was all over, I remember thinking the strangest thing. Honestly, I can't believe I remember this. But then again, how could I forget having a thought like this? I thought 'I've met Impending Doom, and I know how he makes you feel, and I'll take his cousin, Death, anytime.'"

Everyone looked at Quincy as if to say, "What the hell are you talking about?" except for Jack, who was looking at Randy just to see what his reply would be. He didn't know why he liked Randy so much. They were really nothing alike. Four days earlier Jack had been content to be alone every day in his home and his office, only humoring Randy's visits to the latter during Randy's breaks. Now, Randy and this odd group were the people he most wanted to be around, and being alone felt like what only crazy people would want.

Instead of Randy speaking, who seemed too mystified to do so as he was busily pondering over who the hell "Impending Doom" was, Quincy continued. "I know I saw similar visions when Hacker's employer's son showed up and started murdering all my people."

"That's insane!" Randy yelled out, finally granting Jack his hidden desire. "Jack, if he's not bullshitting, and that's the kind of craziness that's coming, you can count me out. I'm finding a cave."

"Okay, Randy, you do that. I'm sure no monsters would ever be in a dark, isolated underground cave," Jack's replied. It felt good to throw that snowball, and everyone laughed. It was another nice break given to them, almost like the kind Randy gave Jack, nightly, from his reclusiveness, which he always pretended, even to himself, that he didn't like. Even Randy laughed a little at his own expense, though something still felt very inappropriate about laughing at all.

The moment of levity concluded, and Sarah spoke. "Quincy, I don't believe you're crazy, and I guess we should take your story as another warning of what may be in store. We have a new guest, though, who, from his story, has just left a great battle and had even been shot. I think this would be a good time for us to relax over a meal."

Sarah made the situation seem normal to everyone, and through her efforts, the others started feeling normal again—at least a little bit—and a little bit of normal in all of this felt like a whole lot of normal in all of this.

Or like a gift.

"I'll help you, Sarah," Randy said. He stood up and followed her as she left for the kitchen.

"That would be fine, Randy," Sarah agreed, and surprisingly, grabbed his hand in a barely noticeable and graceful manner, to pull him along with her. She turned back toward the others. "You boys help Four Winds with whatever he needs. Perhaps some warmer clothes? It is winter."

Four Winds rose to a standing position. No one in the room held a candle to his majestic presence, regardless of how out of place he looked in his clothing standing in the middle of a twentieth-century brownstone sitting room. He started to speak. His tone was mesmerizing, and it melted into their ears.

"The visitor, Byron, told me to tell you this. We will be leaders, and we must seek those who will benefit us in our struggle. We must find the man who sees with eyes that are not of his own, and we must tame those who discern. The end is uncertain, for at the time Byron visited me, he had not yet seen it."

Great, Jack thought, *more messages I don't understand but will most likely be responsible for explaining.*

———◇○◇———

Before the event-filled (but barely noticed date) of February 4, 2007, concluded, four other related and event-filled days had occurred. And they, too, had gone by equally unnoticed—by most. However, the few who did notice, *noticed*.

On June 25, 1876, General Custer and his recruits were going to have a really bad day. It was mostly caused not by the fact they were in a battle and would lose that battle, but by the fact they would lose because fighting would become too difficult when they were busy being faced with the truth (or lack of truth, rather) regarding every single false thing they had ever believed. Gerard Palton, an archaeologist—or "drunkologist," as some called him—was about to be written right out of existence, but not before being burned alive and eaten by a demon. A tracker named Hacker who never got lost would get lost and lose most of his men, while his second in command would be swearing to himself he was seeing visions of Death *or something like it*. Ultimately, Hacker would be shot dead by that very same second of his. A certain young woman named Sarah, who had never hurt anyone, was going to set a man on fire to save another one; afterward, she would believe for years that she had only saved him to subsequently turn him to dust. Sadly, Always Here and The Ancient One would uncontrollably age and perish, leaving those who loved them with a great feeling of loss. Conversely, one more tortured and imprisoned Scroll Holder in an Egyptian tomb would finally be freed from his burden as he also fell into ashes behind a wall separating him from the pile of ashes of his old friend, a very frightened young women, and the woman's dead and charred ex-date.

Several months later, on January 31, 1877, a man named Quincy Davis was going to be fully accepted into a new home in the middle of a frozen wasteland, and he was going to get the new name of Our Future. This same day, our girl Sarah would check herself into a mental institution in Cairo, in order to become forgotten and nameless.

On June 25, 1876, and January 31, 1877, random people around the world would swear they heard something strange, or saw something in the shadows, or had a dreadful doubting of their faith for the first time. A man in Paris would shake his hand in anger after having realized he forgot his money purse while walking down a crowded market. He would swear a man had disappeared just as he turned around making the angry gesture. One little girl in Chicago would tell her parents she was able to start a fire with her bare hands, though she was unable to reproduce the event for them. After admitting this, the girl would be forced not to say another word about it and to stay in her room for nearly a month for having even uttered the word "fire"—that is, given all that had gone down in their quaint little hometown just five years earlier. So you know, that event had *just* been a fire, a simple fire, and not connected with any scrolls or weirdness or anything. Promise...

The date of April 7, 1923, was the next day many similar joyrides in the unnatural would occur. A man named Our Future would watch most of his new family be massacred by the son of a Mr. Sime, a man he used to work for via a man named Hacker. He would witness the rest of them go extinct very shortly thereafter and would degrade into a man without a name who wanted no name. A woman in an Egyptian asylum who had been lost to the world for forty-seven years would get her name and her family back, having been found by her loving sister, Jessica.

That day, a lonely worker by the name of Paul Dunsford would transport a scroll from a cardboard box to a metal one and place it back onto a shelf among many other articles stored in a warehouse contracted by the US government. He would have sworn to himself he had heard something scuttling around in the warehouse, breathing heavily for at least five minutes after handling the scroll. He thought he had even heard a laugh—an evil laugh. He didn't link it to anything, especially not to the box he had just opened or its contents, which he had just refiled. In fact, he didn't really give much thought to it at all. He was too fixated on his plans for that evening. He would leave work that night, go home, have a nice glass of wine, and put a shotgun to his head.

He did all of that, even got the shotgun square between his eyes. Fortunately for him, as he was pulling the trigger, he was distracted by the appearance *or presence* of Death...*or something like it.* This caused him to pause and rethink the decision to off himself. Fortunately for him, he changed his mind, and instead he just went about finishing his wine. It was unfortunate for Impending Doom, who was getting really sick of people mistaking him for his damned cousin on his mother's side. And if I.D. had been much of a thinker, he'd have thought it quite ironic that his very presence had put a damper on his whole Impending Doomness, at least, in this particular case.

However, January 31, 2007...now that was to be a day. Scroll number four was found again, and its discovery by Jack and Randy set off a chain of events like none of the previous dates had. Within four days, all four scrolls would be sitting together in the same room for the first time in, well, that depends on how you look at it. Their actual age dictated it had been thousands of years since they were all gathered together to be looked upon by a single pair of eyes. But their date of origin, the actual date on which they would be written, hadn't happened yet, placing their age on the left side of zero—a negative number, or would it be an imaginary number? Or is it even possible to say? Or is it worth discussing? *Is there a physicist in the house? A priest, then? A psychiatrist?*

A publisher turned to dust. A man coming out of a subway tunnel turned to dust. Actually, quite a few people turned to dust that day. The persons responsible for it pretty much had had the same reaction as Derek. They freaked out, shoved their hands in their pockets, and ran home. One exception to this pattern occurred with a sixteen-year-old boy, Terrance, who watched his parents turn to dust at the dinner table while he reached for the green beans. In his case, he *left* home…with his hands in his pockets.

An entire congregation of homosexual-hating Baptists in Topeka, Kansas, all realized for about two minutes they had their heads completely up their collective ass in how they were behaving. The two minutes were up, and back up went their God Hates Fags signs. One person did leave the congregation after the experience. One positive outcome. If anyone in Topeka cared enough to even pay any attention to them at all, they would have noticed that for at least 120 seconds, the protesters looked like real human beings with hearts and everything.

Three fires were started accidentally in Oklahoma City, Montreal, and Kolkata by people without matches, lighters, or anything in their hands. Except, that is, for the fire in Oklahoma City. That man had been holding a burrito from Taco Bell. A California swimming pool mysteriously froze solid while a nine-year-old girl was climbing out of it. Her left foot got stuck. The pool melted a moment later, so it went unreported, no one having the nerve to tell a reporter without evidence. An executive in Saint Louis lost his golf game because the wind changed directions on him while he swung his last drive. A new religion started when a village in the rain forest of Brazil saw one of their elders float off the ground and drift away. When he was found later, several hundred yards away, battered and dead, having fallen through the trees from a great height, one would think the new beliefs would have stopped, but they didn't.

The list could go on and on, so no need to bore…well, okay…a few more…

A man in Italy nearly doubled his grape yield by touching a vine. He saw it happen. He tried over and over again, but two grapes for the work of one was all he was destined to get that day. A quarry worker in Colorado leaned up against a wall of solid granite, only to see his hand melt right into it. Lucky for him, he pulled it out right away because he didn't retain his ability for too long. If Byron hadn't seen it, no one would have ever known about it. He sure didn't tell the other guys on his lunch break.

In the sight of one homeless man, another homeless man was dragged off by two monsters that rose out of the slime and mud in the middle of the alley in which the men had been sleeping. After this sight, and after being off the juice for one whole week, the remaining homeless man started drinking again, eventually dying from this falling off his wagon. But, shoot, if it hadn't been the monsters rising from the ground and dragging off his alley mate, it would have been something that pushed him off the cart. He hadn't been *that* dedicated.

A Sarah Dubois stirred out of her waking sleep to save her nephew, Derek, from slipping into one, and a Quincy Davis left his typical corner in the Village, wandered up toward Twenty-First Street, and sat down for no real reason he could think of.

The following day a few people mentioned to their better halves weird events, sightings, or feelings they'd experienced during the day before. Others stayed quiet or shook it off as nothing, or as just one of those things, or they'd had too much to drink, or they'd had too little sleep, or they'd been daydreaming, or whatever. Anything was better than admitting they were crazy, or they'd seen a demon flying in the air, or they had set their own hair on fire while shampooing it, or they had watched their entire garden die after getting angry at their tomato plant for not producing enough tomatoes, or they had frozen their hands together while in church saying a prayer, with only the humidity in the air.

And of course, the greatest aftershock of the previous day's events: Jack Johanssen went into work on his day off.

Book IV:

The Beginning of the End

CHAPTER 30

HARVEY AND MEG
DECEMBER 2, 2012

———————◇○◯◯○◇———————

"CAN I FILL 'ER UP, Harvey?"

"Huh? Oh, yes, Meg. Thanks."

Meg, a waitress in her early thirties and a permanent resident of Claremore, Oklahoma, filled up Harvey's coffee at the counter, just like she said she would. Just like she always did. She'd just punched in on the clock. Harvey, as usual, had already been there for an hour.

She followed the fill-up with "Hey, Harvey, are those new glasses?"

"Uh, yes, Meg, they are. I picked 'em up yesterday. They don't look good, do they?" He sighed.

Harvey was a lanky sort of fellow. He was of medium height, but real thin—not anorexic thin, but the kind of thin that's noticed. He wasn't unattractive in a repulsive kind of way, but he wasn't much to look at either. Nice enough, not a creepster or anything, but he did tend to talk a lot if you got him going. And he talked about things most people wouldn't be able to wrap their heads around or even care to try. Confidence was an issue, making him even less attractive to women. He'd shut up if you told him to, though, and he could register "I'm not interested" in people's body language, so this kept him out of the "completely annoying" category of humanity.

His new glasses were actually fairly hip. Rectangular, with thick black plastic frames. On an attractive man, the glasses would have added style and character. On Harvey's face, they just made him look like he was trying to be something he wasn't: cool.

So Meg lied. "No, Harvey, they're cool. You look good in them. Better than the last pair." That last comment wasn't a lie. He did look better.

"Thanks, Meg," Harvey replied with obvious zeal at the nice comment from the most beautiful girl in town, as Harvey had surmised Meg to be. "The lady at the optometrist's office said they were a big seller this year, so I took a risk and got something different. I'm just not sure if they're me or not."

"Well, Harvey, if you make them you, they'll be you," Meg said.

"My prescription changed a lot. I'm officially blind, I think."

Meg focused on Harvey's thick lenses but tried not to look like she was looking.

"I know they're thick," Harvey grunted. "Here—try them on." As he offered, he slid the spectacles off his face, giving her little chance to refuse. He handed them to Meg. He was now squinting in a world gone blurry.

Meg humored Harvey and slid off her own glasses. Handing them to Harvey, she said, "Here, you can try mine!" Meg's flirty side was never absent.

"Okay," Harvey answered, full of glee at the idea of holding anything that belonged to Miss Prettiest Girl Ever, this being another variation on the title he'd given her.

"Meg! We got customers!" called Jimmy, the manager and owner of Jammer's Café, from the other end of the counter. He knew Harvey could monopolize his staff's time if he didn't pay attention. "Harvey, let Meg do her job, all rightcha?"

As Jimmy was barking his order, Harvey placed Meg's glasses on his face and turned toward Jimmy's voice. Harvey's prescription was strong, so Meg's light-astigmatism script wasn't going to do much for him. Being a bit more farsighted than nearsighted, Harvey could just make out Jimmy's shape down by the register.

"All right, Jimmy," Meg answered. "Harvey, I'll need my glasses back. We can do this later, okay?"

Harvey turned toward Meg, thinking for a moment he'd seen something odd as he turned from Jimmy. When he looked back at Meg, he was overwhelmed at the sight of her. This wasn't the normal overwhelmed. Something different was going on. She was glowing. It was unmistakable. Harvey about toppled backward off his stool. As he struggled to catch his balance, he was mesmerized by the colors before him.

"Harvey, really. I need my glasses back. Come on, please."

"Meg! You're glowing!" he gasped. All Harvey could see now were blues and golds and greens emanating from her. It was the most beautiful thing he'd ever seen. He lowered the glasses in order to look at her over the rims. The glowing was gone. A blurry version of Meg had returned. He slid the glasses back up his nose and voilà! She was radiating light.

"Ha! I don't know what to make of this!" Harvey exclaimed.

The patrons of Jammer's Café were starting to take notice of Harvey, and Jimmy was steaming at being ignored by both Harvey and Meg. He began to march down the counter length toward them.

"Harvey, I like you. You know that!" Jimmy yelled. "But I got a business to run, and Meg's my waitress, not yours. So give her back her glasses and drink your coffee."

Jimmy's insistence made Harvey turn again in the direction of Jimmy, who was now much closer. There was no aura around Jimmy. He was blurry, and then he wasn't. No, Harvey's eyesight hadn't improved. Jimmy just—wasn't. No blur, no Jimmy.

Then Jimmy was back again, blurry as ever. And then Jimmy was gone again—blinking, apparently, in and out of existence. Harvey squinted at the illusion, and the faces he made as he looked back and forth between the glowing waitress and the disappearing manager were starting to catch the attention of other patrons. Harvey had never caused any problem at Jammer's and had been showing up almost every morning for most of his adult life—which, at thirty-five, made the year count about fifteen or so. He'd talk a bit too much sometimes, but nothing one couldn't handle, so this display was quite out of the ordinary. A murmur arose in the restaurant, and Harvey became self-conscious. A quirky "Please forgive me" smile arose on his face, and he turned to the other customers to appease the awkwardness he could tell he was creating. Doing so made him feel more uneasy than ever, and it wasn't because he was embarrassed.

About fifteen people were sitting at various tables to his right. But to Harvey, they didn't look like people at all. Instead he saw an array of colors. Several people seemed to be glowing in the same way as Meg. One couple sitting in a booth seemed to pop in and out of existence, like Jimmy was probably still doing behind him. Two patrons at separate tables were glowing a hideous mixture of red and something else. Harvey gasped.

The Passing Out of Harvey Winestall at Jammer's Café—A Strange Tale concerning December 2nd, 2012 was written into the *Annals of Unmistakably Strange Things* when Harvey next observed a demon-like face—a face direct from Dante's *Inferno*, accompanied by a bonus package of long sharp teeth and piercing red eyes—appear in front of him, not six inches away. His psyche decided right then to pack up and take a trip. It was leaving Claremore, Oklahoma, immediately, and heading directly to Faintville, Almost Coma.

———◇○◇———

Meg rushed around the counter, and Jimmy followed. Harvey lay sprawled out on the diner's floor, face up. The other customers were also getting up, save two who appeared not to care less. They were the two whom Harvey had seen glowing red and something else; they continued to eat their food and sip their coffees and read their newspapers.

Meg knelt next to Harvey. She removed her glasses from his head and put them on. "Harvey, are you okay?" She turned to Jimmy. "I think he hit his head pretty hard. Maybe you ought to call an ambulance."

By the time the medic unit arrived, Harvey had come to. His own glasses had been returned to his face, and he sat at one of the booths near the rear of the café, still slightly disoriented, with his head hurting badly. Later, at the hospital, he learned he had suffered a slight concussion. Released later the same day, he called Jammer's to see if someone could give him a ride home. Meg said she would.

A conversation began at the turn of the key in Meg's car. "Harvey, I don't think you should try on other people's glasses anymore! I think your eyes are too bad to handle it!"

"Yeah. Guess you're right," Harvey answered, deciding not to divulge further details about his experience. "How'd the rest of your day at Jammer's go?"

"Oh, 'bout the same as always. I did drop a plate of chicken-fried steak all over Mr. Weathers. He wasn't too happy about that, as he was on his lunch break from work. I can't remember the last time I did anything like that. Been working at Jammer's since I was eighteen. But there I was, placing it down on his table, and the next second, it was in his lap. It's like the plate had a mind of its own. Mr. Weathers is a nice man, so he didn't give me any grief, but I could see he was fightin' hard inside, tryin' not to."

"Yeah, Meg, that is strange. You're like the perfect waitress."

"Aw, thank ya, Harvey. Didn't feel much like one today after that, though."

Harvey wasn't happy to hear about Meg's rough day, but misery loving company and all, he wasn't entirely unhappy to know he wasn't alone. He felt conflicted, like when you're always craving the season you're not in.

"Meg?" Harvey asked after the silence between them had begun to feel just a bit too long.

Oh, no, he thought. *Where are you taking this conversation? What the hell are you about to say?*

"Yes, Harvey? Oh, is this your street up—ah, yep, that's it." Meg turned onto Turley Avenue. "What?"

Harvey paused. "Ah, nothing."

"Come on, Harvey, you can't do that. Say what you were gonna say."

Harvey had been going over the morning's events in his mind all day long at the hospital. He knew he wasn't crazy. He'd put on Meg's glasses, and the whole world had gone crazy, not him. He wanted to say something to Meg just to have someone to talk to about it. But he knew if he wasn't careful, it would sound like any one of the hundreds of other philosophical rants he'd gone on about over the years. If there was one thing he was known for, it was talking about things no one but him seemed to understand or ever think about.

There was the time he'd tried to explain to Jimmy that he thought time was meaningless, because we were all made of atoms, and subatomic particles were all moving at velocities close to the speed of light, and when you reached those kinds of speeds, time effectively stopped or slowed down to almost nothing, and therefore, since everything was made up of those same particles for which time barely crawled, maybe time had barely passed at all for anyone or anything.

All Jimmy had responded with was that he'd just watched some time pass away that he'd never get back and that other customers were waiting for more time than they should have had to because he'd had to listen to Harvey's baloney again.

There was also the time he'd made Meg cry during another subatomic-themed rant. He'd mentioned to her that if we could see ourselves at the atomic level, we would be mostly empty space—would hardly exist at all—and because the outermost edge of an atom was only infinitesimally small electrons flying around in empty space, repelling each other's negative charges, then no two things ever really touched. Even two people who loved each other were, at their atomic level, only electrons being repulsed by each other.

"Oh, Harvey, just shut up" was all she'd said as she walked away crying with her coffeepot. He'd felt bad about that one.

So how was he going to bring up this morning without just sounding like his old self again?

Answer: He wasn't. So he deflected.

"I was just wondering if we could go out sometime. I mean, just as friends—I don't know, hang out outside of Jammer's once or something?" Of course, the question was scary to ask, but for the first time in his life, asking Meg out was the second-scariest thing in the world.

They were pulling into his driveway. Meg was surprised at the question. Harvey didn't repulse her, but she had never been attracted to him. He was always a little too off in his own world to be considered a friend either. But she figured it couldn't hurt, as long as she made her feelings clear.

"Okay, Harvey, that sounds like fun. But just as friends. I don't see you like that, okay?"

Harvey wasn't stupid. He knew he'd never have a chance with a girl like Meg. She was cute and beautiful, and everyone liked her. If small towns had a town nerd, he'd be it. And not the cool nerd but the dorky, unattractive, slightly annoying nerd.

"No, I know. That's really what I meant. It's just we talk at the café all the time. I thought maybe there could be a chance for a real friendship here. That's all."

"Well, all right, Harvey. We'll do it! How 'bout tomorrow night at seven? We can go bowling down at Strike Acres."

"Uh, I have never bowled, Meg."

"That's good, Harvey," Meg responded cheerfully, "so I'll win."

"Okay, then, we'll do it. Thanks for driving me home. I hate to ask for another favor, but do you mind driving me to and from work tomorrow? I'm not sure if I'll have the okay yet—from the docs, that is."

"Sure, Harvey. I'll even sweet-talk Jimmy and Ricardo into driving your car home for you since you're taking me bowling. Can I have your keys back?"

"Not sure you could sweet-talk Jimmy into doing anything for me right now, but have fun trying, Meg." He handed her the keys from his pocket he'd just placed there a minute earlier. "And thanks for tomorrow."

"No problem, Harvey. I'm glad you're okay. Good night." She waved her cute little fingers in a cute little way that Harvey knew had nothing to do with her wanting to be little, or cute, for him.

Harvey returned the wave as Meg reversed out of his driveway. He turned toward his dark house. It was chilly outside but not windy. He walked up the steps onto his porch, realizing he had no keys because he'd just given them away to Meg. He'd never had to use the key in the flowerpot at the top of the porch steps, but he felt rewarded for having decided to put it there several years earlier. He fished around for it in the dirt. The dry soil was hard, and it took some digging, but a few moments later, he was holding passage into his home.

He'd bought the small two-bedroom on Turley Avenue ten years earlier, after working for a local engineering firm for about a year post graduate school. It was an older home, but he'd done some painting and modernized it with some new furniture. There was nothing inherently creepy about it, but right now it was dark, he was alone, and he had just happened to see the face of a demon that morning at such close range he'd thought its drool might drip on his feet, so the house seemed foreboding as if the tortured soul from *The Amityville Horror* might have just moved in to become his roommate.

Light switch! He fumbled for it, assuming he'd see Amity's window eyes—or worse. Perhaps his scary friend from Jammer's would be staring back at him as soon as the lights came on. But when the switch went up, he was alone. He felt peaceful again, seeing his home as it was meant to be seen: with color, decor, and comfort, not a black void in which anything might be lurking.

Harvey sat down at his dining room table. His head still ached from his earlier fall. Figuring he'd better sleep soon, especially if he wanted to be feeling well enough to attend his nondate with Meg on Tuesday evening, he tried to urge himself out of the dining room chair and make his way around the corner and into his bedroom. His mind was swimming with the unexplained events of the day. He knew his dizziness and fainting in Jammer's hadn't occurred for the reason everyone thought it had. Trying on Meg's glasses had not been the culprit. Not exactly. Harvey had taken a vacation from consciousness because everyone in Jammer's had chosen to start glowing, blinking like a streetlight, or…oh…he didn't quite know how to put it…begin looking like a demon from hell.

Reflecting on his day, about to push himself up and toward bed, he noticed his old pair of glasses sitting in the dish at the center of the table. Various other things like paper clips, pens, rubber bands, and a couple of receipts also populated the dish, but only the glasses caught his attention.

Put them on.

Yeah, that's exactly what I want to do. Test out the whole demon-appearing thing while I'm home alone with a concussion.

Put them on. Just for a sec. Just to see.

He lifted the glasses out of the dish with one hand—*What am I doing?*—and pulled off his new ones with the other. "Okay, I'm just doing this for a second, and then they're off," he spoke to his curious urger—the one Harvey refused to admit was one and the same as the man sitting at his table—*him.*

He set his new glasses down on the table, and with both hands, he slowly opened his previous pair. He would slip them on and pull them straight off if Godzilla showed up. He brought them closer to his face, simultaneously wincing, squinting, and pulling his face away from his hands, making his head appear to be having a fight with his arms. Finally, the glasses were in place, but his eyes were closed.

"Open your damned eyes, Harvey, or what's the point?" he said to himself.

He opened them and looked straight ahead. A tad worse than his new prescription, but he saw nothing unusual. Turning his head to the left and then to the right, he had to admit to the same. He slid back his chair and looked further around the room, and off into the living room. Nothing. Or at least, nothing weird. He guessed that was good, but wasn't quite sure what it meant, as he headed for sleep at the end of a day that *had* been weird.

CHAPTER 31

THE SCROLL HOLDERS CALEB AND SHUSAAB
THOUSANDS OF YEARS AGO

◦◦◦

"**B**RING THEM BOTH HERE TO ME**,**" the pharaoh commanded.
The great doors opened at the end of the chamber. Two men were pushed into the room by guards wearing decorative helmets in the shapes of jackals. The men walked slowly toward the throne.

"Everyone out!" the pharaoh's voice echoed. The guards, servants, and various other people bowed and cleared out. The closing of the great doors boomed and shook the two men more than they already were, as they made their way, cowering, toward the menacing ruler.

The pharaoh stood up and looked down at the approaching men. His eyes focused on one of them, and he let out a bellowing question to the servant on the right. "Shusaab, why did you not tell me there was another like you?" The pharaoh pointed to the other man standing next to Shusaab. Well, neither of them were quite *standing*. Both wavered halfway to the floor, as if their bodies were trying to determine whether gravity was a real thing or not. Pointing to the slave on Shusaab's right, the pharaoh bellowed, "I had to learn of this one from my own spies in the camp of the slaves!"

"My lord, I swear I knew nothing of him. Please, you must believe me."

"I doubt that. You know more than you're saying!" Pharaoh was getting louder with every syllable, it seemed. "What's in that scroll of yours? I'm sure it told you he was here, right *here*, in the midst of us, protecting the very slaves I control!"

"Master of all, you know I am forbidden to look upon the contents of my scroll. It is the only command I was given. I was told go to the pharaoh, and your presence will protect him and his line, but never look upon the writing."

"I can't trust you," the pharaoh accused. "My father told me I should. He said that your allegiance kept his dominion strong, and it would continue with me. He says you have never aged, and I guess I can believe that. But to have another appear like you in the very camp of my slaves! Their tribe will not be protected at the same time as the pharaoh!" He turned toward the man next to Shusaab. "What is your name, as if it matters?" yelled the pharaoh.

The young man, still trembling—not necessarily out of fear of the tyrant before him, but for fear of failing his people—looked up at the pharaoh and answered, "My name is Caleb, son of Jephunneh."

"Well Caleb, so-called protector of my slaves, and coconspirator with my servant. There will be no going home for you."

"Please, lord and keeper of all, I knew nothing of him," Shusaab begged. "I do not understand my purpose or his, but I do believe we are here for a reason. You should protect us, as we protect you."

"As you protect me? I am God! You protect nothing! You are alive because I say you can live! My father was foolish to trust you! I see that now. And you would have me risk you and your cohort spreading lies that you are the protectors?"

The pharaoh beamed his attention back toward Caleb. "Give Shusaab your scroll." The man shook in horror as the pharaoh commanded, "*Now!*"

Like most self-proclaimed gods, what they say and what they believe is not always the same thing, unless they're completely delusional. The pharaoh did believe there was magic in these men, but he was not going to let their power be seen as his power, or allow either of them to be a source of power for his slaves. By removing this man from his people, he would be considered a god even more so by the slaves.

Or so he thought.

"Take the scroll from him, Shusaab. Its power will be in my control now."

The pharaoh's Scroll Holder reached out his hand and took the slave's scroll. He hoped this action was not sentencing his newly found brother-in-purpose to an immediate death. The pharaoh spoke again.

"You both will be placed where you cannot spread your lies, and I will know exactly where you are, and no one else ever will."

Later that day, the self-proclaimed god of Egypt commissioned a small team of slaves to imprison the men in a tomb deep within the city. They were walled up separately in adjacent rooms, never to be seen again by anyone of that time. The slaves ordered to bury alive the two Scroll Holders were executed after completing their task, and therefore, only the pharaoh knew of these happenings by the arrival of the following day.

Alone in the dark, unable to even hear each other, Shusaab and Caleb suffered slow decays into insanity over the next four thousand years. The pharaoh lost any protection he'd enjoyed the minute he betrayed Shusaab. Caleb's tribe eventually found their freedom in a story well known to us all.

The two in the tomb knew nothing of these things. They only knew darkness and loneliness until Sarah and Gerard arrived in the first of the two chambers. That day, they had felt themselves age incredibly fast. It was the first time either had enjoyed any mental clarity about anything for thousands of years. They remembered who they were and what they had been asked to do, long ago, by a strange man appearing out of nowhere to each of them with a scroll in hand, only to disappear thereafter.

After the angry man caught on fire, Shusaab had pushed his and Caleb's scrolls into the beautiful lady's hands and had fallen back into nothingness. The same demise silently befell Caleb on the other side of a wall across the room from Sarah, though she was not aware of the event.

CHAPTER 32

THE NONDATE
DECEMBER 3, 2012

"**Y**OU CAME!"

"Well, of course I did, Harvey. When did I ever give you the impression that I was a liar?"

Meg had shown up on time and was looking great. Their meeting might have been prequalified as a nondate, but the way she was dressed and made up said date-date. Her hair was usually pulled back in a ponytail, her lips glazed only with Chapstick, and, of course, she wore only her waitress digs. But now she stood in his doorway, blond hair down, makeup on, and wearing a fitted black evening dress.

"Never, Meg, never. I'm sorry, I guess it's just a nice surprise to see you outside of the café two days in a row! And you look great!"

"Well, thank you, Harvey." Meg laughed in her girlish way. "I *am* out of my waitress uniform. I don't *always* wear it, you know," she chided. "So, are you feeling all right? I think it is good you decided to take the day off today. Does your head still hurt?"

"A little if I shake it," Harvey replied, his eyes still sparkling at the way Meg looked, "but I'm okay. Not sure if I can bowl though."

"Yes, I guess I wasn't really thinking last night when I mentioned that. We can do something else. That's why I didn't dress for bowling."

"Yeah, I guess you didn't. Wow, Meg. How about we just eat a nice dinner somewhere? Maybe down at O'Tooley's?"

"That sounds nice, Harvey. I don't think I've eaten out anywhere nice in quite some time. Working in a restaurant, you don't think to go to one in your off time, you know?"

"Well, you're my chariot tonight, so lead the way!" He locked his house and followed her to her car.

"Hey, thanks again for these." He held up his keys and shook them. "Not sure how you got Jimmy to do it, but he dropped off my car earlier today."

"Jimmy eats out of my hand, Harvey. You gotta know that." And she let out a small version of her unbelievably cute laugh.

They arrived at O'Tooley's. Nondate or not, Harvey did all the things you should do on a date, like opening the door and ordering for Meg, but he made sure to crack jokes about how he understood it wasn't really a date-date. "I just feel you should get the treatment of a lady, regardless of friends or romance."

"Aw, you're so sweet, Harvey. I never knew this side of you existed, given all your talking about black holes and atoms and everything at the diner."

"Yeah, I probably get pretty annoying, huh? I guess I think too much."

"Well, Harvey, maybe the rest of us just think too little."

"I think you're the sweet one, Meg." Harvey laughed.

The mere fact he was having dinner in a nice restaurant with a beautiful girl seemed to have a positive effect on his confidence. He felt it, and it relaxed him. He was more relaxed than he believed he'd ever been. Meg was responding to him in a way she never had before. She actually seemed to be enjoying herself. In the diner, he had never been sure if she genuinely didn't mind his presence or if she was just being a good waitress. Harvey was enjoying himself so much he found it all the more difficult to reconcile the urge to screw it all up with his next question. But he couldn't help it.

"Meg? I know this is a strange request. But would you mind if I tried on your glasses again?"

"What? Why, Harvey?"

"I just need to know something. Would you mind?" Harvey knew he was treading on thin ice, but he had to know.

"I don't know, Harvey," Meg said with surprise in her voice. "Last time I gave you my glasses you ended up in the hospital, and that was just yesterday."

"I promise I won't go to the hospital," Harvey said as Meg found herself handing him her glasses, disbelief in her eyes that she was doing so.

"I don't know why I'm agreeing to this. You're driving yourself to the hospital if you fall over this time, Harvey."

He closed his eyes and slid her glasses on. With every ounce of strength he had, he told himself, *No matter what I see, I will remain composed. No matter what, I'll just slip them off and hand them back to her. This night is going too well to ruin it.*

He slowly opened his eyes. He hadn't so much as moved his eyelids, and the glow was unmistakably emanating from Meg's body again. His peripheral vision caught several of the same colors in the distance where other people were seated. He tried his very best not to let his face show that anything was different. After looking up, he found he needed to try harder. It was blurry, but he saw hundreds of scaly reptilelike animals crawling all over the ceiling. He swallowed with a gulp and stiffened his lip as he lowered his head, trying to force a smile at his glowing date—or nondate, as it were. He removed the glasses and returned them to her.

"What was that all about, Harvey?" Meg asked. "Are you not telling me something?"

"No, it's nothing. Really. I just needed to prove to myself that passing out is not a new thing for me, you know, just from putting on the wrong glasses."

There were noticeable droplets of sweat on his brow, and Meg didn't buy it. "Harvey, you're lying to me. I can tell it. This may be a nondate-date, but if you don't tell me what's in that mind of yours right now, it will be the last nondate-date we ever have."

Meg couldn't believe she wanted to know what was in Harvey's mind. That was like asking a shark to smile. Both produced the same lack of comfort.

"Meg, really. It's nothing. How's your salad?" Harvey said, changing the subject, or least trying to change the subject, as he tried hard to stomach a bite of his own, given the view he'd just observed.

"Harvey, I swear. You better tell me," Meg demanded. "Wait a second. Yesterday, when you put on my glasses, you said I was glowing! What did you mean by that? I see something in your eyes, Harvey. You're holding back. Are you seeing things? Do you think you have a brain tumor?"

"A brain tumor? Gosh, Meg, that's a bit dark."

"I'm sorry, Harvey. That was wrong to say, especially if you do have a brain tumor. I mean—" Meg was starting to sound as unconfident as Harvey usually did.

"It's okay," he said, not believing he was considering offering up the information she was requesting. "I'll try and explain, but first I need to do something, else, okay? Please don't run away."

"Harvey, what are you going to do?"

"Just wait here for one moment. I need to find out something."

Harvey stood up from the table and walked over to one of the waiters standing at the check station. Meg watched him have a small awkward-looking conversation. The waiter got a strange look on his face, shrugged his shoulders, and proceeded to take off his own glasses and hand them to Harvey. Meg saw Harvey switch the waiter's glasses with his own and look around the room the same way he had at their table. Then she saw Harvey look up. The next moment, she saw a look of horror on Harvey's face. He jumped backward, knocking a tray of glasses to the floor. Ripping off the waiter's glasses, he handed them back, made some apologetic motions, and then he returned to her, taking big tiptoe steps on his way back.

Standing at their table, Harvey then proceeded to say as calmly as possible. "Meg, would you mind if we, maybe, I don't know, left the restaurant? Yes, I'd really like to go now, I think…could we *go?* I'm sure you won't believe me, but if we could just go, I promise I'll tell you whatever you want to know. So, can we?"

"Harvey, there'd better be a pretty good story behind all of this."

"Oh, it's a great story. Not one you'll believe, but it's definitely great," he answered, and they walked out of the restaurant after tossing a couple of twenty-dollar bills at the hostess upon leaving.

⟨—◇○◇—⟩

"Okay, Harvey, let's have it," Meg complained after they climbed into her car. "I didn't get to finish dinner, so I'd better get to the finish of what's going on with you."

"I don't know how to start, Meg. You'll think I'm crazy. You already asked me if I had a tumor."

"Just start, or I'm driving you home right now, and I'll get Jimmy to pour your coffee from now on in the mornings!"

"Okay, okay. Umm…uh—" He stuttered, tapping his fingers together. *How*, he thought, *can I tell her and not get a "You need to see the doctor again" response?*

"Spit it out, Harvey, come on. I promise I'll believe whatever you tell me. I won't think you're crazy, and I'll still be your friend."

"Really?" Harvey asked, trying to take her at her word, if only to grasp at the hope he could get through the telling of what she was demanding he tell.

"Really. Now, go!" she ordered.

"Okay, Meg. It's like this, I guess. You see, I put on other peoples' glasses, and I can see auras around everyone, except for some people who seem to disappear and reappear, and I also see monsters everywhere. Hellish monsters, demons. They're horrible. One fell from the ceiling in O'Tooley's and then scurried across the floor. That's why I jumped back. And yesterday, the same thing happened. You were glowing beautifully, and Jimmy kept disappearing, and then there was this face from hell, literally, so close he could have been breathing on me, and that must've been when I passed out."

Whew! I said it.

Meg was still, and she looked back at Harvey without expression. She was trying to decide if she should even attempt to hold to the promise she'd just made.

"Harvey, I'm driving you home."

"But—"

"Eh!" She cut him off. "Don't speak. Just shush! I'm driving you home, and you're not saying another word."

And that is just what she did.

—◇○◇—

Harvey sat alone again in his house, completely bummed out about his nondate-date with Meg. Why should he have even tried? The whole reason he didn't go out with girls, especially girls like Meg, was because he was Harvey. He knew he'd be declared Town Nerd on Declarations Day if such a ceremony ever arose, and he'd probably be shunned by Town Drunk if Claremore had one. He wasn't quite sure what to be more upset about—the evening with Meg or what had happened with his eyesight. It felt ridiculous thinking he could be upset about both, given the nature of the latter, but he was.

He sat on his couch trying to figure out how to patch things up with Meg, and simultaneously trying to understand why he was seeing such strange things through other people's glasses. Then his cell rang. It was Meg.

"Hello?"

"*Harvey!*" Meg was screaming.

"Yes, Meg. What is it?"

"I don't know what you did, but you need to get over here and fix it right *now!*"

"What's happening? Are you all right?" he asked.

"No, I'm not all right! Do I sound *all right*, Harvey? Would you be all right if you'd just seen the devil walk across your kitchen and hiss at you?"

"What are you talking—never mind. Stay on the phone; I'll be right over."

Concussion or not, he was out the door and into his car.

Meg opened her door after she heard Harvey respond to her scared version of "Who is it?" He burst in, very unnerdily and in a quite determined manner, and made his way past Meg and into her living room. He was not a tall man, nor was he broad, but for one second, he looked like a fireman rushing in to save lives. The second passed, and he was just Harvey again.

"Are you okay?" he said and looked back at her, still standing by the door.

"Yes, Harvey. I mean, *no!* I mean, I don't know! What did you do to me? Your little story, and now I can't even be alone in my own house!"

"So you just got scared? You didn't really *see* anything?"

"I don't know! It all happened so fast. I was turning around from the sink, and there he was."

"Who?"

"The devil."

"The *devil?*"

"Yes, the devil. You know, horns, pitchfork, tail, cloven feet, *red!* The mother-freaking devil, Harvey!"

"But now you're making it sound like you really *did* see it? I don't understand."

"I don't understand, either, Harvey. You'll think I'm crazy if I tell you."

"I'll think *you're* crazy?" Harvey was astonished he was having the exact same conversation with Meg, only in reverse, just an hour after their nondate-date had ended miserably. "What do you mean I'll think you're crazy? After what I told you tonight?"

"Yes, Harvey, but you said you just *saw* things."

Harvey looked back at her, trying to make sense of what she was trying to say. She was right, he had just seen things. He couldn't be totally sure about anything else. "Yes, that's right."

"Well, I don't know what you did or whatever, but you're going to make this all better. Because that thing was there!" She pointed into her kitchen. "I could smell him, Harvey. I could feel the breeze he created as he walked past me. I even felt his cloak hit my leg! He was *here*, and he wasn't some hallucination!"

Harvey thought back to his experience at the diner. Before he had passed out, when that demon thing had been right up in his face. He hadn't felt its breath or felt its presence or anything. He had just *seen* it. Yes, he hadn't had much time before drifting into oblivion and counting rainbows, but he was definitely sure he had only been *seeing*. Now, he wasn't sure what to say to Meg. So he told her the truth.

"I'm not sure what I can do, Meg. I mean, I've just been seeing things. I guess I thought it was real enough to confess it to you, but after it was all said and done, I literally did start questioning my own mind. Perhaps I was having some kind of an episode. I didn't really expect you to be calling me and telling me you nearly shook the hand of Satan while holding a dish towel."

"I don't think this is the time to be funny. I don't really think…I mean I can't think…you know, that it was *actually* here, I think. I mean, Harvey, I can't think that, can I? Maybe you're going crazy and it's contagious or something. That's got to be it, Harvey. We got to figure this out. I can't go crazy, Harvey. And I can't go work at the diner and be making everybody else go crazy either. I have bills to pay, you know. Good grief, I shouldn't have helped you."

As she said this, Harvey looked back at her as if he'd been punched in the gut. He wasn't exactly sure what he felt. He didn't know if her comment had just slapped him in the face or made him feel sorry that he might have gotten her sick. Either way, it was the worst he'd felt in a long time, and for a moment, he hadn't been able to hide it.

Meg looked at him and immediately knew she had crossed the line. She spoke. "Oh, Harvey, I didn't mean that. I'm sorry. I'm just upset. Of course, I'm glad I helped you."

"No, Meg, that's all right. You're right. This isn't a good thing, and if I've gotten you all messed up, that's not right. I should be the one who's saying he's sorry."

"No Harvey, seriously. I was completely wrong. I shouldn't have said that. I really am sorry. Please forgive—"

And she stopped.

Harvey stood in his place waiting for her to finish her sentence. Instead of her completing her thought, Meg just stared back at him, motionless, her big blue eyes wider than ever, and full of fear. Harvey whispered (*Why am I whispering?*), "What's wrong, Meg?" Then he saw something move in the reflection of her glasses.

Harvey spun around, and as soon as he saw it, he started backpedaling. The thing took a step toward him, and then another. It was just as Meg had described. It was the devil, or at least, exactly what everyone had always described the Devil as being.

It raised its arm horizontally and pointed as it came closer. Harvey backed into Meg, who still hadn't said a word, almost knocking her down.

"Come on, let's get out of here!" he yelled, as he turned slightly to grab her arm, pulled her away from the thing, and started leading her toward the front door. She started to move with him, and as he grabbed the doorknob and pulled open the front door, he noticed the thing had disappeared.

"Holy God!" Harvey spat out, his back leaning against the open door. "Meg, I don't know what that was, but I hope you don't think this is my fault now. I don't think mental illness makes Satan appear in your living room at the same time to two different people." Harvey slid down the door to a seated position, and with a voice akin to one used in ghost storytelling, he softly said, "He was here, Meg. That was real."

Looking down at him, Meg sobbed. "What is happening to us, Harvey?"

"I don't know, but we better find out, and hopefully, before that thing comes back. Let's get out of here."

"Where are we going?" Meg moaned.

"Somewhere else."

Somewhere else was Jammer's Café. It was the only brightly lit and familiar place in town. Jimmy had acted surprised to see Meg there—and with Harvey, especially, remarking that if they were on a date, neither of them looked like they were having a particularly good time. "Maybe you two should stick to morning coffee," Jimmy had finished with.

Harvey and Meg barely acknowledged Jimmy's chiding. They went and slid into a booth—not too happy looking, yes, but still looking like they were together, and more *together* than only having arrived in the same car.

"And didn't you just leave here for the night, Meg? Seriously, we don't need you back till mornin'!" The two didn't answer. "Well, don't stay up too late kids. I need her alert when she's servin' customers," Jimmy yelled across the diner.

Meg looked at Jimmy and gave a small grin, emanating "not happy" all the more— but this time directed at him. Jimmy took the cue and stopped talking. As Meg looked back toward Harvey, it seemed that Jimmy couldn't stop being Jimmy. "Well just don't go passing out again, Harvey," Jimmy barked, and then he went back to work.

"It was different at your house," Harvey remarked.

"What do you mean?" Meg asked.

"I mean, I *felt* that thing's presence. It wasn't like the other times I saw things. I wouldn't have necessarily realized it before, but experiencing both what happened to me earlier and then what happened in your living room, I know it's different."

"Harvey, honestly, we can sit here and talk about this like we're not crazy, but look around. Now that we're at Jammer's, it really doesn't seem real. There's got to be some other explanation. Come on, you're the genius; figure it out. Talk about your science stuff. Make me feel better."

Of course, she was right. There had to be some other explanation. "I don't know, Meg," he pondered. "I guess it *could* be some kind of codelusional experience or something. Maybe we were exposed to the same chemical or sickness. My story at dinner combined with yours over the phone...somehow...made us—I don't know—it sounds just as crazy as if we really saw it. But, you know, we saw the same thing because we both had it on our minds. That's all I can think of."

"That's it, Harvey. Codelusional. That's what we'll go with. We contracted some disease or we're high on something and we just had a similar vision. We'll go to the doctor in the morning, and we'll find out what it is." Meg was looking less pale, and for the first time, she seemed glad to hear one of his mind's suppositions. "Let's just stay here awhile in the bright lights; and I'm not sleeping alone tonight, Harvey; and I'm not going back to my house, okay? If I have another hallucination like that, I might die, and that's if you're *with* me. There is no way I'm going through it alone."

Harvey hadn't given a thought to ever spending a night with Meg. Hearing her say she wanted to—even if it was as much a nonsleepover as their nondate had been a date, even if it was only to not to be left alone in case Satan returned wearing pajamas—it was still wonderful, yet strange he could think that, given the circumstances. Never in his life would he have considered this would happen. Apparent codelusion was the reason for it to happen, and that was probably the *only* reason it could ever make such an event possible, Harvey thought. He almost broke a smile. Almost.

"Don't get any funny ideas, Harvey? We're still just friends, got it?"

"No, Meg, no problem. That's not what I was thinking. Promise. I just can't believe this evening, huh?"

"*Oh, what a night* doesn't even begin to describe it, Harvey. Now buy me a milkshake."

CHAPTER 33

THE NONSLEEPOVER
DECEMBER 4, 2012

———————⋄∘C═⌘═⊃∘⋄———————

HARVEY HAD OFFERED HIS BED, sacrificing it for the couch, but instead, Meg had wanted the couch and had requested him on the floor next to the couch. A strange couple of days had just passed, but waking up in the morning and rolling over to see Meg's face asleep, above him, resting on the edge of his sofa, was about the strangest event he'd witnessed. His bad vision kept her just out of focus, so he quietly fished for his glasses next to the pillow where he'd left them and slid them onto his face. As he blinked, a second vision of her materialized. She was his own personal sunrise, and Harvey knew he was in love. Yes, he knew he would need to continue being *just Harvey*, the guy she had nondate-dates, codelusions, and nonsleepover-sleeps with, but he'd never seen anything as beautiful as she was now, regardless of the small amount of encrusted drool that had solidified sometime during the night near the corner of her mouth. He hadn't allowed feelings like this before. It would have been an agonizing crush indeed, to see her every day at the diner all these years if he had. A subconscious pipe dream it had been to love her, and it had stayed nicely tucked away in his mind where it belonged, unable to escape and torture him. Harvey had kept it locked up for so long. But now he was waking up next to her (*below her—on the floor, not next to her, Harvey; live in the real world*), and he found it impossible not to let those suppressed feelings emerge. For better or worse, he knew he would try to protect her, always, and for better or worse for his heart, he let himself fall.

"What are you looking at, Harvey? I look awful in the morning. Close your eyes!" Meg had woken. She sat up quickly after this demand, and with the blankets pulled up over her face, she whisked out of the room and toward the bathroom.

Harvey sat alone, on the floor. Reality had returned, and now instead of *lost in love*, he was feeling guilty for having woken up first. It was funny how women could reverse the tables on you so easily. What a skill.

She wasn't gone thirty seconds when he heard her scream. No coffee at Jammer's was needed to wake up today. He was at the bathroom door faster than he figured he'd ever made the journey…if he'd had time to think about things like that.

When he arrived, he saw Meg in the bathtub, her head against the back wall, both legs hanging up and over the outside edge. Her blanket was intermingled with her body parts, which were covered by the borrowed pair of his maroon-striped pajamas.

"Jesus, what happened! Are you all right?"

"Yes. I tripped on the end of the blanket."

"Thank God, you're all right. You know more people die from falls in a bathroom—"

"I don't need a lecture, Harvey. Just help me out of here." Embarrassed, she reached her hand up to him.

After pulling her out of her predicament, he left her to herself. She closed the door behind him and locked it.

From behind the door, Meg called out, "You thought I saw the devil again, didn't you?"

Realizing he probably had, he yelled back, "Yes! I guess I'm glad you only fell in the tub, now that you're all right."

These were the strangest conversations he'd ever had with anyone and Harvey figured if anyone had heard them talking in the past forty-eight hours, they may have thought they were two *special* people who had gotten married and were *managing*. He almost wished an alarm clock would go off, telling them it was time to take their meds. If what had been going on kept going on, that might come true.

On his return to the living room, his wandering thoughts were stopped, as something on the dining room table gleamed from the sun coming through the dining room window. The *something* was Meg's pair of glasses.

I'll just try them on again—just to see.

And he did. It seemed that each successive delve into this new hobby of his was needing less self-convincing.

His eyes were closed, and he was holding on tight to the back of one of the dining room table's chairs. Slowly, he opened his eyes, passing from a squint to a full, open gaze, Harvey saw nothing out of the ordinary, besides his dining room table being considerably blurrier. He turned around to face the rest of the house's interior, and his heart sank. It took all his will to stay calm and quiet. He didn't want to startle Meg into falling again in the bathroom. He couldn't make out everything, but there was definitely movement all around him, stretching as far back into the living room as he could see. He saw figures large and small walking around—each with its own shape and its own hideous gait. Things were crawling on the walls in various directions. One of these *things* made its way down toward the floor, and Harvey got the scariest feeling yet. He didn't want to look down. He didn't want to know.

But he did.

It was bad. Not as bad as it could be, because it appeared this experience was more like his first one. Only a vision. He couldn't feel the presence of any of what he was seeing. The things on the walls were also on the floor. They were crawling this way and that way around his feet. He couldn't make out detail, but the creatures were various shapes and sizes and looked a bit like beetles, only huge beetles, five or six inches long. He wanted to take off the glasses, but he knew he needed to figure out what the hell was happening, so he held on for a little longer. *For Meg's sake*, he thought, and he found the strength to keep observing. That's when he noticed the oddity.

The scarabs—for lack of a better word, given that Harvey didn't know what in the hell they were—were bumping into his foot and then moving away again. They surrounded him on the floor, except for about a thirty-degree arc on his right side, which was completely void of the scarab-beetles. As he looked closer and followed the vacant spot away from him, he noticed it was actually, a path. On this path was *nothing*. No crawling scarabs, no creatures walking. Figures, resembling various versions of a scaly Igor, were avoiding the "path," and Harvey then saw it led to his front door.

He'd had enough. He ripped off Meg's glasses—fortunately, just before she opened the bathroom door. He placed them back on the table where he had found them. An eerie feeling encompassed him as he backed away from the table, wondering if he was stepping on the beetlelike things that had infested his home—on the *dark* side. The pathway (and that's exactly what it was) had him thinking, and he stopped caring about what was at the bottom of his bare feet in Mystic Vision Land.

Is it a pathway? Yes. If so, where does it lead? I don't know. Maybe it's like a red carpet to Satan's chamber? Maybe it's a road to safety.

"Harvey?" *Back to reality.* Meg was speaking. "You haven't moved far." She had made her way from the bathroom, taking a few short paces through the hallway leading to the dining room, which sat adjacent to the living room (i.e., Demon Zoo) at the front of the house.

"Yeah, I know," Harvey responded, "I was just thinking...you know, about everything that's happened."

"Yes?"

"Well, what if it *is* real? I mean...what do we do *if* it's *real?* I guess that's the question. I mean it's not like anyone is going to believe us, and we can't just sit around and live with demons and hell-spawned insects and who knows what else."

"Maybe we ought to cross that bridge if it comes, Harvey. I, for one, just want to put it behind me. I think we ate some bad food or something. I think it will pass if it hasn't already."

Oh, it hasn't passed, Meg.

Meg continued, "I feel pretty normal this morning, outside of waking up in your house."

Well, I don't feel normal, Meg.

He felt a lot of responses in his head, but Harvey didn't know what else he could say. If and until she had another experience, it appeared Meg would only believe this so-called botulism hadn't run its course. He changed the subject to breakfast while his mind spiraled around the questions he'd posed her.

——⊂⋄⊃——

It being December 2012, almost six years had passed since Jack and Randy had opened Box 2347 at 23:47 the night of January 31. The changes to the world's landscape as the scrolls' myths had released their prophecies was gradual, noticeable only to a few who were up close and personal like Meg and Harvey. To the rest of the population, the world appeared to have just more of the same—typical superstitions, tabloid reports, and the ramblings of pop-culture news.

Those suffering *up close and personal,* like parents who realized their children could start fires with only their will, or a spouse who realized his wife could sweep the floor by *wanting* the broom to move, kept it quiet and tried to control it. One couple, whose child could freeze water by touching it, tried taking their son to a doctor. This only prompted scientists to be notified, who in turn, had a field day running tests. The parents experienced horrible guilt for seeking a solution in the first place, and some government officials had a blast using their cover-up skills to cover it up.

There were people who complained about seeing real monsters, but those kinds of things happen all the time, anyway, right? The only difference in these cases were the people complaining were *actually* seeing monsters—*for real.* Of course there was the occasional case in which a "real monster" would kill or eat a "real person," but unless you were there to see it—which no one ever was who wasn't also killed or eaten, too, that is—as far as the police were concerned, it was only another missing person's case or another grisly unsolved homicide.

The world is a big place, and the scarcity and distance between these occurrences kept the threshold needed for mass awareness from being reached. Little could be done by those experiencing these problems, and without a global viewpoint, they could assign little meaning to their circumstances.

The Myth of the Hereafter left some people having lost their religious beliefs because they realized they weren't true. Some realized their husband or wife or partner didn't really love them. Others discovered their parents favored their sister or brother over them. Even a few who found out the world wasn't flat, like they had truly believed, didn't create a megamedia stir. These random people just became people whose mindsets had changed. Of course, some of those mindset changes caused suicide, despair, or an occasional act of violence, but they never manifested on the news as "caused by supernatural events, and now back to you, Bob." A few added themselves to the count of sidewalk preachers, preaching their newfound realizations, sometimes with a pamphlet in hand, sometimes with a sign hung over their shoulders.

But mostly, the few having these experiences only readjusted their personal views and went on with their lives.

After Jack Johanssen had translated the scrolls, the most obvious strangeness leaking out of them were reports of people decaying into grotesque forms akin to a hunchback, a pig, a rat, and insert-other-gross-adjective-here random animal. But even those were few in number—at least, until all hell started breaking loose.

There were the few like Derek, as well: people who realized putting their hands toward the right person would turn the "right person" into a billowing dust cloud. Some people who gained this power stayed at home at first, many times grieving because their respective spouses or children had been the "right people." Eventually venturing out into the world again, they only became petrified to learn there were other "right people." This, in turn, drove them back home and into self-imprisonment. A few of these occurrences did make the nightly news in a town or two. However, the sparse reports amounted only to a quick blurb where eyewitnesses agreed on camera to Bob the Reporter, that they, indeed, had seen a man or woman disappear into smoke right before their eyes. Strange, but not provable and, therefore, not cause for a worldwide stir.

Ghost Hunters remained a hit show, and a few others like it popped up on the old zone-out plasma screen, placating the fancies of a public who was still into reality TV and explanations of the unknown. Psychiatrists got a few more patients between 2007 and 2012. If these medical professionals had all been able to compile their sessions, they might have noticed a strange pattern centering on seeing demons and monsters—many patients insisting they were more than visions. But, to a psychiatrist, a vision's a vision, no matter how real the patient tries to explain it is. Police had a few more homicides and suicides to deal with, but rarely in the same place. A few strange cases in which wives or husbands pleaded in their own defense that they *were* "really trying to shoot the Boogeyman standing behind their spouses in order to protect their children." *Yeah, right, I'm sure you were. But, for now you have the right to remain silent.* There was the incident with that high school in Kentucky, but even that never got the full attention it deserved, and for the most part, went unnoticed. Here and there, a sad note was written by a teenager before ending his or her own life, in which they had described how they were haunted by demons.

Aren't we all, kid? Aren't we all?

There was no worldwide stir from any of this, and for one simple reason. A story on a local television station in Boise, Idaho, was not heard by anyone but Boiseans. And if it didn't happen elsewhere, or if no one made the connection to another report months or years later in Zimbabwe or Albuquerque or Nepal or Krakow, then it was forgotten, and, therefore, it might as well have been in Timbuktu or Kathmandu to anyone else. Even when a town named Bumfuck seemed to pop into existence in Egypt, fully populated with people who seemed all well and good and believing they had lived their whole lives there, the report was short-lived in the media, and once again, no connection was made to any other "happening." And later, when they popped out of existence, many wondered if it had happened at all.

Most of the time, things didn't happen again, or in the same way, or near the same place, or get reported at the same time, or even in the same language. A Duster would get scared and stay home. A Fire-Starter would relish in his or her gift and keep it quiet. But most were all off the grid. People weren't declaring their sudden abilities on Main Street, and everything was too few and far between to be put together by anyone.

Well, almost anyone. There were the conspiracy theorists. There are always the conspiracy theorists. Most of the time, their reading of articles and microfiche and surfing the web and correlating their results into finger-pointing is bogus, and that doesn't help their credibility. But sometimes they're right. Sadly, when they're right, the only people to believe them are fellow conspiracy theorists. There was the couple who put two and two together and then discussed their findings on a late-night radio show or two or three. And they were paid attention to by the avid listeners for their hour time slot. Then the next crackpot was on, and it was on to the next conspiracy, at which the avid listeners were dazzled by New Crackpot's theories. The only difference between them and the next crackpot was that in their circumstance, they were correct. But even so, they didn't know the whole truth, and the only thing they were *right* about was that "something was going on."

And, really, what good is that?

CHAPTER 34

THE SCROLL HOLDER, ALWAYS HERE THOUSANDS OF YEARS AGO

───────◇○◯◯○◇───────

"YOU ARE JUST GOING TO HAVE TO believe me! *Okay?*" Byron hollered. "I don't understand! They will never accept me or take me into their people," said the man lost in a blizzard, way north of his home, to the other man who had found him, who had come from farther away than the imagination could imagine.

Blinding, biting whiteness. To the two men, this was all that existed. The wind howled and gusted past them as if direction had no meaning and wind had always blown from everywhere, to everywhere. The sun tripled the blinding effect of the wind and snow, reflecting white into white between every powdered snowflake whipped by the air. Each man winced as the thrown flakes pierced his skin; the wind's randomness was only an illusion used to mask its well-trained ninja skills. The men's voices were raised to yells not only to hear one another, but also to stifle their respective pain.

"Yes, they will! I've seen it happen," the man in twenty-first-century clothing bellowed through the gusts. "Listen, do I look like anyone you've ever seen before?"

"No!" the man wrapped in hides of polar bear and seal roared back.

The conversation needed to get somewhere fast, and Byron knew it. He should have dressed better for this meeting. It's not like he hadn't *viewed* it first. But viewing was viewing, and, now, it was very clear that doing was *doing*.

Byron fought for the thought of what to say, regardless of his preknowledge. "And—I speak your *language!*"

"Perfectly! *Yes!*"

"I don't know your language! I know that's not proof. You wouldn't understand. I don't understand. Damn, it's so cold!"

"You should have more clothing to warm you," the ancient Eskimo warned, but his words sounded like a demand because of his need to force his voice through the cold hell between him and this strange visitor. "How did you appear from *nothing?*"

"I am not a god, if that's what you are asking. But I might be here because of God. I don't have much time, so please just do what I said! Take the scroll I have given you, and never look at it! It will keep you young. You will live for generations with the people of the tribe living in that direction." Byron pointed to his right, his throat getting drier with every word. Even at his strongest scream, he would not have been heard even a meter away. "Head that way, over that crest of ice, and you will find them. As long as you are with them, they will be protected!"

"They won't accept me. Why can't you lead me back to *my* home and protect *them?*"

"Your tribe isn't chosen. Somebody has to be chosen, and I am telling you where those people are! Speak to their leaders and tell them what I have told you." It was hard for Byron to get out the words; he was shivering, almost convulsing. "I don't have much time! Make your plea to Father and Questions Father. They will listen. You must trust me! What do you have to lose?"

"*My* tribe! *My* family!"

"You're lost! You may not even find them again."

"You could help me!"

"I don't know where they are! Listen to me, take it as a sign. I appeared and saved you by leading you to a nearby tribe you would never have known is over that ridge! You have been chosen because of your character, and this is important to all people. It is a small price to pay for the gift you're being offered. You will hand down the knowledge and wisdom you learn continually until the end of everything."

The wind seemed bent on stopping the two men's communion, and Byron could think now only of the cabin's fireplace, burning and warm. He was holding his body tight, fighting for composure in the frigidness of what would one day, far in the future, be north of Northern Northern *Northern* Canada.

"I've got to go! Please do what I said," Byron pleaded. "Take my leaving as a vision to find truth in my words."

Byron took a step backward from the man and vanished. Byron was back in his cabin, and the man he had just been talking to (*screaming at*) was standing still in a distant past, contemplating his vision of a strange man, as he decided whether or not to turn east and head for the people of Home Now in an attempt to make it his new home.

"Oh my God!" Byron shouted out as he clutched his body in the middle of the cabin. Rubbing his arms with his hands, he moved closer to the fire. "I sure as hell would have chosen another desert over that!"

He sat down by the fire and looked into the flames. They danced, making repetitive leaps in the reflections of his eyes. He was beginning to heat to normal levels again, and chills raced down his spine with every deep breath he took. Exhaling the last of these, he spoke to the flames. "Well…that's number three. One more to go."

"Yep, one more."

Answering himself had been occurring for over forty years, and in no way did it seem odd to Byron any longer. In his long state of "prophet-hood-ness," or whatever one wanted to call it, the behavior had become so natural that even an outside observer may have felt compelled to answer either "speaker."

"One more. The *Horsemen*. And great," he huffed, "it's going to be winter there *too*."

"After everything, could not I have picked the time I go to them, huh?" Byron spoke to the empty cabin but this time not to himself. "It had to be winter. Winter, winter, *winter!*"

All in all, most of the world got along just fine until December 21, 2012. And even that night, the night when the Kansas City's Channel 5 anchorman seemed to set the weatherman on fire by patting the meteorologist on the back, didn't faze many at first. Had there been a creature looking like Death, *or something like it*, standing behind them both laughing his ass off while said weatherman burned to a crisp?

To most, initially, that was just good TV on the day the world was supposed to end anyway, according to the Mayan Freakozoid Conspiracy Theorists (well, that would have been the name most people would have given them if all those who believed in the 12-21 calendar prophecy had organized themselves into a single entity and tried to give themselves a legitimate-sounding name like Society for the Research of World End Events). Even when the entire San Diego news team appeared to be gruesomely slaughtered during the ten o'clock news by two hell-spawned demon-looking things, the craziest comment heard in any living room, was, "Whew, Molly, they'll do anything to keep their ratings up nowadays. At least they waited till the ten o'clock for that bloodbath."

These mild reactions were short-lived, however, for soon after, barbecued friends *and enemies*, hideously disturbing metamorphoses of neighbors into slimy hunchbacks, and the serving up of a human or two on a demon's dinner plate became more common, more visible, and much, *much* less escapable.

Initially, reporters tried valiantly to keep up with the stories, but soon enough, they themselves were becoming the stories, and this just made it too hard to concentrate on the note-taking and microphone holding. It would be nice to say that many people were somehow able to go on with their daily lives, being unaffected by Hell Day, as it would soon become referred to, but it would only be *nice* to say that. By the first of the year in 2013, pretty much all hell *had* actually seemed to have broken loose on the planet, and so the "Hell Day" name had been adopted wholeheartedly in turn.

CHAPTER 35

JACK'S BACK
DECEMBER 2, 2012

————————◇○◁◯▷○◇————————

"JACK?"

"Yes, Randy, it's me."

"Ah. You don't sound like you over this phone. You all right?"

"Yes, Randy, I'm fine. Why the call?"

"We're just wondering if you plan on joining us soon. We really think this Mayan Calendar thing is going to be it."

"Randy, I've told you all before. I have a job here. I can't just keep taking off work every time you believe the world is coming to an end."

"I know, Jack, but a lot has been going on. We haven't talked in a while, and—"

"It's been six years, Randy. I think we need to accept the fact that maybe nothing is going to happen. Maybe—"

"Jack, come on. You know the people we've found and what they can do. You're the one who translated the darned scrolls in the first place. I can't believe you would start to disbelieve. What about Sarah, here? And Quincy? And *Four Winds!*"

Jack didn't have an answer. He knew he believed, but soon after translating the scrolls in February of 2007, it had become very clear that if anything *was* going to happen, nobody in their little circle had the foggiest idea when. Even Randy had agreed after his vacation time had been used up that he'd better go back to work. Like Jack, he had to eat; he had bills to pay and school to finish. Spring semester had already started before the sojourn to find the Duboises, and he'd missed a week and a half because of the visit.

The group kept in touch and continued to float ideas past one another. Derek and Sarah had taken Quincy and Four Winds in as permanent guests, and by the time summer arrived, Randy couldn't bear being away from Sarah any longer. He left school and moved into the Dubois home at Sarah's first offer of the idea.

Jack had told Randy he was crazy. Absolutely nothing strange had happened since their initial parting. He felt Randy leaving school was quitting at best; at worst, he was running away to live off the Duboises. "Eventually, they are going to realize nothing is happening, too, and wonder why they have five people living in their home eating their food," Jack had told him...and Randy had ignored him.

And Jack had been wrong. While he had continued his profession of "misanthrope in dark office in basement of warehouse," the others had started a sort of research team of the strange and unexplained—whatever fit the mold alluded to by the scroll's prophecies and warnings. Inviting Jack to come and join them had come to no avail several times. Even using flattery of needing his fun-loving self *and* his knowledge around didn't produce the effect they desired. Not that they thought it would. He had declined, repeatedly, telling them he was more than willing to help with anything they sent him or wanted to know, but he preferred to be a silent partner for now and continue to receive a paycheck.

They updated him on discoveries they made from various sources: Following leads from magazines like the *National Enquirer.* Scouring the bottomless pit of the internet. Bogus lead after bogus lead had been investigated, and the calls to Jack had become fewer and fewer as months and years progressed. As he heard less from them, life had become more or less normal again. Their searches would eventually die out, he thought; the lack of findings would bring them to their senses eventually. When he'd answered Randy's call today, it had been over a year since he'd received any word from any of them. The quiet normalcy of his office was about to be broken. Randy, somehow, was perching on this desk again, telling him to open a box—only this time with the help of a little toy invented by a man named Alexander Bell.

"Six years, Randy," Jack said in a smug tone.

"I know, but we have more now."

"What do you have? More photographs of men in monster suits? More Art Bell newsletters? I believe the world will end, Randy, but it's most likely going to occur when the sun burns out around 5 billion CE. So, for now, I'd better just keep my health insurance. This job has better benefits than the one you're offering."

"Jack, we have a Discerner." Randy sounded real serious. Even with six more years of maturity and having assumed the role of husband to Sarah Dubois, now Sarah Haverstamp, seriousness had never been his forte. His tone caught Jack's attention, even if it was unwillingly.

"You mean, like Derek?" Jack asked, slightly intrigued. Not intrigued enough to quit his job and become a conspiracy chaser with them, but intrigued nonetheless.

"Yes. He's from England, actually. And we did find him through a late-night radio talk show. He had a website of the 'strange and unexplained' and was using it as a lure to find others like him, just like we do. And Jack, he *has* found others. And we have also! I mean, he's the first Discerner we've found, but Riley—that's his name—and we have recently located people who can do other things. It's all happened in the last five months. Before that, as you know, there was nothing, at least nothing substantial. We would hear from a teenage kid here and there who claimed to have done something once or twice, but most of them couldn't prove it, and it felt too risky to be digging into people's children's lives, so we backed off those responses pretty quickly. And you remember the one man from Russia who could freeze and melt water three years ago, right? I think we told you about him."

"Yes, I remember. But he only did it once for you before he couldn't repeat it. And 'finding one telekinetic human being does not the end of the world predict,' is what I remember saying to you."

"Yes, I know, Jack. But like I just said, in the last five months, we have found over twenty, and Riley—he's located four Discerners and about fifteen people who can do various things with the four elements. And their 'gifts' aren't going away. Doesn't that sound like something's coming?"

"It sounds like something, Randy. Don't know about the coming part."

"Just hear me out," Randy sighed. "Yes, he's being Jack, Sarah," Randy had answered his wife, who must have been listening off the phone to their conversation.

"Tell her not to worry," Jack murmured. "I'm listening. Go on."

"Okay, there's all the hoopla in the news and everything—you know, about the end of the world when the Mayan calendar takes a restart in about three weeks. So this idea hit us a month ago, when everyone started talking about it more and more. We thought, maybe it's the reason we have been so successful in our efforts recently. Maybe it really is the end!"

"Randy, even if you've found thirty or forty people, have you even checked them all out? And you know what you sound like? You sound like every other kook and cult out there on the airwaves right now. Listen, I'm sorry, I'm not trying to put you and the others down. I don't want to say I don't believe. It'd be nice if I didn't. I don't like having to worry whether I'm going to wake up one day and all the stuff in those scrolls is manifesting in my bedroom. And I'm not putting you and Sarah and the others down for holding onto the torch for so long. But exactly what do you want from me? What can I do, Randy? I have a job. I have a mortgage and bills. Remember those?"

"I don't know, Jack. We were all thinking…um…okay, here goes…the Mayan end is near Christmas anyway. You could take a few days off early and come here. If nothing happens, great, we spend the holidays together. It's been a long time, Jack, and I guess we would all feel more comfortable if we were all together, just in case."

Randy sounded sincere, and not just about the "in case" part. Jack thought, *For a misanthrope, I sure am getting a special holiday Mariah Carey Christmas feeling right now. The kid's making a pretty good point—regardless of the mumbo-jumbo hocus pocus stuff—and for some reason, the eggnog is calling.*

Jack made him wait a little longer than he had to, just to be Jack, and then answered, "Okay, Randy. I'll come."

Jack heard Randy deliver a "He said yes!" and cheers in the background returned almost too quickly—as if not just Sarah but also the rest of his pals had been hovering over the receiver waiting for his answer.

"You know, Jack, Sarah made me call."

"Why?"

"She said she knew if she had called and asked, you may have come only so as not to disappoint her, as a gentleman. But if you said yes to me, you must really care."

He felt like he'd just entered the end of *It's a Wonderful Life* or something.

Oh, Sarah. Oh, Randy. Ah, come here, Four Winds—I'll never leave again. Oh, Quincy, put 'er there, old friend. I love you all. I love you all. Merry End of the World, and hallelujah!

Although strangely compelled to say what he had just thought, just to get a laugh, he took the Jack route instead and said, "Tell your wife she's a pretty smart lady."

He glanced down at his calendar, resting under his elbows as he sat at his desk in his dark office in his quiet basement in his civilian-owned government-contracted warehouse—the place where all this had begun nearly six years earlier. The squares marking the days of December were as empty as November had been, and October, and the months before that—he wondered why he even had a calendar. The twenty-first was on a Friday. A week off for friends—he could do that.

"I'll see you all on the weekend of the fifteenth. Bye, Randy."

Jack hung up the phone, still staring at his calendar. Guessing he had never removed it, as useless as it was in his life of uneventfulness, because no one ever removes them; the damn thing won't fit in a trash can, and you're too lazy to walk it to the dumpster when the thought sinks in that you're sick of looking at it. He took his pen and drew a line from the fifteenth through the twenty-sixth—the first meaningful thing he'd put on any calendar since his university days while marking exam dates. God knew the few doodles he'd made on this particular calendar weren't meaningful. He figured he'd need a day after Christmas for traveling back. He focused on the so-called ominous date sitting in the middle of his coming vacation—the date everyone was going nuts over lately. He drew a large *X* through the day, thinking how it might be the thing they were looking for, but if it was, it sure wasn't a treasure. He broke the silence in his office/incubator/cave with his own voice: "So that's when you think it's all going to start, guys?"

You and everyone else.

He wrote *12-21-12* at the top of the calendar page for December and circled it.

Something looked really familiar with the numbers, and he felt a little chill run up his spine. Randy had just phone-perched on his desk, and now it felt like Randy was poking his head back through Jack's office door to tell him some strange numerical coincidence like he had six years ago. Jack picked up the phone and dialed.

"Yeah, Jack? You didn't change your mind, did you?"

"Randy," Jack replied, "you're not going to tell me you didn't notice this, are you?"

"Notice *what?*" Randy was engaged.

"You're the one always fidgeting with numbers and telling me they're prime and everything."

"What do you mean?" Randy asked.

"Write down the date you're so gung ho over," Jack directed.

"*What?* Okay, hold on."

He heard Randy ask Sarah to get him a pen, and then he came back on the phone.

"Okay, done, Jack: 12-21-12. Written."

"Randy, this may be stretching it a bit, but I think this feels like something you'd do."

Jack began his instructions, sounding as if he was making fun of Randy and respecting him at the same time for inspiring his own odd deductions.

"Randy, you ever heard of a palindrome?"

"Yeah. That's when something reads the same in both ways, directions."

"You got it. There're so many tweaks I can make with this, I don't know where to start, so let's start with the one I noticed first."

"So first, 12-21's a palindrome, and 21-12's a palindrome, and the whole date's practically a palindrome if all the numbers keep switching back and forth really fast. *Why* would they do that? I don't know. But don't they kind of look like they would— I mean, if they *could?* So for kicks, let's subtract six off the opposite sides of the date."

Randy answered with a question. "Why six, Jack?"

"Hell, I don't know, Randy," Jack scoffed. "How 'bout there's six of us? Or there's two twelves, and twelve divided by two is six? Or two times twelve is twenty-four and then if you add two and four you get six? Hey, if you add the digits of the mirror image, 1+2+2+1 or 2+1+1+2, you get six! Or how about just the fact that when I *see* twelves, I think *six!*" Jack was laughing out loud by the time he finished answering Randy's question, almost, but not quite, maniacally.

"Okay, okay, Jack. Six it is. So, you mean twelve minus six, right? You know this is pretty simple math—that's *six*, Jack."

"Right-o, Randy. So, you got 6-21, huh, 21-6, on the other side, correct?"

"Yeah, Jack, I guess."

"Where'd we find Quincy?"

"Holy shit!"

"My thoughts exactly."

"I can't believe I didn't see it. I guess just too much on the mind, anymore—"

"—and you needed someone on the outside to take a look, huh?"

"Yeah. Maybe."

"God, does there have to be meaning even in the fact that I left you guys? There *has* to be some purpose in me being aloof. I just don't get this thing, Randy. Why? That's the question. I feel like I'm being pulled right back into this, like in 2007. But if this was all going to happen, why now? Why the wait? I don't understand."

"Maybe we're not meant to, Jack. Maybe we just have to ride this thing out."

"Maybe you're right. Maybe you've been right. I'll see you soon." Jack paused, as he looked at his prophecy-math on the calendar in front of him. Another chill went down his spine. "Hey, Randy?"

"Yeah, Jack?"

"Randy, this is probably stretching it too far, but if you then switch that middle number, 21, to 12…I don't know, like its 'antiself' to 12-12-12, and then subtract six from each number, you kind of get 6-6-6."

"Jack, let's hope that is stretching it too far. We'll see you on the fourteenth or fifteenth, whenever you let us know, okay? And don't play with any more numbers. That's my job. Plus, yours are scarier."

"Deal," Jack answered and hung up.

I wish I was back when all of this was just gnarly, Jack thought.

CHAPTER 36

A JOURNEY BEGINS
DECEMBER 22, 2012

THINGS HAD REMAINED QUIET for them both between the time Meg had begun staying at Harvey's up until the twenty-first. Meg was considering going back to her place the night before Hell Day, but that plan went out the window, along with her belief in concussion-induced botulism, the day they witnessed the stories coming out about what was happening around the world. Harvey and Meg were two people in America who didn't think they were witnessing special effects and ratings boosters.

When CNN revealed local broadcasts on the twenty-second of December of demons devouring newscasters on the twenty-first, Harvey knew he could finally approach Meg with a subject he'd had been dying to bring up.

Meg sat on the couch staring at the TV, jaw dropped open. The thought that everything happening to them three weeks earlier had validity was almost too much to absorb for the waitress. A barely audible "Harvey" escaped her nearly frozen-in-place lips.

"I know, Meg. I see," was his response. "Meg, we need to talk."

"About what, Harvey?" She was still staring in disbelief at the newscast. The response had been one of autopilot, not of true curiosity.

"I think we are meant to leave, and leave now."

"Huh?" She snapped a bit back into "listening to Harvey" and not just "hearing Harvey." "I don't want to go anywhere, Harvey. Do you see what is going on out there?"

"Meg, you have to believe in me. Remember the night you called me because you thought you saw Satan in your kitchen?"

"Yes, Harvey. That is why I live here. How could I forget?"

"Well, that should tell you we're not safe—even in our homes."

"And we'll be safer outside?" Meg shot back.

"I've been seeing something. I was afraid to bring it up to you, because you were so hell-bent on wanting to believe nothing had happened. I figured you'd just call me crazy and ignore me."

Harvey went on to explain that for the past two weeks, he had been periodically placing her glasses on and that he had perpetually seen a path on the floor where no demons or beetle things would pass. He believed it was a path they needed to follow, and the only place they would be safe.

"Why do you think we need to follow it, Harvey? How do you know it's a path for you?"

"I don't know, Meg. But it's all I've got. When I put on those glasses, sometimes all I see are scarabs racing around on my floor and walls and ceilings. Sometimes I see more grotesque figures, dangerous figures. If they are now coming out of this veil of invisibility and hurting people, then maybe some of the things I see will, too, right here in this living room. I have been watching the path for two weeks now. It has become more defined, and it's always there, leading right out my front door. And it starts in the dining room. I think if we're not on it, we could be sorry."

"Harvey, this is crazy. It's not that I don't believe you see what you're seeing, but what do you expect me to do? Just follow you out your front door to who knows where?"

"Let me just see your glasses for a minute."

She gave them to him with a huff. He took them and put them on. They always made his head hurt, immediately, given that his eyesight was so bad. The pain increased the longer he had them on. The path being outlined by "scarabs not crawling past some invisible barrier" was unmistakable, and so was the huge green demon standing behind Meg. Harvey gulped. The thing didn't seem to be aware of them. It was looking around like it had lost something. Harvey then saw it reach a hand toward his wall and scoop up a handful of scarabs off the wall and devour them alive and whole. Disgusting, yes, but Harvey had actually seen it before, and as crazy as it was, he had become somewhat used to the visions of grotesqueness these creatures displayed. He had a strange thought filter into his mind. *Had he been prepared for this? Whatever this was.* What he wasn't prepared for was what happened next.

The demon had been paying no attention to him or Meg whatsoever, as if they weren't even there. Then, suddenly, its eyes flickered, and it looked down at Meg, and he heard it breathing heavily. Harvey had never heard a sound during one of his visions, and he froze. It seemed Meg had heard the sound too. As Harvey froze, she turned quickly, only to see the thing's arm swipe at her head. She ducked and fell to the floor just in time not be hit. A claw had grabbed a few hairs, but that was all.

"He's here, Meg!" Harvey yelled. His joints moving again, his arms instinctively reached down to her, only to find himself freezing again in a half-bent-over position. The demon had looked up, surprised to hear Harvey, and jumped over Meg and came right at Harvey. Harvey closed his eyes, brought his arms up as a shield to guard against the inevitable end, which was next to come, and screamed, bracing himself for some horrible, goring impact. The scream went on too long. He should have been dead by now. Still croaking out the end of his yell, he peered through the blurry crack between his raised forearms and saw, felt, and heard the monstrous thing staring at him, only inches from his face.

This sort of situation—when it happens, that is—usually induces immediate panic in most people. Harvey, however, had two things on his side protecting him from more screaming, running, or the permanent need for a straightjacket and padded room. He was armed with a desire to help Meg and a little bit of knowledge. And a little bit of knowledge can make a man dangerous, as they say. The human fight-or-flight system did have two sides. Fight. Flight. In the millisecond it took his brain to register the demon's corporeal status and proximity, it also worked through the emotional response Harvey was having toward Meg's precarious position, and it even burrowed through a little experience and information Harvey had just been trying to explain to Meg. Processing all this data at lightning speed, drawing conclusions, and then deciding to run was what most people's brains would do when hit with a shot of adrenaline and the sight of a demon. But on this occasion, it was Harvey's mind processing information, and that was something he was especially good at.

"Don't say anything," he whispered to Meg as the thing stared him down, drool dripping from his mouth so close, Harvey knew this time it had to be falling on his shoe, "but, Meg, I need you to listen to me." He kept staring the demon straight in its eyes. It looked angry and confused at the same time, sniffing and moving its skull back and forth slightly, as if trying to determine if Harvey was there or not.

"I don't think it can see me anymore because I'm standing on that path I was telling you about, and I think it's forgotten about you for the moment. If you make a noise, you're going to die. I need you to take a leap of faith here. You need to find a way to get between me and the front door."

Meg almost said, "*What?*" but swallowed her almost-speak, and her mind tried to choose fight over flight as well.

"I will try to distract it for a moment toward the dining room, but you're only going to have that moment."

He had no idea whether she was listening or if she would do what she said. He couldn't see her. The demon had blocked his view. He could only hope her silence signaled a beginning of her willingness to follow his instructions, and not that she just couldn't hear him—or worse, that she had passed out.

"I'm going to count to three, like one, two, three, go. Go on 'go.' I hope you do this, Meg. We're getting one shot." Harvey then walked a few paces to the beginning of the path located in the dining room. "Okay, here goes." And he began counting.

"One. Two. Three!"

Upon finishing the count, Harvey screamed, "Goooooooo!" and immediately threw his right arm out toward the dining room, away from the front door and outside of the vertical border of the path. The demon yelled and went after the arm. Meg sprung from her place on the floor behind the demon. She jumped as hard and far forward as she could. Harvey felt the demon's hand start to wrap around his forearm, and he pulled it back close to his body in reflex. The demon hand closed on air, and again it was looking apparently for something that *wasn't there anymore*. Harvey turned from the demon, and he saw a blurry Meg on the living room floor crawling toward the front door.

Meg had been imaging what the invisible path looked like. A moment before, she might have been squawking at Harvey concerning it, but now it felt like the only thing that mattered in the world. She had envisioned a narrow walkway existing between Harvey and his front door, and she hadn't been too far off in her calculation. The demon turned and saw her, and it took a lethal, screaming jump at her. She rolled out from under its pounce and made a straight line with her body between Harvey in the dining room and the door, pulling her arms in by her side. The demon landed where she had been less than a second prior.

Meg was panting on the floor. "Is this what you mean? Harvey? Am I in the right place, Harvey?"

Harvey looked down at her. He couldn't believe the sight, and even more so, he couldn't believe what she had just done. A minute later the demon was gone, busting through the front window. *The real front window.* There was no mistaking these events for fantasy, delusion, or disease any longer. Meg and Harvey watched, silent and frozen again, in complete disbelief, as the thing destroyed most of the front of his living room, as if in a tantrum, before exiting the house with one final destruction. They both let out a sigh of relief. Somehow relief could still occur in a situation where relief had no meaning.

"Do you think I can get up now?" Meg asked.

"Yes, I do." He reached for Meg's arm, and his foot began to take a step toward her. Upon doing so, he noticed movement on the floor directly in front of him. He instinctively focused on the movement. He had to kneel to understand what he was seeing, but then realized he was no longer on the path. Scarabs where crawling all around him and even up and over his shoes. The beginning of the path had moved about three feet in front of him, near where Meg's feet were currently resting in her reclined position.

"I think we've got to follow this path now if we're going to stay safe. It's moving away from me." He quickly leaped over the scarabs and toward the path's new beginning.

"Harvey, now? We don't even have our coats."

Upon her statement, it moved again. Meg was now sitting only halfway on the path.

"We have to go, now. It's moving again."

"Harvey!" Meg screamed. "Look out behind you!"

BOOK V:

THE END

CHAPTER 37

VIKKI
DECEMBER 26, 2012

---◇○◁═▷○◇---

"*S*HIT," Vikki uttered in disbelief. "Holy…no way…shit. Shit, shit, shit, shit, shit, shit, shit!" Her repeated phrase of choice escaped her lips in a frightened, hushed whisper. She didn't currently know it, but she had just become the only survivor in her small North Dakota town, having managed, with little effort, to escape the carnage a slew of demons and Slugs had just concluded on every other citizen. She was huddled under a desk inside an upstairs grocery store office, which had a small viewing window of the shopping area below. After hours, she had stayed late to work on the year-end paperwork. It was December 26, 2012. There was a small TV in the office, and the local news had been on while she was working. Strange stories had burned across the phosphorus of the older style TV screen during the last few days she had come to work. Everyone in town had been glued to the tube during news hours, and morning coffee meetups had rehashed what had been seen the night before. The end of the world hadn't happened, but something seemed to be up because the bizarreness only found in check-out-aisle tabloids had been appearing in credible anchorpersons' reports on the major networks. There had been people who had mutated into the most grotesque things Vikki had ever seen. The newscasters were warning the audience before interviews not to look at their screens if they had weak stomachs. And they had been right to do so. All Christmas Day celebrations in New York City had been called off because no one could deny that on Christmas Eve, actual demons had shown up and destroyed the Macy's flagship store. It may have been nighttime, but it was New York—and with all its lights and being the city that never sleeps and all, people had pretty much been able to see what the hell had happened (*What the hell had just happened?*), and so could their cameras, and digital recorders, and iPhones, and…

People everywhere were being interviewed, having had strange personal revelations. They didn't believe in their religion anymore. Their favorite politician was a liar. Their dog didn't enjoy running alongside them while they were on a bike. Their father really *had* left them because he didn't care. Their husbands weren't faithful like they thought, and Elvis was actually dead, not alive and living undercover as undercover people live. People said crazier things than these. Some cried about how everything they had ever thought about anything they had ever known for sure to be true had actually been false. Even newscasters themselves had broken down on the air. Regular TV had Jerry Springerized. A San Diego anchor crew even appeared to have actually been killed and eaten alive by monsters on the twenty-first—and it hadn't been a ratings ploy for the big day. The Macy's event on the twenty-fourth confirmed it all.

Vikki Parsons was making fun of herself sitting up in the small office. She had continued to come to work every day. With all that was going on, she wondered if it really was all that important to continue the mundane paperwork of her job. However, her little town hadn't seen anything major happen, and no one had seemed to be complaining about personal revelations they had had. No matter what the event, everything seemed so far away when you lived in North Dakota—even she had joked about it being the possible end of the world. The majority of the public didn't know what to make of the apparently supernatural events taking place and neither did the isolated people of her town. The few days of transition between the twenty-first of December and when things really went to hell on the twenty-sixth, were a time of supposition, onlooking, denial, and confusion. Most people in Vikki's town just kept doing what they always did—only now they didn't miss the news. And if one was a web surfer, one had stayed one—big time. It would be safe to say that productivity in the workplace all over world had taken a giant dip, and it wasn't because of Christmas. In fact, for Christmas-goers, Christmas primarily came and went without notice that year.

Regardless of her self-jest a few hours earlier, she had completed the work and had leaned back in the chair and put her feet up on her desk to continue reading her book.

It wasn't too long after that she found herself huddled up under the desk waiting for the demons to leave—the demons who had destroyed her town and killed everyone in their path while doing so, the demons who were now destroying her store.

"I have to get out of here," immediately followed "Shit, shit, shit, shit, shit, shit, shit!" But she didn't follow suit with her desire. Instead, she used every ounce of her will to force herself to stay right where she was and completely quiet the rest of the night.

The morning came, and Vikki hadn't slept at all. Almost every part of her body, however, had gone to sleep. She jostled herself enough to become off balance and fell over onto her side. Now, out from under the desk, she slowly tried to push her legs out straight and uncurl her arms. She felt nothing, and nothing but pain, at the same time. Moving was excruciating. Waiting for her body, full of pins and needles, to wake up was worse.

After a few minutes, she felt like she could stand. She pulled herself up using the edge of the desk. The back of her leg swept the edge of the office chair, making a sound she didn't expect, and she went back down to the floor, fearing for her life. Events of the night still had hold of her psyche, apparently, but it was quiet now, and time for her to go.

The screams outside the store had started around midnight, and she had listened to the things come into her store downstairs, destroying, it seemed, just for the sake of destroying. Vikki had felt an occasional beetlelike thing crawl up and over her body as she sat still under the desk. She imagined all the grimaces of repulsion and shudders and kicking and screaming she would do if it were possible, but Vikki knew if she had made a sound, the things downstairs would have noticed the small one-way mirrored window overlooking them from the upper corner of the store. Her office would have been found, and she would have gone the same way the rest of her town had: *the way of the dodo.*

She stayed in the office a few more hours that morning. Wrestling with her own fear to go, she finally commenced a small conversation with herself. It started with "I can't do this" and ended, reluctantly, a few minutes later with, "Fine. I can't believe I'm doing this." Déjà vu didn't begin to explain the experiences she was having as she rose from behind the desk a second time. She made her way downstairs, outside, and eventually out of town. She was driving on a full tank of gas with several gallons in the trunk, blaring The Decemberists on her MP3 player plugged into her car stereo. She had thrown a hiking pack of supplies in the back seat, which she had put together after scavenging two or three of the now-vacant stores on Main Street.

By the time Vikki was heading down the highway the morning of December 27, most order in the world had started to break down. So many things were changing that no one could keep up with it. People were confused, having lost the firmness of their beliefs. Momma didn't love them most, their son wasn't an honest person, there was no vicarious atonement for sins, and no one had a free pass to heaven. No people were chosen as special. If you didn't believe in life after death, you realized you were wrong. If you did believe in life after death, you realized you were wrong about how to get there, or you realized it wasn't what you thought it was, but you still didn't know what it was. Nobody was 100 percent right about religion or God, and after the second scroll did its number on humanity, people realized they had been a lot more wrong than they had been right about pretty much everything. Staunch atheists were confronted with their error, and people who strongly believed didn't know what they believed anymore. Very few found any comfort in what was happening to them because people weren't being given truth; they were only being revealed falsehood. No one knew why or how it was happening, and most didn't confess their experiences at first. Any conclusions drawn from this eye opening were done on an individual basis, causing even more pandemonium and isolation in how people related to their new world.

Demons—and demons, for sure, they were—were appearing at night and weren't taking prisoners. This didn't give people a lot of time to reflect on their new mindsets. Towns all over the globe became full of people running for their lives, being killed or worse the minute the sun went down.

Slug numbers began to increase, as well. Some humans were turning into the most hideous, repulsive, *leaking* creatures anyone had ever witnessed—yes, leaking. Up until this week, the world had only seen a few of these people, and by "the world," this almost means that only the inanimate object of "the planet" had really seen them. There had been so few in the previous six years, only those close to people who had changed even knew of them. A few had been deemed victims of a strange, noncontagious disease, and didn't make much news. The rest had decided not to make a public appearance…ever again…and understandably so.

"Slug" was a term that quickly became utilized in the States because of how they looked. They were shunned and chased away. Completely unrecognizable as to who they had been before the metamorphosis, it became easy to forget they were even human. Fear of a contagion made people keep them at bay, and as everyone became busier and busier, trying to survive, the Slugs weren't given much thought other than "Keep away!" As rumors began to spread that some people were actually joining—fighting—with the demons, especially the Slugs, they became despised even more.

By day Vikki drove fast, and by night she lived in shallow graves she'd dig for herself, wrapping a plastic bag around her head and poking a straw up through the dirt to breathe through. For a month, now, she'd been following this ritual and had yet to be eaten by a demon or killed by anything else. She had made it from North Dakota to Missouri before she had finally run out of gas, having not been able to a replacement car or find a station functional enough to fill up for the last three hundred miles. The daily ritual of her journey became "walk during day instead of drive fast," but this would change whenever she found a car with keys still inside. Useful cars were rare, however, because a car *with keys* usually existed only because its driver was still inside the car. The problem was those drivers were dead and they were usually dead because they'd been attacked by something really nasty which had treated their car like a punching bag or a play toy, and this had left the car as not much use to Vikki, no matter how present and pristine the keys might have been.

She followed a rule of staying hidden from anyone and everyone. No point in sorting out *good or evil?* Not worth the risk. She had weapons but didn't need the hassle. Saint Louis finally produced what she was looking for.

Vikki spotted the boy and immediately hid behind a large chunk of building—yes, chunk of *building*—which could have come from thirty stories up at one time, for all she knew. The kid looked high school*ish*, as he was wearing a letter jacket and was sitting in the middle of a park. After a few minutes of watching this peculiar sight of a boy, sitting in a major metropolitan area, completely alone and surrounded by buildings toppled by who-knows-what, she saw something remarkable. The boy raised his hands, and benches, stone pillars, and some building parts in front of him started to rise off the ground. Higher and higher they lifted, coming to rest a couple of stories up, Vikki estimated. The objects arranged themselves together in a sort of *sky pile?* in the air in what appeared to be a small demolition-remnants ball. He proceeded to throw his arms forward, and the conglomerate of downtown park paraphernalia flew through the air and crashed into the remains of a building at the far end of the park.

Vikki jumped up from behind the stone she had been concealing herself with and held up her hands in a surrendering position and yelled out to the boy.

"I'm unarmed, and I'm one of the good guys! Don't shoot! Or whatever you call that."

The boy jumped hard enough to convey that he may have believed he was the only human left on this great blue ball flying around the sun.

"Wh-who are you?" he stuttered.

"I'm your friend, and now you're mine," Vikki answered, walking toward him, her hands still in the air. "You're going to protect me."

"I-I can't."

"Sure you can. I just saw what you did. That, boy, is a protective skill." She laughed out loud.

The boy was standing up by this time. "I don't know what you think is so funny! I tried to protect people. I tried to protect everyone. I was the only one! I was the only one!" The boy started crying uncontrollably and collapsed to his knees.

Vikki ran toward him, seeing it as an opportunity to show some compassion and get a new friend out of the effort. She dropped her backpack and rushed down onto her knees near him and placed her hands on his shoulders.

"I tried everything. I even tried using the buildings against them. I couldn't fight them all, and I ran. Oh God, I ran." And he cried more.

"Kid, you can't expect to be Superman. What are you, fifteen?"

"I'm a coward. Everybody's gone. I should be with them. I should have stayed with them."

"Well, that's great. I could really use your help now, and you're telling me you wish you were dead with all these people. Thanks a lot, kid. Exactly, how am I supposed to feel knowing I have to go off alone without your help because you want to sit here and sob about how you should be demon dinner?"

"But—"

"No buts. You're one kid. You can't protect a whole city, and from the looks of these buildings, you gave one hell of a good try. If there's a but, maybe it's 'but' you can protect *one* person. Me. You game? I have been out here alone for five freaking states. I could use the company, let alone the firepower. Now whaddya say? I'm Vikki." She pulled a hand off his shoulder and offered it to him for a shake. She hoped her Psych 101 class was going to pay off.

The kid looked at her, still sniffling in self-pity. Then he looked down at her hand. He muttered to himself, "Protect just one of you. Yeah, maybe I can do that."

"Good. Now shake my hand and tell me your name."

"I'm Sam." He shook her hand.

"Good, Sam, now let's go." Vikki stood up and continued her instructions. "We've got a lot of ground to cover. I hope the bridge over the Mississippi is still there."

"We don't need a bridge," Sam answered.

"Really?" Vikki responded.

"I can control anything solid. Watch."

Vikki watched as he raised his hand and a large slab of marble fallen from the base of one of the once-polished downtown skyscrapers began to rise off the ground and float toward them. It stopped hovering just above their feet.

"This is how I ran away. I flew away," Sam explained and motioned for her to step up onto the slab.

She did so, and he followed. They sat down, and she shook her head. "It's a whole new world, Sam." Vikki chuckled. "I knew you could do this." As she said this, they rose up into the sky and floated through the Gateway Arch and across the mile-wide river.

"So? Tell me about yourself, kid." Vikki snorted as they soared above Illinois on a piece of black marble.

"What do you want to know? And why does it matter anyway, anymore?" Sam answered reluctantly.

"Kid, you can be a real downer. I guess I can cut you some slack, though. You probably lost your family, right?"

"Not really. It was just me and my dad, and he was pretty much a rotten drunk. I'm glad he's gone. He actually *joined* them. I left as soon as I discovered my power, which was the day before Hell Day. Later, I saw him fighting on their side. I couldn't believe it."

"Geez, that musta sucked, huh?"

"I guess it makes sense, but to see it and know that's where you came from…I think it made me fight harder. I didn't want to risk ending up like him."

"Sins of the father, kid," Vikki retorted. "Whadda they say? Can't be placed on the son?"

"Yeah, well they also say, 'like father, like son.'"

"Yeah, they do, I guess, don't they? Well, what do you think? You don't seem much the demon-lover type."

"I don't know. I guess not. But the way things are going, or at least how they went back home in Saint Louis, it makes you think. Maybe, it'd be easier...safer...to join the other side."

"Well, they wouldn't be kicking your ass, that's for sure."

"It's so weird. I went to Catholic high school. I never believed whatever they taught, but at the same time, to now know I was *wrong* about there not being a God. But then to see all that's happening. How *can* there be a God?"

"I believed in God," Vikki said, looking ahead.

"Do you still?"

"Of course. I guess it's the opposite for me. I believed, and it's one of the things that didn't go away after, well, you know, you experienced it too. So I guess afterward, I *still* believe in God. By the way, we're going to need some blankets up here; it's mother-freaking cold. Fly down to the next house you see that looks safe and empty."

"Uh, yeah, you're right, okay." Sam continued, "Yeah, it was weird when it happened. It was a couple days ago for me. I beleived there was a small chance my dad loved me, you know, but just couldn't show it through all the drinking. But then I just knew. I had convinced myself he didn't blame me for my mother's death during my birth, but then I learned I was wrong. I guess he was just too chicken-shit to finish me off, so he just tortured me instead. As for God, living in that hell, I didn't believe, either, or the shit they were teaching me at the school he was making me go to, but then all of a sudden, I knew I was wrong in my disbelief—I mean, my disbelief in God, that is. But that's all I knew. I didn't know any details past that."

"Maybe you don't need any details past that," Vikki replied. "You seem to have a pretty good handle on right and wrong, even though you grew up with a man who probably couldn't find the word 'right' in a dictionary where 'aardvark' through 'rhombus' had been ripped out."

Sam sat quietly for a while and then rebooted the conversation. "Yeah, but why would a God do all of this? Make us choose sides. Make us fight it out?"

"Kid, we choose sides every day. What difference does it make whether you're screwing your best friend's girlfriend in high school or you're throwing buildings at demons trying to save a bag lady crossing the street you don't even know? There's supposed to be a 'final battle' battle between good and evil, right? Isn't that what they always say? 'They' being the nutjob hypocrites on those cable channel shows who are always stealing old ladies' money. Well, Sam, looks like you're a lucky one who gets to be around when it happens. So, Sam, what's this Hell Day you mentioned?"

"December twenty-first. When everything started happening everywhere. Guess that whole Mayan calendar thing was right. It's the end of the world."

"Ah, yeah, I remember that being said," Vicki replied. "I was seeing the things on the news, and I heard the 12-21 talk. Guess things just take a while to percolate up to North Dakota, even demons. Nothing really happened there until the twenty-sixth. Of course, when it did, my entire town was wiped out."

"Geez, sorry. Did you have family?"

"No, Sam. I moved there to get away from mine."

"Oh, sorry, again." Not knowing what to say next, Sam changed the subject. "So where are we going, anyways, Vikki?"

"This way." She pointed straight ahead. "When it gets closer to sunset, we'll set down, though, and I'll show you how to bury yourself. I'm not getting into fights with demons every night if I can help it." She laughed. "Ha!—with your powers, burying ourselves is actually going to be a hell of a lot easier."

"*Bury* ourselves?"

"Yeah, *kid.* It's all the rage nowadays!"

—◇○◇—

"Let's get something to eat over there. It looks pretty deserted," Vikki instructed Sam after they landed in a badly damaged town somewhere in South Terra Haute, Indiana. She was motioning to a Walmart, or what was left of one. Half the building was caved in, and all the front windows looked like an LA riot had occurred in the vicinity. "Can openers and food better be on the unsmashed side too!" she said to Sam and laughed again. Laugh or cry, laugh or cry. Laughing is the one thing she *had* chosen.

They entered the store, stepping through one of the large panes. Sam had waved his hand, and the jagged glass had jiggled out of the pane and flown away from them and down the street. It was a cloudy day and later in the afternoon, so the inside of the store was dim. They took light steps, not wanting to announce their presence to any unseen unfriendlies. They weren't exactly having much success in their stealth with all the broken glass on the floor, but they tried. Crunching and scraping with every step of their boots, they finally gave up their plan and started to walk normally.

Within a few seconds, both heard movement coming from deeper inside the store.

"Shit! Did you hear that?" Sam whispered, his heart pounding.

"Yes," Vikki answered, continuing to move deeper into the store. "Let's see what it is. Be ready, okay? But careful."

"Are you crazy?" Sam answered, panicking. "Let's just leave, Vikki. We can find food somewhere else."

Vikki reached back and pulled her rifle from the pack on her back and kept heading in the same direction. She looked back at Sam, and said, "It's not demons, Sam. I think you can handle a few people with your tricks if they're trouble."

Sam, still not liking the idea, but assuming she was probably right, continued to follow. A moment later they heard more rustling coming from the right side of the store, perhaps a couple of aisles over from where they were. Vikki took off running following the sound. She rounded the end of the store aisle she thought the sound was originating from and started yelling. Sam chased behind. When he caught up with her, he almost puked from the scene at the end of the aisle.

Vikki had yelled "STOP!" at the creatures and followed it with a shot from her rifle pointed toward the ceiling. The Slugs at the end of the aisle had obeyed and huddled together, showing signs of fear and holding their hands up, showing they were unarmed and requesting not to be harmed. They were wearing human clothes, but that was practically the only *human* thing about them. Everything else seemed like God had tried to remember how to create a human after suffering from a bad case of God-Alzheimer's and had given up halfway through when he couldn't remember what he'd been doing.

There were four of them. They were breathing hard as if the same God had forgotten how to make functioning lungs as well. They all looked different from one another. Some had folds of skin covering an eye, or some were missing an ear (or ears), while others had one shortened arm or a neck and head that all seemed to be oversized and run together in one gelatinous mass with their shoulders. They stood crookedly and shuffled, as they backed up, instead of taking steps, which, at least, might have conveyed they had experience with walking as upright beings at some point in the past.

One of them started to speak through the heaving breathing. Its mouth was disgusting, and the generic word "orifice" was better suited in describing it. Sam had to look down as the thing started to form words with its misshapen lips, which revealed missing teeth—if there had ever been teeth. Well, maybe that thing there was a tooth. Hmm…not really sure.

"Please, don't hurt us," the thing gurgled.

"And why not?" Vikki countered, aiming her rifle and continuing to march closer toward them. She was about halfway down the aisle. "You're in league with him and those things that come out at night! You're not taking any of this food. You don't need it since you'll be dead."

"No," the thing pleaded. "We don't want to be dead. At least we think we don't want to be."

"What does that mean?" Sam exploded "You think you don't want to be? Come on, Vikki, let's just get this over with. I can't stand the look of these things. I've seen them before; they're always on the other side." Sam raised his arms. Grocery goods on either side of where he stood began to rattle.

"Stop, Sam! Wait," Vikki ordered.

"We know," the thing quickly answered, "but *we're* not. Don't judge on how we look." It took a deep, grotesque breath, putting an image in Sam's mind of a plunger and a garbage disposal working in harmony, to make some very wrong kind of music. "We've learned that lesson the hard way." Then, more junk-music breathing punctuated the end of its sentence.

Vikki smiled, and she lowered her rifle, looking back at Sam. Sam caught the grin on her face and couldn't believe she was taking the gun off them.

"What are you doing? We can't trust them!" He started to raise his hands again to blow some shit their way.

"Sam!" Vikki shouted. "Put down your hands! We're letting them go."

"But—" This was how many conversations with his new companion seemed to be ending now.

"Trust me, okay? They're not going to hurt us. Go and gather something tasty for us all to eat. I need to talk to these guys. I think they know some things."

Sam stood there, dumbfounded. He'd gone from Super Telekinetic Man who fights all evil to Errand Boy for the Slugs "R" Us Club. "I don't understand," he said, like a five-year-old being told the sky was blue because of dust particles and ultraviolet rays.

"Just do it, Sam. Then we'll be on our way. We're fine."

—◇○◇—

"I can't believe you just let them go," Sam said as they climbed aboard a park bench—his and Vikki's next ride. "They're Slugs. They work for the other side. You didn't honestly believe all that crap they grunted about learning the error of their ways...wherever they're headed, it's going to be somewhere they can inform someone about us. And where the heck are we headed?"

"Sam, you can't just kill people," Vikki answered. "Not if they haven't attacked you."

"Well, we could have taken them prisoner, or something. We just walked away and left them to their evil deeds. And they're not people anyway."

"They *were* people," Vikki responded, slowing her words to make a point.

"Yeah, well someone, and we know who, upstairs, decided they didn't pass their Humanity Merit Badge because they ain't people now" was Sam's last comment on the subject as he lifted them off the ground and started heading south.

"So?" he asked Vikki a couple minutes into their continuing journey. "I asked where we are headed."

Vikki looked over at the kid and calmly said, "Kentucky."

"Kentucky? What's in Kentucky?" Sam asked. "Didn't you say you came from North Dakota? Who the heck do you know in Kentucky?"

"I have an acquaintance there I need to meet," Vikki said.

"How do know they're there, or even still alive?"

"I know. I found out just before the demons attacked my town. He'll be okay, I'm

268

positive."

"Is it a large group?" Sam asked.

"Yes, it's very large, and I need to get there, so the faster the better, kid."

Sam could tell from Vikki's tone she didn't want to talk anymore, and after being with the Slugs and arguing with Vikki about the Slugs, Sam decided to drop this topic, too, and take a break. At this point, she was the only friend and companion he had, and he didn't want to push her away. Instead, he chose the passive route and muttered to himself just loudly enough for her to hear. "Well, I hope there are others like me there. Some help would be nice. Plus, I'm sick of sleeping in a living grave."

CHAPTER 38

A DUBOIS HOME CHRISTMAS AND A 'SOMETHING' NEW YEAR
DECEMBER 24, 2012

"HOLY MOLY, GUYS! Do you see that?" Randy was yelling at the television set. "Those are demons!"

The six of them were finally together again with Jack's visit, and they had watched the world quickly change into complete chaos a week later. Jack admitted they had been right about December 21—especially seeing what he was seeing now. Randy's outburst was being prompted by the Macy's store destruction being caught by news crews on Christmas Eve. Except for Randy's voice, only somberness hovered within the room.

"Oh my God," Sarah whispered under her breath. "This is it. This is really it."

"I'm afraid that's what it looks like, Sarah," Jack responded solemnly.

"I'm just afraid," Sarah answered back. "Isn't there something we could have done? We knew about this for the last six years."

"I don't think so, Aunt Sarah." Derek broke his jaw-hanging stare at the television long enough to answer her. "The scrolls made it pretty clear that it was coming, no matter what."

Randy looked down at his cell phone. It was vibrating over and over. "I'm getting texts and emails like crazy."

Everyone they had found, along with Riley from England, was contacting them, given what they were also seeing on the news concerning downtown New York.

"They're wanting to know if we know what this is about," Randy conveyed while scrolling through his messages. "Riley says he doesn't believe we have much time, so we better get organized."

"Organized? To do what?" Jack asked.

"Remember? We told them all about the scrolls," Quincy said. "We told you that when you first got here. I think the Elementors are keenly aware they are supposed to be the first line of defense in the coming battle."

"They're okay with that?" Jack asked.

"Some," Quincy replied, "and others, not so much, and I don't blame them. But they're going to start using their powers to defend themselves, regardless, when push comes to shove. We're trying to make them understand they'll stand a better chance if they work together and ally with one another. If not, we may lose the people who can be our greatest assets."

"How can you all stay so calm about this?" Jack begged. "You sound like a military strategist, Quincy. Do you see, there, on that television? Demons from hell are tearing apart the Macy's building the night before Christmas!"

Jack had about lost it. He was mad at the scrolls, he was mad at the situation, but mostly he was mad at himself for having ignored it for so long, offering so little help to his friends who had been much more right than he had ever come close to being.

"We have to, Jack," Derek said, trying to calm Jack down. "We've got to act quickly and be smart about this. Don't hate yourself because you didn't think this was coming. I had my doubts, too. Maybe you didn't disbelieve—maybe you just had more hope than the rest of us—for a better outcome. If Sarah hadn't been a relative of mine, I probably would have done the same thing as you. But because I didn't, I can tell you we have been planning for this constantly. We have procedures in place on what to do, if and whenever hell broke loose on the planet. The downtime had to be used—for something. And it's all been pretty much useless because we hadn't found hardly anyone who fit the profile of a Discerner or Elementor."

"Where did 'Elementor' come from?" Jack asked.

"From this kid, Brian. He contacted us from Iowa. He can do amazing things with a little fire. He came up with the term when we read to him about his gift described in the fourth scroll. It just kind of stuck."

"This is the end of the world, but it sounds more like a comic book," Jack replied. "You guys know this isn't funny, right? This is the *actual* end of the world."

Four Winds chimed in, in his usual way.

"The end of the world, only as we have known it. When I met him, Byron did not yet know what the true end would be. The scrolls refer to the good being given gifts to push back the evil. I believe we are to fight so that the world does not end."

"Fight?" Jack asked. He held out his arms and glanced around the room, pleading for some sanity. "Besides you, do any of us look like fighters, Four Winds? Do you see what's on that television set? Even you wouldn't be a long-lasting meal for those things, and the rest of us, for sure, would just be appetizers."

"Jack is right, Four Winds," Sarah acquiesced. "None of us seem to have any abilities. I don't think we'd survive long, up against that." She pointed to the scene on the television also.

"And I only seem able to kill humans that aren't even really there," Derek moaned, disgusted with the little use he believed himself to be.

"A great chief once told me it is not important whether you believe you can win; it is only important what you are fighting for. We may not believe ourselves to be strong or that we can survive, but does that mean our decision should be that we do nothing? That we will sit here and wait to be killed? I don't believe so. I believe we will do what we can. And, therefore, we should stop discussing all that we can't."

Four Winds had forced the others into a new conversation, as they realized the only real option for them was to get busy *doing* instead of continuing to whine. The conversation led them to contact Riley and all the others they knew about with the procedures they had created yet had never put into practice. They gave them set times to check in to give their status on the situation, wherever they were. They were to be on the lookout for any new Elementors and bring them into the fold. While electric power remained, they would use cell phones, and after that, everyone would most probably be on their own, taking charge in their area. It wasn't a great plan, but it was something.

"Riley's on board," Derek said, filling in the rest of the group after getting off the phone. "He didn't sound very hopeful, though, and I think he's right. We know of only forty people around the world who can do anything special, and up against what's happening downtown—I don't know...doesn't seem like much...or enough. Most every one of them is in a location far from the other. They won't even be able to work together to protect one another."

"Yes, Derek, but at least they now know they are not alone and someone cares," Sarah said, in her typical wise way. "Having a purpose and knowing you have someone who believes in you can do a lot for one's hopelessness. I know. I heard it in the voices of some of the younger people I spoke with, like Brian. He sounds much readier to believe he can help...was meant to help."

"I hope you're right, Aunt Sarah. I hope you're right...for everyone's sake."

Sarah was right, for the most part. In the beginning, most people stayed in their homes, afraid to go anywhere, but then the demons would appear in their towns and start slaughtering people, whether they were indoors or outdoors. When a person would accidentally discover they were an Elementor—although unaware of the term coined by "a Brian from Iowa"—many Elementors stayed indoors, afraid of themselves, after finding they could freeze their couch or blow out the windows of their home by just moving their hands. But after Hell Day, when a demon appeared in their living room with them, survival of the fittest took over, and they found themselves freezing a demon, frying a demon, burying a demon, or blowing one through a wall and down the street, in an effort to keep from being chewed up and spit out by a demon. Or when they saw their neighbor had a gift, as well, and saw that neighbor light some demons on fire by pointing at them and shooting fire from their fingertips, they began to be less afraid of themselves and more confident they could make a difference in what was happening around them.

Sarah was informed by the Elementors she knew that her words were inspiring and to keep them up, but this didn't last long. Within a week, there were no more cell phones, and contact became almost impossible.

Soon, however, there were many towns and cities who had bands of Elementors helping to protect people from the demons that would appear at night. During the day, fighters would gather supplies and gather together, developing plans to move to bigger cities in hopes of finding more like themselves. In greater numbers, there was greater protection…they hoped.

—◇○◇—

By the first week of January 2013, it became blatantly obvious to Jack and the others that the Dubois brownstone was protected. The nightly destruction had eventually shown up on their street, and almost everything around them had been decimated in a single night. If the same swift reckoning was happening elsewhere, they surmised the world was going to be looking like a very, *very* different place, very soon.

"I think we can all agree they're looking for us," Jack said, turning from the front window out of which he had been looking.

Jack was referring to the facts they knew. They knew that every night for over two weeks, the beasts had been destroying the city. Based on what they heard every night before the television stopped broadcasting, the destruction had appeared to be completely random. As of yesterday, their idea had begun to change. Yesterday, a group of Slugs and Traitors had appeared on their street. It was a group of about ten. They had weapons and were knocking on the brownstones' doors. If people came out, they were shot on sight. If people didn't come out, the Slugs broke in. If they found anyone inside, they were brought out into the street and shot.

Randy was peering out the upstairs window, trying not to be seen. He saw one of the men pull a map out and start directing part of the group in another direction.

"It looks like they're surveying the area," Randy told the others. "If people come to the door; they're shot. If they don't, they go in, find them, bring them out, shoot them, and then move on to the next house. And you gotta see this."

The others joined him at the window, being careful not to be seen.

"I guess we know what the people who are affected by the first scroll turn into, huh?" Randy said pointing to the Slugs in the group across the street.

"Oh, dear God, it's horrible." Sarah gasped.

"I know, and look at the others. They're completely normal, and yet they joined the other side. What kind of sick bastard do you have to be to—I just don't understand."

They watched as the group had walked right by the Dubois home as if it wasn't even there. That night the demons came and flattened the entire block, except for Sarah and Derek's house, which also had been completely ignored by the monsters.

When the things had shown up, the group had stayed away from the windows, so none of them saw much. It wasn't clear, either, which situation would have been more frightening: being able to see the things materializing from the hellish mind of humanity's myths, or doing what they did—sit huddled together, waiting and wondering what was going to happen, only able to *hear* the sound of demolition and the grotesque noises of the beasts responsible for it taking place outside.

When it was all over the next morning and the street was empty and only their home stood, completely untouched, they debated for hours on what it meant, the reason for it, and where the power of protection was coming from. Finally, Quincy threw the wrench in the conversation machine, stopping all their flapping lips of theory.

"Somebody's going to have to find out."

"Find out what?" Randy asked.

"Well, I think we can assume if it's not us being together as a group that's protecting us, then it's the scrolls being here with us, just like they protected the tribes in the past. We need to find out," Quincy concluded.

"And why?" Randy followed up with an even deeper question than he had just asked.

"Because we can't just all safely sit in this house while the rest of the world is destroyed. We already had to hold Four Winds back from running out into the street yesterday when those things were executing neighbors. He was right. We have to help."

Quiet filled the room. It made Four Winds think of Strength From Inside, and he wished his friend was here. If they were going to be battling soon, he'd have felt more comfortable with Strength along his side. Several years had passed since he had been fighting Custer's army and had seen his friend. He hoped somehow when this was all over, they'd meet again.

Four Winds spoke. "Quincy is right. We must not sit here enjoying protection we don't even understand. We should find out and use whatever knowledge we gain to assist in whatever way we can against the destruction we are witnessing."

"Four Winds said we would be leaders," Quincy continued. "Leaders don't hide in the basement."

"Ah! I hate this!" Randy yelled. "We know everything, and we know nothing! What the hell?"

"Randy, it's okay. We all feel like you do," Sarah said, trying to comfort her excitable boy, who wasn't a boy anymore. He was about the same age Jack had been when this thing had started, and without the power of the scrolls controlling her age, she was too. She turned to Quincy. "How do you propose we find out?"

"Someone is going to have to go out there alone and see if they make it," Quincy answered. "I guess, since this is my idea, that someone will be me."

"No, Quincy, I will go," Four Winds insisted.

"No, Four Winds," Derek objected. "I think we all have to do it."

"But we've only got four scrolls," Quincy responded, "and there's six of us."

"I don't think any of that matters," Jack said, stopping their mutual heroism. "We don't know why we're protected. Is it because we're all together? Is it because we have the scrolls? Is it because the scrolls are together? Would each one of us be protected on our own? Do you need to have a scroll with you to be safe? Or is it this house? We don't know anything. The fact is, I agree—fearfully and reluctantly, yes—but I still *agree* with Quincy. We have to find out."

"How do we do that?" Derek asked, "We can't try out all those scenarios, see what works until it doesn't, and one of us, or all of us, are dead."

Jack had resumed his place on the couch and leaned his head back in his usual way, thinking for a moment. Clearly, it was not an easy question to answer. Why risk it? Why risk anyone? Why risk themselves? They were safe. Maybe they should just be happy with that.

But is that the right thing to do?

"*Right?* When did I have to start caring so much about *right?*" Jack spoke out loud to the room.

"Who ya talking to, Jack?" Randy answered.

"Damn it, everyone!" Jack yelled again. "I didn't ask to be in this position."

He stood up and walked back to the front window of the sitting room. He put his hand on his head and rubbed his brow, his other arm resting on the wall as he looked out the window at what had become of everyone else's homes and lives for the five or six blocks' distance he could see. After a moment, he slowly turned back toward them. The others watched, waiting to see what he would say. Whether they had held an election or not, he had become the leader of the group, which he thought was funny. *Really* funny.

"I guess that's it," Jack said to himself, looking at the floor. He raised his eyes back up to look at his strange group of friends. One was a wannabe archaeologist rent-a-cop who had quit school and his job. Two were over 150 years old. One was a Discerner, bringing a whole new definition to that word for Mr. Webster to type into his book. And one was back from the dead. He had somehow become their leader, which was so ironic, he laughed every time the thought crossed his mind. He was a loner, a man who didn't like to be bothered. He wasn't like them. Randy was the closest person to him existing in the realm of *normal,* but he and Sarah were together, so that still made Randy more a part of the group sitting in front of him than the part of the group standing against the wall—namely, him. Yet he was here, and it was they who had dragged him back after six years. And he had come, more willingly than unwillingly, which he didn't like admitting to himself. The world was falling down everywhere around them, and it seemed a part of him knew almost every word he said, every decision he made, was somehow impacting the very future of humanity's existence. Whether he liked it or not, he guessed that was the situation.

"Whaddya say, Jack?" Randy asked. "Didn't quite catch that."

Jack pondered a bit more, still leaning against the wall. Then he began his world-changing speech by saying, "I don't want to be here. I sure as hell was happy with my job back in 2007, in my basement—only bothered by Randy a couple of times a night, and bothered about nothing of consequence, at that. But then I look around this room, and I wonder if how I feel is true for any of you. Sarah? You and Quincy have been able to live to see things you would never have seen. And the same with you, Four Winds. Maybe it's not exactly what you wanted, but it is a gift. You and Randy have each other." Jack looked at Sarah and Randy directly. "And Derek has you too. I guess what I'm saying is I only know how *I* feel. I don't know how you feel. Do *you* wish this had never happened? Wish to know what your lives would have been without it? Would you choose that life over this one? I know that's not a choice we have, and honestly, the more I stand here looking at you all staring back at me, the more I second-guess myself; the more I think *I* would choose this life over that old life. Hell, I don't know, and I'm pissed I don't think the choice is easy. I guess what I'm trying to say in the end, if I'm saying anything at all, is I think the only choice we have is to value our friendship and do whatever we can to help this situation with whatever we've been given. To do that, we have to find out what we've been given. The only other option is to walk outside and join that group that came down this street yesterday killing people. So...I think we draw for it," Jack concluded.

I don't know what I said to make Sarah cry, Jack thought as he saw the tears start to run down her cheeks. She let go of Randy's arm, stood up, and walked over to Jack, tears flowing, and hugged him. One by one, the others joined her. They didn't all cry—that's not everyone's nature—but Jack did, probably for the first time in his life.

And so did Byron. Remember, he's always there...or you wouldn't know any of this.

Jack regrouped himself after the family hug began to unfurl. As he watched Sarah and Randy walk away, her hand loosely resting in his, Jack didn't notice Four Wind's hand heading for his head to ruffle his hair. Four Winds was wearing jeans and a T-shirt, the outfit he had quickly taken to back in 2007, and Jack still hadn't gotten used to it.

Back then, Derek had gone out and returned with some suits for Quincy. Quincy hadn't said anything, but Derek had seen it all over Quincy's face when Derek had opened his closet to find something to wear the day he had been found by the group. As for Four Winds, Derek had struggled to find anything that would fit the young man, given his size and height, besides jeans and T-shirts. Regardless of this Four Winds had liked the choice, and it had stuck. As for Jack, the first moment Four Winds had walked through the Dubois door and stood in front of them in authentic Sioux warrior dress had imprinted on Jack's memory, making any other version of Four Winds seem not quite right and pale in comparison. Jack smiled up at Four Winds's towering self, and the moment ended with the brave walking away as well.

Derek and Quincy were wandering back to find a place to sit, too, and everyone appeared to have a dazed and confused feel about them. After everything that had happened and everything they'd been through and seen, a sense of disbelief appeared to descend on the group at the same time. Jack stared, thinking to himself. *It's not disbelief they're feeling. If they're feeling what I'm feeling, then it literally is "dazed and confused."* He and Randy had been "tripping" six years earlier, and now the whole group was getting a heavier dose of scroll fever. It had induced love and compassion and blended those emotions with fear and hallucinations, which, sadly, weren't hallucinations. But now it was time to snap out of it and start discussing the plan again, as much as the whole thing just sucked. And it did. It all just sucked.

Jack began again. "I think it's safe to assume having a scroll in our vicinity might be the source of protection. Having a scroll had kept its people safe, so maybe a single scroll protects. But there's always the chance that it's having all *four* of them *together*. We draw, and whoever draws short takes a scroll outside tonight and wanders the streets. The bastards will show up, most likely. Since we don't know the true source of protection, this still puts everyone at risk."

"What if we're all destroyed?" Sarah asked.

"I think that's highly unlikely, but the fact remains we don't know what we are supposed to do, why we are here, why we were selected to be in this thing the way we are, or how we're supposed to be leaders. And if Riley is ever successful with his plans to secure a shortwave radio, then I think we better have a better handle on all of this. We're going to have to find our own HAM, and that's not happening by sitting here. I think we better own up to the fact that whether or not we are protected, we are going to have to venture out of this house if we are to accomplish anything worthwhile for humanity."

"You sound like Four Winds," Derek balked.

"He's a good teacher."

—◇○◇—

March 2, 2032 CE: Entry 7,124

"I guess it's me." Randy said this today when he drew the short straw. He had to take a scroll and walk around outside at night, hoping he wouldn't be eaten or ripped apart by a demon, and hoping if he wasn't,

that the Dubois home would still be safe and intact, when and if he returned. It was January 8, 2013. The demons approached him but did nothing. Thank God! I was so scared. I like Randy, and I didn't want him to get hurt. It is so hard watching and not being able to do anything. I hate going to the times after Hell Day. I feel so useless. Always arriving back here in the safety of my cabin, having watched more senseless slaughter. It's a nightmare. And to see them take such a risk when they were completely safe in that house. I honor them. Maybe I should do the same. Maybe I should be out there fighting instead of here writing this useless garbage. What's the point? I'm supposed to stay here if I want to save my parents. That's what I was told. If anyone finds these writings, please don't judge me too harshly. I also believe I am here for a reason, like all of them, though I don't know what it is yet. Those scrolls have an amazing power, it seems, and their power of protection has returned. I wonder where they came from. I am trying to keep straight all that has happened, the dates, the places, the people. It's so hard to understand it all when I am in one time and then another. I hate the after–Hell Day times. I hate it. I don't want to go there anymore.

Okay, so this is what happened when Randy went outside...

(Journal entry continues.)

———◇○◇———

"Well, that answers that!" Randy said, still breathing heavily. He found himself immediately fighting off hugs and kisses from Sarah.

"I guess it does," Jack answered. "It appears the power is in the scrolls or us. I say we go with the scrolls and don't risk any more tests."

"So that means, at most, only three of us can leave on our own safely," Derek postulated.

"If we're reading this right, yes," Jack offered.

"Well, I'm not going off on my own anytime soon after that," Randy said, panting.

Jack laughed. "Randy, don't worry; you won't have to. What you did tonight deserves a medal for bravery. Wish I had one to give."

"I'll take her kisses." Randy kissed Sarah again. Then, breaking away for long enough to finish his thought, he said, "But, Jack, that was damned scary. I was literally praying for God to make it quick when they showed up. Being bait is no fun. No fun at all." Sarah let go of Randy's waist, and he added, "And there's another thing."

"What's that?" Jack asked.

"I think those scrolls offer some sort of range of protection."

"Whaddaya mean?"

"Well, Jack, we couldn't quite see it from inside, here, but the brownstone on either side of us is fine, too, and the one behind us."

"Huh. You mean like a radius?" Derek asked.

"Yeah, that's the word I was thinking," Randy said, nodding.

"If that's true," Jack followed, "it might give us the ability to create a base of some sort—a safe haven for people. It's a stretch, even a little risky to try out, but it might work."

"I see what you're saying," Quincy said. "If we spread the scrolls out away from each other, maybe we could create a perimeter or something that could keep evil forces out."

"You got it," Jack replied. "I don't know how far we push it, but once we had some help, we might be able to test the boundaries a bit if we knew we could fight them off if we judged ourselves a little thin. Damn, I wish Riley knew this. We don't even know if he's been able to survive since the cells went out."

"I'll go and find out," Derek said.

"Go? He's in England!" Sarah gasped. "How can you go to England?"

"I'll fly. I have a pilot's license, Sarah," he explained. "An Atlantic flight takes a lot of skill. I don't know if it's possible, but if I've got a scroll, maybe I can make it. We need to see what's going on over there anyway. Maybe I can help. He's the only other Discerner we know about. Maybe I'm supposed to help him."

"How do you figure?" Quincy asked.

"Four Winds told us Byron said we had to tame the Discerners. I don't know what that means, but I figure two of us working together to figure it out is probably better than being apart. I should have left as soon as we found him before all this happened. I just didn't…I guess, I just didn't want to. I was in as much denial as you, Jack, even if I pretended to myself I wasn't. I feel like such an ass, especially knowing how much I've known for how long."

"Do you think you can make it?" Jack asked.

"You're not serious about letting him do this!" Sarah shrieked. "You're not going anywhere, Derek, especially not over an ocean!"

"Aunt Sarah, I think I've got to do this. I don't know why, but it feels right. And I think I'd better do it soon before they destroy so much of the area, I can't even find a plane to fly."

A flash of light caught everyone's eye in the front window.

"Was that lightning?" Quincy asked.

"I don't think so. The sky was crystal clear when I was out there," Randy answered, starting to look out the window. "Holy shit, I was wondering in a city of nine million if one would ever show up. It's a Fire-Starter! Hurry, yell him down; I think he's in trouble!"

Four Winds ran to the door and threw it open. A man possibly in his twenties was running down the street being chased by some sort of gargoyle-looking thing in the air above him. He was shooting fire out of his hands. The man took the chance to turn around, but the demon was quick to react and was gaining on the young man. Men with guns were rounding the end of the street and starting to take aim. Four Winds yelled to the man to head the way of the brownstone's front door. The man looked at Four Winds, but he didn't really have the ability to change course, given the pursuit he was under.

"Four Winds, out of my way," Randy yelled and pushed past Four Winds as he ran out the door.

Randy ran out into the middle of the street and grabbed the man, pulling him back toward the brownstone. A shot rang out in the dark. One of the men down the block had fired. The demon had flown past Randy and the Fire-Starter, under its own inertia, but it was changing direction to head back toward the men.

Sarah ran up to Four Winds with a scroll in her hands. She pushed it into Four Winds's hands and yelled, "Go get him; he doesn't have this!"

Without hesitation, Four Winds ran out into the street while the others watched the gargoyle's claw grab at Randy's shoulder as he ran behind the Fire-Starter, pushing the man back toward the Dubois home.

Randy felt himself being lifted off the road, and then…he was falling. The thing had let go of him. He landed on his feet, trying to keep his balance and nearly twisting his ankle. He started running again, following the man he had run out to save, who was already at the base of the Dubois front stairs. Four Winds was running toward Randy. Whatever power the scroll in Four Winds's hand had, it had gotten close enough to Randy to ward off the demon attack, and the men down the street had ceased their efforts also. Randy wasn't paying any attention to this change, however, and was only racing to catch up to get back inside the house. Not being picked up by that thing again was the only thought in his mind. When it had touched him, he had felt heat begin to seep from his core, as if he was beginning to be cooked from the inside out.

Four Winds and the Fire-Starter were inside the door. Sarah was yelling at Randy to hurry, even though she could already tell it appeared he was safe. He made it up the stairs and into the brownstone and slammed the door behind him.

"Moly!" Randy exploded. Randy had yelled "Holy!" as the demon thing had grabbed his shoulder and begun to carry him away. Somehow, he had suspended that thought, finishing it now, as the door was latching behind him. He stood bent over, hands on his knees, breathing hard. Sarah went to him and grabbed his shoulders and placed her head on his back and cried.

Upon hearing her tears, he raised his head and body, and she followed. He held her and kissed the top of her head and said, "I'm all right…it's okay." He looked at the others and continued, raising his right hand to the back of his head, "I thought it was all over there for a moment…guys, you do *not* want to be touched by one of those things. It was horrible. It felt like my heart had entered hell and the rest of me was following it."

The man Randy had saved looked around the room, amazed he was alive and amazed the people inside this house were too. He looked to be in his twenties, most probably late twenties. He looked like an academic, either a young associate professor type or one of those lifetime students. He was wearing jeans and a multicolored, horizontally striped, button-up sweater over a white T-shirt. He had reddish-brown hair and a scruffy yet well-edged beard.

"Thanks a lot," the man said, breaking into a smile, fueled by the sudden realization of how happy he was to be alive. "I have been fighting off attacks like those for a week, trying to find someone—anyone else—who's alive. I thought this was it, game over."

"What's your name?" Sarah asked.

"I'm Stuart. I am, eh, *was* a student at NYU. I was studying linguistics. Wish I'd been studying weapons now." The man, shaking his head, asked, "How is it that you are all alive? These are the only buildings standing for blocks."

Jack intervened, seeing Sarah wasn't sure how to answer and was already beginning to look in his direction. "That's a bit of a story. But for now, just know and be happy that you're safe here."

"All right," said Stuart. "Honestly, that's all I need to know right now."

"Good. Don't worry. We'll fill you in later. You mentioned looking for others. You're saying you haven't seen anyone else out there except for us between here and NYU?" Jack was alarmed. This man's ability made him easy to spot. Jack was surprised there were no survivors who might have come out of hiding to band with him in order to gain some protection.

"No, not really. I mean there are those bastards who were shooting at us, helping the fuckers! And you've seen the…I don't know…whatever they are, right?"

They all knew, from the disgusted look on Stuart's face, he was talking about the Myth of Man's targets…victims, sufferers, getting-what-they-deservers, depending on one's viewpoint. Those who had degraded into some sort of subhuman mass of grossness due to hate and arrogance they had harbored in their hearts.

"Yes, we've seen them," Jack said, biting the corner of his mouth and shaking his head. "I guess it's possible there are people out there. This is a big city. Maybe they're just too afraid to come out from where they are."

Quincy followed Jack's statement. "Jack. The scroll protected Randy once Four Winds got closer to them. I think we need to go out and start looking for others."

"I think you're right," Jack said, nodding quickly at the idea. "I think we need to start right away, too. If we don't, I don't think anyone out there has much time left."

"And I need to start looking for a plane," Derek announced.

CHAPTER 39

BRIAN, AN ELEMENTOR
JANUARY 31, 2013

"T HERE'S PEOPLE down the road!"

Brian had been leading what was left of his hometown of Tipton, Iowa, for two weeks toward New York City. They had found a wind-blower and two ice-makers/water-movers along the way and were doing pretty good against the enemies of the night. The four Elementors took shifts sleeping in cars, getting a whole new brand of daymares, as they tried to rest to be prepared for the real nightmares materializing in the dark.

Several weeks earlier, Brian hadn't been much more than any normal seventeen-year-old Midwestern small-town kid. He played football for his Tipton High School team. He was good but wasn't going to be going to college on a football scholarship. He had been a big freshman, and that had been enough for the coach to seek him out three years earlier. Knocking people down was a fun way to spend your afterschool afternoons, and it gave his bulky body some exercise, and that kept it from getting bulkier. It was his third year playing for the team, and he was finally getting some real play time. Being on the football team wasn't bad for his social life, either, and considering his size, he might have had more trouble in that area if he hadn't been known for slamming rival school's team members to the ground on weekend nights.

All that was before. Now he was known for something else. He was the only one in Tipton who could fight demons by producing spontaneous fire from his hands by sheer will alone. And when a demon wanted to tear you into pieces or drag your friends off to some unknown location to enjoy them as a snack, being able to fry that demon became a real popularity booster.

Popularity didn't really matter to Brian anymore, however. Staying alive did. And he knew he wouldn't be able to hold off the attacks indefinitely. They were already losing people every night to this new horror of a world.

He had convinced his remaining friends and fellow town members—numbering around three hundred or so—that they needed to leave, to try to find others like him, or they wouldn't survive for much longer. The part he didn't tell them was his plan was to head to New York City because of some *other* friends he had met on the internet prior to Hell Day, which is what everyone was starting to call the twenty-first of December. He was afraid people wouldn't understand that he had known anything about *anything* prior to that date. He really hadn't. He knew he woke up one morning in October and nearly cooked his dog when he told Bernie to *get the hell outside* because Bernie had pissed on his blanket. When he came across the Duboises' website and contacted them, he had learned the group in New York had suspected something might happen on the twenty-first, but they weren't for sure. Even if they had been sure, who would have believed him, anyway? But now, with twenty-twenty hindsight, they would all want someone to blame for being so unprepared. Better to stay their hero than the man who knew too much. At least for now.

There was a lot of hemming and hawing about leaving the safety of the town for the open road, but Brian said he was going no matter what, and no one could really argue, considering that he was the only thing that had stood between them and total annihilation up to that point. They had already lost most of the town, even with him doing everything he could.

Brian needed to move. He wasn't going to last much longer by himself. Two nights after they left town, the group was attacked by the first group of flying demons they had ever seen. The townspeople fired guns trying to help, and they did—*some*—but Brian was still thrown to the ground by an aerial attack and almost killed.

As he was seeing his life flash before his eyes, and the monster's jaw was coming, lowering quickly toward his face, the damned thing had frozen solid and then had flown apart into a million pieces, blowing away toward the other side of the road. And that's how he met James and Paula. They were a brother and sister from nearby Wilton, one of the rival towns Brian played against. *(Used to play against.)* They were on the run, the same as him. They had heard the screaming from down the road and had come running to see what was happening. James was an ice-maker, and his sister was a wind-blower. Together they made quite an awesome pair of freeze-and-blow-to-bits demon killers.

"Thanks, a lot!" Brian yelled in relief as James pulled him off the ground. James was a lot smaller than Brian, so he didn't really pull Brian up, but it felt to Brian like he did, considering, at that moment, Brian felt as if he was rising from the dead.

"No problem. Come on, we gotta help those people!" James had yelled and took off following his sister.

Brian followed as quick as his legs could carry him, and together, they finished off a couple of more enemies down the road beginning to attack the townspeople up ahead.

"That's some pretty amazing firepower you've got there. My name's James Alboy, and this is my sister, Paula. Nice to meet you. We're from Wilton. Where you from?"

Brian answered, "Tipton. I'm really glad you showed up. I thought *I* was over." He held out his hand. "Brian."

"Yeah, us too. We were running so hard. We saw that thing knock you down. We didn't think we'd get close enough in time," Paula explained, still out of breath.

"Well, thank God you did. Thanks again." Brian said, still fighting through heavy breathing to speak. "She freezes, and you pulverize. Pretty great combo. I have *really* been hoping to find more like me to protect these people *and me.*"

Brian turned to the rest of his group. "This is exactly why we needed to leave. We need to keep searching for others, or we'll never survive!"

The townspeople nodded, and the men with the guns reloaded.

"You're quite the leader here," James said to Brian as they walked away from the crowd. "By the time Paula and I had discovered we were different, out on our farm, everyone in town was already dead or gone. We just took off after we were attacked in town, investigating if anyone was still around. We knew if we didn't find people fast, we weren't going to make it alone, no matter what we could do."

"Agreed. Felt the same way," Brian responded. "Did you have any family?"

"Nah, me and my sis have been living on the farm alone since our parents died in a car wreck three years ago," James replied. It appeared easier for James to say than for his sister to hear, from what Brian saw on their faces.

"I'm sorry," Brian said.

"You got any? Parents, I mean. Are they in that group of people?" James asked.

"No," Brian said, knowing the question was coming. His eyes felt a quiver, and rather than go the route of letting it all out, he squeezed his eyes and shook it off. "They were killed on Hell Day. They were in a movie theater."

"Oh God, sorry, man," James responded. "Didn't realize. That's still pretty fresh. You all right?"

"It's all right. I brought 'family' up. And hey, we *have* to be all right. Gotta stay alive, keep these people alive. We're heading east. That okay with you?" And he started to walk away, wiping at his eyes.

"Sure, how far?" James called.

Brian stopped, turned around, and came close again. "I haven't told anyone yet, but—can you keep a secret?"

"Uh, yeah," James said. Paula was nodding.

"Well, I talked to some people in New York City prior to Hell Day, and they seemed to know it was coming. I mean they weren't totally sure, but they were looking for people like us and said they were banking on the Mayan calendar date actually meaning something. I wouldn't have believed them if I'd just met them on the street with all the wackos on TV and everything talking about the end of the world on 12-21 and all. But I had found them through a website they had made explaining they were looking for people who had abilities like us. I felt I didn't have anything to lose, you know, so I called. Anyway, they were nice and sounded normal. I think we need to get there, find out what else they know. I was talking to them until the cells stopped working. We're supposed to listen to shortwave radio. They said they had a plan to hopefully, eventually, communicate that way. We need to find a shortwave radio, I guess, on this trip too. If you know anything about that, that'd be great. They also said to do exactly what we're doing. Find others, help others, and survive."

"That's some heavy shit. People knew this was going to happen?"

"Sort of. They tried to explain it to me; they said they were almost as much in the dark as anyone else, but they had come across some prophecies or something that had been almost too undeniable to deny. They had no concrete answers, though."

"Well, Brian, if they have no concrete answers, then why we going all the way to New York City?"

"I figure they know what they know for a *reason*. And I figure being around people who know a little is better than being around people who know nothing."

"Can't argue with that, I guess," James said, knowing he was sticking with Brian and the group, regardless, even before he asked the question. "Fine, we'll head with you."

—◇○◇—

"What the hell was that, Brian?! Are they insane?" James was yelling after a fight a few weeks later. He was stomping back onto the pavement of the highway. "Why would people join with the freaking monsters?" He then saw his sister lying on the far side of the road and took off running. "Paula!"

—◇○◇—

A little earlier, another group had been walking down the same highway. Brian had seen the people down the road, and everyone had picked up pace to meet them. It was getting late, and having more to help before night fell couldn't hurt. They now numbered in the neighborhood of 550 people, plus they had met Gene, an earth-mover from Walcott. They had hoped to pick up more people in Davenport, but it had been almost completely wiped out. They were currently close to Chicago. The weather was getting colder, and the moving was getting slower. Brian being able to start fires was a really good skill to have in the winter, and Gene flying in firewood complemented it very well.

The group of people up ahead turned out to be less than beneficial. As they got closer, it got darker. The long, straight roads of Illinois farmland had made the strangers appear a lot closer than they were. As the gap between the two groups closed, James had noticed something strange in the way some of the people were moving. He said to Brian, "Do you see how some of them are moving? You think they're hurt?"

Brian had replied, "I don't know. They look a bit weird. Look. There's several of them, all moving like that."

"Think we should be worried?" Paula had asked.

"Don't know," Brian had said, "hard to tell. They probably just need help."

Their slight concern had been correct. The group they were closing in on ended up being populated by people who didn't appear to have any of Brian's or his group's best interests in mind. The ones James had thought might be injured were disgusting, inhuman creatures, and they were even worse to look at when they were up close trying to kill you. Night had fallen when the groups reached each other. Within moments, a fight to the finish had ensued, along with demons, who commonly liked to make their appearance.

Brian, Gene, James, and Paula did everything they could to protect everyone and each other, but the fight never organized, given the surprise attack by the strangers. Everyone was fending for themselves. They lost over fifty of their group by the time it was over, and Paula had been shot in the arm.

<hr/>

"Paula, it's not that bad," James said, relieved after assessing his sister's condition. "I thought you were dead! Thank God it didn't hit an artery." He had torn off a part of his shirt to wrap her arm with. He looked up at Brian, who had come running to Paula after James had seen her on the ground from across the interstate.

"Those were people! Helping them? And what were those *things*?!"

"I guess we're dividing, right?" Brian answered.

"Dividing? What do you mean?" James responded.

"You know, good and evil."

"Good and evil? That sounds like a bunch of religious bullshit, and we all know now that religion is a bunch of bullshit."

"Not necessarily, James. Ever since Hell Day, I have definitely known that my church was full of crap, but I don't feel like my belief in a God is."

"Yeah, fine. I guess I can't deny you got me there, but the way you make it sound is this is some sort of end-of-the-world battle. The freaking apocalypse."

"Maybe it is. Do you see what we've been doing, what we've been fighting against?"

"Listen, I'm just out here to save my own ass from being eaten by one of those things. How does that make me good?"

"Well, you're not fighting with them, are you? If you want to just save your ass, then go join them. We now know others are."

"Dammit! Stop making sense! You're supposed to be a stupid football player, lughead linebacker type. I'm not joining a bunch of *shitfaces* like that ever. They can eat me for dinner first."

"I think we need to get to New York, fast," Brian concluded.

"Yeah, okay, Brian, it's six states that way. We'll catch up when you're tired of jogging."

"James, don't be such a butt," Paula barked. "We're all scared. Let's just try to make it through the rest of the night and hope we don't run into any more enemies. Another demon could appear at any time."

"I'm watching." It was Glen. He had joined them as well, but his eyes were peeled to the skies.

"All right, Paula," James conceded softly, finishing the bandage.

"I think we lost a lot. Maybe fifty...or more," Gene informed them. "Fathers, sons, brothers, little sisters. Shit, it's horrible."

"We've got to find more like us...and quick," Brian remarked.

"Yeah, right after we get to New York, *quick*."

"James," Paula said curtly, "you're not helping."

CHAPTER 40

THE PATH
JANUARY 2013

<hr/>

"BY THE TIME THE MACY'S INCIDENT in New York had occurred, Harvey and Meg were already on the strangest of journeys. If anyone had seen them, the "enginerd" and waitress would have appeared to be the blind leading the blind—on a tight wire.

Harvey and Meg had been walking their awkward walk for over three weeks. The day was easier than the night. As long as Harvey kept an eye on the path, they only had to stay directly on it if they saw other people. They had discovered that while on the path, they were invisible not just to the demons but to regular people, as well. This fact had at least given them the ability to run into a convenience store or two to gather food and drink to carry with them, and then run back to the path for safety, effectively popping out of existence to anyone who may have caught sight of them. They had also been able to sneak away from the path long enough to loot boots and pile on winter clothing. If they *had* been visible, any onlookers might have commented, "Look. There go two Inuit doing a conga line." But Harvey and Meg *weren't* visible, so nothing like that happened.

The warm clothes didn't come soon enough for either of them. During the first night of their walk, they had nearly frozen to death. The path's beginning was moving with almost every step Harvey took, and they had to keep going all night long so they wouldn't be seen by the demons that were hitting Claremore. They started jogging to keep up their body heat, trying to create some slack between where they were on the path and where the path was shrinking, someplace behind Harvey. It was difficult for Harvey to see the path in the dark. His headache had become ferocious from not using his own prescription. Meg followed close behind with her hands resting on his hips. Besides following an invisible path to who knows where and having no protection from the wind and cold, they also had to endure watching their town and the people in it get slaughtered by a horde from hell. By the time they were downtown and saw Jammer's, it had already been hit. No one seemed to be able to see them, and both of them had been afraid to step off the path for fear of what might happen if they were seen by anyone or anything.

It was the middle of the next day before they reached another town and found a clothing store Meg could run into while Harvey watched the path. Both of them had succumbed to some level of frostbite on their fingers and toes. They layered up in the middle of the street in the clothes and coats she had returned with, but not being able to get warm first wasn't making it easy to button and zip.

"We have to get something to start a fire, Meg," Harvey said, shaking as he was putting on the last of the layers. "Our fingers are going to fall off. I can barely move them to do this."

He tried to help her with her coat as she was struggling, just the same.

"I know, Harvey. Why is this happening to us? What's it for? My hands hurt so bad."

He didn't have the heart to tell her that her nose didn't look too good either. He was almost positive a couple of her fingers were heading beyond saving, no matter what.

"I don't know, Meg. This is bad, but at least we didn't end up like the rest of the town. We'll get through this. There has to be a reason I can see this path. If we keep moving fast, we can make enough ground on its disintegration behind us so that maybe we can rest for a while."

Eventually, they had to rest. Meg had run into another store and gotten some boxes of wooden matches and thrown some fire-starting logs into a backpack. They set fire to one of the logs and finally began feeling human again. They took turns sleeping during the day. Meg would wake up Harvey every so often on her shift, so that Harvey could keep checking that the path hadn't outrun them. They kept moving all night when the path was harder to see, as they were afraid they might lose it. Harvey didn't know what he would do if the path ever veered off the road.

—◇○◇—

The wave of *Hereafter realizations* hit Harvey like a rock in the gut. Harvey's long-held belief that somewhere, down deep, Meg had begun to love him was apparently dead wrong. Most of his theories on the universe were completely off the mark, and Jimmy at Jammer's Café really wasn't faking how much he hated Harvey's conversations.

Meg and Harvey were sitting down with a fire log burning between them. It was the middle of the night. It had just gotten too cold, and they had needed to take a break. They had been doing their routine for a little over three weeks, had traveled from Oklahoma through Arkansas and were nearing Dyersburg, Tennessee. If anything, Harvey's realization about Meg had hit him the hardest. He had started to convince himself that somewhere down deep, she really had feelings for him, that somehow he'd grown on her once she really got to spend some time with him, away from the diner, even being protected by him on this journey. But he suddenly knew this was a complete fallacy in his own mind.

"What's wrong, Harvey?" Meg asked. "You don't look so hot."

"Yeah?" he replied, not knowing what to say. Sticking his foot in his mouth, he followed his interjection with, "I guess that's the whole problem, huh?"

"What?" Meg asked back, confused.

"Meg, we, ah, nothing, it's nothing. Never mind."

"Harvey, whatever this nothing is, you better tell me right now! We've just walked through two states in the middle of winter, following some invisible path while watching demons flying and killing all around us. I don't think this is the time for secrets!"

What am I going to say now?

He'd opened this can of worms with his stupid comment. She'd never understand whatever had just happened to him, so he figured he was stuck, needing to say something believable to her. She may not love him, but if they were going to need to keep traveling together, he didn't want her hating him either.

"I guess I was just being stupid. That's all," he said to her.

"Stupid? About what?" she asked in return.

"Listen, Meg, I know we're just friends, and this has been to you probably the longest nondate-date you could ever imagine having. I guess I just thought, that somewhere…somehow…after everything that's happened… all we've been through, you'd—"

"Harvey, are you trying to tell me something?"

"Well?" He knew she was getting it and was now trying to lead him into spilling his guts. He wasn't going to roll over that easily.

"Harvey. Do you see the situation we're in? And you're thinking about relationships? Men. You never cease to amaze me, you know? Does that brain of yours work on any other channel?" She started laughing.

Fun for Harvey he would not define as her "laying it out" for him, but her laugh was more of a "with him" kind of laugh, so he figured it was best to let the sleeping dog lie and laugh at himself too. He wasn't so dumb to realize the conversation he had started could have gone south really quick, making their situation even more uncomfortable than it already was.

"I guess you're right, Meg. Men! Ha!"

After a little more chuckling, Meg made a comment on a much more pertinent subject.

"Two of my fingers are dead, Harvey. And I really don't know what to do about that. I also don't know if I can do *this* much longer. Sometimes I just want to step off this narrow lane of safety you've shown to me and let those things take me."

"Meg, no!" Harvey freaked out. "You aren't giving up. This path leads somewhere, and we're going to get there, and everything's going to be okay. Let me see your hand."

She slid it out of her glove, and she hadn't been kidding. Her hand didn't look good at all. Her pinky and ring finger on her right hand were definitely gone. They were going to infect her hand soon, and he knew what had to be done. Harvey also knew he was the one who was going to have to do it.

"Meg, we're going to have to remove them. You know that, right? Or you're going to get gangrene, and you could lose the rest of your hand or arm, or even die."

"I know, Harvey," she answered. "Why do you think I want to let them take me?"

"Meg, I can promise you that whatever it is they do to you, it's going to hurt more than what we've got to do to save your hand. We need to do it now."

The look of fear on her face tripled. It was one thing to have a pipe dream of flinging yourself in front of a truck, or in her case, a demon, in order to remove all her woes and sorrows. There was fear associated with such a thought, yes, but it was still a daydream—a something you *might* do or *could* do. It was even one thing to be afraid, in the background of your mind, of the coming inevitability of having to sit there while someone cut off your fingers. But it was a whole different thing to be told that it had to be done *now, right now,* and knowing they were right.

"I can't do this, Harvey. Can't you hit me in the head with a rock and knock me out or something?"

"It doesn't work that way, Meg. I'm sorry. I could beat you all day, and you might just end up with a bad headache, or a concussion, or dead. Any of those three, but not unconscious. You're gonna need something to bite on."

"Oh, Harvey" was all she could get to escape her lips.

"I'm so sorry, but we have to do this," he answered.

He turned to get the knife out of their backpack of supplies that had been slowly amassed along their journey. He stuck it in the flame. Harvey knew what he had to do and wondered if he had the strength to do it. He figured causing her that much pain might put him out cold on the spot. He was already seeing a bit gray.

If you love her, you can do this. This was the thought he needed, and he focused on that.

"Meg, you're going to have to lie down on the path and put your hand out in front of you. Scoot back. I've got to get on the other side of this fire with you." Realizing his body was going to block the light of the fire, once he climbed over it, he dug in the pack for a flashlight as well.

She did as she was told, wanting to and not wanting to at the same time. *Get it over with,* Meg kept telling herself. *You hid it long enough, but you brought it up now for a reason,* she further convinced herself. Harvey was trying his best to be gentle about the situation, and she appreciated that. It made her feel more at ease if that was really possible. She backed up and lay on her stomach. He had told her to move her feet a little left because they were slightly off the Path to Wherever. She stretched her damaged hand with its gray and black fingers out in front of her on the highway, and Harvey stepped over the burning log and sat down in front of her hand.

"Meg, it's going to hurt. But I don't think as much as you think it will." He had no idea if this was true, but it was a thought he had in his head, and he figured it couldn't hurt. "The fingers have lost all feeling, and you've never had a sensation like this. Your mind might not quite know how to register what's happening till it's over." Once again, he knew he could be feeding her a total load of Harveyesque bullshit, but it didn't matter. She seemed to be focusing on the "won't hurt as much as you think" part and was nodding in submission to the idea. Harvey laid the flashlight down on the road so it would be pointed at the mini–surgery area he had created. He reached back to remove the knife from the flame. Meg took her nylon glove and put it in her mouth, laid her head on the pavement, and closed her eyes.

He raised the knife over her hand and carefully announced, "Meg, I'm going to have to do one at a time. I love you." He had no idea where that came from, and he pushed down through her hand and listened to her scream.

CHAPTER 41

THE JOURNEY'S END
FEBRUARY 13, 2013

⟨⟩○⟨⟩○⟨⟩

I T WAS MID-FEBRUARY 2013 when Harvey and Meg came up and over the last crest
of Kentucky they would be walking over together. It was after dark, and the sight
they saw could safely be said to be the most disheartening one either of them had
ever thought they'd see.

Between the road where they stood and a tree-covered mountain far to the east,
there lay a valley several miles wide in between. Various shades of brown carpeted
the valley, and winter had left it with a desolate and lifeless-looking feel, compared to
what was most probably a beautiful picturesque view only a few months before.
However, the scenery would have still reminded an onlooker of a captivating scene
of nature, if, that is, the center of all that is evil in the world hadn't set up camp at the
far end of the valley.

Harvey squinted to see that far away through Meg's glasses but he couldn't get a
clear image. He glanced down at the road to verify they were still standing on the path
that had led them to the fate in which they now found themselves. His eyes followed
the path away from them, past Meg's feet, and he noticed it was the first time the path
had ever veered off a road or walkway. It appeared to lead down the hillside straight
toward the horror existing across the valley.

Harvey took off Meg's glasses and handed them to her. She would have been
grateful to wear them again at any other moment. But to see better what she had
deduced she was seeing was not on her bucket list, and never would have been, either.
Harvey pulled out his own thick spectacles from his coat, placed them on his face,
and peered across the field outstretched before them. He didn't need Meg's glasses
to see demons because they were fully visible to the normal eye. Hundreds of them
seemed to be flying and walking around the encampment. It was too far away to see
much detail, but it was safe to say that the demons looked quite at home at the camp.

"Harvey," Meg whispered instinctively, although their time on the path had taught
her they were completely safe where they stood. She looked away from the site they
had discovered and back toward him. She continued, the dread apparent even in her
whisper. "The path led us to them. What the hell are we supposed to do now?"

Harvey's first thought was to turn back. There was no point following it anymore.

He kicked himself for not having predicted this. They had passed people they could have joined, as they had silently continued on their now-debunked path to safety. Now, they were completely alone and headed right into the lion's den—the only weapon being an offering of some beef jerky and the canned goods in their backpacks. His secondary thought was they couldn't go back. The path had continued to disintegrate slowly behind them as they had traveled. Whatever safe passage the path provided, it was one-way protection. The irony was superb and ridiculous at the same time.

"Why be kept safe, just to be led to those who will murder us?" he asked, not expecting any answer to come with any truth. The path had been a lie. Why not everything else, from now on?

Meg was noticeably distraught. She'd lost two of her fingers. She'd walked across four states in mid-winter. Harvey knew she'd kept hope alive that they were being led somewhere they could be protected. Now she had nothing left to grasp at. She appeared at the edge of a breakdown. She began shaking. She grabbed Harvey by the shirt and began yelling profanities at him. She accused him of doing this to her, of being aligned with the forces of evil. He tried to calm her down, but she just kept screaming. He tried to stop her hands once they began landing punches on his chest. She was losing control.

In the mayhem, Meg had taken a step to the left—off the path—and Harvey had his arms out toward her, trying to calm her down. In an instant, he was no longer staring at Meg's face, but instead he was looking at her waist, and then her feet, and then...nothing. He didn't have enough time to attempt to hold on to her, or even get out a yell. When he recognized what was happening, an automatic signal went down his spine to command his arms to pull in close to his body—a maneuver they had gotten very used to on their journey. *Stick inside the boundaries of the path.* Harvey looked up, it finally having registered that Meg had been picked up and carried off by something. He saw her figure high in the sky, being held by a monstrosity with wings. She was headed toward that base from hell that lay below him in the valley.

He stood still a moment longer, making sure he wasn't seen and wasn't going to experience the same fate. After a calming down session of the mind, which consisted of Harvey telling himself to get a grip (for Meg, if for anything), he knew what had to be done. He was going to have to follow the path wherever it led (*you know where it leads*), with the hopes that somehow, he could rescue Meg. He looked down to get his bearings, in order to view the path. As he did so, Harvey immediately realized he was wearing his *own* glasses.

CHAPTER 42

BYRON DISCOVERS HE WROTE THEM
JUNE 2047

---◇○◁❍▷○◇---

BYRON LAY ON THE FLOOR by the fireplace in the middle of his cabin. He couldn't move…or rather didn't want to move…had no desire to move. What he'd just witnessed had floored him. This pun, he thought, wouldn't favor a laugh till later, when he was writing these events in his journals. At this moment, Byron didn't know what to think. He told himself he should have known, that it had been staring himself in the face for years. Nevertheless, the idea had never occurred to him. The Enigma machine had been sitting in the cabin when he had arrived there as a boy, yes, but at most he had thought perhaps there would be some additional scroll he was meant to find and translate himself. He'd never postulated that he was to be the author of the scrolls his distant friends had found.

"How can it be?" he asked himself. "How can I have written them?"

How in the world would they get to where they eventually needed to go: thousands of years in the past?

Byron had just experienced another one of his eerie chicken-and-egg viewings of himself. The viewing had placed him in his own cabin a few weeks in the future from the current date in June, calendar year 2047. He had watched this future version of himself pull the desk away from the wall and discover a large sealed envelope attached to the back of the desk. From the envelope, he had pulled out several pieces of very familiar paperlike pages. The pages were identical in material to what he had viewed all these years as the paper the scrolls the four myths were written on. Future Byron had then proceeded to pull a Russian-English Dictionary off one of the shelves in the living room and had headed back to the desk. Byron then viewed himself write, encode, and transcribe the scrolls onto the previously hidden papers. He watched in almost horror, confounded by disbelief in what he was seeing. Later, he would wonder why this discovery felt so impossible, given everything else he had witnessed in his life. Maybe he was most surprised because he hadn't seen it coming.

The strength to get off the floor came upon remembering the Russian-English dictionary from his vision. He turned his head toward the wall and the few shelves built into it, the same wall as the fireplace. Could it be possible that it had been there all these years and he had never noticed it? As his eyes scanned across the book back, he realized that—yes, it could have. There, in the exact place he had seen himself in his viewing remove it from, sat the dictionary. It was mixed in with several other books the German man had left in the cabin, which Byron had never had a desire to read, nor the time to do so anyway.

He raised both of his hands to his forehead and tried to shake off the absurdity of it all. Eventually Byron rose up from the floor, still trying to understand what it all meant. This was only the first of several very strange viewings he was about to have. Physically being able to step into another time, at will, was really going to knock Byron out when he realized he was also the person who would hand the scrolls to four men who lived a really long time ago.

—◇o◇—

October 21, 2034 CE: Entry 9,342

Jack and the others were able to secure a military base today, with Brian's group's help. Many of the military underground installations are still manned. It seems the personnel stayed put in many of the important command centers. Some have been destroyed internally by either demons appearing within the facilities, or by actual soldiers battling it out between themselves because some would choose the bad side. But with shortwave, they're able to communicate with Derek and Riley in England and are hoping to make the base their protected encampment. If one of them can eventually leave and do the same somewhere out West, they believe they may be able to have a pretty wide range of communication available to those who are out there fighting across the world. Since Brian, James, Paula, Gene, and the rest showed up in New York, things have really started looking up. I hope this continues. They have a lot of weapons now, and real soldiers who can train them.

I still have so many questions, though. I can't believe I've been doing this for twenty-seven years. Does the war really last this long?

CHAPTER 43

TO SAVE OR NOT TO SAVE
FEBRUARY 13, 2013, CONTINUED

H ARVEY HAD NO CHOICE but to sit down on the road for the rest of the night and pray the beginning of the path didn't catch up to him before morning, exposing him to view. At daybreak, he would hike back to the town they had passed a few miles back, staying out of sight of anyone, if he could help it, and find another pair of glasses. If he were lucky, and he'd have to be damned lucky, he could reach back to where he was and find the path again and follow it into the valley without being seen, caught, killed, carried off, or eaten. His mornings had become so different from the years of coffee at Jammer's. He barely recognized his current state of being as even being his life anymore.

Morning arrived and Harvey had gotten lucky. He hadn't needed to walk all the way back to the last town. There had been a car on the side of the road. The car had been badly destroyed and the driver killed. He remembered having passed it with Meg when he was about halfway back to it and had hoped he might find some glasses on the driver or somewhere in the car. Even a pair of reading spectacles would be something. Once arriving at the spot where the car lay in the ditch on the side of the road, he soon discovered he would not easily find a pair of Walgreen's reading glasses in the glove compartment. Instead, he had the pleasure of sliding them off the face of a burnt corpse, both temple pieces stuck to crisped skin. His stomach crawled as he wiped the glasses off, having to scrape away a bit of flesh on one temple arm, the cooked skin having pulled away from the dead man's skull along with the glasses. Add necro-pick-pocketing to his new life and list of morning activities no longer including reading the paper at Jammer's Café or annoying Jimmy with some new theory he'd thought of. Ah, those were the days.

He placed the glasses on his face, grimacing as he fought hard not to throw up again. This mission was all about trying to find and save Meg. Harvey didn't have the luxury of complaining about glasses that were "as clean as he could make them," yet *unclean* as they were. He wasn't sure he could call finding these glasses luck, either. The glasses allowed him to see the hidden things in his new reality, but they forced him to squat near the ground to do it. The prescription seemed to be the opposite— if that was a proper term in optometry—of everything his eyes required to see properly, and he found it difficult to even catch the outline of a scarab. When he held his hand up in front of his face, he only saw a flesh-colored blur. It could have been another person looking back at him, for all Harvey could tell. He thought momentarily about continuing the hike back to the town to see if he could find any other pair that might allow him to see more clearly, but he had to shake that idea away, knowing he may never find the path again if he didn't hurry back up the mountain. Meg and Harvey had tried very hard to move fast and keep moving early in their journey, not only to stay warm but also to make a lot of headway on the incredibly shrinking path. He estimated they had possibly made a day's worth of gain on the thing, but he couldn't be sure. He had already lost nearly twelve hours and had no certainty the beginning would not have moved past the spot where he had lost Meg. If he had to travel too far down into the valley just to find the darned thing, he would risk being seen by the inhabitants of Hell's Canyon. He needed to get back, and pronto.

He slipped his newly found pair of glasses into his pocket and sliding on his own glasses, he brought the world back into focus and took off back to where he'd come from that morning. Harvey hadn't seen any sign of life on his trip down the mountain, and he hoped the same for his return.

The stretch of highway Harvey was traveling on would have been beautiful in the summer. Pastures spread out on either side, and the road up ahead was heading into a tree-covered mountain of the Appalachian chain. Some grayish-green conifers littered the view, but everything else had the dead, wintry look. Add on the cloud cover, the fear of monsters, human and nonhuman that Harvey knew were on the other side of that mountain, and the sights offered nothing close to beauty.

He moved quickly, but the dismalness of his surroundings and the worry that Meg might already have been on the dinner plate of two or three different demons and might now be digesting in their stomachs left him feeling unmotivated, and questioning why he was moving so fast. He was tired, and the more he thought about Meg, the more he felt like he was losing hope. He thought about where he was trying to get back to and what he was trying to find: a path he once believed was a road to safety, but instead had led them to likely destruction. Meg was gone—most probably dead—and he was probably hours from the same fate if he kept going forward.

Just turn around Harvey. Leave. Why do you want to go find that path and follow it right into their camp? To save a dead girl who didn't even love you anyway? There's nothing but your own demise waiting for you up that hill, behind those trees. Turn around, find others, and survive.

Harvey stopped. These thoughts had been circulating through his mind for several minutes and he was now standing at the base of the mountain. The road was feeling steeper, and he had started to get more out of breath from the walk. He felt like an idiot. This quest had taken on a ludicrous nature. What was he trying to do? What was the point? And even if he got to where he was going, what did he think he'd be able to do when he got there? His plan was antithetic to foolproof. There was no reason to keep going. He would just get himself killed. Meg may not have loved him, but she would not want him doing this. She would want him to save himself, so their journey didn't end in complete vain. In fact, when he lost her, she had been angry with him, had been hitting him. She had lost faith in him, so why was he risking his life on a suicide mission to save her? She was already dead, anyway.

Yeah, forget it. Not worth it, he thought.

He turned around and looked at the open road behind him. It seemed nicer than before. It wasn't so dead and ugly after all. Winter had its own peaceful beauty. The frost was still glistening in the light of the morning, the landscape had the hope of spring in its bones, looking forward to rebirthing, to living again. Live again. Live.

I need to go back to that town, start looking for others. Safety in numbers. Your previous path of safety is gone. Meg would want that.

He wouldn't survive alone. That was true. And the path that had protected him was shrinking and had pushed them right into the enemy's hands.

He moved his left foot forward one step. Then his right. Then his left, again. It was getting easier as he found himself walking away from the mountain, walking away from certain death and feeling better, safer. He had made the right decision. He looked ahead and saw hope again, and with his own glasses, he could see it all the more. He had barely worn them for two months. His headache was gone, and his eyes didn't hurt. It felt good, good to be himself again. He looked down at his hands. They were crystal clear. He looked at his feet. He could *see* them. He saw the granularity of the pavement below his feet. Most of this journey that pavement had been nothing but a blurry black-and-gray surface.

And blurry scarabs outlining that blurry road.

Yep, that's all that was missing. Those nasty bugs on either side of his steps. He stopped again. Not knowing why, he was ripping off his own glasses and pulling out the ones he had just confiscated and put them on. He looked down at the road. The scarabs couldn't be seen clearly, but the ground appeared to move beneath him, so he knew they were there. Harvey dropped to his knees, and they came more into focus. Hundreds, millions probably, maybe even trillions of them, if he imagined the whole world where they were running over it in all directions. He turned to his left and right, only to see more of the same. He thrust his hands down into them and started crawling on the road. As long as he couldn't feel them, it was okay—at least that's what he was telling himself. From a distance, he would have been a strange sight to see. A grown man crawling this way and that on a Kentuckyian highway, face close to the ground pretending to be a bloodhound in pursuit of a trail.

After making a couple back and forths on the asphalt, Harvey stopped and sat back on his heels. The path was gone. He and Meg had followed it the day before on this road. Wherever it was, if it still existed at all, it was not here. It was somewhere, *hopefully*, up that mountain.

You love her, Harvey! You fool! You don't walk away from the woman you love to save your own ass, even if she begged you to. If there's a chance she's alive, you're going to find her or die trying.

He felt like the biggest louse on earth. If this new motivation hadn't been Meg—driving him to do what needed to be done—he would have just laid down on the road and become one with the scarabs—become a later dessert for a random demon after it had finished dining on the mystical roaches now blessing the entire planet's surface with their presence. He felt no better than them for having turned around and changed his mind, even for a moment. If he saved Meg, he wasn't sure if he could ever confess this waffling to her, this decision he had made to leave her, to just assume she was dead. Meg needed him to be a hero, but after what he had just done, he knew, even if he succeeded, he would never be able to convince himself he was one.

The path wasn't here; he hoped to God it was still up there, somewhere on that road. He took off running.

CHAPTER 44

VIKKI AND HARVEY
FEBRUARY 13, 2013

—◦◦◦◦—

"WE'VE BEEN FLYING over these mountains for days, Vikki." Sam moaned and started to lower the park bench toward a small rest stop he had spotted on one of the highways. "I don't think we're going to find this camp you're looking for that has your friend in it."

"Don't worry about it, Sam," she answered. "You do the flying, and I'll do the worrying. We may need to change our strategy, though, so set us down for now. I need time to think."

Vikki really meant she needed time to pee, but Sam didn't need to know that. She had already decided what they needed to do if she was going to find what she needed to find.

They finished their pit stop and munched on some of their processed, preservative-filled snacks. While she sat there eating a Twinkie and chasing it with a Red Bull, she wondered if people who had been all organic and vegan before Hell Day would be dying off soon, their bodies unable to resort back to Cheez Whiz and Hostess for sustenance, like normal people.

"I love the fact that I can eat a Twinkie and no one is going to look at me funny anymore," Vikki commented after her previous thought, yet seemingly out of the blue, to Sam.

"Yeah, I guess," he replied.

"Aw, you wouldn't understand, Sam. You're not a girl." She laughed and took another bite, feeling the cream sink into the grooves between her teeth. She smiled at the feeling and the taste.

"Why do you look so happy, Vikki?" Sam asked. "We are hardly in a position to be happy about *anything*."

Still with her mouth full of Hostess, she answered, "Sham, ith-suh Twinkie, my *Gawd*!"

He just shook his head and turned away in his usual mopey manner. "Well, you can have fun with your Twinkie, but I'm getting tired of flying around up there in circles. Eventually somebody on their side is gonna spot us and take a shot at us."

"That's why we're going to look at night now," Vikki replied.

"*What?*" Sam shouted, jumping off their chariot park bench. "What do you mean, search at night?"

"Hey, you said you were tired of sleeping under a pile of dirt," Vikki said calmly and with a grin that bled sarcasm. The comment didn't make Sam any calmer, nor had it been designed to do so.

"Vikki, I want to know what your plan is! You sit there and eat Twinkies with a smile, and now you're telling me we're going to fly around with the demons in the sky looking for a needle in a haystack, and you expect me to just go along? Go along, like I went along with you talking to a bunch of Slugs like they were better friends with you than me…and then letting them go, you believing every word they said."

Sam wasn't making a dent in Vikki's demeanor, and that fueled his anger even more. She wasn't reacting, and he wasn't getting any answers. He felt like he had in gym class when he couldn't make a free throw—ever. The ball would barely make it to the rim unless he jumped when he threw it. No points there, no points here. He wondered why he couldn't have had his newly found ability then, just once in gym class, so he wouldn't have had to be the only boy who couldn't get the ball in the hole. Her lack of reaction made him feel like he was being rejected, patronized by any other girl he had experienced that with. Even in Saint Louis, after Hell Day, he'd been a complete failure. He'd lost the city and everyone in it. And Vikki knew it, which made the failure worse. She had said she needed him, and it was okay, but she looked at him now like he was just another stupid kid throwing a temper tantrum.

You are just another stupid kid throwing a temper tantrum, idiot.

"Yeah, well I have a right to!" Sam shouted.

"What?" Vikki said. "Oh, wait, never mind."

Ugh! She had even dismissed his accidental verbalized gripe at himself.

She thinks you're just a kid throwing a fit. You're not impressing her, and she's not going to deal with you. Man up, Sam! Show her you can be the man she said she needed.

He stood there processing these thoughts while she leaned back on the bench swallowing more Red Bull. She was really pretty, regardless of her attitude. He knew her looks had been one of the reasons he had decided to help her in the first place. If you were going to be completely alone—and eventually slaughtered by fiends from hell and all the traitors to humanity—then you might as well do it with a pretty girl at your side. And Sam hadn't been known for having any girl at his side back in high school, let alone a pretty one.

He pushed all his angst out of him, or at least just buried it below the surface the way they buried themselves every night. They couldn't be seen then, and he would hide his fear, his immaturity, as well, but like in the nightly burial, he left a small straw poked out, ready to breathe life back into these thoughts he was locking up—if, that is, he truly felt they needed to be voiced again.

"Okay, Vikki. We'll do it your way. But…can you please tell me how we're going to remain even remotely safe flying around at night with those things that can pop into existence at any time?"

"I think we're in the right area, Sam. And the demons aren't everywhere, all the time. But at night, maybe we can spot a fire at my friend's camp if we go high enough. Get it?" Vikki waited for a response and got none. "Sam, it's a risk, but we gotta take it. What we're doing, it ain't working. I knew it wouldn't from the beginning."

This comment prompted Sam to respond. "Then why, Vikki, have we been flying around for days looking for it?"

"I knew you would have to get sick of that before you'd agree to this."

Really? he thought. He'd been played, but what irked him more was that she was right. He really hadn't minded what they had been doing too much. It was as safe as anything else, given the new world order, and he liked being around her. He had never spent so much time with a girl in his life. It had only been in the last couple of days he had started to feel natural frustration born out of noncompletion of the task.

"Fine. I guess you're right, Vikki. I'm sorry if I'm acting like a dumb kid."

Those thoughts got life again, pretty quick Sammy…ugh! Shut up!

"It's all right, Sam," Vikki replied as she unwrapped a Ho-Ho. "I like Twinkies better, ya' know," she said, showing the chocolate in her teeth, "but the last place we stopped were all out, and I'm saving the last I got for later. Let's just stay here and eat more of heaven until nightfall."

"Okay," Sam said.

What else could he say to that? What could anyone say? To Vikki, snack cakes and the apocalypse seem to hold the same level of importance.

Maybe they do Sam. Who knows? What'd that song say about it being a mixed up world?

—◇○◇—

"That's it! Do you see the light, Sam?" Vikki was shouting and pointing down at a glimmer dancing in the far-off distance, shining dimly in the sea of blackness that lay below them. They were flying high in the sky, but Sam had figured that it was not protecting them any more than if they had been lower. He didn't think demons had an altimeter or limit if they could fly and pop in and out of reality at will. He had been in a state of near-panic ever since the sun had set and they had risen into the night sky to look for Vikki's friends.

"I see it," Sam said, "but how do we know it's friendly?"

"I'm trusting my gut," Vikki replied.

Trusting your gut? Sam thought, but he was through arguing with her. He pushed the ridiculousness of her response away, simply saying, "Fine, but let's be careful, okay?"

As they got closer, the glimmer broke into several distinct patches of light. They were keeping a distance, but Sam could see it was a very large and spread-out encampment.

"Set us down here, Sam. We'll walk the rest of the way. Just look for a road as we get closer to the ground."

"I don't know if we'll be able to see a road, even if we get closer," he replied from behind the scarves wrapped around his face.

"We'll find one, Sam; just go down, quickly."

They descended, and she had been correct. He saw a road come into view as they neared the ground, and he set the park bench down on it.

"Okay, we hoof it from here, Sam," and she pulled out a Twinkie. Sam shook his head. "What is it now, Sam? I need one—for this."

Walking at night wasn't something he'd done since Saint Louis. He didn't like sleeping underground with only a straw to breathe through, but he didn't like walking out in the open at night, waiting for monsters to appear and pounce on him, even more. The road was silent, cold, dark—a horror movie waiting to happen.

"Vikki," he began, "now I'm not trying to say for sure what we should do, but I'm thinking, why don't we sleep like usual, and we walk to your friend's camp in the morning? We know the direction now."

It was a reasonable idea. It made sense. He was glad he had said it. Vikki would agree he'd had a pretty good idea, a safe idea.

"Okay, Sam," Vikki said with a tone of complete submission to his idea. She then turned from him and continued walking down the road, a road he could barely see due to the overcast skies and the dark of night.

It took a moment to register what had just taken place. The resulting shock from her quick agreement and her antonymic action of walking away slowed the recognition that he couldn't even see her in front of him anymore, given how dark it was. Suddenly, he found himself existing alone, in a black void, with only the ominous silhouette of trees off to each side. Afraid to stay, afraid to move, a mental coin flip had Sam taking off in a trot to catch up with her. His backpack on his back was bouncing, producing a metal clanking sound from something rattling inside.

His breathing was more of a panting as he reached her asking why she was so insistent on going *now*. Vikki kept walking, picking up her pace. Panting and clanking, Sam sped up, too. Duped into following her by her continued motion, he was now back to doing her bidding.

"Vikki, stop! We're both going to be sorry if those things appear and come at us. Let's just wait till morning."

She ignored him. She was still walking. He didn't understand her persistence. He remembered she had asked for him to come along because she had needed him. He couldn't use that against her, now, because he realized he wanted her around, too.

305

But not if it's going to get you killed. Yes, but she can't do anything—I'm the one with powers. Right, idiot, so you have to protect her. Ugh. This was the only result produced by his internal debate. He was right—and that made him wrong.

"Fine, Vikki, you win! But I hope you know I can only fight so many, and it's *dark!*"

"Okay, Sam, I'll keep that in mind." And she kept moving down the road as he followed along.

"What the hell is Vikki doing? I'm with you, Sam! This is crazy!" Byron said, but, alas, no one could hear him as he walked along beside Vikki and Sam in the dark. Vikki was one strange girl, and she had been since the first time Byron had viewed her in her grocery store, where she had spent the night being a desk's fifth leg. Her attitude had gone from simple grocery store girl to woman on a mission overnight, and Byron had no idea why or what was driving her. At first, he figured it was good to have people like her around who weren't going to lay down and take the crap evil was handing the world, but now, Vikki just seemed to be letting good sense fly out the window. She was going to get herself and Sam killed long before she did any good.

Morning came. They were still alive. Sam concluded that Vikki had gotten lucky. Shit, he had gotten lucky, right along with her. Walking all night down a dark road hadn't been his idea. There were times it had been so dark, he didn't know he had veered off the road until he had felt the dirt shoulder beneath his feet. Every noise in the forest made him jump like Vern on watch with his gun in that old movie *Stand by Me.* Those kids had been afraid of ghosts they probably only half believed were real. Sam didn't have that luxury. He'd expected, at any moment, something with long claws, huge teeth, and an actual existence would come out of the dark and take his head for an hors d'oeuvre. But it hadn't happened, and he guessed he was glad about that. What he wasn't glad about was having had to go through it at all, or *again*, if Vikki chose the same course tonight if they didn't reach her so-called friend's HQ. He may be able to manipulate the earth at will, but that wasn't going to keep him from having a heart attack from stress and fear if she kept putting him in situations like the night before. Hopefully that wouldn't happen. They would find the encampment today, and he would be in relative safety with others—besides Vikki— calling the shots. His grumblings hesitated at the idea that it would no longer be just Vikki and him alone. Bothered by that, Sam found he didn't like the idea she was going to meet others she knew or already had a friendship with. He was only a fifteen-year-old kid, and he had been a complaining kid, at that. He wasn't going to be her first pick for company once they were in a crowd.

"Hey, Vikki?"

"Yes, Sam," she replied.

"I mean, I know I've been a bit of a pain the last couple days. I was just worried, you know. And worried about you too. Uh…I guess…I…"

"Spit it out, Sam."

"Okay, I guess I was just wondering if me and you, you know—are we still going to be friends, hang out some, I mean, once like we're in with everyone else?"

Of course not, Vikki thought.

Of course not, Sam thought, *not if I keep talking like a cross between a boy asking a girl out on a date for the first time and a valley girl.*

"Sam, of course. You can hang with me as long as you want. You just may decide I'm too much trouble, given how much you don't like my decisions."

"Nah! No way, Vikki, it's been cool. Just a lot of craziness, you know." He was feeling better; she definitely seemed to not mind having him around.

"Sam, its gonna get a whole lot crazier before it gets saner, believe me," Vikki commented. She raised her arm and patted her backpack. "Reach in there and pull me out a breakfast Twinkie, will ya, please? And you can grab one for yourself if ya want."

He loved how she talked. He didn't know what to call her accent, but he had commented on it before. She had said she didn't notice hers, but that he didn't quite sound right to her either.

"There's that way you say "*ya*" again. That's so cool!" And he got them both Twinkies.

Near midday, they were heading down a stretch of road that veered left. They could see the trees thinning out up ahead as the left side of the road was opening to reveal the beginning of a valley.

"Okay, Sam," Vikki said. She stopped walking. "I think this is it, but we better stay in the trees till we can get a better look." Vikki said this and started walking off the road and into the forest. Sam followed, feeling his heart rate increase, if only from the act of choosing stealth as their new modus operandi.

They saw the edge of the trees ahead of them after walking for a minute or so, and Vikki dropped her backpack to the ground, got on her hands and knees, and crawled the rest of the way, stopping behind a tree trunk. Sam did the same. They peered into the valley. It was wide and open. Sam followed it with his eyes, down and across, and then his vision fell upon the camp.

"That's it, Vikki. It's gotta be, right?" As he said this, he was pulling out some binoculars. Raising them to his eyes, he looked down into the valley. At once, Sam noticed a group of Slugs talking to men with guns in between one of the tents. He didn't like what he saw, but his first reaction was disappointment. It appeared Vikki's friends were not at this camp. If ever there was a wrong type of camp to stumble upon, they'd just stumbled upon it.

Vikki grabbed the binoculars and took her own look. "This is it, Sam. I was right."

"What do you mean? Don't you see who is down there? It's those Slug things!" He was whispering, but he wanted to scream. Then it hit him. "Oh, man, Vikki, are you telling me your friend is also into the art of believing Slugs when they say they've learned the error of their ways?"

"No, Sam, this is different. They're not here."

"Uh, no, it's not. I saw them." He grabbed the binoculars from her hands to prove it to her and give her the right tents to look at. What Sam saw when looking this second time changed his initial assessment. It was even worse than he had thought. The men with guns turned away from the Slugs, and as they did, they exposed a group of other people, who were tied together and being led away by the men with the guns. One of the Slugs kicked a woman as she struggled to walk.

"Vikki," Sam's voice had become even more of a whisper. No answer. "Vikki." He was still watching the group. They were far enough away that he wanted to stay focused on them, be able to show her exactly where to look. No answer. "Vikki, look at this. I really don't think this is your friend's camp."

Still, no answer. He broke his gaze and glanced over at Vikki. She was no longer looking down into the valley. She was looking at a spot closer to them, straight ahead, and closer to the road. He followed her sightline and saw what she was looking at. There was a man crawling, practically on his stomach, face in the grass, about a hundred feet away. He appeared to be starting a one-man assault on the encampment below. He wasn't armed, and the last thing he looked like was a soldier or a man with any kind of fight in him, for that matter. His army crawl wasn't that good, either, now that Sam thought about it. But that's because it wasn't an army crawl at all, was it? The man was looking for something, something on the ground, and was only trying not to be noticed.

"What is he doing?" Sam asked.

Vikki, once again, was completely ignoring Sam. She had a strange look on her face, almost void of emotion. She didn't seem like the same Vikki, not even the gruff one. She turned and went back to her backpack which she had dropped before they had crawled up to the edge of the forest. Sam watched Vikki search her bag which resulted in the only Vikki-familiar thing about her right now—finding, opening, and devouring yet another Twinkie. Next, she threw on her backpack and began marching back toward where Sam sat behind the tree line. She didn't look like she was going to stop at where they were hiding.

"Vikki, wait! Where are you going?" He was panicking.

She stopped right before becoming visible to the valley. Vikki looked at him with the same blank stare he'd been seeing on her face as she swallowed the last bit of her mouthful of yellow cake and cream.

"You can't go out there!" Sam whispered with a hard voice. "That isn't a friendly camp! They'll kill us."

"Sam." Vikki said to him, blank stare and everything. "This *is* the place. Goodbye."

"What? *Goodbye?* I don't understand," he said, a little too loud. He was in such confusion; he'd forgotten to keep whispering.

"I'm leaving," she replied stoically. "I appreciate you getting me here, but you've got to go...*now.*"

Vikki finished her sentence and walked out into the field toward the man crawling on his stomach. Sam reached out as if to grab her and keep her from doing so, but she continued upon her foolish course. It wouldn't take long for the men down in the camp to notice her walking across the field at the top of their valley. And from the size of the encampment, it *was* their valley.

"Vikki! Wait!" Sam called, whispering again, his heart pounding. "*Wait!*"

She just kept walking. The man on the ground looked up at her, startled to see someone else. When she got close enough for him to hear her clearly, she stopped.

"Hiya. You looking for something?" Vikki asked the man.

"Yes, but do you think you can get down, *please*. I don't want them to see us." The man pointed down into the valley.

Vikki's reply left the man visibly worried. She'd be winning no prizes for man-nurturing today. "Well, then you better find what you're looking for, and quick."

Sam sat still in the trees. He was the one with the blank stare now. He watched the camp to see if there was any sign the encampment had spotted Vikki at the top of the valley. Why had she told him *goodbye*, told him to *go*? As he was pondering over this confusing state of events, he saw Vikki reach back and grab her rifle and point it down at the man. She was saying something to him loudly, but he couldn't make it out. She looked to her left, down the hill, and this prompted Sam to do the same. Once he did, he saw there were several men running out of the camp and up the hill toward Vikki and the man on whom she had pulled her gun.

The scene added to his confusion. What was Vikki doing? Had she used him? This was a horrible thought, but it made the most sense. Why would a pretty girl like her want to hang out with a fifteen-year-old kid unless she needed something? *Shoot! She had started this relationship, stating she needed me.* And she had let those Slugs go, without a scratch, in that Walmart. Sam wrestled with this possible betrayal while deciding whether he should ignore it and step out and do something about those men coming up the mountain. He didn't know if he could fight that whole camp, but maybe he could buy some time. But buy time for whom? Should he save the man

Vikki was accosting? Should he save them both? Vikki had told him to go, and she had been dead serious when she'd said goodbye. He didn't think she would go with him or take kindly to his interference. Would he have to attack her?

He knew he had to do something. If he fought the men off who were running up the hill, it would give him enough time to gauge a reaction from Vikki. But what if she turned on him? Could he fight her? He didn't think he could stop a bullet. He felt he needed to see an object to move it. He wasn't sure he could hurt her. What if she turned on him, and he froze? Sam felt his decision-making time shrink. Panic was starting to take over. He looked back down the hill and saw the men had gained on their approach. They were starting to hold up their guns. As his instincts began to take over and as he raised his hands to attempt some sort of attack on the men, his peripheral vision caught movement, and he heard something coming from where Vikki was standing. Reacting naturally, his gaze shifted over toward her. He didn't see the man, and a second later Vikki was gone, as well—she'd vanished into thin air.

Sam blinked a couple of times, even punctuated the blinking with a squint, to make sure he wasn't hallucinating. It didn't make any difference; they weren't there. The men who had run out of the camp had also stopped. They appeared to be just as surprised as Sam was feeling. They fired a few shots up the hill and then talked among one another. Two of the men broke from the group, continuing to head up the hill. It seemed they meant to verify that Vikki and the man were truly gone. Sam backed further into the trees to avoid being spotted. He would be of no use now, to Vikki or the man, and he didn't need to get into a war by himself.

The two men didn't find anything, as Sam already knew they wouldn't. He'd seen the disappearing act up close and knew it was real. He'd ponder on that later. For now, he waited for the men to retreat. Once they turned their backs and began making their way back toward their camp, Sam leaned back against a tree and cried. He was alone again, possibly betrayed by the woman he'd thought had been his friend, and even if not, Vikki was gone and hadn't wanted him around anymore. It was getting to be midafternoon. Dark would be coming, and he didn't want to bury himself in these woods this close to where he figured Demon Central may be. He was going to need to leave.

—◇○◇—

"Those men are going to kill us!" said the man on the ground.

Vikki grabbed her rifle out of her backpack and yelled at the man, "I'll kill you, too, so you'd better find what it is you need, now!"

"Okay, okay," the man said, facing the ground. "I had it on the road, but my eyes, they don't see too well. These aren't my glasses. I had just stepped off onto the grass, and then I lost it."

"Just find it, quick. They're coming, and I need your help," Vikki shouted.

The man crawled back and forth like he was mowing a lawn with his forehead. The men in the valley were fighting to climb the slope. After several passes, the man called out, "I've got it. This is it!"

Vikki looked down and saw the man crawl forward. She watched as he disappeared, his head first, then his torso, and finally his legs and feet. She followed him where she had seen the last of him vanish and took a step onto the grass in front of her. Nothing seemed different, but when she looked down the hill, she knew something was different to the men coming after them. They had stopped and were looking left and right and then directly at her and the man on his knees in front of her. They showed all the signs of having lost sight of whom they were chasing. Two or three fired their rifles, straight into the vicinity of where she stood, and then one by one they each lowered their guns.

"It's a path they can't see," Harvey said from his hands and knees. "And they can't see us if we're on it."

"I know. I saw you from a vantage point I had," Vikki said. "So? It leads down this hill?"

"I think so. It's vanishing behind us. That's how I lost it in the first place, so we better start moving. I don't know when it will start disappearing again."

"Okay, then. Go," Vikki said, still holding her rifle.

"Keep your arms close to your body; the path isn't very wide," Harvey explained.

"Yeah, yeah," Vikki replied. "Move it."

Harvey was crawling, keeping his eyes peeled to the ground. The glasses were horrible, allowing him to see barely anything of detail. His headache and the variations in the grass weren't helping. He tried to stay focused on the movement of the scarabs on either side of his hands to define the border of the path in front of him. He couldn't be sure the path would lead them directly into the camp below. Perhaps it would turn before it got there. He decided not to mention this thought to the girl with the gun. She appeared to be glad she was hidden from the men who had started to come after them, but he couldn't quite determine whether she was on his side, either. He and Meg had been separating themselves from the action and goings-on around them since nearly the beginning of this nightmare. He hadn't thought of the possibility of a "third" side to this war between good and evil that had appeared to erupt on earth, but he really had no way of knowing exactly what was going on with this woman's intentions, so he assumed that anything was possible at this point. And if there were more groups besides good and bad, did that then mean he couldn't necessarily assume he was part of the good side? Another point he hadn't considered. He and Meg had walked past a lot of horrible things and had just kept walking. He had convinced himself there was nothing they could do—they would only get themselves killed if they had tried to help. Had this been an easy rationalization to make themselves feel better about saving themselves? Were they possibly part of a group who weren't necessarily evil but, at best, could only hope to be awarded a trophy for "Most Complacent in Humanity's Fall"?

Harvey had begun to surmise, after everything he'd seen, that some sort of apocalypse was upon them. Harvey felt he knew very little truth after that, besides a belief in heaven and hell. He hadn't believed in those, or God either, before his realization the night before about Meg's total lack of love for him. But whatever spell had been cast on him that had wiped away his false beliefs had only left Harvey knowing what was *not* true about his own beliefs. The only truth he could discern after that could only come from deduction based on what he had learned to be false. This didn't provide a lot of detail to fill in the blanks.

He spent his crawl down the hill contemplating these ideas. Before, he had not believed in God staunchly. He now knew that to be false. Along with that belief, he had not believed in heaven or hell. This belief had also been negated. Any thoughts he'd had about heaven and hell prior to choosing not to believe in them, regarding what they were like, how you got into them, et cetera, appeared also to be wrong. He had to admit, most of those ideas were very childish and not very sophisticated, and it had been nearly since he was a child that he had believed those simple explanations, anyway, so he wasn't able to deduce much from their negation. He just knew that heaven was not this white cloudy place where all good people go, and hell was not simply a fiery place where all bad people go, and that was about it. He knew it was more complicated. Only that. He pondered one nagging question. If hell wasn't what he had thought, he wondered, *Where in the hell are all these demons coming from?* No pun intended.

Harvey didn't quite know what to make of his new situation. Just when he thought life could get no stranger, he had come up the mountain that morning after fetching his new pair of "extremely useful" glasses, hoping the path would still be there. He had found its beginning nearly where he had left it. If he had arrived much later, he may have never found it. He was glad he had jogged up the mountain as much as he had. He had found the path on the road, but when he had stepped off the road, trying to follow it from a standing position, he'd lost it—either because his vision was so bad or because it had jumped forward again. Regardless, he had dropped to his knees and started looking for it when this girl with the shotgun had shown up. His original plan, foolish or not, was to follow the path down into Hell Camp No. 1 and try to save Meg, figuring it out as he went. Hopefully, she was still alive, and hopefully, he could do something about it. Now, Harvey didn't know what to do. Not having much of a choice, guns being at the bottom of the hill and one behind him, "go with the flow" was the only idea he had left. Harvey guessed this was about as close to his original plan as any, so, what the hell? *And once again, no pun intended.*

The path never veered left or right, and the girl walking behind him never asked him about the fact that they were getting closer and closer to the camp below. He found that strange. His hands and knees were hurting from crawling on them down the mountain. He had landed on more than one pebble and stone along the way. The girl had seemed in no mood to talk the couple of times Harvey had tried to complain, or chitchat to feel her out. He didn't even know her name. The only other question in his mind he wanted answered was what vantage point she'd had to know what he'd been looking for on the hill.

"I gotta know," Harvey said, "why did you…I mean…how did you know what I was looking for?"

"Shut up" was the girl's response, and since she had the gun, Harvey followed instructions. One more detail avoiding clarification. Nothing new here. Move along; move along.

And so he did. Maybe she had seen him appearing out of thin air when he had lost the path while stepping off the road. She then had hoped he knew how to find a way to disappear again when he began looking on the ground. Yes, that was it.

When Harvey and the woman had reached the edge of the camp, Harvey had expected her to finally realize the path wasn't going to turn, and she would want to stop moving forward, so he stopped crawling. Immediately, he felt the end of her gun pushing into his back.

"Keep going," she said.

He followed suit, but her response made him wonder even further what he was going to do. He was trying to save Meg. He didn't know if he could, but his plan had been to try. Now that he was at the camp, Harvey felt he needed a little autonomy if Meg was alive and was going to have a chance. But this new companion of his appeared to be on a suicide mission or something, and that wasn't going to give him any control or ability to plan his next move. They were both, most likely, minutes from dying and everything he had done since Meg had been carried off would have been done in vain. He felt helpless. Having nothing to lose, Harvey spoke again.

"Listen, I'm trying to help somebody," he pleaded. "She's a friend of mine. Meg. I don't know what you're all about, but I'm trying to save her, and you don't seem to be interested in hearing anything I have to say, let alone help me."

"You're right. Keep moving."

Her response was exactly what he had feared it would be when he began this final attempt to make a dent in this woman's ridiculous momentum. They entered the camp. They walked right by Slugs and soldiers. Men and women were exiting and entering tents. There were campfires and weapons laid out on tables. Harvey noticed everyone they passed was avoiding *the path* in front of them on—what could best be described as—a subconscious level. Harvey looked around, trying to get a feel for the layout, to see if he could recognize anywhere that looked like a place they might keep prisoners.

Most tents looked the same. They were military issue. It was obvious by the clothing and demeanor that some of the people working this side of the aisle had come straight from the US Armed Forces. He assumed the weapons and equipment had also been supplied by the same. It seemed chanting slogans about honor and God hadn't done their job on everyone in the military. "Good" was going to have a lot of very bad days ahead, based on what Harvey was witnessing.

He was able to stand up at the camp. The inhabitants' footsteps had trotted all over the main walkable areas, and seeing the scarab boundary was easier. The path had not turned even after taking Harvey into the camp. It had come straight down the hill, continuing to where he was walking. The woman was still pushing him along with a nudge here and there from her rifle, and they now appeared to be on a collision course with the opening of a tent at the center of the compound.

As they approached the tent, Harvey kept on the lookout, hanging onto hope that the path would turn before taking them inside. It didn't. Just as he realized this, he felt a hand on his back, grabbing his shirt. He was being pushed forward through the doorway of the tent. He didn't have time to react verbally, and before he knew it, he was being pushed to the side, away from the path and into the realm of "visible to others." He wasn't sure what had happened to the girl—how someone else had been able to see him and push him off the path—but the question became meaningless a moment later when he heard the girl's voice erupt behind him.

CHAPTER 45

AND THE DEVIL MAKES THREE
FEBRUARY 14, 2013

"SIR, I FOUND THIS ONE up on the mountain!" the woman who had just forced Harvey down the mountain said, as Harvey realized he was in full view of everyone in the tent he had just entered.

Harvey couldn't be sure what he was looking at, given the glasses he was wearing, but he knew something wasn't right about the figure before him at the far end of the tent. He ripped off the glasses. This action alone improved his vision slightly, and he knew his assessment of the figure had been correct. He saw a being, deep red in color, and though he couldn't be sure, Harvey thought he saw something like a tail—and, worst of all, he felt familiarity. As the thing began to speak, Harvey was pulling out his own glasses and wrestling them onto his face. He didn't know what was going on, but he knew he needed his sight, first, if he was going to figure it out.

As the conversation continued, Harvey saw his worst fears realized. The woman who had brought him down the mountain was joining forces with this group and was using him as proof. *And* the figure standing before them was unmistakably the devil incarnate, and the same figure he'd seen appear two months earlier in Meg's kitchen.

"Who are you?" the devil said.

"My name is Vikki Parsons. I was at the top of the hill when your foot soldiers started coming at me. I didn't want to be shot before I had a chance to offer you something, so here he is."

"They wouldn't have shot you. They would have interrogated you," he replied, and his tail moved forward and pointed at Vikki on his second *you*.

Harvey couldn't believe his eyes. Even with all the things he'd seen, this was unbelievable. It hadn't even occurred to him the actual devil would be running part of this show, but now that he thought about it, he guessed it made some sort of warped cosmic sense.

The devil continued. "They said they couldn't find you. How'd you get into the camp?"

"This man, here, he can see things, things others can't. He found a path which led straight here, into your tent. It kept others from seeing us."

"Is that so?" the devil replied, turning his attention to Harvey. "A path that leads to me. What were you planning on doing when you got here?"

Harvey stuttered. He saw how it looked. He began to answer, still not quite comprehending how he could be talking to whom he was talking to. "I-I honestly didn't know where it was taking me, until we got here. I mean it. I didn't have a plan."

"Hmmmm." The devil raised an eyebrow, creating ridges on one side of his red forehead. He was as real as anything else, and yet at the same time he looked, to Harvey, like he'd been drawn into the room with computers like they do in movies based on graphic novels. A strange thought floated across Harvey's mind he couldn't control. *I'm standing in a room where the devil just said, "Hmmmm."* The devil followed his verbal summation of Harvey's answer with the question, "And who else will be following this path the girl speaks of?"

Harvey saw where the question was leading and knew he needed to put this thing's possible fears at ease.

"No one. The path is virtually gone, I swear," Harvey answered, trying to sound as honest as possible, figuring the more he tried, the less he'd succeed, but he tried anyway. "It was disappearing behind us—fast. I was safe on it, so I just kept walking."

"Well, it appears it's brought you to the right place, as far as I'm concerned," the devil commented. "What's your name? And what other things can you see?"

"I-I'm Harvey," he said, stuttering again. Vikki glanced his way with a surprised look on her face. "There's really nothing else I—"

Just as Harvey started this lie, Vikki swung around fully to face him. Pulling her rifle out again, she jammed it into the space between Harvey's throat and his jaw. She was now pushing him backward toward the far side of the tent. He felt the back of his knees hit something, and he fell away from Vikki. He was now sitting in a chair he had fallen into.

"Don't lie! You wouldn't shut up on the mountain. Rambling on and on about your journey! You wouldn't shut up!" Vikki was screaming and had a look in her eye like she would pull the trigger any moment if he didn't do exactly what she said. "Tell him how you can see demons during the daytime! Now!"

"All right, all right. It's true, it's true!" Harvey had fallen into a chair, and the gun's barrel was still up against his neck. He hadn't remembered telling her that, but it had been a long crawl on his hands and knees, and he had attempted several times to converse with her. Everything was happening so fast; there just wasn't enough time to process this information.

"Harvey, it appears you have a gift to see the unseen. We wouldn't want you falling into the wrong hands now, would we? Wouldn't want anyone following any of my messengers or pets."

The devil came closer to where Harvey sat on the chair, his throat still in pain. "Let him up, Vikki," the devil said, and he placed his hand on her shoulder. She didn't flinch and turned to the devil with a look of pleasure in her eye. The devil noticed it and appeared to take delight. Harvey noticed it and wanted to throw up. Vikki lowered the gun, and Harvey slowly got to his feet again, unable to comprehend how the beautiful girl he saw before him could be remotely interested in the thing standing next to her.

"We'll keep you. You may prove handy, Harvey," the devil said, leaning in close to Harvey's face as if to get a really good read on Harvey's next answer. Harvey could feel the hot breath of the monster slide over him as if the air between them had turned into invisible gravy. "You'll help me when I want it, right?"

Then Harvey mustered up the biggest lie ever. "Yes." He was happy to know that God hadn't given this monstrosity a built-in lie detector. It was poetic justice, he thought, to be able to lie to the devil's face, given he was supposedly the father of lies.

"Vikki," the devil said authoritatively, "take this man and put him with the other prisoners. One of the men outside will show you where they are. Then, I want you to come back to me. I think we will have some more business to attend to, now that you're here."

"Yes, my lord," was Vikki's reply as she grabbed Harvey by the arm and exited him out of the tent.

Shut up! These had been the only words he'd gotten out of Vikki on the march to wherever he was being taken. He had managed to get out "How could you—" of the longer sentence *How could you possibly be interested in being here, and even more so, interested in that thing?* Her response was predictable, given their time together, but he had had to try. She had accosted him and had continued on. The only other thing she had done was pull off her backpack, grab another Hostess Twinkie, and start eating it. He had a lot of questions, but at present, his attentions shifted to a thought that hadn't occurred to him during the mayhem that had taken place inside the devil's tent.

If Meg's alive, she may be where I'm headed.

———◇○◇———

When the prettiest, sweetest girl ever kisses you, you kiss back, right? Well, he wished he had—immediately—when she had jumped into his arms, planting one on him, but Harvey was so surprised by Meg's reaction to his presence, it took him a moment to process. She had almost pulled away at his lack of response. In the undefinable, infinitesimally small moment before Meg could believe he wasn't interested, Harvey let everything he'd been through fly out the window. He pulled her closer and kissed her with all his might, and for a moment, there was no devil, no journey, no path, no demons, no Hell Day, no end of the world, no nothing. Only her.

After the impromptu kiss-fest, which had been the most passionate thing he had ever experienced, he embraced Meg hard, pushing his face into her hair, which still smelled good, somehow, even after all that had happened.

"Meg!" he said, eventually pulling away and looking at her face. "You're alive! I knew it. I knew it was the right thing to do to come after you."

"You're here because of me, Harvey?" she asked.

"Yes. I couldn't leave after that demon carried you off. I wanted to believe you weren't dead."

"Oh, you stupid man!" she yelled. It was apparent to them that a few of the other prisoners were now paying attention to their drama. "Why'd you go and get yourself caught, just for me? They're going to kill us, anyway. Oh, Harvey, I'm so sorry."

Meg began to cry. She even hit his chest once like she had done the night before, when he'd lost her.

"Kill us? Why?" he asked.

"I heard them talking," she replied. "Prisoners all over have been taken, and tomorrow night their going to make a display of us. They're going to mutilate us, Harvey, all over the world, in front of as many people as possible. To scare everyone. To let everyone know that, whenever possible, if prisoners are taken fighting *him*, that this is what will happen. That it's better to join with him and be his slave than to fight against him and end up like us."

"Meg, that's horrible." Harvey was mortified. To think he had come so far and found her, only to learn she was going to be murdered. Then Harvey remembered, as crazy as his situation was, he might have some clout. "Wait! I think I have an idea."

"What?"

"He wants me alive. He thinks this gift I have of seeing the unseen world could be useful to him. Maybe I can strike a deal with him to keep you and these people here alive."

"And if not?" Meg asked.

"Then we die together, Meg. I'm not living without you, and he won't get to use me if he hurts you. I swear."

"Harvey, I don't know if that's the stupidest thing I've ever heard or the sweetest. I can't believe I'm so glad to see you."

"I don't know what you feel, Meg, but I love you, and I just want you to know that."

Meg looked back at Harvey after his declaration. She realized it was only in this kind of a screwed-up world for it to be possible that her emotions could go down the path they were headed, but she found, suddenly and somehow, that the kiss she'd just given Harvey hadn't just come from excitement in seeing a familiar face, and it hadn't come from some deep-seated desire to just feel good for a moment. She realized she loved Harvey, here and now, his lanky and talkative self, and it felt wonderful to be in love no matter what, given what the "here and now" had actually become.

"*Make a deal with me!*" the Devil cried out, materializing back in his tent, looking as if he'd been created out of smoke right there on the spot. "I'll destroy this world before I make a concession to anyone!"

Vikki rose from the chair she had put Harvey down in the day before and walked calmly over to the raging leader, placing her hands on his shoulders.

"What happened? Tell me about it," she requested of him in a smooth, soothing voice. Then she leaned in and kissed his leathery lips.

"That Harvey. He said he'd kill himself if I killed any of the prisoners, anywhere tonight. He said he could see other things like fear, dishonesty, and defeat in good people, and he would use it to help me win the war, but not if I killed people aimlessly. How dare he? I don't need his parlor tricks! Tonight, I will do what I mean to do, and tomorrow this world will be razed by my demons. I'll have soldiers launch missiles. I'll destroy every home and building. Cave in every cave. I'll burn this earth to a crisp. There won't be a livable spot left on the planet when they're done!"

"Then where will I live?" Vikki asked and pushed her body into his. "How will we remain together?" His tail automatically wrapped around her back, and she could feel his desire for her as the tail pulled her tighter against his thigh. "I came all this way to be with you, to find you. And you'll have me die in an inhabitable wasteland?"

Her actions made him forget his anger at Harvey, and he became compelled to act on the hunger she was showing for him.

"What is that taste...on your lips?" he asked as he lowered her to the ground.

"It's Twinkie."

"Maybe there is another way to bring this world to submission," he said as he crawled on top of her.

"I'm sure there is," she whispered in his ear.

"Harvey? Can you really see those things in people?" Meg whispered in his ear, after the devil had vanished.

"No, but I had to say something—make him think I'm useful to him," he whispered back. "Seeing a path that's not there anymore and seeing demons he already knows about doesn't offer him much."

"But you see other things. You told me. About how we look?"

"Right, but I don't know what it means. And until I do, I don't want him knowing about it. I have some ideas, though."

"What?"

"I would just rather not say, right now. I have no idea who's listening. For all we know, those fucking scarabs running around our feet can understand us. I just hope it worked."

"If it did, Harvey, I owe you my life. And—to what you said earlier—I love you back." Meg kissed Harvey for the second time in twenty-four hours.

CHAPTER 46

AND THE DEVIL MAKES SIX
SEPTEMBER 11, 2013

—◇○◁∽◇○◇—

RANDY POKED HIS HEAD IN THE DOOR of the office. Jack was sitting at the desk having a conversation with Sarah, Quincy, and Four Winds.

"Jack?" he said, interrupting their powwow. "Brian says he's here. And by the way, Brian also wants to know why they can't just blast him. Those were his words."

"Send him in, Randy," Jack responded. The others moved away from the desk to give him a clear view of the door. Jack smiled and continued. "And tell Brian, he and his friends need to trust us and not do anything provoking."

"Gotcha. You oughta see the kid, though. The Dark Lord appeared in front of Brian, outside the gate. The kid runs to tell me and didn't appear to have a flinch in him."

Randy left the office to ask Brian to show Satan *(Ha! Is this really happening?)* in. A lot had happened in the last several months, but you just didn't get used to things like this, Randy thought. Brian left the compound, and a few minutes later, the devil was standing in the office, with all five of them. The thing began to speak.

"You don't need special powers, Jack, to see the nice little circle of protection you've got around this place. Must be nice to know you're safe and snug when you go to sleep, while I go to town on everyone else."

Jack, ignoring the devil's smugness, replied with a direct question. "What do you want?"

"I've come to be a reasonable negotiator," the devil replied. "Don't be so harsh in your tone. Your side is losing, Jack. Our numbers are growing by the millions, and you know it."

"Out of fear."

"Perhaps," the devil said, and he curled the side of his smile further than it seemed possible. "And perhaps you should follow suit if you've got any sense. You've put up a good fight, Jack, you and your dreamers, but in less than one year, an overwhelming majority has voted for me, and *not* for your useless gang here, as their new leadership. Me. Over you, you could say."

"Quality over quantity," Jack replied. "You've got a lot of really dumb followers. They'll probably start kicking the ball into *our* goal because they forget the rules."

"You're funny, Jack. It took me a while to find you, and I didn't realize you'd be such a crowd pleaser. But you and your friends, here and everywhere, need to know something."

"And what is that?" Jack asked.

"I could have crushed you all a long time ago if I had wanted."

"Oh? Is that right?" Jack questioned. "Then why pretend to let us win all those battles?"

"Jack, those battles, as you call them—little towns, shopping malls—they aren't even on my radar. I could unleash enough power from hell to crush mountains, overturn their rubble on your heads."

"Then why don't you, Mr. Mountain Crusher?" Randy said from the side of the room.

The devil turned his head. Randy stood his ground off to the left side of Jack's desk, but the devil could sense the twinkle of fear in the young man's eye. The devil's tail rose from the floor and pointed in Randy's direction, and Randy raised his hand quickly as if to block an attack.

Ugh! I flinched, Randy thought.

"Ha, ha, ha! I'm not going to hurt you, Randy. Don't get yourself looking so weak there in front of your girl. Answering your question is all I'm doing, and that answer is, I happen to like mountains, Randall. In fact, I happen to like a lot about this world, which is why I have tried my best not to let my underlings destroy it completely. And Randy?"

"Yes?" Randy asked back.

The Devil was beaming. "Randy's cool. Randall Haverstamp—not so much. Too bad your lady over there had to have that typed on her marriage license."

The devil turned away from Randy again. Sarah squeezed his hand and looked at him with her sweet, old eyes. She was telling him he didn't need to worry about what was just said, but it didn't seem to be helping.

The devil had placed his attention back on Jack. "People are coming to our side in droves, Jack. Do you really want to lose this fight, in a *fight?*"

Jack stood up, angry at even the idea of what he felt his foe was suggesting. "What are you asking for? A surrender? Some sort of Appomattox?"

"Jack, I may not be the ruler you would prefer, but I am a ruler. A ruler needs subjects. Do you really want boys like Brian out there at your gate, and all the rest of them, to pay the ultimate price for your pride?"

At this, Sarah spoke. "Maybe death isn't the ultimate price."

"Ah, the prodigal Sarah Dubois. Out of the institution, back on the wagon, talking again. Baby steps, Sarah. One day at a time. Keep it up; you'll go far," the devil said as he turned on his cloven feet and made his way toward her. Randy stepped in front of her.

"Don't come any closer," Randy yelled, "or I'll—"

"Or you'll what?" the devil said, cutting him off. "Coward!" He moved his head over slightly to see Sarah behind Randy. "Well, you'll go far after you dump this little boy, and go back to dating the real men you were known for enjoying." He said this to her as he tilted his head slightly toward Randy.

"You're not protected here. We are!" Randy swung his fist at the tilt of the monstrous face before him. The devil vanished and reappeared in the middle of the room, leaving Randy swinging through air, losing his balance.

Satan disappeared, reappearing at Jack's desk again, where he had been a moment before. "I may not be able to hurt you here, but you can't hurt me anywhere, boy. You know, Ms. Dubois, I was there in that tomb with you; one of my pets ate your boyfriend, Gerard, after you so graciously cooked him medium rare. I even grabbed a bit of him for leftovers while your drunk self stumbled to safety."

"Leave her alone!" Randy scolded. "She doesn't have to answer to you."

"Didn't know I asked a question, *Randall*." The devil was on a roll. "Does she have to answer to you?" The devil leaned back and sat on Jack's desk, it's tail heading back toward Jack's face as it continued to address Randy. "You know, she's the older and wiser one. Well. She did choose you. Let's drop 'wiser', shall we? So just older. Ha! Maybe I should show you what you really married and show you how old she really is—all sagging and osteoporosying."

"That's enough!" Jack demanded. "So what are these terms you're peddling to save humanity?"

Quincy spoke up from the opposite side of the room as Randy and Sarah. "You're not seriously considering surrendering, are you, Jack?"

"No," Jack answered, "but he's here, so let's hear him out."

The devil seemed more interested in making acquaintances than discussing politics, and he turned to Davis. "Mr. Davis. An old friend of yours is on my side now. He looks a bit different, but he has all the same nice-guy characteristics you loved about him when he was your boss."

"Hacker's with you?"

"Why, yes, of course, he is. Gerard would have been, too, Sarah—" he glanced back at her, his tail turning with his head again "—but as I said, I let my pet eat him. But Hacker, he's been a bundle of joy to have around. Wouldn't have wanted to give up that skill of his of finding things that can't be found. The man found dirt in the Arctic! A little credit's in order for that, don't you think? Of course, you stole his thunder, didn't you? I told him he doesn't need to worry about that. You two will have your day soon enough, and then he can drill a hole between *your* eyes. And by drill, I mean *drill*." And the beast laughed at his own idea after telling it.

"Well, I'd sure like to talk to that bastard!" Davis belted. "I knew he wasn't that great of a guy, but to be helping you, to be on your side, that's just too much."

"I know, Davis. He is actually responsible for my little visit today. He *does* know how to find things." The devil began to laugh. "I'm sorry. You look defeated, Davis, or is it Quincy now?" The devil paused for a moment, reeling in delight as he stared Davis down and developed his next dig. "Or is it, perhaps, Our Future. Ha! What a silly name! All you brought to those people was pain and destruction. And they called you Our Future. I pity you and your failure."

Davis and Sarah were visibly affected by the comments he was making. Randy was about ready to start punching again but felt it was useless, so he held back. Four Winds stood like a rock at the back of the room.

Jack couldn't figure what the devil was here for. It appeared the thing's goal was only to play mind games with the enemy's leadership. Again, Jack tried to deflect the devil's low blows by returning to the topic at hand. "What are your terms, dammit? Explain why you came, and leave!"

At this outburst, the devil's demeanor completely changed. He seemed to grow from six feet tall to nine. He came toward the desk Jack was standing behind and brought his fist down on it hard. He leaned forward with his red face and horns, his tail coming up and over the desk again, and right up to Jack's eye. In a commanding voice he boomed, "You don't give orders to me! You take them!"

Jack didn't budge, but every part of him wanted to, badly.

The devil continued, his bellows loud enough they were probably heard outside the building. "I'm giving you one chance! This chance is it, for what's left of your side of this affair! You're outnumbered in the billions. You can't count on your guerrilla warfare and small-time battles. It's just playing games. It's solely by my bidding that the world is still in as good a shape as it is. Or perhaps you'd like my demons to start playing around your nuclear power plants? Don't push me, Jacky Boy. The terms are simple. Total surrender, and by doing so, you relinquish all power. I will command you as I do everyone already with me. You won't like it, but you'll be alive."

"You call that alive?" Four Winds, it appeared, finally had something worth saying. "Slavery is not living. Soullessness is not being human. You bring deceit and are not worth listening to."

The devil disappeared again, coming back into being, still in motion at the back of the room, stopping in front of Four Winds. It appeared this in-your-face tactic was one the devil was used to using and getting his way with. "Your foolish words will be the words that destroyed humanity if you let them infect the others here into not agreeing to my gift of a peace. Just like your foolish people would not acquiesce to the European when he came. Perhaps if you had, your people would have become something more than a nation of alcoholics, debtors, gamblers, and drug addicts, most of whom aren't even here anymore to fight for humanity. Your foolish pride. Worse than Jacky's. At least he's listening."

The devil turned away from Four Winds and back toward Jack. "Think hard, Jack, before you decide—for all time—what becomes of the human race. Don't catch what Mr. Winds has got and make yourself the one responsible for your species' end. When did you ever want to be a leader anyway? Didn't you like it back in your hole at Archive Central? You have twenty-four hours to decide, or I'll put you all in a hole, and you won't be getting government benefits."

Jack thought on the words just spoken to him. Everything this thing was saying was true. He remembered his mother saying, "Even the devil tells the truth sometimes." Is this what she had meant? How had he gotten into a position where he was deciding the fate of humanity? Jack Johanssen, misanthrope. The irony was ironic. It was too much for him to decide on this. It was too much to make the decision in twenty-four hours. And from the looks of the others in the room, none of them deserved the right to be making this kind of a decision for everyone else either.

And that's what made it all the more ironic when Jack replied with what he replied.

"We don't need twenty-four hours."

"Ah, you're a smart man, Jack. I knew you would see reason. All you have to do is take this—" The devil came closer to the desk, beginning to remove something rolled up from under his cloak.

"I think you are misunderstanding me," Jack said, putting his hand up like one of the Supremes to stop the devil from moving forward, bringing balance to the world, as the world must have. Jack had made the same motion several years earlier to a nice security guard to keep his sneezing nose out of a certain box. "You can put that right back in your pocket." Jack pointed to the paper the devil appeared to be pulling out for him to sign. "I've seen enough scrolls for several lifetimes, and the last one I want to see is yours. We don't need twenty-four hours to tell you you're full of shit, or to go to hell or back to hell, or to tell you 'Up yours' or 'Fuck you.' We're not surrendering. Humanity will defeat you, or we will die trying, but none of us will lose who we are to become your slaves!"

The devil seemed to become a deeper shade of red, if that was possible. For all his power, it appeared Jack had gotten the best of the devil's emotions. He looked a bit speechless as he turned to march out of the room. Right before reaching the door, he did, however, turn back to the room's occupants, apparently to make a final statement—to get the last word, all tantrum-like, Jack thought.

"If you want your Armageddon, your battle of the apocalypse, I can make it happen; don't worry, if that's what you want! And you'll watch in one fell swoop as all of you are destroyed! You will regret this day, Jack! I'll keep you alive long enough to see it." Then he was gone, really gone, apparently remembering at the last moment that he needed no door to depart from the office.

The Dark Lord's presence lingered in the room the way body odor clings to a path the unshowered walks, and the devil had left a dark cloud of gloom and doom in everyone's hearts instead of a gross soup in their noses. Even Jack, who had felt pretty damn strong a moment earlier, now felt hope loosen her reins a little. A momentary sink into depression washed over him, leaving the feeling of defeat as inevitable as the coming sigh he would produce next.

Sigh…

Then it was gone. A moment before, everyone in the room had been dealing with personal comments the devil had hand-delivered to each of them. But now, the ethereal shadow he'd left in the room had dissipated, as if it had never been there in the first place.

The group spent time talking about the meeting, which hadn't gone anything like anyone had expected. None of them could describe to themselves what they had expected, but they all knew that how it had gone was *not* what they had expected. Up to the point where the devil had walked through their office door, they had only heard vague reports about him, an occasional sighting during a battle. If not for the fact they had proven having three scrolls at their base gave them protectdion, they would have expected it would have walked into the room and slit their throats with the blade located at the end of its tail.

Surrender, they knew, as Jack had told the fiend, was not an option, but the devil had made it sound (and convincingly so) like he had been holding back. This was not a piece of information they had considered. Up to that point, the team had believed their side had a fighting chance of holding their ground. Reports on the HAMs were coming from all over the globe describing battles won, even when they were outnumbered. Slugs didn't have the power and speed to withstand Elementors or plain old normal humans with weapons; Dusters were able to take out some filler, and the demons and monsters—the biggest problem, by far—were still fightable, killable.

But if the devil wasn't lying and hadn't been using his full powers, and he was, in fact, trying to keep the world in some sort of inhabitable shape for his future rule, then this new knowledge left them with a big unknown. Did humanity even have a chance in heaven, for victory?

"He made a good point with the nuclear reactors, Jack." Randy said. "I mean, if he just wanted to win, why not set off all the nukes, destroy all the reactors, and let the world fry? Whoever's left would be dead in a year from radiation."

"I know. It makes you wonder," Jack said.

"The demons only come out at night, and the rest aren't too much of a problem during the day. That always gives us a fighting chance with the ability to regroup in the morning."

"Randy, I understand; that's true," Jack agreed, "but he said something else that bothers me."

"What?" Sarah asked. "Only one thing? He said a lot that bothered me."

"Yes, I hear you, but the thing I'm thinking of," Jack went on, "is how he said he could use his power to crush mountains."

"Or if we wanted our battle of the apocalypse, he could make it happen," Quincy added.

"Right," Jack shot back. "He seems to be saying he has the power to destroy us even within his own self."

"That doesn't make any sense," Randy said. "If he can do that, why not just do it? Wave his hand, and voilà, no more 'our side.' Crushed, like a mountain, like he said."

"It goes back and forth, I know," Jack said to Randy. "Why not destroy us like that? But if he can do that, why does he need to use his demons to destroy reactors? And why does it matter how many people are on his side?"

"A lot of whys," Quincy responded.

"A lot of lies." Four Winds had spoken again for the first time since the devil had accosted him and his race.

"I don't know, Four Winds," Jack answered. "I heard a lot of truth when he was here, almost too much."

"Truth mixed with lies is the greatest veil. The villain spoke truth without context and blended lies as punctuation," Four Winds assessed.

Four Winds's voice left a new resonance in the air, much more welcome than what Satan had spewed, seemingly, from his very pores. The effect of Four Winds's resonating voice always made you want to remain silent while it…resonated. The effect also produced a desire to ponder his words. And that's what they all did. The other four remained quiet and thought about what he had said. Randy finally broke the silence.

As usual, Byron thought. Remember Byron? He's always *there*.

Randy said, "So if what Four Winds says is true, then how do we know what's true? What *can* he do? What *can't* he?"

Four Winds answered, an anomaly, for he was usually a one-comment kind of guy. "We may not know until later, but we can know that if he could crush us, there would have been no need for him to come here today. I do not believe the only reason he came was to get us to sign treaties or to make friends with us because he is lonely."

"He came to scare us," Sarah announced.

"Correct," Four Winds replied.

"And it didn't work…*completely*," Randy followed, still showing signs of regret that he hadn't been slightly tougher in the thing's presence.

"Which is why he left so angry," Jack said, smiling at Randy, and at the turn in the conversation Four Winds had brought to the table. "That was not the display of a leader being disagreed with. It was the tantrum of a child who has just lost a game." Jack looked at their favorite Sioux warrior, and struggled to offset their foul visitor's baseless accusations. "Four Winds, you are an asset, and your people are, too, no matter what that thing says about them." The words felt flat to Jack and he groaned inside, feeling as if he'd tried to repair the centuries-long decimation of Native Americans with a one-sentence four-hundred-years overdue apology.

Four Winds acknowledged Jack's efforts with better words, as was his style. "All good people are an asset, and all bad people are a liability. And all peoples have a mixture of both."

At the end of the conversation, it was agreed none of them knew what the devil was capable of, but that hope didn't appear to be lost, if they had read the situation correctly. A message was sent to Derek and Riley in England, via shortwave, with the details and conclusions of the meeting.

"Well, you got me on what all that means," Derek responded after being informed of the meeting. "I guess what you guys think is about as good as anything. I don't like the idea of all this fighting having been a ruse. I hate to think he really could finish us off that easily. If that's true, what's the point?"

"Right," Jack answered, "that's what we figured. But I don't think he's just going to take what I told him lying down, either—just continue the status quo. That worries me too. Maybe I shouldn't have been so antagonistic."

"Don't beat yourself up, Jack. From the sounds of it, he wasn't holding back either. It sounds like it was strutting time for both leaders, and you didn't do so bad."

"Leader? Geez, Derek, you act like you five elected me or something. We're all in this together."

"Yeah, but you are the one behind the desk!" Derek laughed. "We put you there for a reason. That's where the first bullet goes when they execute us."

"Thanks a lot." Jack sighed. "So? What is going on over there? Anything new?"

Derek explained how he and Riley had couriers traveling with messages and shortwave equipment all over Europe, and some were attempting to use planes by day. Derek wanted to reach farther into Asia, but those plans weren't being held as top priority because of the fighting they were dealing with in closer countries.

"We can only do so much. We figure people everywhere have power over the elements. We have to hope they are banding together and making a stand wherever they are," Derek explained. "We've got a pretty good handle on the plan for this continent and are finding many people who are beneficial to our cause."

"What about Discerners?" Jack asked. "You made any headway on locating more and figuring out what 'taming them' means."

"We don't have a clue. Our best guess is to follow it literally. Get 'em to keep their hands in their pockets as much as possible. Not quite sure why. Riley's got a theory."

"What's that?"

"Well, he was thinking, maybe all this excess in humanity's ranks is meant to give us manpower to fight with. If we Dusters start randomly wiping them out of existence, it could hurt our cause."

"Dusters?"

"Yes. That's what some of them are calling themselves—the few we've found. I even had one kid ask me if I was a Scrooger."

"Scrooger?"

"Yes. I guess it's another slang someone dreamed up after I explained a bit about this power and what it does. I guess it has something to do with that line in *A Christmas Carol* where Ebenezer says it'd be better to let the poor die off so as to decrease the excess population."

"Wow. I guess it is good to 'tame' a group who could feel the need to identify with that guy! But...I see the point. One thing, Derek. I get what Riley offered as an explanation, but it still leaves one unanswered question, doesn't it?"

"What's that?"

"What are you guys for, then? What are you supposed to do?" Jack asked.

"Right," Derek answered. "I getcha. We'll mull that one over some more. Maybe we can find the answer in Hans Christian Andersen."

BOOK VI:

THE MYTH OF THE WAR

CHAPTER 47

ONE YEAR OF HELL
11/12/13

I T WAS ALMOST ONE YEAR after Hell Day. Things weren't going exactly great for humanity, per se, but at least the people at the top had a plan, and they were putting it into action. Battles *were* being won. People *were* joining together and making a stand. However, it was also clear that good was quickly becoming outnumbered by bad, even if one took the demons and monsters out of the count. From what could be seen, it appeared the old adage "There is more good in the world than bad," in reality, was quite opposite to the truth.

The David and Goliath metaphor inspired some, but typically in the moment, decisions to keep from being swallowed whole, or torn in half and then swallowed in bites, were what brought out the fight in individuals. Those holding mystical elemental powers fought at night, and the rest stepped it up to fight against Slugs and Traitors by day.

—◇◦◇—

It all goes great until someone changes the rules, they say, and the rules all changed November 12, 2013. In a single moment, the rules changed. The game changed. The landscape changed, the battle changed, the war changed. And pandemonium immediately ensued. Up to this point, the previous twenty-four hours had followed most twenty-four-hour periods: fight to stay alive against all foul things. November 12 came, and with it came *out* with "the usual" and *in* with "the unusual"—new and improved style. In an instant, a blink—the amount of time it takes to have a thought—everyone was in the same place. Everyone.

A moment earlier, where there had been nothing but a vast plain, above it the sky and below it the earth, a billion-plus people now stood. Many people stood shocked. Many immediately assumed battle stances, peering at one another. Some backed away from the surprised stranger they saw in front of them, only to bump into another stranger behind them. They'd spin around and find the other doing the same.

"Are you good? Are you bad?" one would ask.

"Stand back!" another would respond.

"Quieto!"

"Arrêtez!"

And the list of questions and responses, all in various languages, went on and on down the line, so to speak.

Any chance for order was on the verge of oblivion. Elementors raised their arms to attack anyone who might make an aggressive move. Those holding weapons did the same. The roar of voices raised to a level that could be heard in space—where sound can't be heard. It was the last scene of *Reservoir Dogs* times ten million.

All conversations could be summed up by one Elementor's shout: "I swear to God, you people make one move, and I'll turn the earth upside down on you!"

Jack, Randy, Sarah, Four Winds, and Quincy had been separated by the event. The phenomenon had shuffled their entire species like a deck of cards.

Byron watched in horror as what was left of the good in humanity assumed stances, ready to attack itself. As they hollered and threatened each other, Byron believed it would be an impossibility to hear anything louder than their combined yelling and banter. That was, until the cheering behind him from the other side of the plain commenced. More than five billion voices erupted in elation, drowning out the one billion cries of fear and suspicion. As the sound attacked eardrums, all present on both sides, dropped to their knees, stunned by the pain and holding their heads.

With hardship comes ease, and the trauma did allow Jack and his billion band of merry men and women to notice the several billion minions of the devil, who were also kneeling a mile across the plain from them. Inner tension in their group relaxed, only to be replaced by twice the amount of dread. For the first time, a true visual existed of the enormous threat good was up against, and the great disparity existing in their respective numbers with bad.

Slowly rising from their knees, both sides stared at one another in silence while recovering from their ringing ears and heads. Humanity's Last Chance Army pondered on what might happen next. Was all-out war seconds from beginning? Should they take the offensive, believing that God would not let them down? Did they have a chance in heaven or hell of winning? Where was their leadership? Some still wondered if they had leadership; not everyone had become aware of Jack and his circle of "in the know" comrades. No one wanted to make the first move, but all feared a first strike by the enemy.

And then the newly assumed rules disintegrated, changing again. The new tension built in the last few moments dissolved as a man and a woman emerged from the enemy's ranks and started making their way across the field. The man and woman covered approximately a one-half-mile distance to the center of the field and were standing patiently when good produced a seemingly random set of human beings out of its folds and out onto the field as well. Although seemingly random, they also all appeared to be emerging from the same general vicinity—somewhat centered along the miles of people existing in either direction—and across from the two who were standing, apparently waiting to be met in the center of what might soon be a battlefield.

Jack Johanssen had noticed the two representatives marching out of the leading edge of the enemy's force because he had been standing right across from them. *Coincidentally?* He thought not, although he had very little energy to invest in that kind of thinking, given everything he felt he should be thinking about at that moment. Jack shook his head at himself as he felt compelled to start his own trek out of the crowd to find out who this man and woman were.

One by one, Sarah, and then Four Winds, followed by a mix of a few unknowns, at least to the Scroll Holders, and then Randy, Derek, Riley, and finally Quincy, trailing in the rear, followed as Jack was arriving at the center to meet the man and woman waiting on the plain.

CHAPTER 48

THE VIKKI SITUATION

"HELLO. I'M JACK JOHANSSEN."

"I know said the woman. She continued, "Well, sort of. Anyways, I'm Vikki Parsons, and this is Harvey."

As the others from his side started to gather around Jack, he curtailed his curiosity to ask what this was all about until everyone had arrived.

"I think I'll wait till everyone's here to hear what it is you've come to say," he explained and turned around, not waiting for an answer, hearing her acceptance of his statement as she replied to the back of his head.

Jack wasn't surprised to see his friends, but he was curious as to who the others walking toward him were. He made his way back to meet those who were coming so they could discuss any ideas developing in their minds away from whoever these two were to whom he had just introduced himself.

"Hi, Sarah, it's good to see that everyone appears to be all right. I think I see Quincy way in the back there." He pointed.

Sarah nodded happily at seeing everyone she knew and loved, walking toward her and Jack, but her smile slowly returned to a look of seriousness, which was the obvious choice of emotion, considering the situation.

As the unknowns began to arrive, introductions commenced. It appeared many people believed themselves to be leaders in the last year's war, and they were from all over the earth. Fortunately, most spoke English. The ones who didn't tried to pick up on the cues of comradery developing among the forming group. Jack eventually communicated to Quincy that he should return to the front with the few who didn't speak English in order to search for translators. He wasn't fond of the idea of having to make decisions again that could affect everyone—and by the look of things, it now appeared that "everyone" literally meant everyone. He was even less keen on the idea of making decisions within a group of people that consisted of many he had never met. He thought it was very important to get everyone believing they were involved and create as much of a unified voice to those waiting behind him. The last thing he wanted to convey was that they distrusted each other more than those whom they were fighting.

There were some strong personalities in this impromptu huddle, and some of the new faces, new at least to Jack, had obviously been through the thick of it. Seeing them, Jack realized the bubble of safety he and his fellow scroll bearers had enjoyed—even if it hadn't been by their choice—had been a true gift. They had missed out on a level of seasoning and battle scars that the rest of this new leadership group *had* acquired. And by the looks of them, that seasoning had not been acquired easily.

Each explained where they were from and their marvel at the new event that had brought them all together on this morning. Some knew of Jack, Derek, Riley, or knew others that knew them, and had been following whatever guidance they could from HAM communications. Jack tried to explain to others who Sarah, Derek, Randy, Four Winds, Quincy, and he were, and to explain how they had found the scrolls, the information contained within them, and how they had tried to use that information over several years to develop a plan for the war they believed might come to pass—the war that had come to pass about a year earlier, commencing on Hell Day. Hardness may have developed in these warriors' outer appearances as a result of God knew what experiences that had shaped them over the past months, but their nature was far more understanding and cooperative than what Jack would have expected. This wasn't a group that was mimicking a United Nations meeting, including leaders of various levels of honesty, goodness, corruption, or whatever. These were leaders who had emerged through trials and hardships and had the wear to show for it, but they had still been born out of a group of humanity who had chosen good over the force led by Mr. Red, and had done so with firm conviction.

Jack explained he was more than willing to run a vote on who should be the front man to the meeting waiting behind them. His speech of acquiescence to the group ended up being the very thing to put him right back in the position he had never asked for from the beginning—Numero Uno. "*All that and a bag of chips,*" Jack heard an old high school friend's phrase echo in his mind. Some of this group, he had discovered were even Elementors. All that power, and they still had not been corrupted by it. They had just handed the scepter to him with barely a thought. God had given the right stuff to the right people. That was for sure. But why had he given any stuff to the wrong people? He thought he might never know.

The group turned to face the two who had presented themselves out of the devil's ranks: Vikki and Harvey. *What names*, Jack thought, *representing all that is wrong and destructive in the world*. When only a few paces remained between Jack and his meeting of monumental proportion, a vague voice of panic could be heard erupting from behind him. It came into form, growing louder and closer, and the group turned again, away from Vikki and Harvey, to see who was producing the disruption.

Jack and his group—it really could be, officially, called his group now—looked back at their own front and caught the image moving toward them. It was a young boy, a teenager. He was standing on two stones that were carrying him through the air like a magic carpet would, if magic carpets existed. Jack actually thought about this as he watched the kid approach. *With everything that exists now, magic carpets are still just a story.* And he chuckled.

Byron gasped, invisible and unbeknownst to the rest of the group, as he realized it was Sam, the boy Vikki had left in the woods of Kentucky.

"Waaaaiiiiiit!" Sam yelled as he gained speed. Jack's group wouldn't have noticed, but to Vikki, Sam looked weathered. The last several months had taken their own toll on Sam. He had come a long way with his ability, but he appeared to be using considerable concentration to balance on the rocks he was moving under his feet.

The group stilled as they wondered what the boy could be so concerned about—other than the obvious that *everyone* was concerned about. Two or three of the fighter types in Jack's group turned around, instinctively, making sure nothing was happening on the devil's side that may have sparked the boy's reaction.

Sam landed in front of them. He started speaking faster than he'd been flying. "I know her. You can't trust her! Nothing she says is the truth!" Sam was out of breath, frazzled and pointing at the woman standing behind then all.

"Who are you?" Jack asked.

"My name's Sam. I traveled with her. I met her in Saint Louis. She tricked me into taking her to the devil's camp. I thought she was good. I thought she was my friend. But she's not! She's a liar!"

Sarah now spoke, and again, as usual, in her saving-the-day manner. "Sam? I'm Sarah Dubois."

Sarah's beauty and charm could probably send a rushing bull into instant sleep, and so too, it ran its course on the boy. He calmed a little…enough…and replied with a little more composure than before. "Uh, hi, I'm Sam. I mean, well, you know that, but I'm just trying to explain. I know her—"

"We understand, Sam," Sarah said. "Thank you for alerting us. I don't believe anyone from that side can be trusted. But we are glad you are here. You may be able to help, since you know her."

"Sam?"

A voice only Jack had heard up to this point spoke. When Jack heard Vikki's voice, he thought for a moment how patient *The Two* had been up to this point.

Sam immediately responded, "What? I don't want to talk to you! You're a liar!"

"I know you hate me, Sam," Vikki responded. "I don't believe you're wrong in feeling how you do."

Sam moved forward, closer to her, and raised his arms. "I ought to blast you all the way back to Kentucky right now, and give you what you deserve. You left me alone in that forest, and now you're that thing's spokeswoman! What's *wrong* with you?"

"I don't expect you to understand, but I request you hear me out before you make any rash decisions. There is still hope for everyone here. And I know you care about that, Sam. If anything, you care about that, Sam. So just listen."

—⊂○⊃—

Sam didn't want to listen. He hadn't even thought about listening. He had thought about attacking first and asking questions never. But when she said that, it was like she had read his mind before he'd thought the thought. The truth was, he did have hope; he did want to hear what she had to say, and he didn't know why on earth that would be the case. He hated her, didn't he?

...but hate was sometimes just love hurting, wasn't it?

Sam quieted, and with a small show of reluctance, he pursed his lips and lowered his arms. The group gathered closer after Sam turned off attack mode. Vikki's last words had made more than Sam want to listen.

Jack, having been voted official leader, spoke. "Sam here says we can't trust you, but I think we would all like to believe there is a way to end all of this. So, if you have something to say in that vein, get on with it, Miss Parsons."

Ruining the moment as easily as she had created it, she answered, "You're not going to like all of it."

CHAPTER 49

THE VIKKI SITUATION ON ACID

⸺◇○⟨⟩○◇⸺

"REALLY? Jack responded. "Honestly, I haven't liked much since about 2007, so I don't think you're here to surprise me."

"I can't believe this is happening. Some of it is verbatim what I remember," Vikki said.

"What are you talking about?"

"We're being watched," Vikki replied to Jack, throwing in a suspicious glance by bopping her head to the left, eyes moving in that direction also.

"Obviously," Jack said, "there's about five billion of your kind right behind you. Speaking of which, why is the big guy not out here? The way I see it, he'd love to watch us shaking in our shoes right now."

"I convinced him to let me come instead."

"You convinced him? And how exactly did you—" Jack didn't finish his question. He could see the answer on the girl's face. *Oh my God*, he thought.

"Yes, you're right, Jack. I know what you're thinking," Vikki said, looking down at the ground.

"Now listen, Miss Parsons, I'd like to believe you have something to offer here, but I'm really starting to lean toward Sam here's thinking. I mean if you're…" Jack paused, not knowing how to put the surmising he'd done into words. "I mean, if you're his…uh…"

"His woman?" Vikki filled in for the struggling spokesman for all that is right and good in the universe.

Jack felt embarrassed with the topic and his fumbling of it. He picked up where she left off. "Well, yes. It's just in my opinion if you're with *him*, you're needing a straitjacket—or you're…" Jack struggled to finish. "I don't know. But able to trust? That's a big pill to swallow. You see all these people behind me? They're what's at stake here for me, and I'm supposed to believe, forgive me, that the devil's girlfriend can *benefit* us?"

Vikki leaned forward and whispered to Jack. "I had to do it. It was the only way to gain his trust and be standing here, discussing saving humanity with you."

When the rules keep changing, you can get off your game. Thrice in one day. Game board changed before; pieces were changing now. Had the face of the

340

opponent's leadership just changed? Jack was expecting to look down and see himself wearing a skirt soon, the way things were going. This was a wrinkle in the conversation he hadn't expected to ponder. Traitorhood on the devil's side. The possibility of such devotion to his own side that someone might have actually done what she was claiming to have done. It was worth considering. But it was also risky. It was so much easier when you could just say, "They're bad, and we might not be great, but we're not them." Here, before him, stood a girl who was as evil, disgusting, and dishonest as they came, or she was the one person—out of all who there ever was—who had sacrificed everything and, therefore, should be listened to and even protected.

"Listen," Jack answered, "I don't know yet if what you are saying is the truth, but I haven't heard any of what you say you've come to say, so let's just continue with that, for now." Jack didn't want to dismiss her efforts if she was telling the truth, but he didn't want to offer too much sympathy if she was lying.

"Okay, I know where I start, but even though I know that, I'm finding it difficult to know where to start. And the sad part is, damn it, I know I was going to say this, and I didn't have to, but here I am saying it, and *he's* going to write it down."

"Miss Parsons—"

"I know, I know. I'm not making any sense. You know when I said earlier, we're being watched?"

"Yes."

"I didn't mean by Big Red. What I meant was, there is someone else here."

"What do you mean? Someone else?" Jack asked it, but everyone around him was thinking it, starting to look around for that someone else.

"We can't see him, and I only know his name as Byron, but I don't think that's his real name. Just like I know you as Jack, and her as Sarah, and him as Randy, and only learned your real names after the devil met with you. All I can say to convince you is: the man I know as Byron is the same man that visited your Native American friend—the one who likes jeans and T-shirts. This Byron has been watching *all* of us through some kind of visions—for years—and writing down everything that we do."

Jack didn't know whether to laugh because of how little sense the girl was making, or cry because he really did feel sorry for her—she had obviously lost all sense by going through whatever she had put herself through as Satan's lover. Jack couldn't speak, which left an opening for Vikki to continue.

"I know you have no idea what I'm talking about, but I know things. Things that can prove what I'm going to tell you is the truth, if you'll just hear me out. I'm the only one who seems to know them. It's crazy. I can't believe that no one else read it, but if so, why hasn't anyone else said anything? I don't know. Maybe people did and they're dead, or maybe they have said something, but haven't said it to anyone that would have been in any position to do anything with the information. Or maybe they were ignored, or maybe no one realized it because they weren't specifically talked about like I was, and so it didn't click. Once again, I don't know. All I do know is I was reading a book the night the demons came to my town in North Dakota, of all places, and I had just read a part in the book describing exactly where I was, what I was doing, and then the demons came, and I just knew it was me. I didn't want to believe it...but I couldn't escape it. It was exact."

"Really, Miss Parsons, I don't think any of us are following you." Jack had no idea what she was trying to convey, but whatever it was, she was definitely trying to convey it.

"I know, I know. Just wait. I have to get it all out, and it will start to make sense. The next morning, everyone was dead or gone, and when I finally got the guts to move, instead of running out the doors of my grocery store—because honestly, I didn't know what might be waiting for me—I stayed in the office and finished my book. It turned out, I wasn't just mentioned in the book as a character who stayed huddled up under her desk while her town got devoured. I discovered I was the one who was going to help bring an end to it all. It was insane. The kid had even written down the several 'Shits!' I had yelled out when I got to the part of the book that made me realize I was really going to have to do what it said I was going to do. It's nuts because I read that part before I did it, and I still did it."

Jack had to stop her. Her rambling wasn't anything he could follow, so he could only assume the rest were lost also. "Vikki, you need to go slower for us. You're not making *any* sense. What book are you talking about?"

"It's a novel. A book—*The Four Myths*. It came out a few years ago. I guess not a big seller, probably because it was some unknown author. But it's about the end of time. About all of us! About you and Randy and how you found an ancient scroll and translated it from Russian with an Enigma machine, and you, Sarah, and your nephew, and how you—"

"Whoa, Miss Parsons!" Jack stopped her. "How do you know about that? How do you know about the scrolls? We know the devil doesn't know about those."

"I'm telling you...this Byron kid. Well, he's not a kid now—well, he is—but not the one that's here, now—anyway...he's watching us. We can't see him because he's invisible. He's viewing us, he's been viewing *everything*—in pieces. He's writing everything down, and somehow this author guy is going to find his notebooks and write a novel about it. The novel I *read*. It tells our story. It tells all of *this*. It tells how it ends. And I know how to save us."

"Honestly, this is insanity," Jack said, somehow starting to get an inkling of what she was trying to describe. "A novel about all of us? That already exists? That anyone could have read, already? Then, why haven't *we* read it? Why don't we know how it all ends? Why doesn't he? Even if I could believe you—which I can't—you're asking me to believe in the impossible and risk everything on a preposterous story of which you have no proof. I don't even see you offering the book in your hand for us to check out for ourselves."

"I know. I burned it. I couldn't risk it being found, knowing where I was heading. Plus, I learned that I burned it—*from* it—anyways. I was heading right into the pit of his organization, as you know, so I couldn't very well have it with me, could I? But that's why Harvey's here."

Vikki pointed to Harvey as she said his name, and Harvey, who was just as confused by all he was hearing as Jack, looked up, surprised to be mentioned.

"Me?" he said.

"Yes. Harvey here's a prisoner, but a prisoner with some weight because the devil's been convinced he's got a useful ability he doesn't really have."

"And what's that?" Jack asked, deciding to keep going along with this, whatever *this* was.

"Harvey can see things others can't see when he's wearing other peoples' glasses. I told the devil he can sense people's sincerity, so he's out here to report back on whether we should believe you if you say you'll agree to his terms."

"*Oh?* And what terms are those, Miss Parsons?" Jack asked, now realizing this was the *real* meat of the discussion he had been waiting for, but then found he was wrong, yet again, with her subsequent response.

"I'm not here to discuss his terms with you, Jack. I am here to tell you there is a way to defeat him. You just have to continue to hear me out." Vikki was talking fast again, trying to stay calm, yet trying to explain quickly while trying to stay believable. He could see all this in her efforts. The one thing Jack could gather was she was definitely trying. That was unmistakable. Trying to *what* was still the question.

"Harvey can't really do that gauging of sincerity thing, but he can—"

"Jack?" It was Randy interrupting this time. "You hear what she just said?"

"What's that Randy?"

"Come over here, for a sec." Randy decided it was in their best interest not to give away the information he had just come to remember.

"It's okay, Randy!" Vikki called as Jack started to walk away. "I know what you've realized. You just remembered Four Winds told you Byron said to find the man who sees with eyes that are not of his own."

"His name wasn't Byron," Four Winds said.

"I know," Vikki replied, "I just explained that the book has everyone's names changed. I don't know his real name."

Jack knew there had been a chance the presence of the scrolls could have possibly made it to the devil's ears. They had had to inform some people of their existence to gain trust in the early days. But only the six of them knew of the message Four Winds had brought from the man who had brought Four Winds to their doorstep after his fateful day at Little Bighorn. The rules had been changed to the game, but the new rules were starting to make sense, as little sense as they made.

Jack once again turned back toward Vikki, and although only Jack and six others in the group behind him had fully started to understand what the girl was talking about, the entire entity behind Jack was starting to pay close attention to her every word. She was obviously hell-bent on convincing them of something that could save them all, and the man they had voted spokesman looked as if he might be beginning to believe her.

"Miss Parsons," Jack began, as he decided to give the first indication to her that he might be giving her her due, "if I were to believe you—believe that you read this so-called novel, *and* that it told you about all of us, and the scrolls, and how it *all* ends, *and* that you have done everything you have admitted to doing so you could be standing here with us, today, to tell us how to win—if I were to even consider believing you, to actually decide our strategy against that incredible force behind you, and God knows what is coming when night falls, should be what you are going to describe it should be, then what kind of proof, if anything, can you give me to even attempt to convince everyone here, that I should go along with it? You have to give me *something*, Miss Parsons. Because all I have right now is an impossible story. I will admit, you have a few pieces of information you shouldn't have, but not necessarily impossible to have—and Harvey there looks about as clueless as I feel."

"The book said I'd bring Harvey, and he'd help convince you. Harvey has a gift, but he doesn't really know what it means. But I do. When he puts other people's glasses on, he can see who they are."

"Like their name?" Jack asked.

"No, like their type. He sees a beautiful aura around them if they are good, something really sinister in color if they're bad, or—"

"You know what I can see?" Harvey interrupted.

"Yes, Harvey."

"And you know what it means?"

"Yes, Harvey, I do."

Welcome to Mind-Blown Harvey. "I didn't know why, Vikki, but I have been willing to accept you had your reasons for trying to keep me from getting killed. Figured it was some selfish and evil reason, like everything else around me." He looked at Jack and the others. "She's right about me. I can see what she says, and there is only one other person who knows about it, and we haven't discussed it since practically the beginning of all of this. There's no way she could know. Wait!" Harvey turned to Vikki again. "There's a third type I see. I don't know what it means. Do you?"

"It means they're filler, Harvey." It was Derek who answered, not Vikki—or rather, Derek had made a pretty good educated guess. Harvey was right back into can't-speak-mind-blown mode, not understanding what Derek's answer meant.

Wouldn't you be?

Vikki responded, "He's right, Harvey. It means they're not *really* human. They just make the world go 'round."

"But then what are you?" Harvey asked Vikki.

"I don't know," she answered.

"What does he mean by that?" Jack asked. "Aren't you one of the three types he claims to see?"

Harvey cut in. "No. I noticed it about her the first time I saw her. She's the only one I've seen like her. She doesn't do anything. No aura, beautiful or otherwise—nothing. She looks the same either way, when I wear other people's glasses or my own, blurry or not blurry. That's it."

"Well," Jack said, "that's convenient. I guess you'll tell us we have to believe in you on faith, right?"

"I really don't know, Jack," Vikki responded and held her hands out in front of her and palms facing up in an "I give up" pleading manner. "I know what I know, and I know what I don't know. I know you'll agree to go along with me in the end, but I don't know what happens to me or you or any one of you, really."

Jack listened to her description of her knowledge and its unfortunate self-proclaimed "holes." He didn't know what to make of this girl. She was convincing enough, and Jack thought if she was telling the truth, she had taken one hell of a chance and put herself through one hell of a hell. She'd risked everything for the sake of humanity on a hell of a chance she was right about a novel she just happened to be reading when all hell broke loose on this new hell of a planet.

"If Harvey truly has this gift, and he's the one we've been searching for…" Jack stopped and turned to Sarah and Randy, raising his hand in a defeated way as if to say, "What do you think? You believe her? Can I get some help here, please?"

He then turned back. "The one we've been searching for—and I guess that's not as much of a secret as we thought it was—then how does he help us? He can't tell us whether you're good or evil, truthful or lying." Jack chuckled inside as he realized this girl's very state of being changed the rules on him again.

"Harvey isn't here to convince the devil of your sincerity or you of mine. He's here to *prove* to you what I say is the truth."

"What else do you have to say…that's the *truth*?" Jack asked

Vikki spoke to the crowd gathered and listening behind Jack. "Someone give Harvey some glasses. Someone with a strong farsighted prescription would be best."

A pair of glasses came forward through the group and was finally placed into Jack's hand.

"Now," Vikki explained, "when Harvey puts them on. I want you to all turn away and act like you're fed up with the conversation and start to head away from us. I will plead for you to come back in a moment, and you will. Harvey? When they turn away, you're going to turn away, as well, and I want you to take a good hard look at the army of the Devil, and then just follow my lead." Vikki looked up at Jack. "Now hand the glasses over slowly to me like you're going to shake my hand. When I have them, turn in disgust and storm off like you're changing your mind."

Jack felt he understood the point of this ruse she was creating and went along, still not believing he had considered anything she had said so far to be true. A moment later, Jack and the rest were marching back toward their side of the field, and hollers and cheers were starting to come from the enemy's side. Then he heard Vikki calling, as if demanding them to return to the discussion. They stopped after she hollered for a few seconds, and one by one made reluctant but abiding gestures to her request, each playing their part in what was, most likely, their first acting gig. Vikki also called to Harvey, who also turned back around to face the group.

When they had all come together once again, Jack stopped the ridiculousness and asked the obvious question. "Okay, Harvey, what'd you see?"

Harvey looked like he'd seen a ghost. He was staring intensely past Jack, past the leaders behind Jack, and apparently past the horizon behind the army behind the leaders behind Jack.

"Harvey. Tell them what you see. Please," Vikki urged. "We don't have a lot of time. This war needs to be over before nightfall. Harvey!"

Harvey snapped out of his gaze. "Uh...I'm sorry. It's incredible. I don't know what it means, but it's incredible."

"What is? What's incredible?" Jack asked.

"Everything...but their army, it's—it's almost completely—it's like one big, blinking light. I mean, there's definitely a lot of red mixed in it, but over ninety percent is there one second and gone the next."

"Does that mean something to you, Jack? Derek?" Vikki asked with a smile on her face, not being able to help herself, given how long she'd waited for this moment. "Can you help Harvey understand the importance of his discovery?"

"Wait," Harvey continued. "There's more."

"Right," Jack prompted. "You were looking at our army too. What'd you see there?"

"It's the most beautiful thing I've ever seen," Harvey yelped. "It's like Meg times a trillion."

"Meg's the woman he loves," Vikki said, filling in the gap.

Derek once again felt the urge to say something. "Harvey, you mean to tell me, you don't see any filler on our side?"

"I don't see any blinking, if that's what you mean. I mean the light is beautiful, but it's not blinding. It just goes on and on, continuously like a perpetual field of aurora borealis on steroids."

"All the filler drifted to the bad side," Derek stated rhetorically to himself. "It gives the devil false confidence. Jack, this is big. This could be the reason we were told to tame the Discerners. If we had let our hands out of our pockets too much, it might have become apparent what the situation was. I don't think the bastard knows about us."

"He doesn't," Vikki affirmed. "He doesn't know that if all of you charge his army at once, the largest part of it will disappear in a cloud of dust."

"Oh my God," Derek said as if a great weight had been taken off his heart. For the first time in seven years, he didn't feel like a leper, like someone who had to be worried constantly about who he might disintegrate with his very presence. "That's what we're for. Oh, thank you, God." The smile was on his face was one Sarah hadn't seen in years.

"See?" Derek continued. "There is more good in the world. I wanted to believe that so badly."

"It's not that simple, though, Derek. This is a war, and there will be casualties. Your Dusters and those covering them are your front line, so to speak."

"We have some protection, though," Randy said. "We can take the scrolls on the battlefield with us," Randy said and then chopped his own words. He had said this quickly, and immediately realized he had just given up one of his side's greatest secret defenses to a party no one had affirmatively decided to trust.

"Randy!" Jack turned, putting his proverbial hand over Randy's proverbial mouth.

Vikki spoke, breaking the need for any further disciplinary action. "Jack, don't be too harsh with Randy. I think you'll find we're all on an even playing field now. I don't think any one of you had a scroll in your hand when you were transported here this morning, did you?"

CHAPTER 50

THE DECISION

*T*HE FACT COULD NOT BE DENIED, Jack thought. Whether the girl was telling the truth or not, whether she was on their side or lying, the fact remained she had just made Jack and his small circle of scroll finders aware—for the first time since Randy and him had peered upon a certain mystical relic at the bottom of a metal box nearly seven years earlier—that they were like everyone else, and only a few hours before night came, and the demons that came with it. A war was going to be fought on this plain, very soon, whether he wanted it to happen or not, and his gang could offer no more protection for anyone anymore. They would be up against a force more than five times their size and that force would include god-awful things coming out of the darkness on land and in the sky after day fell away. The only thing he could do in his position that could possibly make a difference now was to *make a decision*—or convince the group behind him that they should make the decision to believe this girl—with no proof other than Harvey. Harvey, who, for all Jack knew, could be lying too. He needed more.

"How long do we have to stand out here and talk like this, because to be frank, I'm not sure what to think quite yet?" He'd buy time by asking about time.

"I'm not sure, Mr. Johanssen, but after our little show we just put on, I'm sure it would be in all our best interest to wrap this up quickly."

Randy broke in from behind again. Protocol didn't seem to mean much to him. "You said you know we can win. You said you know the end, but you don't know what you are, what happens to us, or how long we talk? I don't get it."

"I only know what was in that book, what was conveyed in the story. I know we continue to talk awhile longer, and you decide to believe in me. I know we fight, and I know our side prevails."

"*Our* side?" Randy asked. "And what *side* is *that?*"

"Listen, I'm here. I'm telling you what I know. I'm telling you I want you to win. My side is your side."

"What else can you give us about the battle that's coming?" Jack asked.

"I can tell you it goes well into the night. I was hoping to change that by making this session quicker but didn't have much hope it would happen, given I say it in the book, and the battle still carries into the night. I can tell you that even when you

348

surprise him with the Discerners, you're going to have a hard fight on your hands."

"Tell them about the Slugs, Vikki!" It was Sam again. "I don't think you can believe her, Mr. Jack!" He was yelling from the side. "I just remembered. We met a group of Slugs in a town while she was getting me to take her to her devil, and she just let them go."

"Is what Sam is saying, true, Miss Parsons?" This was the first time Jack honestly felt he might have been had.

"Do you know what the Slugs are, Jack?" Vikki answered with a question she knew he could answer.

"Yes."

"And?"

"They're people who thought they were better than others, who hurt others because of their arrogance. Could be racists, Nazi types, or I guess just plain assholes."

"That's right. But do you know why they became deformed?"

"I guess I can't say I know for sure, but it was explained their pride is one of the worst of sins, and that they would be punished with the experience they gave others. They would be shunned, reviled, et cetera, et cetera."

"I think a lot of people have pride, but not all hurt others at the same level. I think sometimes a lot of people learn that kind of hate from their parents too. I do think many people who are fighting over there with the devil are there because they want to be. They truly have forsaken good over bad. But I think some of those Slugs are there because no one else wanted them. And some of them have even learned a hard lesson."

"I'm not sure I'm following you." And then a moment later he thought he was following her. He had read the scrolls over and over and now he was remembering the end of *The Myth of Man.* Jack muttered, "Perhaps they will learn, but most will probably not."

"Yes, Jack," Vikki answered. "The Slugs I met, the ones Sam is talking about, were a group who had not yet joined with the devil. They were contemplating it for their own survival, knowing if they met any of you, they'd be shot first and thought about second. But they had discovered the errors of their previous life. Many exist like them. I told them they should join with the bad people, but there would be a time in the future when they could redeem themselves. They should seek out others like themselves and wait patiently."

Jack heard this and thought he understood what she was saying, but there was so damned much to process, especially in light of the fact he was still standing in the middle of a far-off land, staring at five billion foes just waiting to destroy him. It was a little hard to stay focused on all the complicated turn of events this girl was describing.

"Why don't you just tell it to me straight, Miss Parsons? What can we expect, if we surrender? If we don't surrender? Just tell us what you know. You said it yourself—we don't have a lot of time, and you're the one who had a desire to get this thing finished during the day!"

"Jack, listen to me. You can't surrender. I'm out here because he wants you to surrender so he can subjugate you and torture you and feel like the devil. But he's not the devil. He's a made-up monster, just like all the other things. He holds all the qualities relating to the myths humanity has had about a 'devil.' He wants me, and I'm the only reason he didn't scorch the earth to make it just another hell he could rule."

"Subjugate us?" Randy asked. "If he could do this, have the power to bring us all in one place, why didn't he do it before? Why doesn't he just use that same power to enslave us?"

"He's arrogant. He's a tool. He enjoys toying with you. He doesn't really have the power to destroy you with the whoosh of his hand, like you'd think. And he doesn't like admitting, even to himself, that when you were winning battles, he was actually losing ground. He has one power only, really—he gets to tell his demons what to do. He thinks he has the power to choose the form of Armageddon, but I don't believe he has that power either."

"Well, he brought us here, didn't he?"

"Yes, but I've thought a lot about that. He believes he could have destroyed you all, using your own weapons, like nukes and such, against you, but chose not to in order to keep it hospitable for me. He believes it was a great decision to bring everyone all together to fight this final climactic battle, but honestly, I'm the one who put both of those ideas in his head. And who am I?"

"Well, that's the question we're still all trying to answer, I think," Jack replied.

"Who I am, Jack Johanssen, is a girl who's always been on your side from the beginning. And a girl who was privy to a book telling me just how I'd play the devil against himself. Did you read your own scrolls? They're all about humanity being subjected to its own crazy ideas, its own myths. You want prophecy? Well, here it is. You wanted a battle between good and evil at the end of time? You thought it was such a great thing that you kept bringing it up and discussing it all the time? Well, okay. Here it *is*—served right up for ya'. I don't think he had any more choice in these decisions than any of us had in preventing them or stopping those scrolls from being found by you all. He's our devil and this is our apocalypse. This is the battle we wanted, and here it is. So the only question that remains is: Do you play out your role of the good that never quits and risks sacrificing everything to fight an insurmountable evil, on faith alone and for the sake of good, or do you give up?"

The group had listened to Vikki intently as she gave her philosophical stance on everything that had been their life for the past year, and maybe their whole life, when they thought about it—if they had had much time to think about it—and continued to look like they were listening for at least a minute after she finished speaking.

Somewhere, in the back of the crowd, a voice spoke up. The group turned to hear what the voice had to say. "I don't think we have a choice either." It was a translator Quincy had found for an Asian man. The Asian man was older, tough like the rest of this crowd, and looked like he might be Vietnamese. There was a pause as the man spoke more to his translator, and then the translator concluded with a final sentence. "We're the side of good. We don't give up. That's what good *does*—for evil would take over the earth, Jack, if good did anything else." The man gave a nod to Jack after the translator finished speaking, as if to tell Jack, "I just made the decision for you. You're off the hook."

"I was waiting for him," Vikki said. "Now, Jack, tell me since you know he's right, you might as well take my advice on strategy and hope for the best. After the first tide turns, there will be many Slugs who will turn on the devil, your Elementors will fight the demons, and the rest of you will just fight."

"And what will you do?" Jack asked.

"I go back and tell him you're surrendering and that Harvey said you were sincere."

"Why would I tell him that?" Harvey asked.

"Because, before I tell him the result of this little meeting, I'm also going to tell him that part of the deal is that you and Meg are to be released, be allowed to leave this battlefield—that it's the only way you're willing to use your gift to help him."

"You'd do that? You're going back just to save Meg?"

"I'm not going back alone. We need the element of surprise, and he wants proof anyway. After your surrender, he's already informed me he's going to unleash all of hell on you. Many will be killed, immediately, just so you fear his power."

"What kind of proof?" Jack asked.

"A leader from your side needs to return with me."

One decision *had* been made for Jack. But number two...Jack knew, would have be made by him.

Rules...

CHAPTER 51

I Guess I'm Having What She's Having

JACK AND VIKKI were walking together toward the opposite side Jack had started from that morning. Harvey and the rest had been left behind. As five-sixths of the population of earth grew nearer to Jack, and he realized it was filled with those wanting him dead or enslaved, he felt smaller and less like a leader than he already had, given most days. He had hugged Sarah and Randy and Quincy and Four Winds. Derek had nodded Jack's way, hands stuffed in his pocket, afraid of what his Scrooging range might be. Each of them, and even a few behind them, had tried to offer themselves to return with Vikki. Jack had immediately told Vikki it would be him who would be going with her. He, of course, wouldn't have it that any of the others would go, and Jack knew they didn't deserve it. His small group had worked hard toward the goal they hoped they were about to attain, for years, while he had waffled back into his dungeon of a warehouse. And the others—they had fought for their lives every day and night over the last year. If anyone was needing to step up and prove himself, prove his faith in all of this and in them, it was him. This was his battle, and he knew it as soon as Vikki had explained the terms.

"So. What are we going to do once we get over there?"

"Jack, I only know what I said to you in the book at this moment."

"And what was that?"

"I'm going to try and kill him, and if you have the opportunity, I'd like you to help me."

"Oh."

Yep, that's what I figured, and it makes sense—we'll be closest to him.

After a few more paces of silent thought, Jack asked, "I assume you don't know if we succeed or not, huh?"

"I think we do, or I do...or you do. But I can't say I *know*...ya know?"

"Right, you already explained. You've got nothing on what happens to individuals. I guess that'd be kind of like cheating, right? Now that I think about it."

"Yeah, I think that's the point," Vikki followed.

"Yeah, I think I get it. I can't believe that I *get* I get it. But I think I do."

"Jack, I asked you to help because, for all I know, I'm gone as soon as Derek and his bunch wave their hands. And then it might be up to you."

"Yeah, I hear you, but I don't think you're filler. Why on this earth God would make you do what you had to do to get it all this far, I'll never understand. How did you read a book and find the courage to do what—" Jack halted at the subject matter he was bringing up. He'd rambled into no-man's-land. "I'm sorry, Vikki—I shouldn't have."

"You're right, Jack, but I forgive you. And…I don't want to talk about it. I don't know the 'why' in all this, and I don't know what to think about this Byron guy—the one I said was watching us and writing it all down? You don't know he's one and the same with the one who wrote the scrolls, gave the scrolls to their original bearers, and that, of course, made all this happen, do you? I just don't know what to think. He seemed tortured when he discovered these facts himself. I don't know whether to hate him or feel sorry for him."

"How much do you know about him?" Jack asked. "I really only know he sent us Four Winds, and now you're telling me about the scrolls."

"I know what the book described. I wish there was more time, but we're approaching the camp. Best not look like we're friends, chatting about the weekend."

"I guess you're right. I hope we get out of this alive."

"It'll all start soon, Jack. Be prepared for a long night."

CHAPTER 52

IMPENDING DOOM AND THE IMPENDING DOOM

H E'D BEEN BUSY...*really* busy. There had just been so much doom everywhere that had been so damned impending. Well, he was always busy, he guessed, but the "impending" had been a lot different this last year than he'd witnessed before. So maybe he had been the same amount of "busy;" only, lately, it had been so much more fun—so many new types of scenarios—and it had only *felt* like he was way more busy, than usual.

And the kind of busy he was about to be was the best yet. Impending Doom saw he was practically stretched across the horizon. If he had been able to be seen, he would have blocked out the sun. He was flying in from the heavens toward millions of people who were all just standing there watching a group five times their size march slowly toward them. From I. D.'s viewpoint, the stationary mass was about to be decimated, and he was readying his skills.

<hr />

Derek and the other leaders were walking back to join their side. Each of them took a glance every now and then over their shoulder to see Jack walk away with Vikki. Harvey waited in the middle with Four Winds, for Meg, who Vikki had convinced them she could deliver, once she returned to lie about their surrender.

"We may never see him again," Randy said to nobody, anybody.

"I know, Randy," Sarah replied, holding his arm and resting her forehead on the side of his shoulder.

"Damn it, Jack! He never takes no for an answer."

"It's not right, this whole thing. It doesn't make any sense," Derek complained. "But if we are going to believe what that girl told us, then we've got to get prepared. Jack will do his part. We'll just hope for the best."

The others stopped for a moment and looked back at Derek. Everyone offered their answer of what they believed preparation meant.

"Well, we obviously are not going to be able to go back and tell a billion people everything we know in the time we have. We can try to grapevine the important parts as quick as we can, use people like Sam to fly down the line and get anyone who knows they're a Discerner to get ready, but there's no way it'll reach everyone."

"Then, what do you suppose we do?" Quincy asked, followed by lots of similar questions from the others.

Derek would have scratched the back of his head in an effort to scrape an idea out of his mind if his hands weren't still stuffed in his pockets. Instead, he just looked back at them, raised his eyebrows and pursed his lips as if to say, "Hell if I know."

"I think we have to do what we'd do anyway. We fight."

This came from one of the leaders the Scroll Bearers had just met in the meeting with Vikki.

"I guess she's right. What's your name?"

"Charlotte. I'm from New Zealand."

"Who'd have ever guessed, with that accent?" Derek laughed. "Okay, everyone. Charlotte here, stated the obvious and that's exactly what we've got to do—we fight. As soon as we get back, all of us spread out down the line as fast as we can. We'll all have to start the charge; you know that, right? And then hope to God it inspires everyone behind us to follow, after they see what happens."

The looks on everyone's faces said, "Yes...love the plan and hate the plan."

"If what Vikki told us is right, then I guess we've got a chance."

"A chance doesn't mean we'll all walk away from this battle," Randy said, holding Sarah. "She's not charging!"

"What? Randy!" Sarah yelled.

"You're not! I won't see you wiped out in the first minute of this thing! What the hell would I be fighting for, then?"

"Them! Randy!" She pointed to what was left of humanity. "What's still good in the world…"

"I don't want to lose you, Sarah," Randy cried. "This may be our war, but you're my girl, and I love you."

"I love you, Randy. But we fight together."

"Who's comforting who there, Aunt Sarah?" Derek was trying to get Randy's mind off what was an obviously suck-ass position to be in. "Randy's right. Sarah's right. Everyone? Find your resolve, because this is it. We're all where we are because we aren't over there with that son of a bitch. I think it means something about all of us, so just remember that. Anything after that is out of our hands."

━━◇○◇━━

Thirty minutes had passed since they had all returned to the front line. Derek had stayed with Randy and Sarah. It had felt appropriate. They had done their best to explain the plan to those around them, urging it to be passed on. Derek witnessed something on the battlefield and leaned over to Randy and said, "Maybe there's your resolve, Randy."

Derek was nodding at Harvey and Meg, who had just been reunited in quite an amazing spectacle of purity, given the landscape they were the centerpiece to. After embracing and kissing like something out of a movie, and even more so because of the unlikely pair they appeared to make, Sam was sent to fly in, grab them, and fly them off to safety. However, instead of disappearing into the horizon to the left, they appeared to be arguing with Sam. A few moments later, Sam was flying them toward the front a little further down to the right from where Randy, Sarah, and Derek stood. They didn't creep into the back. They apparently had decided they weren't going anywhere.

Randy, watching this and responding to Derek's comment, said, "I want to believe that Vikki, believe we'll win. But I tell you. If our side is made up of people like them, then we at least deserve to win." He squeezed Sarah's hand, which he was already holding, even tighter.

As Four Winds approached from his walk back from the middle of the plain, Randy spoke again. "I was thinking. Maybe even the word 'Allied,' which Jack found all over the fourth scroll, actually had some meaning, too, after all."

—◇○◇—

"Harvey!"

"Meg—" Harvey said, barely getting a chance to finish her name before she nailed one on him, simultaneously wrapping her arms around his waist.

The kiss and embrace lasted longer than normal, and they spun themselves around an axis as it went on. Four Winds looked down at the ground, giving them symbolic privacy, considering almost all of humanity could see the sight.

"How did you get me out of there?"

"I didn't, Meg. I wanted to, but I didn't know how. It was Vikki's plan that got you here for me."

"Oh, Harvey, I don't care! If you hadn't come back for me in the first place, I'd never have survived. I love you!" And the kissing started again.

"You need to go." Four Winds had given them their time, but Sam had arrived, and there were other important things to understand.

"Ye-yes, Mr., uh, Four Winds was it?" Harvey stuttered. He turned back to Meg. "Meg, you have to go. They have a plan to win this war."

"Really? But they said you were surrendering. They told me they saw no reason why I needed you so bad, considering they'd be taking us all over soon enough."

"It's a ruse," Four Winds explained. "There is much to explain to you, Miss Meg. Sam will do it as he flies you *both* away from here."

And you know the rest. Argument, argument. Courage, courage. And no one flew anyone off to anywhere.

CHAPTER 53

WELL, HERE...IT...IS

EVIL WAS CLOSING IN ON GOOD. Their orders had been given to them, even before Vikki had gone out to convince Good to surrender. If she was successful, they were to approach the last of the rebellion, and in a surprise, destroy many, immediately, to place fear in the remaining souls being destined for servitude to the Dark Lord. The greater killings and mutilations would occur after dark, when their comrades from the hidden world arrived again.

Impending Doom was beyond ecstatic as he moved in from above, for the coming attack. As described before, Impending Doom didn't really care who was getting the impending, as long as he got the doom part.

Everything had been clear. One moment he was moving in for the kill, knowing it was coming. And the next moment, everything changed. The front line of the smaller group he was heading for started charging. I. D. still headed for them. The ones at the front would be easy kills for the horde coming at them from the other side. And if their sudden movement had placed some on the other side in the impending category, so be it. He didn't take sides, he took lives.

The thing was, though, these several men and women charging on the side he was headed for began to raise their hands, and Impending Doom found himself in a confused situation where he had no idea what to do. For the moment, he did not sense there was anyone about to die anymore, on either side, which was the exact opposite of what the scene itself was portraying.

As he turned to the larger army, thinking that somehow the tide was going to turn, regardless of their numbers, there was no "impendingness" to sense there either. This seemed utterly impossible to I. D. Two armies totaling over six billion people were facing off against one another on a battlefield the size of a small country, and he didn't have anyone to kill on his register. If *Death* had dreamed this shit up, he was going to have words with him later.

As he watched, an incredible event happened. People, or something—he didn't know what they were because he wasn't picking them off…and he didn't see his jacked-up cousin anywhere—began disappearing by the dozens, and then the hundreds, and then the thousands. And every time I. D. thought, "Well, that's gonna make the ones behind them feel some impending doom, for sure, he'd instead sense nothing, and then those 'people' disappeared too. He didn't have anything to do and it was pissing him off.

And then he saw him.

"You!" I. D. yelled. "Did you set this up?"

"Set what up?" Death responded.

"Well, you're here, and something strange is going on. Two armies. One vastly outnumbered that I was homing in on to destroy, and then 'nothing'...no destroying. A lot of people are dropping off like flies, but I'm not doing anything. So it must be—"

And then, they both got busy. I did say it was only a moment that I. D. was confused.

Impending Doom and Death each had their work cut out for them over the next several hours, and well into the night. As the devil's army began to witness its numbers decline rapidly—the bulk of their soldiers having gone up in smoke—most of it began to feel a lot of impending doom, and I. D. was happy to oblige as much all-out doom as they needed to get them "over the hump," so to speak. The lesser army had miraculously turned the tide of the war and didn't seem to be feeling anything impending at all, except for their believed victory. Of course, they would not all make it because it was still a war, and both sides were fighting, and that's where Death's job mostly took over, working the crowd of good souls, who were dying, yes, but who weren't feeling any doom, impending or otherwise. Death didn't have the same temperament as I. D., and he felt a little sympathy when he took a young, yet old, and beautiful woman named Sarah, as a stray random bullet buried itself in her temple.

Vikki had lied about knowing this. And she had read about her lying about this, right here.

The war ended, if it really was a war at all. Set up from the beginning, most obviously to end like it did. Bad destroyed. Good, with devastating losses, but victorious. The Elementors fought ten demons each or more and saved lives tenfold over that, many times giving their own lives in the process. Eventually, there weren't many demons left, or perhaps Vikki and Jack had been successful, and there was no longer a certain crimson someone left to call his demons from the other world. Byron, if he witnessed that, did not write it in his notebooks. I swear.

Byron was about to learn a harrowing fact at the end of this viewing. The final battle started and ended less than one year after Hell Day. Yet it had taken Byron almost forty years to witness everything he wrote down. He only became aware there had been a world going on outside his doors for over thirty years on January 31, 2048. He didn't take it at all well, nor did he take well the other event of which he learned. I'm sorry for his loss, and the agony he will feel in his responsibility.

CHAPTER 54

SO, "VIKKI", ARE YOU GOING, ALREADY?

January 31, 2048 CE: Entry 12,347

I realize now I am alone. Not alone in this cabin, but completely and utterly alone. Everyone is gone. I was not always aware of dates, and I did not see everything in the order it occurred. I have been confused, and they had been through so much, I couldn't always tell their ages anymore. I hadn't seen the end. Now I've seen the end. It was a long time ago. Thirty years ago! And now, they're all gone. They won, but they didn't win. The ones who were left are rebuilding, forging a new future. But you said if I went with you, I would be saving my parents! You're a liar! Why did I listen to you! If I'd never come, there would have been no scrolls! Who are you? Were you one of these demons I unleashed with this task you put me on? Were you? Answer me, damn it! I want my mother back! I want my father! Why am I here? Why did I sit here in this cabin for my whole damned life, doing your bidding?

January 31, 2048 CE: Entry 12,348

Things are as hopeless as ever now. I am cursed. I have had another vision this evening, and it is the scariest of all I have seen. I arrived at my home the day I left it. I was viewing from the side of my house when I saw the man arrive. He was a few paces to the left of me closer to the front corner of my home. I heard myself as a boy playing in the front yard. Before the man disappeared, he turned toward me, almost as if to show he knew I was there. That's when I saw his face. It was me! He whispered something that, now, I spit on. He said, "Trust yourself." How can I trust myself when I see I am the very cause of everything? I'm the one who tricks my younger self into running off

*and starting everything. I even lied to myself and destroyed the world. I
didn't save anybody, and I killed almost everybody. I am alone. I could
never leave here knowing what I've done. And everyone I've ever loved
is gone. It's all over. I'm sorry. I hope you all learn from your mistakes,
and you never know the likes of a prophet like me in your new destiny.
I will wait for my death in the bed where the previous inhabitant of this
cabin waited for his.*

—◇○◇—

JANUARY 31, 2005

That was the last entry in the last notebook I found in Byron Henning's cabin. If
all this is true, then I am not sure what to make of it all. Honestly, typing these last
few thoughts after everything I've read, and discovered, I find it a little nonsensical
to be making the statement "if all this is true." Nonetheless, I'll make the statement,
if only for the benefit of those who are reading this as they try to make their own
determination.

Is Byron evil? Is he good? Was he a pawn of the universe, of God, of something
worse? I don't know. I don't believe I am meant to stop it. I don't believe I could.
And if I try to stop Jack Johanssen from translating his relic, will I be *able* to? If I told
you his real name, his real location, would you try to stop him? And if we did, would
we stop anything? Perhaps, all we would do is enter the same future, but with no Jack
Johanssen, no Sarah and Derek Dubois, no Randall Haverstamp, no Quincy Davis,
no Four Winds, no Harvey Winestall, no Vikki Parsons, and no book.

I'd like to conclude with answers instead of more questions, but I don't have
anything to provide by way of guidance other than what Byron appears to have had.
If anything, I would say: prepare. That is, you might ask yourself which side you think
you'd drop down on, if it all happened tomorrow. Because, honestly, I think it's going
to.

THE END

EPILOGUE

THE PREVIOUS PAGE concludes my "original" book—the one I didn't write, yet somehow...I did write. Let me explain, if I can, the *whole* truth, regarding the finding of Byron's notebooks, no matter how bizarre it may seem or how it might weaken my credibility as an author.

Obviously, the significant dates mentioned in the accounts of this novel have come and gone, and none of the events described have come to pass. I hope the following epilogue will shed some light on this matter, explaining the truth about the origin of this book, which I am finally compelled to share with its publication. Most assuredly, "*What should I believe?*" will be your question. And "*What should I do?*" has been mine. At one time, I even conceived of writing my own death into this epilogue to escape any scrutiny, discovery, or risk of being labeled a plagiarist.

Yet here we are. You and me, together having to deal with the ramifications of all of it, from both sides of the page. Does adding an epilogue, and thus modifying the original book, have an effect on the future? What if I am wrong in disclosing all the facts? On the other hand, if I don't, you may not take its contents as seriously as you should, especially since nothing happened.

So here goes.

It is true that I had been vacationing that summer of 1999, away from the world, trying to contemplate the details of the next story I would write. I took long hikes every morning in the thin air, hoping the higher altitude might get my thoughts flowing if less air was crowding my brain. The moment in which Byron appeared before me, like Scotty had beamed him off the *Enterprise* and into my morning jaunt, left no room for second-guessing. I hadn't been looking down, only to look up and see him there. He hadn't walked out from behind a tree or a burning bush or something. I had stopped to take a breather, and *voilà!* He materialized two feet in front of me, my eyes wide open—and we were face to face, just like that. There was no mistaking what had just happened, even if I most surely did not want to believe it.

I about fell over backward, and after the typical "Holy Gods," "You're shitting mes," and introductions—that typically happen in these kinds of meetings—Byron went on to try and explain his story—a story that would equate with multiplying the word "unbelievable" by some number you used to make up when you were five.

Byron explained the contents of a book he proceeded to hand to me. As I held this book and turned it over in my hand, I was slightly perplexed because it appeared to have a pen name of mine—Robert Reisler—printed upon it...and I hadn't told that name to anyone, hadn't even written it down. He said he was giving it to me right away to produce a frame of reference to some (*insane*) ideas he wished for me to believe and even more insane favors he would be asking me to do. It was way too much information to take in, and I'm surprised I walked away from the experience with even one coherent memory of the conversation. Byron was nervous. Looking back, I can now assume he was likely caught between believing his idea was brilliant and scared to death it wouldn't work; and, all the while he fully understood that this part of his plan was probably the toughest to execute—that is, make a complete stranger do what he wanted him to do on faith alone, only to persuade the stranger with what could be considered a couple of parlor tricks. Maybe he had banked on the fact that he'd done it four times before, right? The only difference with me—as I understand now—was that he was lacking the luxury of a *viewing* to know this attempt's outcome.

Byron told me he had a plan he believed was the culmination of all he had witnessed—a final thought while lying in his bed, wishing not to eat or drink anything, ever again, as he would wither away and die for the crimes he had committed and put an end to the losses he had experienced.

"Robert," he said to me in the woods of his mountain, "I believe my story is meant to be a myth, in and of itself. A guide for those who will listen. I once told myself to 'trust myself,' but it was at a time when I would have *thought* I would be doing nothing but planning my own destruction—and the world's. Lying in my bed and waiting for my death, I realized something of great magnitude."

"What was that?" I asked Byron, still in disbelief I was even having this conversation.

"I realized I personally had not gone back yet, to tell myself to come to that cabin!"

"What do you mean?"

"I mean that I had seen and done everything else that is in your book. I had even traveled back in time to my home to see *me*—there—about to vanish and start whispering in my boyhood ear to leave my parents for good. But I hadn't, actually, done that yet myself! I hadn't actually been *The Voice of Prophecy!*"

"Oh." I was really trying hard to wrap my mind around what he was trying to explain, but I wasn't being very successful. Remember, I hadn't even read one journal or my own book—the one I apparently was holding in my hand. At this point, you all have more information than I was running on at the time. I was still fighting my own desire to call him—or myself—crazy and run away.

"I figured there had to be a reason," he continued. "It's really the only task left to do. Go back and convince my younger self to run away, and then finally deliver all the notebooks to the cabin for you to find here today. I started racking my brain trying to understand. He—I mean *'I'*—had known I was there. He (*I*) turned around toward me and said, 'Trust yourself' and was smiling. Then it occurred to me. Why not just *not* do it? Don't go back. Don't kidnap myself."

"Right," I said. It was really all I could say.

"Because, Robert! Because there had to be a reason for all of this. To not do it, I had the same fears you had when you thought about not writing that book. What if the end happens anyway, and we have no one to help protect the good in the world?"

"I write that, in here?" I said, pointing down at the book in my hand.

"Yes, you do. Actually, turn it over. [*Which I did.*] You write it on the back cover. [*Which I then read.*] I didn't exactly have the same thought as you. I knew none of it would happen if I didn't go back and kidnap myself. No kidnapping equals no scrolls equals no prophecy. But I still feel there is a reason for everything that has happened. It's why I brought you that book." And now he was pointing at what I was holding in my hand, as well.

"So what's your plan?" I asked.

"*That* is my plan." He pointed to the book he had given me again. *(The one with my pen name on it, the name that no one in the world knew I had been thinking about using, remember? I think that's the only thing that had kept me engaged, and I guess Byron had bet on that too.)* "The very fact you are holding that book means it happened. It all happened, even though I've decided to try and stop it from ever happening. I think that's why I was shown what I was shown. I think it's how I save my parents. I think it's what I'm supposed to do."

"I don't understand, Byron."

"You publish that book, like you did before, so people know my story and it can serve—"

"Whatever purpose it may serve." I found myself saying in unison with Byron as he finished his sentence. I had just read the back of the book a moment earlier, and the sentence now felt…eerily…*me.*

"Well, it served its purpose. And now, it will serve another one," Byron finished.

"But, Byron, I didn't write this. I can't do that. It's plagiarism." I was back in disbelief—in reality. Part of me knew that was a much better place to remain. "I could be discredited as an author."

"You *did* write it, and you'll just have to believe me. Read it, and you'll know I'm telling you the truth." Byron was starting to look scared, as if somehow my reluctance was something he hadn't expected. His face wrinkled in determination. He wasn't leaving unless he was convinced I was the embodiment of "yes." "You have to, Robert, or all I've done will be for nothing. Please, promise me."

I thought for a moment. I needed time. Appearance out of thin air. A book with my pen name on it. Yes. But, seriously? Maybe it wouldn't hurt to humor this guy and just *say* yes. If I changed my mind later, no harm done. Unless of course he *was* a madman—which wasn't out of the question—and later, he appeared on my doorstep, ready to use more forceful persuasion tactics.

In the end, I think I actually took a leap of faith.

Don't we all sometimes?

"All right, Byron, I'll read it, and if what you tell me rings true, I will publish it as my own."

Byron sized up my answer. I'm not a man to say things lightly, and I really meant what I told him, regardless of how much my rational mind was calling me an idiot. After a moment of sizing up my answer, he sensed the legitimacy of it, and the deal was done.

"Thank you," he replied and then asked for another favor.

"Something *else?*" I was intrigued by what else he could possibly want. I figured I had just handed him the golden egg. Perhaps he should be happy with that. Now he wanted that egg on golden toast glazed with golden butter—and all prepared by Mrs. Golden Goose, herself.

"Yes, please. If my plan succeeds, I'm not exactly sure what spiraling effect it's going to have on the future I live in. I believe I may never have the luxury of knowing if I succeeded. So please, find out for me, so at least you'll know, and if you believe me, others will know, too."

———◇○◇———

Knowing all I know now, I do believe in the man who handed me the book you just read, and I do believe in some strange manner, in some other timeline, in some other reality, I am the one who wrote it. From his telling, and now my belief, it was to be that morning—the morning Byron appeared to me—that I would have stumbled upon a cabin filled with notebooks, which would perplex me and consume me for the next several years. However, because he visited me on that walk and I had agreed to his requests, I did not find his notebooks.

Instead, after this meeting, I went back to my hotel and began to read the book he had handed me and think about what had happened during that hike. I did eventually return to the mountain to find the place. Ironically, it was me, this time, who was responsible for burying a dead German hermit who had died there. There were no notebooks for me to find, but the old man had left a diary. Upon my subsequent reading of it, I found that it had no mention of a Byron or his appearance. Only the sorry ramblings of a man riddled with the guilt of his past, the loss of his bride in his youth, and the sad, crushing loss of her picture in his last days. I found Lucina's picture outside and away from the cabin—uncracked because no young Byron had taken a fall on top of it. I buried it with the German. In this, there was proof of nothing. Byron could have found the cabin before me and made the whole thing up, but this experience only relates one of my fact-finding missions.

———◇○◇———

I had to wait a few years, but I decided to take Byron up on his last request from our conversation on the mountain. So, I took a trip. This trip would find me traveling to Byron, although I would not meet with him, as he met me. I traveled for two days to a street in a small town near an address Byron had given me. I got out of the car on that brisk, *not too cold* of a day, and headed off to my date with destiny. It was January 31, 2007.

There I hunched, feeling like a stalker crouched behind a line of bushes bordering the house I had come to observe. You don't have to believe me, but it is that day I finally decided to publish my book. And if I'm being honest, I don't know why I am writing these pages now. Byron had told me to publish the book he handed me; he made no mention of it being okay for me to add to it. Will it have repercussions? Will it affect the power of the message his story is meant to invoke? Am I arrogant enough to think my story will have any power to invoke anything? If I tell the truth of my self-plagiarism—if that's what you'd call this—will it lessen Byron's life struggle to others? Perhaps I'll burn these pages once I've completed them. I need more time to think on this.

In requesting this favor of me, I don't think Byron had really considered all I'd see that day, and for what I saw, I, too, can say I wasn't prepared for it. I had read the account in "my" book, yes, but a movie is always better in the theater. The experience really registered on the weird scale when I saw a lightly bundled-up child of eleven years or so run out of the house to play and hearing his mother announce, "Byron, it's just a few minutes, and then your mac and cheese will be ready." A few minutes later, I saw the older version of Byron appear on the side of the house in identical fashion to how he had appeared to me eight years earlier. He peered around the corner and saw the smaller version of himself playing. He smiled, and then he turned around toward the back of the house. From my angle, I couldn't make out what he was saying, but he seemed to say something to someone who wasn't there or whom I couldn't see. As he turned back toward the front of the house, his eye caught me hiding in the snowy bushes. He gave me a quick wink, and a look of accomplishment flashed across his face. It was followed by a look that seemed to say, "Hide!" so I ducked down further. Then he was gone.

The very act of spying puts you in a bit of a panic. I was afraid of being seen by the child, by the neighbors, by a passerby. I hadn't even thought about being seen by the older Byron, or the other invisible Byron, but that's what the visible Byron was afraid of. I think he hadn't wanted to confuse the *viewing* Byron with my presence. Perhaps it would corrupt the message he was trying to send *that* Byron, which would plant the seed of this plan. Could you follow any of that? Anyway, I stayed hidden further down in the bushes. I think when it was all over, I wished I could have grabbed the boy and told him something, anything, just so he'd know. Maybe I could go find him and tell him now? Or maybe not. Chicken. Egg. What started it all; what finishes it? Who's in charge? I hope not the butcher. In the end, I could only sit and listen to what happened next. A moment later, still huddled in the bush, my Peeping Tom self heard a mother's voice call from inside the house.

"Byron?"

No answer.

"Byyyyyyyyyronnnnnn!"

"Yes, Mommy?"

"Come inside. Your lunch is ready."

"Okay."

And I watched the boy go up the porch stairs and enter his home, swallowed by the present, a hot lunch being the only certain thing in his future. From inside I heard, "Go wash your hands, Byron; you're all dirty."

No, Byron, you're all clean.

POSTEPILOGUE

I was afraid of adding an epilogue, and here I go throwing in a "postepilogue." However, who knows? Maybe all of this was supposed to be published with the rest of the content of my original book, from the beginning. Perhaps all these epilogues should have been titled *Book VII: The End of the End*. I have seen and witnessed so much since the completion of the last epilogue; I hardly know what to believe anymore.

I told you it was that day outside Byron's house that I finally decided to publish, but the *when* I would publish, and the *how* I would publish—those were yet to be decided. Just because I was no longer a skeptic didn't mean I didn't want to know *more*. You may remain skeptical because I will not disclose the real names of the individuals whom Byron claimed to view during his life of solitude. I choose this because it's what I chose to do the first time I published *The Four Myths*, and I do so this time, as well, for their protection, privacy, and the right they have to disclose themselves if, or when, they wish to.

When we had met on the mountain, Byron told me his real name and location, as well as that of several of the individuals related in this account. I feverishly began taking notes at his request—caught between acceptance and rejection of the whole ordeal—while standing in the middle of trees that would have given those of Tom Walker a run for their money.

After witnessing young Byron run inside to eat his lunch, I became obsessed with the need to fact-check as many of those names as I could. Initially, I found that the owners of those names existed. But that wouldn't have been too hard for "Forest Byron" to fake. After finding and observing them, I could see nothing in their actions leading me to believe they knew anything about what I knew. This left me in a quandary. Maybe I had been tricked and deluded myself into wanting to believe. Maybe my own ego had become intoxicated on the idea that I was part of something important, something world changing. I decided I needed to wait. I needed to wait and see if 2012 brought a Hell Day. This had been a fear of Forest Byron, and apparently "Other Timeline Me." If there was no "Prophet Byron," perhaps instead of stopping Hell Day, we would only produce a Hell Day with no one aware of why, and no Jack Johanssen to be leader of *All Those Whose Faces Will Not Be Melted*.

Well, as you all know, 2012 came and went. By the end of 2013, Hell Year, the war, and the beginning of rebuilding would have come and gone, as well. But, *lo and behold!*, this is when things got interesting. It had been over six years since I had decided to crouch myself behind some kid's neighbor's bushes in the middle of winter and spy, and now I was really beginning to second-guess everything. I was probably feeling a bit like Jack did after he had left the gang to go back to work in his warehouse. But like Jack got a call from Randy, I suddenly got an idea.

Check again.

So I did. And this time, I made contact.

I don't know what the reason is behind what I found. I can only make guesses. I tracked down everyone I knew of again, but this time, I discovered they made up two groups of people. I can only assume if I knew everyone who was ever mentioned in the novel, the number of groups would still hold up as only two. The first group consisted of people who walked away from me thinking, "Who was that guy?" and "What exactly was he trying to get me to say, without being remotely clear about it?" Yet the second group was entirely different. They knew *everything*. This group consisted of all the major players in the scroll-bearing group. They already knew about each other and were already in contact. A few others (not in the original six) also remembered everything from their lives depicted in the novel form of my book. Everyone told the same story. Around the middle of 2013, they all started to remember a completely different life they had led. It appeared, like me, they could only guess as to why they were chosen to remember, but I believed as they received more information from me and were able to read this book, which they had only heard about from Vikki's account (*in another life*), that we all came to a similar possible conclusion.

Nobody believed Byron was a magician or some mystical being. In addition to him only being a teenager, at present, and seemingly one of only two key players in this whole story who didn't remember any of it, we could only assume he was a chosen and innocent prophet—a tool utilized to bring forth this message and whatever effects it will have on the people who read it or learn of it. Since I know you're wondering; the second key player spared her memories was "Vikki." I found her to be living, comfortably oblivious, in "North Dakota."

The others, however, had not been chosen to forget. When I met them, they were all continuing with living their lives. The only difference for them was that they had a new set of friends and new lines of communication that did not exist before. "Jack" had not found anything especially significant at work the night of January 31, 2007. Another interesting factoid "Jack" informed me of, was that he couldn't remember, in any way, having ever had a class in college that gave assignments related to an Enigma machine, although he did remember it in his other life. "Randy" was never going to have the fortune of meeting "Sarah," and I could tell it wore on him, as it was obvious that he yearned for their life together. He told me he wouldn't wish her life on anyone, including her, so that gave him some peace. "Derek" is still writing, but he said he tends to walk with his hands in his pockets more, nowadays. He misses his aunt, the same as Randy, and said it's very odd remembering two different childhoods: one in which he grew up with Sarah and one where he didn't. Remarkably, however—and honestly, this really stunned me—it does appear Sarah was gifted with the knowledge of her other life also. She had written long letters to Derek and Randy. I saw them, so I know they exist. She had given them to her great-nephew, Derek's father, when he was a boy and had instructed him to give them to his son when he grew up and reached Derek's current age. It was done as part of some guise wherein she had given many letters to be given to many family members who would be her descendants. The letters were supposed to contain stories of the journeys she'd been on in her life and the lessons she had learned. A few "extra" journeys were discussed in two of the letters, in particular. Interestingly, she had written that she had tracked down Gerard Palton, and he had curiously never contracted the funds he'd needed to do the dig in 1876, as described in my book, and therefore was not the one responsible for finding the City of Abydos. Randy and Derek felt this fitting due to what *The Four Myths* had described of him. Davis and Four Winds were never heard from, or at least in no manner, as of yet, but they were discussed and mentioned often. They were holding out hope that at some point, a Western Union telegram or a Sioux descendant might appear on one of their doorsteps with a message from the past.

The group I had the fortune of spending time with had not decided what to do with the very real fact that they all knew everything that had happened. They wondered if they were supposed to be messengers of some sort. They asked me if I was still planning on publishing. I replied with a yes, with still no answer as to how or when. They figured they'd wait to see if my book was to serve a purpose or open a door of insight for them on what they should do, if anything. Perhaps, they told me, their memories were only to convince me to go forward with its publishing.

I believe any or all of these ideas may be correct, but everything still begs the question *why?* I have put a lot of thought into this. I wonder that maybe this is not the first time this has happened, or something like it. I wonder if the stories and lessons of old, which seem inconsistent and historically unprovable, and even sometimes apparently corrupted, yet speak much truth, regardless, are all somehow the same as Byron's story. Could it be that the Armageddons of the past, the present, and the future have happened, do happen, and will happen, but at the same time never happened and won't happen?

For what purpose? Why have the end of the world without the end of the world? Why provide prophecy of its coming, only to reverse it, leaving only loose ends and improvable evidence behind? I do not pretend to know the mind of God—if that is, in fact, whom we are talking about—but if this is really the way it works, maybe it's only to remind us. Perhaps there are always things we will not understand, but there should always be great stories telling us the same message. No matter what the situation is, whether you see the signs or you don't, whether it's the end of the world or just another day—perhaps, it only matters what side you are on. Are you struggling to do the right thing, or are you drifting toward other ends? In my research of all these kinds of things, I came across an interesting statement a Muslim friend of mine told me. He said prophet Muhammad had uttered the following words. I believe the statement gets very close, in spirit, to what I have concluded, as well. He said, "If 'The End' comes while you are planting a tree, then keep planting the tree."

In this novel of Byron's accounts, only a handful of people *saw* the signs of the coming End—the actual End—not the many kinds of Ends people crazily dream up every time a new date is mentioned in *The Enquirer*. Yet how many people sit around and talk about prophecy, and signs, and what's going on "behind the scenes"? It seems like an awful waste of time when one could be out building a home for a poor family, or reading to an elderly relative, or being at home playing with one's children. And if this story is true—which I am convinced it is—then the signs we are waiting for and the prophecies we are trying to read are only leading us to something that has already happened or the next something that will happen, but we won't remember. End of the world or not, it was the daily choices people made in the minute-to-minute decisions they were faced with that placed them with the leader by whom they were led.

I don't know the answers, and I can only make my own inferences, like you. But I do know I don't want to end up playing for the losing team described in this story. Whether I die in bed as a jaded and bitter old man, with not a nice word to say on my lips, all alone in a *normal* world, or as a younger man fighting alongside a demon, against people like Jack and Sarah during a battle at the "supposed" end of the world…either end is essentially the same, isn't it?

I've stopped looking for major road signs and started looking at the everyday small signs telling me to yield to the more difficult and less traveled road. For, as they say, the road to hell is paved with ease.

And the road to heaven? Well…it's not.

THE END—END

About the Author

Robert Reisler is an American author and part-time philosopher. Attending Purdue University and Kansas State University, he holds a Pre-Medicine degree with a minor emphasis on the Arts. Faith, miracles, and the metaphysical intrigue Reisler and he continues to study different religions and the nature of belief. A lover of a good thriller or mystery and a traveler at heart, Reisler has raised five children while living in India, SE Asia, Africa, and Europe, as well as several locations around the United States. A Kansas native, he now resides in Atlanta, Georgia.

Made in the USA
Columbia, SC
03 March 2021